Rushing Amy

By Julie Brannagh

Rushing Amy
Blitzing Emily

Coming Soon:
Catching Cameron

Rushing Amy

A Love and Football Novel

JULIE BRANNAGH

AVONIMPULSE
An Imprint of HarperCollinsPublishers

EPub Edition FEBRUARY 2014 ISBN: 9780062279729

Print Edition ISBN: 9780062279750

JV 10 9 8 7 6 5 4 3 2 1

To Grandpa Dick and Grandma Elaine
You have shown me what it means to live
life to the fullest.
I hope I live up to your example every day.
Love, Julie

Acknowledgments

I HAVE so many people to thank for their help with *Rushing Amy*.

Thank you to my wonderful agent, Sarah E. Younger of Nancy Yost Literary Agency for all her hard work and encouragement. She chose me out of the 2,394,073 submissions she gets yearly, and I will always be thankful.

Amanda Bergeron is my terrific editor at Avon Impulse. I still can't believe she chose me, either. Thank you for all your hard work and making my books so much better than I ever dreamed they could be.

My husband Eric had no idea he'd be dealing with the high-stakes world of publishing when he married me. Thank you, honey, for all your patience and support. I love you.

I'd like to thank Greater Seattle Romance Writers of America. Without their advice, encouragement, and writing workshops, I'd still be thinking *Someday I'd like to write a book.*

I am so lucky to be part of the Cupcake Crew. Jessi Gage and Amy Raby, you make Friday the greatest day of the week, and always want my best work. Thank you so much for everything.

Thanks to Cupcake Royale in Bellevue, WA, for continuing to harbor the Cupcake Crew.

Thank you to my incredible mentor, Susan Mallery. I treasure every bit of hard-won advice you've ever given me. And yes, I will get back to work immediately.

My life changed as the result of a five-minute phone call on March 25, 2011, when I learned this book was named a Golden Heart finalist. I'd like to thank Judy Wiebe and Anna Muzzy for making sure I was in New York City to enjoy every minute of RWA National. I can't ever thank you enough for your friendship.

Thank you to Schatzi Schricker of Duvall Flowers and Gifts, Duvall, WA, for answering my research questions, too. Owning a small business is not for the faint of heart!

Thank you to my unaware muse, Howie Long. I got the idea for this book shortly after listening to an entire roomful of romance authors rhapsodizing over him. (He is the definitive alpha male.) I'd also like to thank Mrs. Howie Long for sharing her husband with the women of America for an hour each Sunday morning from September to February.

I'd like to thank former and current Seattle Seahawks for interviews they've given in various forms of media that helped me with my research.

One final note: Matt is a character invented in my imagination. Any artistic license is mine. Any mistakes in the research are mine, too.

I'd also like to thank YOU for buying my book. I hope you'll enjoy it! I'm at www.juliebrannagh.com, on Facebook, and on Twitter as @julieinduvall.

I love to hear from readers!

Go Sharks!

Chapter One

THE WEDDING WAS over, and Amy Hamilton stood amongst the wreckage.

Every flat surface in the Woodmark Hotel's grand ballroom was strewn with dirty plates, empty glasses, crumpled napkins, spent champagne bottles—the outward indication that a large group of people had one hell of a party. A few hours ago, Amy's older sister Emily had married Brandon McKenna, the man of her dreams.

Three hundred guests toasted the bride and groom repeatedly. Happy tears flowed as freely as the champagne. The dinner was delicious, the cake, even better. The newlyweds and their guests danced to a live band till after midnight. The hotel ballroom was transformed into a candlelit fairyland for her sister's flawless evening, but now all that was left was the mess. The perfectly arranged profusion of flowers was drooping. So was she.

Amy arranged flowers for weddings almost every

weekend. Doing the flowers for Emily's wedding, though, was an extra-special thrill. She'd seen it all over the past few years, first as an apprentice to another florist, and then after opening her own shop a little over a year ago. It meant long hours and hard work, but she was determined her business would succeed.

Amy took a last look at the twinkling lights of the boats crossing Lake Washington through the floor-to-ceiling windows along the west wall. She couldn't help but notice she stood alone in a room that had been packed with people only an hour or so ago. She'd been alone for a long time now, and she didn't like the feeling at all. She picked up the black silk chiffon wrap draped over yet another chair, and the now-wilting bridal bouquet Emily had tossed to her. Obviously, she'd stalled long enough. She wondered if the kitchen staff would mind whipping up a vat of chocolate mousse to drown her sorrows in.

HEAVY FOOTSTEPS SOUNDED behind Amy on the ballroom floor, and she turned toward them. The man she'd watched on a hundred *NFL Today* pregame broadcasts strolled toward her. Any woman with a pulse knew who he was, let alone any woman hopelessly addicted to Pro Sports Network.

Matt Stephens was tall. His body, sculpted by years of workouts, was showcased in a perfectly tailored navy suit, but that didn't tell the whole story. The wavy, slightly mussed blue-black hair, the square jaw, the olive skin that seemed to glow, and the flawless, white smile were exactly what Amy saw on her television screen each week during football season. Television didn't do him justice. After all, on her TV screen he didn't prowl. He locked eyes with her as he crossed the ballroom.

She glanced around to confirm she was still alone in the ballroom, and the beeline he was making was actually toward her. She couldn't imagine what he wanted.

She knew a lot about him. Matt was a former NFL star, and a good friend of her new brother-in-law's. When Matt got tired of playing with the Dallas Cowboys (three Super Bowl rings and six visits to the Pro Bowl later), he'd played in Seattle for the last two years of his career, afterward embarking on the wide world of game analysis and product endorsements. Guys wanted to be him, and women just plain wanted him.

Well, women who were still on the playing field wanted him. She was putting herself on injured reserve. After all, *once burned, twice shy,* and every other cliché she'd ever heard that reminded her of salt being poured on the open wound that was her heart.

Mostly, guys who looked like Matt weren't looking for someone like her: A woman more interested in being independent than being some guy's arm candy.

Matt stopped a few feet away from Amy. The deep dimples on either side of his lips flashed as his mouth moved into an irresistible grin.

"Hello, there."

"You're late." The words flew out of her mouth before she realized she'd said it aloud.

His smile cajoled. The man was clearly aware there

wasn't a woman on the planet who could hope to resist him. She could, though. She would. He slipped one hand into his pocket.

"Oh, I'm definitely not late," he said. "As a matter of fact I'm right on schedule."

She let out a gasp of outrage. In other words, he'd missed the wedding on purpose.

His eyes slid over her from head to toe. Slowly. They made a few stops along the way, too. Amy dragged a shallow breath into her lungs. She resisted the impulse to smooth the wrinkles out of her dress, shove the hairpins back into what was most likely the wreck of her updo, and press her lips together in an attempt to salvage lipstick smudged off hours ago. She reminded herself that she was dealing with just another male. Even worse, this one evidently believed the rules in life applied to everyone but him.

"Were you actually invited to this event?" she asked.

He looked a bit wary. Even if Matt were the most gorgeous man she'd ever met, he was not getting away with this. She was busting his chops. After all, someone had to do it.

"Yes, I was invited." He tried to look sheepish, but she wasn't buying it. "McKenna's going to kick my ass."

"Why do I think it won't be the first time that's happened?"

Matt lifted one eyebrow, seemingly unused to any woman who didn't collapse into a quivering mass of flesh whenever he chose to make any effort at all. She saw his mouth twitch into a smile.

"It seems we've gotten off on the wrong foot. Maybe we

should try this again." He took a couple of steps toward her and extended one hand. "Hi. I'm Matt Stephens."

Amy tried to surreptitiously wipe what she was sure was a sweaty palm on her dress before her hand vanished into his much larger one.

She nodded a bit and tilted her chin up as if she were introduced to guys who made *People*'s "Sexiest Man Alive" issue every day. "Matt, huh?"

"And your name is?"

Her mouth evidently had a mind of its own. For some perverse reason she blurted out, "I'm Fifi."

"Fifi." He looked a bit skeptical.

"Yes." She squared her shoulders. "My parents were— imaginative."

"Is that so?" He glanced around for a brief moment, and his eyes moved back to her. "I'm a little thirsty. Are you thirsty, Fifi? Let's have a drink."

Amy deliberated for about half a second. Despite the fact she was fairly sure she'd just met the most arrogant man in the world, she was dying to see what he was going to do next. Broken heart or not, she was in.

He didn't wait for her response. His fingertips brushed the small of her back as he nodded for her to precede him out of the ballroom.

Matt led Amy to the small bar tucked under a grand, winding staircase in the hotel's lobby. The bar resembled an old-fashioned bookstore. Bottles nestled in crackle-painted, indirectly lit shelving, sparkling-clean glasses lovingly flanking the alcohol. The five barstools were made of highly polished hardwood, padded in leather, and pulled up to a dark wood bar. There wasn't a neon advertising sign, a paper umbrella, or a test tube shot in sight.

Amy laid her bouquet, wrap, and purse on the bar, and then gathered the skirt of the vintage copper silk Vera Wang gown she wore in both hands, hiked it up, and attempted to plop herself down on a barstool. It would have worked so much better if the petticoats she wore underneath cooperated with the general idea of sitting down, or if she knew the specific location of the barstool itself. Needless to say, she missed.

She grabbed frantically for the edge of the bar.

Matt's hand shot out, grabbed her arm, and righted her before she hit the floor. "Easy, sport. Let's try that one again."

She managed to get both feet under her. Maybe if she held onto the back of the chair, and scooted herself on . . . Yeah, right. If she let go of the dress, she couldn't see the barstool. If she didn't let go of the dress, she was going to end up on her ass—and what an attractive picture that would be.

"Need more help?" Matt asked.

"I'm fine," she insisted.

"That's some dress, Fifi. Did you lose a bet?"

She glanced up at him, ready to rip off a strip of his flesh with her tongue. He held down the barstool with one foot, gripped both her upper arms, and lifted her up. He had set her down on it before she could get a word out. She found herself speechless as a result. Of course, that problem quickly resolved itself.

"Okay. We need a drink," he told her, sitting on the barstool next to her. He directed his next comments to the bartender. "Greg, two Herraduras."

Amy glanced over at Matt, and back at Greg. "A shot of Jose Cuervo Gold, please."

Matt let out a snort. "Friends don't let friends drink Jose Cuervo."

"Don't be a booze snob."

"You're intending to get naked wasted drunk, then? I'll join you." His lips curved into an infuriating smirk.

"I am *not* getting naked wasted drunk. I'm having a drink. There is a difference," Amy informed him. Her new drinking companion just laughed.

"So. You want Cuervo, you want Herradura—" It appeared Greg was having difficulty keeping up.

"Anejo, Greg. Skip the Cuervo."

"We've got Herradura Silver."

She turned to the caveman next to her. "I can order my own drink—"

"Obviously, you can't." Matt shook his head. "The silver will do." He turned to face her. "What's a nice girl like you doing in a place like this?"

"Hey, 1975 called. They'd like their pick-up line back." Amy took a breath. Well, as much of a breath as she could. Even the effort to talk to him left her breathless. God, he was unbelievably cute. Other women could handle this stuff with style and grace. If he had any idea her stomach was in knots and her palms were still sweating, he'd probably laugh at her. "Why don't you ask me what my sign is as well, Sparky?"

"You're not going to remember the first thing I said to you tomorrow, anyway." Matt's heart-stopping grin belied the sting in his words. "Why should I make the effort?" She resisted the impulse to make a rude hand gesture in response.

The Herraduras arrived. He nudged one glass in front of her, picked up the other, and said, "Drink up, sport. Shall I demonstrate?"

"Excuse me?"

"You sip this. You don't slam it." He touched his glass to hers and sipped. Full, and what she imagined to be soft, lips brushed the rim of the glass. His Adam's apple bobbed as he swallowed. He chased a stray droplet of tequila out of the corner of his mouth with the tip of his tongue. He made love to a mini-snifter, and she wondered if he was that good with a female. He set his glass back down on the bar. "I'm waiting."

"And this would mean what to me?"

He challenged Amy with his eyes and a quick nod toward her glass. His eyes were darker than the navy blue of his suit, dappled with tiny gold flecks. Even high-definition television failed to capture their color. The edge of his mouth curved into another smile.

"Don't make me drink alone. We're getting drunk together, remember?"

"You're getting drunk. I'm having a drink." She took a sip. It was smooth all the way down. "This is pretty good."

"So, you'll manage to choke it down?"

Amy narrowed her eyes and took another sip. There were a few other guys in the bar area. They seemed to be circling. Even through the slight haze of fine tequila, too much emotion, and little food or sleep, it was apparent to her that she must be wearing an invisible sign around her neck. After all, she wore an expensive—albeit, wrinkly—maid of honor gown and had a semi-wilted bouquet sitting on the bar next to her. Besides, it was getting close to closing time. She was a desperate bridesmaid, ripe for the picking.

Matt signaled the bartender for another drink, and one of the guys approached. Judging from the college-man attire and his straggly facial hair, he must have been on a weekend pass from the frat house. He leaned against the bar, gesturing to Amy's glass.

"What are you drinking, gorgeous?"

She gave him a quick grin, but Matt broke in before she could even respond.

"She's drinking a shot of back the hell off."

Amy's mouth dropped open.

"Greg, my man," Matt stated, turning to ignore the frat boy leaning against the bar. "I think my new drinking buddy needs a refill."

Greg made his way over to them. Amy still had half an inch in the bottom of her glass. Quickly, she laid one palm over it.

"Maybe later," she whispered. Greg gave her a nod.

Mr. Tragically Hip glared at Matt. "She can speak for herself, can't she?"

Matt's expression didn't change.

Amy caught the other guy's eye. "Thank you, but no thank you."

"You're sure about that? Why don't you ditch Gramps here, and we'll take you someplace better?"

Considering the fact that Amy was closer to Matt's age than his, it must have been his idea of a compliment. However, the guy in question evidently had no experience with waving a red flag in front of a bull. Matt bent a look on him that must have been an NFL leftover.

The guy's buddy grabbed one of the frat rat's arms.

"Do you know who that guy is?" he hissed. "You can't tell me you don't know who Matt Stephens is. Let's get the hell out of here before he rips your head off and pisses down your neck." He turned toward Matt and Amy, and spoke up. "My buddy's had a lot of beer. Sorry."

Amy stifled laughter as she watched the look of abject horror that crossed the face of the frat rat's friend. He extended his hand to Matt. His voice was sheepish. "I'm a fan. Sorry."

Matt shook his outstretched hand. "Thanks."

The other guy didn't seem to know when to quit, however: "So, is Falcon as big of a dick as he seems to be on the show?"

Sean Falcon was the former Super Bowl-winning, six-time Pro Bowl quarterback of the Welders in the eighties and the biggest star on Pro Sports Network's Sunday morning coverage.

Amy heard a burst of male laughter behind them, and Sean Falcon strolled through the bar area with three of his and Matt's Pro Sports Network co-stars. They'd all been at the wedding. Brandon knew everyone, or at least it seemed like he did.

"Oh, he's an even bigger dick," Falcon called out. "See you later, Stephens." He turned to one of his companions and said loudly enough for everyone to overhear, "Stephens is at the reception for twenty minutes, and he manages to hook up with a bridesmaid. I just don't get it, man."

Matt lifted one hand over his head with his middle finger extended; everyone laughed, and they were gone. The guys who'd been trying to talk to Amy were struck silent. She gulped down the last of the tequila in her glass.

"That's my girl." Matt signaled the bartender. "Hey, Greg, we need another refill down here."

She'd had less than ten hours of sleep in the past three days combined. She hadn't eaten much in that period of time, either. The flowers for Emily's wedding took precedence over everything. When Amy wasn't working on them, she lay awake, brooding over Brian like a lovesick idiot. Sleeplessness, no food, and alcohol weren't a good combination. Right now she had a definite buzz going from just one drink.

Matt turned to her as Greg refilled his glass again. She caught Greg's eye and gave him a nod. In for a penny, in for a pound. Greg poured a shot into her glass.

"So, where's your date?"

Amy had to give him snaps for being observant. The third finger of her left hand was naked as the day she was born.

She took a sip. "I gave up dating for Lent."

"Is that so?" He raised an eyebrow. "Interesting choice."

She took another sip and then swirled the tiny amount

of tequila left in the bottom of her glass. The frat rats had evidently found more promising prey out on the patio overlooking the lake, she thought as she watched them lope away. "Yeah, I'm on the wagon."

Matt appeared to choke back a laugh. "You're shitting me."

"No, I'm not." She enunciated carefully, or at least, as carefully as she could. "No dating for me, Sparky."

"So, what brought this on?"

Amy watched Greg's head snap up as well. He was polishing glasses, but she had his full attention. "Isn't the bartender supposed to be asking these questions?"

Matt's voice dropped to a conspiratorial murmur. "He's busy. I'm filling in for him. You can tell me."

"Don't you have something else to do?"

"Nothing more important than what I'm doing right now," Matt assured her. He casually rested one arm around the back of Amy's chair, while making perfect condensation circles with the bottom of his glass on the bar in front of them.

"Greg?" she called out. "May I have another drink, please?" Just thinking about Brian made her want to grab the bottle out of Greg's hand and chug it till it was gone. Brian wasn't her soul mate by any stretch of the imagination, but he'd managed to break her heart anyway.

"Are you sure about this, sport? Stuff's got a kick like a mule," Matt warned.

"I can handle it," she informed him. "Maybe I should order a double."

"This'll be good," Matt muttered.

"What are you talking about?"

Greg poured another inch or so of tequila into her glass, and Matt leaned toward her a bit.

"Nothing. You were saying?"

The late night, exhaustion, and a fresh drink conspired against Amy.

"I dumped my boyfriend. Yesterday. I'm done with men."

She was lying, but how the hell would he ever know? She wasn't a liar by nature, but she wasn't about to confide to a guy who appeared in *People*'s "Sexiest Man Alive" issue that she'd gotten dumped.

She lifted her glass. "Let's drink to single women everywhere."

"I'll drink to that," Greg assured her.

Matt didn't drink. "So, you're hanging it up?"

"Yes, I am." Amy tipped her chin up and threw her shoulders back. No self-pity for her.

"You're just going to let him win?" Matt insisted.

"What are you talking about? Win? Are you kidding?" She gestured with her glass. The few drops of tequila slopped dangerously close to the rim. "He moved to New York. I don't care about him."

That's why she'd watered Emily's wedding flowers with her tears yesterday, and why she'd had to soak her face in ice-cold water this morning. She concealed her broken heart well. After all, she'd had lots of practice.

"You don't say."

"He got on a plane this morning. He couldn't even wait until the wedding was over. *Win*? That's insane. There is no winner here." She took another sip of tequila.

"Then again, I'm the winner. Fine. I don't want him. He doesn't want me, either."

"That's the spirit, Fifi." Once again, Matt appeared to be smothering laughter. "I thought you dumped him."

"I did. I totally dumped him." She polished off the last few drops of her drink.

"So, I take it you'll be joining a—what do they call it? A nunnery? Maybe there's some kind of 'down with men' club you're checking into?"

"It's called a convent. Didn't you pay attention during catechism?"

"As a matter of fact, no, I didn't." He captured the bowl of pretzels Greg had just put onto the bar and held it out to her. "I'll bet you look great in black. Snack?"

"No, thank you."

"So, let's get back to this whole 'we hate men' thing. I'm intrigued. Is it all men, or just your ex?"

Even with the buzz, Amy knew Matt was teasing her. There was an expression in his eyes she couldn't read. At the same time she got the feeling he didn't want to spend the evening alone. He was in no hurry to leave. She didn't want to spend the evening alone, either.

Amy let out a sigh.

"I don't know what they want. They say they love you, and then they don't." She waved her arms for emphasis. "I shower. I'm reasonably nice. I know how to cook, and I'm somewhat financially stable. I'm not clingy, demanding, or crazy. I do not get it."

She turned to face Greg. "Greg. You're a guy. What is it that they want?"

"Damned if I know," Greg reassured her. "Who cares about them, though? They're obviously stupid. You're hot."

"Thank you." She beamed at Greg, and glanced over at Matt. "I love him."

"You're not helping me right now, Greg," Matt informed him.

Greg moved down the bar a bit. Matt took another sip of his drink, and turned to study Amy. How could he drink so much more than she had, and still appear to be sober? This was just another of life's inequities. He patted Amy's hand.

"So, sport, what are we going to do about this?"

"Do about what?"

"You shouldn't be running around in public alone."

"I am *harmless*—"

This time, Matt laughed out loud. He threw his head back, closing his eyes for a moment. The sound bounced around the room.

"It's late." He leaned closer to her. "Maybe the best thing to do is to make sure you get home safely. Let's try that first. Do I need to call a cab?"

"No, no." She shifted on the barstool. "I have a room upstairs. I'll be fine."

"Got it. Well, Fifi, I think you've had enough."

"Nope." She waved the snifter at Greg the bartender, who took it out of her hand before it went flying. Her reflexes were somewhat unsteady, but she knew exactly what she wanted. "More."

"How about a cup of coffee instead? It's on the house." Greg was all efficiency. Matt slid his credit card across the bar, and Greg scooped it up. "I'll make a fresh pot, just for you."

"No. No coffee." She held up one hand like a traffic cop. "More tequila."

"Not tonight. Let's leave some for the other customers," Matt said, and rose from the barstool. He and Greg had some sort of murmured conference. He signed the receipt, and took Amy's elbow. "It's time for you to get some sleep."

"I'm not tired. Are you tired? I don't want to go to bed yet."

Her feet wouldn't reach the floor. She couldn't figure it out. Plus, the dress had a mind of its own. She couldn't seem to get it untangled from the barstool. One minute she was sliding off the barstool, the next minute she was toppling over. Matt caught her in his arms. Again. It probably had something to do with the fact she also managed to put the stiletto heel of her sandal through the tulle that made up the underskirt of the gown.

"I can walk," she protested. Man, he smelled good, like fresh air and laundry soap. She was a little more buzzed than she thought.

"I'm helping you."

"I don't need your help." She heard the tulle rip as she yanked the underskirt away from the heel piercing it. "Fixed it," she informed him proudly.

"Where's your room?"

For some unknown reason this was hilarious. She had an overwhelming impulse to giggle. "Upstairs," she managed to choke out.

"Do you remember which floor you're on?"

The room was tilting. Was there an earthquake? Nobody else seemed to be worried.

"Of course I do."

Matt pulled the black evening bag out of her slack fingers, opened it, and examined the room key. "No room number."

"It's on the third floor. How hard could it be to find, anyway?"

She tried to move away from him. Though the tulle had torn away from her heel, the dress still wound around her ankles. She pulled it free, reached out to grab her purse out of Matt's fingers, and attempted to walk. She grabbed at one of the barstools in an effort to right herself.

"That dress is dangerous. Come on, Fifi. I'll walk you to your room." Matt took her elbow.

After a series of trial and errors, Matt and Amy managed to find her room before hotel security was summoned. The keycard only worked in the correct door, so they didn't disturb anyone else. Amy pushed the door open, and Matt followed her inside.

"Thanks for walking me back to my room, but I'm okay now. Really. You can leave." She held the door open with one sandaled foot and pointed into the hallway with a somewhat unsteady finger. "Out."

Matt actually snickered. He still held her elbow. He marched her across the room, plopped her into the easy chair by a sliding glass door, opened it a bit, and tossed his jacket on the bed.

"I'm going to buy you a very large glass of water and a

couple of aspirin. You need to get it all down." She tried to push herself out of the chair. He was having none of this. "Just relax."

The room was spinning, but it wasn't unpleasant. Amy realized that she had a much more immediate problem. Her dress had thirty small, fabric-covered buttons down the back. How was she ever going to get this thing off by herself? Plus, it wasn't smart to ask someone else she didn't know, no matter how cute he was or how many times she had watched him on television, to half-undress her.

Matt was on the phone with room service, and she stood up from the chair. For some reason, it didn't feel like she stood up straight. She felt crooked. She shoved the slider further open, and ventured out onto the balcony overlooking Lake Washington.

Matt was on the balcony in a flash, too. He surprised her by grabbing both her shoulders in his hands.

"Oh, no, you don't. You shouldn't be out here."

"It's cold." The chilly air slapped Amy in the face. "Why are you still here?"

"I'm earning another Boy Scout merit badge." His voice was a mixture of amusement and exasperation. "I'll leave when I know you're settled in for the night."

She grabbed the balcony railing with both hands. The sky shouldn't be spinning. "There's just one problem."

"What's that?"

"I . . . I can't get this dress off by myself."

She heard a low chuckle in her ear. "You know, I've heard this happens to other guys." He moved closer and murmured, "Dear *Penthouse*: She begged me to take her dress off."

"I can handle this," she stubbornly insisted. "Never mind. I don't need your help."

"You'll be wearing that dress for the next week if I don't help you, sport. Let's see here." Matt's fingers grazed the top button.

"We're outside and it's dark. You can't even see."

"I work by braille," he assured her. "How'd you get this on in the first place?"

"My mom helped me." Emily and Amy's mom had some colorful things to say about Vera Wang by the time she was finished. "People will see us! We should go inside—" She felt cool air on her skin as another button opened.

"Well, Mom's not here now, is she? Dizzy, Fifi?"

Amy's knuckles showed white as she held the balcony railing in a death grip. Matt's warm breath tickled the back of her neck. His scent filled her nostrils—fresh air, clean skin, some musky stuff that must have been him, because it wasn't like any other men's cologne she'd ever smelled before. It mingled pleasantly with the cool night air.

Her hands slipped off the balcony railing as his quickly moving fingers set her free from a smooth prison of fabric. Of course, the building mood was shattered instantaneously. He stepped on the ripped underskirt at the back of Amy's dress, she lost her balance, and her arms flailed as she fell against his chest. She also managed to get him in the gut with one elbow.

"Damn, Fifi, what the hell was that?" he wheezed.

"I'm sorry! I didn't mean to hurt you! It was an accident! I—"

He grasped her forearm for balance. "You're just a menace, aren't you?"

Amy left her dress in a pile on the bathroom floor. Her slip, pantyhose, and bra followed it. She'd get the hairpins from her former updo out in the morning. She washed her face with soap and water, wriggled into the t-shirt and shorts she brought from home, and walked back into the room once more.

A tray with water, pain relievers, and a napkin-draped basket waited on the computer desk. The scent of freshly baked bread made her mouth water.

"Sleepy," was all Amy could get out.

"I'll bet. First, though, let's have some bread. It's still warm." He held out the basket. Matt looked more delicious than the bread: He had perfect muscles; he smelled good; he was taller than she was, which was always a good thing.

"Sleepy," Amy repeated. "It's time for bed."

Before she knew it, she was tucked up in the bed, alone. He was explaining something to her. All she had to do was concentrate.

"I'll leave the light on . . ." His words floated back to her from somewhere in the room.

"Thank you." She rolled onto her side, closed her eyes, and took a deep breath. Realizing Matt was still there, she forced her eyes open and attempted to focus on his face. "Do you always rescue women?"

"Only the beautiful ones," Matt assured her.

Everything was wonderful. As a matter of fact, everything was perfect. She was finally horizontal. The room didn't spin as long as she lay perfectly still.

Matt sat down next to her. It took a few minutes, but she realized he was slowly pulling the pins out of her wrecked hairdo. He was still talking.

"Just sleep. It'll all be better tomorrow."

"No, it won't. Brian left."

"Who's Brian?"

"He's a lawyer." Amy let out a gusty sigh. "I don't like lawyers."

Matt let out a snort. "I don't like them, either."

"I shouldn't be sad about him." She flipped onto her back, squeezed her eyes shut to stop the spinning, and threw a forearm over her eyes.

"No, you shouldn't, Fifi."

"I hate men," she insisted. "Well, except for you."

Matt made a sound somewhere between a choke and a chuckle. He sounded like he was smiling, though. "It's good to know that. Why don't you get some sleep, huh?"

"Why were you late to the wedding, Matt? You should have been there." If she could get the bed to spin in the same direction as the room did every time she moved, it would be a good thing. "It was perfect. Emily was so beautiful. The food was really good, and Brandon was so funny during the toast, and . . ."

Matt interrupted her. "I hate weddings."

"Why? Too mushy, or no tequila till the reception?"

"Someone always gets married." Matt was still carefully extracting the pins from her hair. Amy opened her eyes to see him studying her for a long moment. "Do you like weddings?"

"I have to go to a lot of them because I do the flowers. But, truthfully? I'm not sure I like them, either."

"I thought all women liked that stuff."

She wrinkled her nose and tried to shake her head before deciding it wasn't the smartest move. "Nice stereotyping, Sparky."

"Come on. You know I'm right."

"It's not the wedding so much as the rest of it. Mostly I want a family. If I have to go through it to get one, I will."

They both fell silent for several minutes. Amy was half-asleep. Strangely enough, it was comforting to hear Matt speak, and listen to his breathing in the darkened room. She had the vague thought that maybe she should be keeping an eye on Matt. He was a stranger. It wasn't good to be alone in a hotel room with a stranger. Plus, she was telling him about Brian. She was going to give this some serious thought later on. At the same time, it was all she could do to keep her eyes open longer than a few seconds at a time.

"Sleepy yet?" Even in her less-than-sober state, there was something in his voice that made her open her eyes once more. He looked sad. "It's time to say goodnight, Fifi."

"Maybe." She snuggled down into the blankets. "My name's not really Fifi."

"I know it's not."

"It could be."

"Oh, I'm sure it could. I'm guessing the only thing you have in common with the other Fifi I've met is that you probably like bacon."

"Everyone likes bacon," she sighed.

"The other Fifi was a lovely standard poodle owned by my former next-door-neighbors. She enjoyed long walks on the beach and sunsets, too." She had to smile a little, and he pulled the blankets up to her nose. "Shhh. You'll feel better in the mor— That's a damn lie. You'll feel better eventually," he muttered.

She wondered if she was sending some kind of Morse code with her eyelids.

"I've got it." Amy snapped her fingers. Well, she tried to. They weren't working correctly. "It doesn't matter if I ever get married, does it? I could still have a baby. I'll just adopt. Everyone's doing it now."

"Sure you could. It can't be that hard."

"If the adoption thing doesn't work, I'll   well, I'll just find a sperm donor. He doesn't have to have anything to do with me or the baby. It'll be great!" Matt flinched. "Are you cold? There's lots of blankets. Here." She sat up, and let out a groan. "If the room would just stop spinning . . ."

She tried to pull the blanket at the foot of the bed out from under him, but she couldn't budge his weight.

"I'm fine. Lie down," he said.

A few minutes went by. Maybe she imagined it, but she heard him say, "Why would you be in the market for a sperm donor when the old-fashioned way's a hell of a lot more fun?"

THE NEXT TIME Amy opened her eyes, sunlight streamed through the hotel room windows. She was alone.

A small army had set up shop inside her head, pounding something incredibly intricate on her brain pan with miniature hammers. Her mouth felt like she'd wandered the Sahara for a week. When she wasn't suffering from terminal cotton mouth, the room was still spinning.

"Uhhh," she groaned. Silence greeted her.

She focused her eyes long enough to see an orderly pile of hairpins next to an envelope on the nightstand that read "Fifi." It wasn't her imagination. She'd spent most of the previous evening with Matt Stephens. She flopped back into the pillows with the envelope in her hand, and let out a moan. She remembered last night while her stomach did a figure-eight.

Oh, God. What had she said to him, anyway? Snatches of last night's conversation were coming back to her. Of course, the sweet, comforting part was completely lost on Amy when she thought about the reality: She'd just spilled her guts to a guy she didn't even know. To make things worse, he was a nationally known, really, really handsome guy she didn't even know.

She'd told him she hated men. She'd let him unbutton her dress. On the balcony, no less! Had she really told him about Brian? She gave him a fake name, which of *course* reminded him of his neighbor's dog. Even worse, she'd said something about a *sperm donor*. . . . Oh, God, no.

No. It wasn't true. She dreamt it all. Amy tore the envelope open, and flinched with the combination of the noise involved and the fact that she knew, deep in her heart, it wasn't a dream.

His business card fell out of the folded note. "Fifi," he had scrawled in a heavy, dark hand. "I had appointments this morning, so I had to leave. I might have a solution for that problem you're having. Coffee? Matt."

Chapter Two

Matt Stephens woke up alone in his own bed the next morning. It would be good to say this happened often, but it wouldn't be truthful. It had happened more and more lately, though, and not due to a lack of invitations. He was less than interested in taking things to their natural conclusion with the vast number of women he was meeting these days. Mostly, he wanted someone to come home to, and he hadn't met her yet.

After "Fifi" fell asleep the night before, he'd made sure she was tucked in and more water and aspirin waited for her on the nightstand, then he'd slipped out of her room after leaving his contact information. He was musing on the over/under of Fifi calling him for the coffee date he'd suggested when he heard a feminine voice calling out to him.

"Matt? Matt, are you awake?" He heard muffled footsteps on the carpet runner in the hallway outside of his bedroom. "I'm hungry. Someone ate the last toaster pastry, and it wasn't me."

His gangly fourteen-year-old daughter padded into his bedroom, clad in a "Team Edward" t-shirt and sweat pants; she had cobalt-blue streaks through her almost waist-length, inky black hair. She shoved the mass out of her eyes, and regarded him through Kohl pencil smeared from eyelid to temple. He wished she wouldn't wear the stuff.

"And you think I ate it?"

"Maybe someone broke into the house and took it," she suggested. She threw herself down next to him.

"Wanna watch cartoons?" he enticed. "I love Ren and Stimpy."

"No, thanks. I need to get dressed. I'm going shopping today. Don't you have a meeting?"

He definitely had a meeting, but he could stall. Right now, he needed a few minutes with the most important female in his life. He propped himself up against the headboard.

"Do you need some money, princess?"

"I have money," she informed him. "We're going shopping, and then we're going to a movie."

"Who's 'we'?"

"Brittany, Morgan, and me. We're taking the bus to Bellevue Square. Brittany's mom is driving us home."

"Brittany, Morgan and I, and you'll be home by dark."

"It's dark at five o'clock now!"

"You'll be home by dark," he repeated. "No getting in someone else's car that I don't know, either. If you need a ride, you call me."

"You're busy . . ."

He cut her off. "I'm never too busy to come and get you. No R rated movies, either."

"But the Rob Pa—"

"No." He grabbed his robe off the foot of the bed, pulled it around himself, and sat down next to her. "I will see it first. If it's okay, we'll go together."

"It's just violent and there's swear words—"

"This isn't a negotiation." He watched her lower lip quiver. "I've been informed that you need a dress for the upcoming dance. If you ask for Michelle at the Brass Plum, she has several on hold for you to try on. She promises me that no, you will not be a laughing stock, however, you *will* look your age."

"Matt! Why can't I pick out my own dress? I can't believe you're doing this! I'm not a baby. I can do it myself! Oooh!" She jumped up off the bed, flung herself out into the hallway, and he heard stomping footsteps all the way back to her room. The door slammed seconds later.

The greatest love he'd ever known started the moment a doctor had handed him a lustily crying infant, wrapped in a soft pink blanket. She had his hair, she had his eyes, she had the dimples at either side of his mouth, and she had his heart clutched in her tiny fist. One smile from his baby daughter, and he knew he would slay dragons for her. His ex-wife teased him that he loved Samantha more than he'd ever loved her. It was true. Matt's entire life hinged on the fact his little girl was never, ever going to find out that he was putty in her hands, wrapped around her finger, and completely smitten. As a result, he set rules that made the Marine Corps look lax.

The silence from her room indicated she was most likely texting everyone she knew to tell them one more time that her dad was the meanest, most unreasonable man on the face of the planet. He picked up the phone on his bedside table, dialed her cell number, and waited for her to answer.

"Samantha, get dressed, and we'll go out for breakfast."

He waited through a long silence.

"I don't like you very much right now," she said.

"You're going to have to try that one on someone else. Come on. After we eat, I'll drop you and your friends off at the mall on my way to the production meeting."

She thought for a few moments. "Fine."

He resisted the impulse to laugh.

MATT PICKED UP the menu at Pancake Corral and pretended he wasn't listening to the chattering of a table full of teenage girls. Pancake Corral wasn't one of those white tablecloth places, and he was glad. The décor was homey. The food was good. He also appreciated the family atmosphere, which came with a side of humor. A sign close to the front door proclaimed, "Unattended children will be given an espresso and a free puppy."

He peered over his menu. "Ladies. Why don't you decide what you'd like for brunch, and we'll all order?"

Brittany and Morgan were frequent visitors at the Stephens residence. They'd befriended Samantha in preschool, and the three girls still saw each other often. This morning, though, a fourth school friend was with them. Natalie had made it clear she wasn't happy about Matt's order to put their cell phones away while they were eating. She wore a tight, revealing knit top he wouldn't let his own daughter purchase, let alone wear. She was staring at Matt, and he was growing increasingly uncomfortable with her obvious interest. Since when did a little girl try to pick up on a man old enough to be her father?

"Chris asked Melanie to the dance. His parents are getting them a limo," Natalie informed the other three girls. "The Hummer one."

"Wouldn't that be sick? Trevor's not getting a limo. His parents are driving us. His dad made a reservation at John Howie Steak for dinner, though," Brittany flipped her long blonde hair over one shoulder. Matt knew Brittany's dad, and he'd be making a phone call. It was hard for Matt to believe that Brittany's parents would go for this kind of thing at all. Fourteen was much too young for a date. Brittany and her "date" were probably having dinner with her parents.

Morgan wrinkled her nose. "My parents took me there a long time ago. The vegetables are good, but I didn't like it."

"You're still a vegetarian?" his daughter asked. "Don't you eat bacon?"

"I only eat it once in a while."

Matt hid his amusement behind the menu. He managed to get the four girls to order an actual breakfast, whether they liked it or not, and ordered for himself. The female, twenty-something server wrote down the order, but she spent so much time looking at Matt he wondered how she managed to make notes.

She winked at him. "I'll keep the coffee coming."

"Perfect." He handed over the menus. She hurried away, and Samantha let out a groan.

"She likes him. We can't go *anywhere*. You just watch. She's going to try to talk to him again, and she'll give him her phone number."

"Nobody flirts with my dad, except my mom," Morgan reassured her. "They kiss in the kitchen when they think I'm not looking. It's kind of gross. They're old."

"At least your mom and dad like each other. My mom calls my dad 'the sperm donor.' She says he'll stick it in any—"

Matt interrupted Natalie. "Ladies. Are you all shopping for a dress today, or are you on the lookout for something else?"

Natalie, Samantha and Brittany began to speak at once, while Morgan glanced down at the table. Matt remembered Samantha mentioning Morgan not only lacked a "date" for the dance, but her dad had lost his job recently. Matt assumed that Morgan's parents were having a tough time financially as a result. He'd always enjoyed his conversations with Morgan and her family. They were down-to-earth people who stressed family time over material things, and he appreciated their influence on his daughter.

An idea took hold as he listened to three girls chatter like magpies and observed the quieter one, who was valiantly trying to seem happy for them.

Breakfast arrived. He handled the typical conversation about "fat" and "calories" well, he thought.

"If you ladies refuse to eat, you'll have to go running with me later, won't you?"

Four horrified faces gazed back at him.

"You'll burn this off by lunchtime anyway. Eat up."

He took a large bite of his omelet. He slid the business card with the server's scrawled telephone number on it that arrived with his breakfast into his pocket. He'd toss it into the trash can outside the front door of the restaurant; he never disrespected a woman with control over his food.

He herded four girls into his car to leave after breakfast, while texting one of his co-workers. He was going to miss their meeting. He needed to do a little shopping.

MATT PULLED INTO the parking garage outside Nordstrom and found a space. The girls scrambled out. He slid his arm around his daughter's shoulders as they walked to the store's entrance.

"Listen, kitten, I'm going to join you for a little while this morning."

Samantha acted like he'd just deleted all content off her iPod. "Matt, I can handle this myself! Don't you have a production meeting?"

Morgan's eyes got huge. "You're still calling your dad by his first name? My dad would—I would be grounded for the rest of my *life*."

"I think it's cool," Natalie opined.

Brittany just shook her head.

"Well, now she's forced to go shopping with me, isn't she?" Matt joked.

Twenty minutes later, he sat in a comfortable chair outside of the dressing room in Nordstrom's teen department. One of the salespeople was bringing dresses in and out of the rooms at a furious pace. He was in the midst of a murmured negotiation with the manager of the department, who was taking notes.

"The little dark-haired one's name is Morgan. She's a close friend of my daughter's, and things are tough for her family right now. I want to pay for a dress, shoes, whatever else it is she needs. We can't let her find out I'm doing it, though. How are we going to work this?"

"You can either give her a gift card, or you can buy the items today, and we'll have them sent to her house."

"Let's have the items sent to the house, and I'd like to put a gift card in there for another fifty dollars or so, just in case."

"Wonderful."

Matt dug out his wallet, handed the woman his Nordstrom card, and settled back into the chair again. He didn't have a lot of extras as a kid. He knew how hard his mom worked to pay for the basics—shelter, clothing, and food. He didn't want to ask her for stuff she would have a hard time getting for him. He still remembered the look on her face when she'd figured out he outgrew more clothes and shoes, or needed something she had to scrimp and save to pay for. He got a paper route as a kid, too. He paid his own sports fees for football and gave his mom the rest of the money for the household bills. It still wasn't enough.

He'd tell Morgan's parents that the gift came from Samantha. In the meantime, he wondered if one of his colleagues might have a job for Morgan's dad. He'd make some calls later.

Samantha emerged from the cacophony of giggling that was the dressing room and twirled around in front of him.

"What do you think?"

The dress was silver, mid-calf length, with thin straps holding up the bodice, and some kind of silver sparkly netting over the skirt. The sash at the waist was black. She'd probably wear Army boots with it, but Matt's heart squeezed in his chest. His little girl was growing up. She would find some boy and fall in love, and Matt would commit some kind of bodily harm on him if that boy ever made her cry. She tried to play it cool, but her shining eyes and flushed cheeks told him she loved the dress. Of course, it was exactly what he wanted her to buy—pretty, but modest. He wouldn't mention that fact.

"I like it. It's a nice dress, and you look beautiful." He raised an eyebrow. "I suppose we need some shoes to go with it." He held up the slender tube of pale pink, sparkly lip gloss another salesperson had brought from the downstairs makeup counter. "They told me you might like this, too."

She thought he didn't know about the pencil she used to line her eyes. His ex-wife, Laura, had put the blue streaks in Samantha's hair herself. She reluctantly allowed Samantha to use a little mascara as well, which turned out to be a mistake. Samantha used as many coats as possible on each application. He knew she was dying to use "makeup." She'd be waiting awhile for that, but a little pink lip gloss on a special occasion didn't hurt anyone.

The young woman in question completely forgot her teen attitude, and flung her arms around him. "Thank you! Oh, thank you. Do you really like it? I think it's so pretty. Plus, the lip gloss is sick. It's exactly what I wanted!"

He breathed in the scent of her hair and some body spray she insisted on marinating in, which would never be as sweet as the babyhood smells he remembered. She was all arms and legs now, but he knew she would be even more stunning than her mother. He was going to spend the next ten years keeping the male population away from her. For the moment, though, his little girl was hugging him. This was a great day already.

She pulled away from him, regarded him with serious eyes, and whispered, "I need to talk to you."

"You do, huh?"

"Morgan needs a dress. Her parents can't afford it, and she's so sad. Natalie is being really mean to her, too. We shouldn't have invited Natalie." She plunked herself down on her dad's knee. "I have about a hundred dollars I saved up that I can use. Maybe you could take the rest of the money out of my allowance. Please?"

Matt felt like the Grinch, whose heart had grown three sizes in thirty seconds. Mostly, he was proud of her. She was listening to the things he and Laura tried to tell her, and she was willing to use her own money to help someone else.

"So, you'll give up your allowance to buy Morgan a dress? It's quite a bit of money," he said.

"I know." Samantha's excitement dimmed a little. "She's my friend, though, and—well, I can babysit or something if I need extra money, can't I?"

"You know I don't want you babysitting during the school year."

Her face fell. She fidgeted with the tag on the side of the dress, and didn't meet his eyes. He saw her chin quiver, and he pulled her closer.

"Listen. It's already been taken care of. It won't cost you a dime." He took a breath and gave her a squeeze. "It feels good to do something nice for someone else who needs it, doesn't it?"

She wrapped her arms around his neck. "Yes."

"Now, don't tell Morgan. It's all going to be sent to her house. I'll talk to her mom before it shows up." He gave her an awkward pat on the back. "You know you can come to me anytime if you have a problem or you need help."

"Uh-huh." He felt her nodding against the side of his neck.

"I'm proud of you."

In a voice so soft he barely heard it over the commotion in the store she murmured, "Thanks, Dad."

Chapter Three

A WEEK HAD passed since Emily's wedding, and Amy hardly thought of Matt Stephens at all. Well, she wasn't thinking about him when she was asleep anyway. Surely he got the hint when she didn't call him back, but her conscience nagged.

The least she could do was buy him a cup of coffee for making sure she made it back to her room safely, not to mention rescuing her from taking a header off the hotel room balcony. Then again, she'd rather be dragged buck naked over broken glass than face him again. Just the memory of that evening made her flinch. Obviously a cup of coffee did not mean a committed relationship, but between her continuing embarrassment and unwillingness to open herself up to more heartbreak, she was not picking up the phone to call him.

Amy let out another groan. Luckily, there was nobody else in her flower shop to hear it. Business had been slow since Valentine's Day. The first day or so, it wasn't that big of a deal. She needed a break after Emily and Brandon's wedding. Now, though, she worried. She was hoping word-of-mouth from both the wedding and the advertising funds she squeezed out of the shop's tiny budget would pay off for her. So far, things were a little quieter than Amy would have liked.

After ten years as a CPA, she'd worked hard to get the financing to open her business. Even with a fairly good Valentine's Day business, she still needed to pay next month's rent. There was always cleaning and bookwork to do, so she headed back into her workroom.

The phone rang, and she grabbed it. "Crazy Daisy."

"Hey, weirdo." Emily sounded like she was in the next room, instead of 2,600 miles away. "How's it going?"

Amy sank down on a stool in front of her workbench. "Fine. How are you? Where's your husband?"

"He's sleeping," her sister said. Amy heard laughter in her voice. "I think I wore him out. Poor guy. He just isn't as young as he used to be."

"Niiice. So, what else have you all been doing?"

"Well, we took a surfing lesson. It's fun. I did a little shopping yesterday. Oh. Mom called. She and Dad tried to call your room after the wedding, and she said you didn't call her back. I just said that you were probably out with a friend or something. Did Brian ever show up?"

"No. He had to work."

Brian had to work, all right. She'd rather keep the news they were no longer a couple quiet until she figured out how to explain that to her family. She also wasn't sure she wanted Brandon to know that she'd spent the evening after he and Emily's wedding getting unintentionally plastered with one of his buddies—the cute one.

Amy restrained another groan.

"So, where were you?" Emily persisted.

"I had some tequila. I must have slept through the phone ringing."

"Oh. Okay." Amy knew Emily didn't believe her, but she was saved by an unexpected source.

A sleepy-sounding male voice called out in the background, "Hey, sugar, who you talkin' to?"

"Gotta go," Emily said. Just before she hit the disconnect button, Amy heard Brandon telling her sister, "You're wearing waaay too many clothes."

"I'll pretend like I didn't hear that," she told the resulting dial tone. Maybe she could use some brain bleach to erase *that* visual. She picked up the mop she was using on the workroom floor once more.

A few minutes later, the bell on the front door jingled, and Amy heard footsteps in the lobby. "I'll be right with you," she called out.

"Take your time," a familiar male voice responded.

The hair lifted on the back of Amy's neck. The mop fell back into the bucket with a splash. Brushing her wet hands off on her apron, she hurried around the corner of the workroom.

Maybe she was mistaken. Maybe it wasn't really him. *Damn.* Matt Stephens gave her a smug grin.

"Good morning, Fifi. How are you?"

Her stomach did a complicated roll. Her heart rate

picked up. Dread, embarrassment, and pleasure washed over her like the rains over Seattle from November to February. The palms she'd just dried off were already sweaty. Of course, he'd seen her, so she couldn't run back into her postage stamp-sized office and lock the door.

"What are you doing here?" she blurted.

Matt pretended great interest in a cymbidium orchid. "You never called. I had to make sure you didn't go deep-sea diving off the hotel balcony, didn't I? Plus, I need to send some flowers."

"How did you find me?" Just speaking was a major undertaking at that point. She'd never met a guy who flustered her like this before.

Matt twirled what Amy recognized as one of her business cards in his fingers. He lifted an eyebrow.

"How'd you get that?"

He drummed the side of the business card on the counter. His mouth twitched with barely repressed laughter. "Just call me Sherlock."

He must have swiped it from one of Brandon's friends. Amy tried to think of a clever retort, but her brain was currently experiencing some kind of power failure. The blood was obviously rushing to the parts of her body that didn't regulate speech.

She'd inched out of the workroom while they were talking, and now Matt stood a few feet away from her. He was casually dressed in beat-up Levis, a blue-and-white checked sport shirt, and a black leather jacket. Despite ditching the suit and tie he wore for his TV appearances, he was still gorgeous. And she still felt like an idiot.

"Speaking of the flowers," he said, "I need some delivered tomorrow. Think you can handle that?"

"Where are they going?" If she could just concentrate on the business transaction, she could hope to get through this without embarrassing herself further. Maybe.

"Are you familiar with the condos across the street from Carillon Point in Kirkland?"

"Yes," Amy said. She pulled an order pad and pen out of one of the pockets of her apron. "What would you like?"

"So, why didn't you call me, Fifi?"

"I was busy," she said.

She fiddled with the pen. Of course, it slipped out of her fingers, and she dropped it on the floor. She bent to retrieve it. When she straightened up again, she couldn't look into his eyes.

"I was concerned," he said.

The silence stretched on for what felt like an eternity but was most likely under a minute. He let out a breath.

"I'd like eighteen pink roses arranged with whatever it is you put with them to make them look nice." He pointed to the paler pink variety she'd picked up from the wholesaler just that morning. "Those."

"Whom are you sending them to?"

He rattled off an address and telephone number and added, "They're for Samantha."

"Does Samantha have a last name?"

"Just 'Samantha,'" he insisted. He twirled the card

holder she kept on the counter, selected one with brightly colored balloons printed on it, and spent a few minutes scrawling a note. He slid the card back into the envelope, tucked the flap beneath, and handed it to Amy. "What's the damage?"

"One hundred dollars plus tax."

"A hundred bucks. I should have gone to the grocery store."

He handed her his platinum card, though, which she swiped through the credit card machine. She resisted the impulse to tell him it had been declined, just to yank his chain. His fingers brushed Amy's as she passed him the card slip and a pen, and she felt a jolt of heat. She jerked away. Her stomach did another slow roll.

"Are you all right?"

She wondered if it was possible to die of embarrassment.

"Fine," she chirped, with a breeziness she didn't feel. "I'll have these to Samantha by tomorrow afternoon." She stapled the credit card slip to the receipt, and handed it to him. "Thank you very much."

"You're welcome, Fifi."

Oddly enough, he seemed in no hurry to leave. He sniffed at a small vase of carnations set out on the counter. Amy tried to look busy and efficient, while she wondered if her brain was melting. She just couldn't get past all the humiliating crap she'd said to him a week ago. It was a new low for her, even if she was a bit impaired at the time. Plus, her behavior that evening was a complete accident. She supposed she could have tried pleading the effects of extreme exhaustion and alcohol consumption, but she hadn't acted like that even in college. She got an hour or two with a guy who gave a whole new meaning to "drop dead gorgeous," and she acted like a reality TV star. *Great.*

She heard him speak once more, and she managed to tip over the small box holding an entire day's worth of receipts.

"Let's grab a cup of coffee."

Her head snapped up. "Are you talking to me?"

Matt gave her a look that could only be classified as another smirk.

"There's nobody else here. Who did you think I was talking to?"

She took a deep breath and reminded herself that he'd just spent a hundred dollars, the shop's rent was due in two weeks, and he probably had women crying on his shoulder every day, which was even more embarrassing. Oh, God. He probably thought she was an NFL groupie. She'd rather die than turn into one of those women who attended a football game in a micro mini and stilettos.

Matt was positively unruffled by their exchange. "How about it? I'll even treat."

"I can't," she informed him immediately.

"You're the boss. You can do whatever you want," he countered.

"I have too much work."

"It can wait."

"No, it can't."

He didn't seem to be listening. "Next time, then."

This needed to stop, right now, even if her toes were curling in her shoes. Even if the laughter he was still fighting to control melted her heart.

"Matt. I really appreciated your help the other night. Obviously, tequila does bad things to me." He let out a snort, and she continued. "It's really thoughtful of you to check on me, and of course I appreciate the business. At the same time, I don't think it would be a good idea for us to have coffee."

He leaned on the counter a bit. "Why not?"

The fresh-air-and-laundry-soap scent she noticed the other night drifted toward her again. Her heart was banging against her breastbone like a loose shutter in a hurricane, her knees knocked, and she blurted out the first thing that came to mind.

"Look. I'm a big football fan, so it was great to meet you. At the same time, I can imagine you'd like to settle down some day, and truthfully, you are the last man on earth I would do that with. We shouldn't date at all." She immediately wanted to bite out her own tongue. It was true, but she didn't have to be so blunt.

"Is that so?" The corners of his mouth dimpled. "What if I'd just like to have a cup of coffee with an attractive woman?"

"I'm not your type."

According to the stuff she'd read about Matt, that was a giant understatement. After all, she had a career. She didn't spend all day Sunday prancing around on the sidelines of a football game in a pair of knee-high white boots, even if at least one of her friends did. She was surprised he wasn't pursuing someone like Mackenzie, an NFL cheerleader whose yoga studio was two doors down. He also seemed quite fond of breast implants, if the photos she'd seen of his former girlfriends were any indicator. They'd never quite made her "to-do" list.

His smile grew. His voice was deceptively mild. "Maybe you should let me decide who is, or is not, 'my type.'"

"I really don't think—"

He cut her off. "The last man on earth." His eyes moved over her face. "Now there's a challenge if I've ever heard one." His voice dropped to a low, sexy rumble. "There must be a lot of other guys you wouldn't want to end up with besides me."

He was the picture of injured innocence—*who, me?*—the wolf whose big teeth Little Red Riding Hood didn't see until it was much too late. Unfortunately for Matt, she'd already spent some time in the forest, and she'd met plenty of guys like him before.

"Again, Matt, good to meet you. Thanks for stopping by. Have a nice evening."

When he finally stopped laughing, he pinned her with his eyes.

"So, I'm guessing that whole sperm donor thing is off as well?"

"I am really embarrassed that I said that stuff—"

"It was the most entertaining date I've been on in a long time." His voice was gentle. "It's just coffee. I promise I don't have a marriage license in my back pocket."

Amy swallowed hard. Obviously, Matt thought the

word *no* was a cue for negotiations to start. She was wavering, but at the same time, she wasn't an idiot. This guy was trouble in gift-wrap. The package was gorgeous, but she was more than a little apprehensive of what she'd find when she tore the shiny paper off.

"That wasn't a date. If it was anything at all, it was the after-after party for my sister's wedding reception." She sucked in a breath. "You date supermodels, actresses, and NFL cheerleaders. I'm none of those things." She moved toward the workroom. "Thanks again for the business, Matt, but no, thank you."

"I'll see you soon, then."

He sauntered out the front door.

Amy waited till the front door bell stopped jingling, and curiosity got the best of her. She slid the flap of the envelope he left on her counter open.

The card read, "Sam, I fell in love with you for the rest of my life the moment I saw you. I love you, kitten."

Chapter Four

"WHAT A CHEATING dog!" Amy cried out in her empty shop.

He sent love notes to some chick named "Samantha," but he asked *her* to have coffee with him. What did he think she was? This just confirmed that she was right to turn down the coffee date he offered. He was just like so many of the guys she'd met before. He would turn on the charm, and then she'd find out that he was the world's biggest creep. Good thing she knew before she got emotionally involved with him. Well, except for that whole "turned her knees to water" thing. She wasn't going to see him again, anyway. It didn't matter.

Amy wanted to throw the enclosure card on the shop floor and stomp on it. She managed to paper clip it to the order form instead, and stalked into the cooler to grab eighteen pink roses, greens, and a little pittosporum. Scum. Poor Samantha had no idea what kind of ass she was with. Samantha was probably some nice, trusting woman who didn't know she was involved with some scary ex-NFL player who dazzled women with his gorgeousness, and then stomped his natural turf cleats all over her heart. If she kept thinking about that, she wouldn't remember the way Matt had slipped the pins out of her hair, one at a time.

The next morning Amy drove to the address Matt provided for his order. She still couldn't afford a full-time delivery driver. It was just another challenge for a small business owner.

The condos across the street from Kirkland's Carillon Point were luxurious, with a price tag to match. They faced out over Lake Washington, which was a tranquil, almost opaque medium blue this morning. She rang the doorbell at the address on the slip. A tall, dark-haired, barefoot woman appearing to be Amy's age and wearing jeans, a worn Ramones t-shirt, black toenail polish, and a mischievous expression answered the door.

"Hi. Are you Samantha?" Amy asked.

"No. Samantha's not here right now." The woman glanced at the flowers. "Those are gorgeous."

"Thanks so much. These are for her." Amy handed over the floral box.

"I'll make sure she gets them. Thanks for stopping by." The woman gave Amy another huge smile as she shut the door. Maybe she was Samantha's roommate. Amy spent the drive back to the shop imagining that Samantha was a beautiful, flawless eighteen-year-old blonde. If she ever saw Matt again, she'd tie his lungs together.

She spent the next week or so worrying about the fact that her business was quiet. It seemed most people were pretty tapped out after Valentine's Day. There were a few walk-in customers, but not the amount of business she'd hoped for. The phone was so silent Amy was almost caught up on the cleaning and bookwork, too. She was thrilled to hear the bells on her front door ring on a cold, rainy Wednesday morning. Until she saw who'd entered the shop.

Matt Stephens stood at the front counter once more.

Today he wore jeans, loafers, and a dark blue v-neck sweater that matched his eyes. Amy took a deep breath. The weasel was back and more gorgeous than ever.

Her momentary elation over having a customer dissolved in a stew of nerves, and the memory of the card he'd sent with the last bouquet flashed through her mind. She hadn't had a reaction to a guy like this since she was in middle school. Take that back, maybe never.

"Why are you here?" she said.

Every time Matt talked to her, she had the feeling that it was all he could do not to burst into laughter. Today was no exception.

"You know, I could have sworn I just walked into a flower shop." Isn't the correct question "How may I help you?" he asked. Amy gave him a stare. "Nice to see you, too."

"Whatever." She straightened the pens in the container on the front counter.

"I'd like to send some flowers," he insisted.

"Sure, you would."

"Someone must have peed in your Wheaties this morning. What's the problem?" He leaned over the counter a bit. "Did you have another tequila incident?"

"No. I'm off tequila, probably for life. May I help you?"

Amy pulled an order pad out from beneath the counter as she picked up a pen. He took a deep breath and tried to arrange his features into a smile. She tried to ignore the fact that her blood was racing through her veins, she suddenly forgot how to breathe, and she wanted to rub all over him like a cat. Maybe, just maybe, she could duct tape his mouth shut so he wouldn't say something to piss her off. Then again, he couldn't kiss her with duct tape on his mouth, and God, she wondered what it would be like to kiss him.

She wondered if he tasted as good as he smelled.

He was a vile seducer, she reminded herself. He asked other women out while he was involved with the wonderful and charming Samantha. She'd never met Samantha, but she was positive that Samantha was a fantastic person who had no idea she was involved with the devil incarnate. Well, maybe that was a bit strong, but he was a lousy cheater, and other women should be alerted to this fact. It would be a service to mankind. Well, womankind. Something like that.

His mouth was moving again; she couldn't stop gawking at his lips . . . Oh, hell. She swallowed hard, which was difficult with the microscopic amount of moisture left in her mouth. She resisted the impulse to fidget.

"Would you make a mixed bouquet of flowers this time? She likes springtime flowers like tulips, daffodils, that kind of stuff." He was writing the card as he spoke. "She doesn't need them in a vase either, because she's got plenty of them. Just the arrangement, please."

"How much would you like to spend?"

"A hundred dollars. I'd like it if they were there by tomorrow afternoon. She's in Laurelhurst."

She nodded. "They will be. I'll need her address and your credit card."

He extracted the credit card from his wallet once more and took the pen out of her now-slack fingers. She'd met guys before that tripped her trigger, but nothing like this. She wished she could rally enough to pretend like she was in control of the situation. He was a player to the tenth power, and Amy couldn't believe she was stooping so low as to help him send flowers to some woman he was probably cheating on Samantha with. This was not what she'd envisioned when she opened her shop.

He'd written down the address on Amy's order pad, and handed her another envelope addressed to "Pauline." In the meantime, he leaned against the counter.

"So, Amy, how about some coffee?"

She wanted to scream. He sent flowers to two different women in the past week, but he wanted *her* to have coffee with him?

"No, thank you," she said automatically. Maybe she could drive the pen through his temple. Someone would have to clean up the mess, though. Obviously, she'd be awarded the Nobel Peace Prize for services to humanity, or at the very least, to vulnerable single women everywhere.

Matt's eyebrows lifted, and he spoke with exaggerated patience.

"Maybe you should surprise me and say "Yes." Do you know the word "Yes?" I'll even sound it out for you," he teased. He captured her chin in one big, warm hand, while bestowing another heart-stopping grin on her. Her heart skipped several beats in response. "Yesss," he said as he nodded. "Yes, Matt, I'd love to have coffee with you."

"N—"

He put his fingers over her lips. "I'm going to keep asking you till you say 'Yes.'"

"The answer is not going to change." It came out pretty muffled.

"Yes, it will," he confidently informed her.

"Uh-uh," was all she could get out. He didn't stop smiling. Amy belatedly realized she'd offered another challenge to a man who believed that only wimps walked away from them. Plus, she was the *tiniest* bit flattered he kept asking.

"I'll see you in a couple of days, Amy." He moved to the front door, turned back and called out, "Don't read the card," as he walked out of the shop.

Of course she read the card.

"Hey, hot stuff," he'd written, "you're still my best girl. XO, Matt."

THE NEXT MORNING, Matt stopped in again. He wore a beautifully tailored charcoal pinstriped suit, a medium blue dress shirt, and a soft gray silk tie with interlocking diamond shapes in shades of blue. Amy couldn't figure out how a guy who probably spent more than her monthly shop rental payment on his attire could still have rumpled hair. Then again, some woman probably spent most of last night running her fingers through it. Not that she cared about what he did or anything like that.

She had plenty of other things to occupy her time instead of mooning over Matt Stephens. Unfortunately the second he walked into her shop, she forgot all of them.

He'd already selected an enclosure card, and was writing away by the time she stepped up to the front counter.

"Fifi."

"Matt," she said, attempting a disinterested smile.

He glanced up for a moment and waited till he caught her eye, and then the corners of his mouth turned up. He didn't say anything. She wasn't giving in, either. They were locked in a private battle of wills. Amy let out a sigh. She wondered how many times she would have to see him before she didn't react like a twelve-year-old girl confronted with her favorite boy band in person.

"Aren't you a little overdressed for doing whatever it is you do during the day?" she said.

"Not for lunch with the PSN executives." He finished his composition, inserted it back into the envelope, and studied her. "Want to join us?"

"Excuse me?"

"We're going to the Metropolitan Grill. Imagine how much sweeter your disposition will be after some nine-layer chocolate cake." He gave her a huge grin. She smiled in spite of herself.

Amy had experienced that chocolate cake before. It was the most delicious thing she'd ever eaten, and the Met's food was fabulous, but she wasn't going there anytime soon on her budget.

"No, thank you." Even if she were going, and she had no intention of doing so, she wasn't exactly dressed for it.

"Cheesecake?" he cajoled.

"Nope."

"Not a dessert girl, huh?" He gave her a pitying smile. "That's too bad."

"I love dessert," she burst out, and then realized she'd just played into his hands. Again. She rubbed her forehead with a free hand while yanking an order form out of the apron she wore. "Can I do something for you?"

The look in his eyes shifted, reminding her of sultry summer nights and tangled sheets—otherwise known as things she would never, ever be sharing with him.

"Of course. Would you please send those big white lilies to the following?" He took the order form out of Amy's fingers, scrawled a name and address, and handed her his credit card. "Let's spend a hundred dollars."

She completed the paperwork, handed him his receipt and his credit card, and he turned to walk away. He paused at the front door.

"My offer still stands, Amy."

"What offer is that?"

"How about lunch?"

She shook her head vigorously. "Thank you, but no."

The dress clothes made his eyes look even more startlingly blue. The jacket outlined and accentuated already broad shoulders. He brushed her hand with his when he took the receipt from her; she almost jumped out of her skin. She was cracking like ice on Lake Washington in March, but she did everything she could to make sure he had no idea. She wondered how many more times he would ask before he finally gave up.

Did she really *want* him to give up?

"See you later, then." He pushed the door open, and strolled through it, looking back with a wink.

Amy scurried back into her workroom with the order and the card. He'd left just in time.

She was such a sucker.

This time, he'd left the envelope flap open.

"Rebecca. Thanks for last night. You were great," she read.

Chapter Five

MATT WALKED INTO Seattle's Metropolitan Grill shortly after he left the flower shop that morning, still laughing. Any chance to see Fifi was the highlight of his day.

He knew she was reading the enclosure cards he'd written at her shop. She was going to go into orbit when she read the card he enclosed in the flowers he was sending to Rebecca, the local FOX affiliate sports reporter. Rebecca had helped him out by letting him borrow her cameraman for the interview he'd done the previous evening with the Sharks' head coach, but Amy would believe they were romantically involved. He couldn't wait to see what she was going to do about it.

The other bouquet went to his mom, Pauline, who'd texted him immediately with, "Loved the flowers. I'm guessing the florist is the one you're currently going broke over."

If this kept up, he was going to have to start sending flowers to women he'd never even met, just for a chance to talk with Amy again. He was enjoying pushing her buttons. Typically women approached him. This time, though, he wanted more. It was refreshing that she made him work for her attention. Cat and mouse was always fun, but it was even better when he knew his plans for her were bigger than coffee or lunch.

MATT GLANCED AROUND the bar area. He didn't see the PSN party, but Brandon McKenna was advancing on him from the lobby. Matt stuck out his hand.

"McKenna."

"Stephens." The two men briefly embraced, and Brandon slapped Matt on the back. "Did you get lost on your way to my wedding?"

"So I was a little late."

"Shane told me he saw you in the bar later on."

"Yeah. I screwed up, man. I'm sorry. Did you get the espresso machine?"

"Yes, and thank you. Emily was thrilled. I'm wondering if I'm going to have to go back to school for another master's to learn how to use it." Brandon shook his head a bit. "One-button latte, my ass."

"The machine comes with a free class on how to use it, big guy." Matt leaned on the bar. "How's your bride doing?"

"Her life is perfect. She's married to me."

Matt had to laugh. Brandon was obviously joking, but he quickly pulled an iPhone out of his pocket, punched a few buttons, and held the screen up for Matt to admire.

"The wedding photographer sent us a file of the pictures yesterday. I keep asking myself how I got so damn lucky. Look at her." The red-haired Emily in her wedding gown, holding her bouquet with a filmy veil cascading around her, smiled out at him from Brandon's phone. "Her ex is a real ass, but I sent him the best bottle of single-malt I could find. He did me a huge solid."

"So, how's married life?"

"We just got back from Kauai last night. My bride was still sleeping when I left the house."

Matt signaled the bartender. "You must be here to meet the PSN guys as well."

Brandon slid the phone back into his pocket as he nodded. "I'm job-shadowing next week. What are you up to?"

"We're talking about the draft and training camp coverage. Plus, I'll get to eat a steak on someone else's expense account, which is always a good thing." Matt ordered a couple of iced teas, and the bartender put some coasters down. The affluent and influential of Seattle were drifting in for their lunch meetings as well.

"Hey. I wasn't sure how to bring this one up, so I'll just spit it out," Brandon told him.

"That sounds ominous. Maybe I should have ordered a couple of beers instead."

"Don't worry about it." Brandon chuckled a little. "What's your status these days? Still seeing the woman you met in London?"

"That would be a *no*. I enjoyed her company, but ten hours on a jet is not my idea of fun. Plus, she has no interest in relocating." Matt handed the bartender a twenty for their tab, and took a swallow of the iced tea that was put in front of him. "Why? Are you asking me out?"

"Emily has something up her sleeve. I thought you might appreciate some advance warning."

"She wants to ask me out, then."

"She's off the market as of two weeks ago for the rest of her life." Brandon touched his glass against Matt's and took a healthy swallow. "My beautiful wife has an equally beautiful sister who's single. Amy's in her mid-thirties, owns a flower shop, and Emily doesn't care for the guy she's going out with. She's convinced herself that you and Amy would be perfect for each other, and she thought we should all have dinner together so it won't look like such a set-up." Brandon put his glass back down on the bar. "Did I mention Amy has had Sharks season tickets for five years now? She loves football. She was quizzing me about Sharks defensive sets the other day."

Matt raised an eyebrow while reminding himself to play it cool. "A Sharks season ticket holder, huh? So, why me?"

"Because I'll know where to find you if you make her cry." Brandon pulled the phone out of his pocket again and scrolled rapidly through the wedding photo file. "This is Amy."

Matt's memories of Amy, otherwise known as Fifi, were a bit different than the dazzling woman who gazed back at him from the photo. Her hair in the photo was perfect, shining, spun gold. Her amber-brown eyes reflected warmth, and her lips, covered in a barely tinted-pink gloss, curved into an artless smile. The copper silk of her dress gleamed in the sunlight like a shimmering, shiny penny, accentuating the pale satin of her skin. She was flawless. He hated it.

He preferred the sleepy, disheveled Fifi, who argued with him over his preference in tequila, allowed him to pluck hairpins out of her wrecked hairdo, asked him to unbutton her dress, and talked to him about things she had no intention of following up on, like sperm donors.

He'd been friends with Brandon McKenna since Brandon's rookie year, but he wasn't about to tell any member of Fifi's family quite yet that he was already chasing her. He preferred securing a date with her (and he would gently persist until he did) on his own. He also preferred flying under the radar.

Matt took another sip of his drink. "She's lovely. So, would you have dated her if you hadn't met Emily first, big guy?"

"There is no good answer to that question."

"Sure, there is. Yes or no?" Matt watched Brandon's brows knit.

"Considering the fact I wouldn't have met Amy if I hadn't met her sister first, that's not really a question."

"So, the answer is yes." Matt grinned. He finished off his iced tea.

Brandon ignored that. "Emily wants to try that new fish place in Kirkland we've heard so much about. How about Saturday night?"

"Thanks for the invite, but Saturday night won't work." Matt took a deep breath. "While Amy is a stunning young woman that I'd undoubtedly be lucky to spend any time with at all, there's someone else on my radar screen right now."

"Maybe another time."

"Maybe." Matt set the pint glass back down on the bar. He saw the execs from PSN walk into the restaurant out of the corner of his eye. When they strolled into the bar, there was the usual backslapping, name-calling and handshakes, but he was a bit distracted.

So, Fifi's family had no idea the boyfriend was out of the picture. She was full of secrets. It would be fun to figure out why.

"THANKS FOR LAST night. You were great."?

Amy would show him. She could still be a professional, despite the fact she wanted to use his guts for garters. She couldn't figure out why he still had such an effect on her, besides the fact he was gorgeous, sexy, and made her laugh. She was also beginning to understand that maybe Matt's love life wasn't all it could be. After all, ordering flowers for another woman while asking out the florist—who kept saying *no*—wasn't exactly the most efficient use of his time.

She pulled a bucketful out of the cooler and got busy on the latest bouquet. The phone rang. She trimmed and cleaned stems while taking another couple of orders. Things had picked up this afternoon, thankfully enough, and Amy lost herself in the scent and beauty of the flowers she worked with. Even if she spent long hours at work, she loved what she did. Her quiet, orderly life of profit-and-loss statements and audits had given way to a riot of color, textures, and scent. She still worried about the shop's profitability, but this morning's enjoyment was a welcome respite from the typically constant *bills, bills, bills* refrain inside her head.

More people called. She made an appointment for a wedding consultation. When she wasn't scrawling orders and taking credit cards, she wondered to herself what on earth was going on. The phone rang again as she was digging under her workbench for her shears, which she'd dropped. Again.

"Crazy Daisy."

"Hey, Amy," an unfamiliar male voice said. "Matt Stephens told me that you can get me off my wife's shit list in short order. I need some help."

The mystery about where the increased business was coming from was over. She had to smile. He was sending her business, which would warm the heart of any small-business owner.

"I'll do my best," she assured the caller. "What would you like to send, and where's the delivery going?"

"This is Tom Reed of the Sharks." Amy's heart skipped a beat. Tom Reed was the Sharks' QB. It was going to be all she could do to keep from gushing over him. "Matt says you're a football fan, so I know you'll get what I mean when I tell you the wife's pissed because I've been spending more time with my playbook than her." He let out a sigh. "I want every red rose in your store. If you'll get her a pound or so of some really good chocolate, too, and deliver the stuff today, I'll throw in a couple of suite tickets for a game next season for you. It's going to our house in Bellevue."

Amy promised Tom she'd have three dozen red roses and a pound of Fran's sea salt chocolate-covered caramels at his house by five o'clock that afternoon, thanked him for his business, and hung up the phone. She was torn between excitement at the amount of money she'd made and the fact she knew she had to hire the delivery driver she now needed desperately. She could put an ad on Craigslist, just as soon as she had five minutes to do so.

WHEN MATT WASN'T stopping by her shop to order flowers he was having his executive assistant order them, and Amy was crafting a dazzling array of arrangements sent to what she imagined was every female Matt had had a relationship with since he hit puberty. A disproportionate number had first names ending with "i" as well. The messages on the enclosure cards were getting progressively more ridiculous. Matt must have had a full-time ghostwriter on retainer. When he wasn't devising new and more ambiguous enclosure cards for elaborate floral arrangements going to a small army of women, he was still asking her out for coffee.

"Come on, Amy. It's twenty minutes out of your life."

"No, thank you."

"I think you really want to go," he said. She could hear the smile in his voice over the phone, too.

He was right, but she wasn't sure she wanted to give him the pleasure of admitting it quite yet. Even more, he sounded like he was getting a cold. That wasn't good. Despite the fact she pretended indifference, she didn't want him to be sick.

"I can't figure out when you'd fit me in. After all, if you're dating all these women you keep sending flowers to, you must be exhausted," she blurted out.

She heard raspy laughter.

"I'll *make* time." He let that one sink in for a minute or so. Amy slumped against the front counter. She closed her eyes and sighed. His voice dropped to an intimate rumble. "I'll ask again tomorrow, Amy."

"Whatever makes you happy, Matt," she said. He let out a snort.

"Tomorrow." He hung up.

AMY'S NEW DESIGN assistant Estelle started at the shop the next morning. Amy told her to answer the telephone.

"If Matt Stephens calls, please tell him I'm dead."

"Matt Stephens, the football player? He's a hunk," Estelle shouted back.

Estelle was somewhat loud when she didn't have her hearing aid turned up, but Amy liked having her around. She was already reducing Amy's workload. Even more than that, it was nice to have someone to chat with when the shop was slow. The phone rang, Estelle grabbed it, and Amy could tell from the blushing and laughter exactly who it was.

"Oh, Matt, you are such a flirt," Estelle trilled. "I wish I could have coffee with you, but Mr. Estelle would have a problem with that. He doesn't like it when I date."

Amy tried to pretend like she wasn't listening.

"Well, I'll make sure we get that order out right away. A dozen pink roses to Mary Margaret, and a card reading, "We'll always have Paris." Amy will put the charges on your statement. Thanks for thinking of us. It's such a thrill to talk to you." More giggles and blushing ensued.

Amy resisted the impulse to lean over the garbage can in her workroom and barf. Estelle hung the phone up with a bang. "He's charming, isn't he?" She fanned herself with one hand.

"He's a lower life form." Amy snipped off some greenery in a savage fashion and pictured doing the same to Matt's neck. She realized with a shock that she was jealous. Maybe she should have answered the phone herself.

"If I didn't have a husband and some grandkids at home," Estelle sang out, "I would have taken him up on it. I've seen him on *NFL Today*. Norm thinks I'm watching the game, but I'm looking at the men. Wait till he hears he has a rival for my affections. *Matt Stephens?* My girlfriends won't believe this." She pushed her reading glasses up her nose and moved away to grab another bunch of daisies out of the bucket for the latest delivery order.

Mary Margaret. Who the hell was *she*?

Chapter Six

AMY SLUMPED OVER her worktable the next morning from sheer exhaustion. She'd delivered Matt's latest bouquet on her way home from work the afternoon before. It turned out that Mary Margaret was actually *Sister* Mary Margaret, one of Matt's teachers in the parochial school he'd attended. She'd taught him French. Allegedly.

Sister Mary Margaret pulled the card out of the bouquet, peered at it through thick glasses, and let out a soft laugh. "That Matthew Stephens is as naughty as he was in school. Wait until his mother hears about this."

The sister was also a very persuasive woman. After a long, appreciative sniff of the flowers she'd received, she set down the vase containing Matt's dozen roses on an occasional table inside the front door of the retirement home she lived in.

"It's nice to meet you, Amy. I wonder if an old nun could ask you for a favor." Her faded blue eyes sparkled as she took Amy's hand in hers. "Do you have plans for the evening?"

"No, no. Not at all," Amy stammered. The only thing on tonight's schedule was laundry. "What do you need?"

"It's almost dinner time, and we're short one server. If you'll help us with the dinner service, I'll introduce you to some more of Matthew Stephens' former teachers. I'm sure you'll enjoy their stories." Sister Mary Margaret was surprisingly strong for an older woman. She slipped her hand through Amy's arm, pulling her toward what Amy imagined must be the community dining room. "We'll get you an apron and a hair net. Plus, it's spaghetti and meatball night, which everyone's always excited about. It'll be fun."

Amy spent the next couple of hours serving dinner and helping to clean up afterward. She forgot her exhaustion after a long day in the shop when she realized how happy those in the facility were to spend even a few minutes chatting and laughing with a younger person. She couldn't say no when they offered to teach her how to play pinochle, either.

She didn't make it home until after eleven o'clock that night. She was up at five the next morning to go to the flower wholesaler's.

THE NEXT MORNING, Amy was in desperate need of a nap. The wholesaler's bill was the size of the national debt. It was only ten o'clock, and Estelle wouldn't be in for another hour. The phone rang again. She was in the midst of cleaning a new shipment of roses, and she clutched the phone between her shoulder and her ear.

"Hello, Crazy Daisy."

"Hello. My name is Samantha Stephens. I would like to send some flowers to my dad. Would you help me with that?"

"Sure. Let me get my order pad." Amy barely avoided dropping the cordless receiver into the bucket of water she pulled roses out of. She grabbed the pen and order pad out of her apron with two fingers while juggling her shears. "Who are they going to, and what would you like to send?"

"Well, he likes blue. A lot. It also needs to be something a man would like. He used to play football, so it can't be pink or frilly," she explained. "His name is Matt Stephens. He lives in Redmond."

Stephens. Used to play football. Maybe it was a huge coincidence. Amy took a deep breath.

"What's the occasion, Samantha?"

"He has a really bad cold. We were supposed to go to the father-daughter dinner at my school, and he's too sick to go. My mom says that some flowers might cheer him up. I liked the ones that came from your shop."

So, she was the same Samantha of the eighteen pink roses. In the meantime, Amy attempted to cover her surprise with BS. "Irises are nice. They're a little more purple than blue, but they have yellowish centers, no scent, and men seem to like them."

"Okay. What else?"

"How about a few yellow Gerbera daisies to go with them? They're the larger daisies."

"Let's do that." Samantha paused for a moment. "Please make them really nice. My dad gets me flowers every month on the eighteenth because it's the day I was born, but I've never sent him flowers before."

"It must be great to look forward to." Maybe it was better not to tell Samantha Amy knew her dad.

"Yes. I like it a lot." Amy heard the grin in Samantha's voice. "I'll put my mom on the phone. She's paying for it with her credit card. Thank you for helping me," she said.

"Thank you, Samantha. I'll do my best to make an extra-special arrangement for him."

She heard another "Thanks!" followed by some muffled noise, and then a woman's voice came over the line.

"Hi. I'm Samantha's mom, Laura. It must be time to do the paperwork, huh?"

"All I need is your credit card and Samantha's dad's exact address." Amy's glance fell on the card rounder on the counter. "Actually, that's not true. I never asked Samantha what she would like on the card."

"Just a moment," Laura said and partially covered the mouthpiece of the phone with her hand. "Honey, what would you like written on the card for your dad?"

"Just say 'I love you' with some kisses and hugs," Samantha called out in the background.

Laura and Amy finished their business, Amy thanked her, and they hung up.

Samantha was Matt's *daughter*. Mary Margaret was a nun, as were several of the flower recipients she'd met last night. He'd sent a huge number of arrangements to females all over the city, while leading her to believe he was romantically involved with all of them.

Matt was a dead man.

LATE THAT AFTERNOON, Amy rang the doorbell at Matt's house. It was nothing like she'd expected, and she glanced around as she waited. He lived in a Craftsman-style, one-story home beside a small lake on Redmond's Novelty Hill. The house was beautiful, but it wasn't huge.

"Be right there," a voice called out.

A very rumpled, sleepy-looking Matt opened the door. Amy pushed the vase of flowers into his chest.

She couldn't think of anything else to say besides, "Thanks for telling me you have a daughter." She turned on her heel to go.

"Got somewhere to be, little girl?" She turned back toward him. He really did look awful. His voice was raspy, and the end of his nose was red.

"I have to go back to work."

"No, you don't," he argued. "You close at six. It's twenty after."

"Bookwork. Inventory. Payroll. Gotta go."

She was pulling it all out of her butt, but he wouldn't know that. Something was wrong. Besides the red nose, his hair was matted to his head, he was pale, and his clothes looked like he'd slept in them.

"You're here. You might as well have some coffee with me. Better yet, how about some chicken soup?"

"I'm not hungry."

"I am. Will you make some for me?"

He really did look miserable. The next word out of his mouth made her bite her tongue instead of telling him one more time how busy she was, as she'd intended.

"Please?" He reached out one hand to her but didn't touch her. "You probably shouldn't come near me at all right now. Maybe we could lay down some kind of Lysol barrier." He regarded her for a moment.

"Fine," she said.

She knew she was risking the worst cold this side of bubonic plague, but he was obviously so sick he needed help. If she ended up with whatever he had as a result, she deserved it for being such a sucker, but she reached out to push the door open a bit further. He backed up as she stepped over the threshold of his house.

Amy glanced around the entryway, which was surprisingly neat. His car keys and wallet rested on the hall table next to another vase of wildflowers. She indicated the flowers with a nod.

"One of your many admirers?"

"My mom sent them." Amy resisted the impulse to ask why his mom didn't order flowers for him from her shop.

"Does she live here? Maybe you should call her to come and take care of you."

"She's in Seattle." He rubbed one hand over his face. "She's—ah, she's elderly, and I don't want her driving after dark." He gazed down at her. "Hey. What's your favorite flower?"

"Excuse me?"

"You must have one. What is it?"

"Sweet peas."

"That's interesting, Fifi." He probably didn't even know what they were.

Matt gave Amy a shadow of his typical smirk and led her into the kitchen. Now, this was more like it. The sink was overflowing with dirty dishes. It looked like he'd spent the past several days with enough strength to feed himself, but that was about it. Even now he swayed a bit as he put the flowers down on the center island.

"Matt." Amy quickly snaked an arm around his waist to steady him. "You need to sit down." She wrinkled her nose at the evidence that he hadn't changed his clothes for a while.

"Just tired," he informed her, but he didn't resist. He looped his arm around her shoulders, walking them through an informal dining area to what must have been the family room. The coffee table was covered with more dirty dishes, used Kleenex, and multiple cold remedies. There were two bed pillows and a couple of blankets on the leather sectional by the gas fireplace. Matt must have been camping out for several days.

"When was the last time you ate?" she asked.

"Last night, I think. Good thing Amazon Fresh delivers."

"You. Sit down."

Amy gave him enough of a push to let him know she meant business and adjusted the pillows behind his back when he collapsed onto the couch. She draped a blanket over him. He needed a shower, but he needed food and some orange juice first, if she guessed correctly.

"You're going to feed me, right?"

She propped her hands on her hips. "Yeah, I'll feed you, and then I'm going to yell at you. Why didn't you call anyone to come and help?"

"I'll be fine—" Matt was racked with a fit of coughing that scared the hell out of her. She shoved more tissues at him.

"How long has *that* been going on?" she cried out.

"It's better than it was." He lay back against the arm of the couch and threw one arm over his eyes. "Maybe I'll cough up a lung."

"Okay. You're having something to drink, something to eat, and then we're going to the doctor. Let me see if you have a fever. That cough sounds awful. I can't believe you . . ." She laid the back of her hand against his forehead. He tried to brush it away.

"I'll be fine," he repeated.

"Yeah, right. Don't make me call your mother," Amy threatened as she grabbed a plastic grocery bag off the table. She saw the ghost of a smile in response.

"Aww, Fifi. You care. How sweet."

"I just don't want you to die while I'm in your house."

He let out something that sounded like the combination of a choke and a snort. She quickly cleared the crumpled tissues and napkins, shoving them into the plastic bag. She took the dishes into the kitchen and returned to him with a glass of orange juice.

"You need to drink this."

"I'm tired," he said.

"Too bad. Drink it." She folded her arms and watched

until he drained the glass. "Samantha said you were supposed to go to the father-daughter dinner at her school, but you were too sick."

"Yeah." The normally confident—hell, arrogant—Matt seemed to deflate a bit. "I hate missing any of her stuff. I would have just gone anyway, but if she'd gotten sick, too, I would have never forgiven myself." He shook his head. "She's growing up so fast. Pretty soon, it'll be guys and cars. She won't even want to be around her old man."

"That can't be true."

"You don't have a teenage daughter, do you?"

"No. I don't. No kids." Yet. Amy stifled a sigh as she felt another stab of pain. She wondered if she would ever have a kid, let alone a daughter of her own.

"How did you feel about your dad when you were fourteen? I couldn't wait to be an adult. I love my mom, but she treated me like a baby." His expression was wry.

"What about your dad?"

"He left when I was two. I was the man of the household." Even in the dimness of early evening, she saw something pass over his face she couldn't quite identify. The normally laughing, somewhat sardonic Matt didn't want to discuss this. At all.

"I'm so sorry."

"Yeah. Me, too." He glanced up at her. "Soup?"

"As fast as I can get it made." He closed his eyes, and Amy readjusted the blanket over him. Maybe he'd sleep for a while.

The chicken noodle soup warmed on the stove while she loaded and started Matt's dishwasher. She wondered how many other women had been in this kitchen before and whether or not they were dressed at the time. She couldn't figure out why she was doing housework for a man she didn't even know, but truthfully she was worried that he seemed so sick. The zillions of women he'd had in his life were, evidently, nowhere to be found. Shouldn't they want to take care of him at a time like this? Maybe she was just an idiot.

She dug around in one of the kitchen drawers till she found a notepad and then started a shopping list—he'd need more tissues, more soup, and some bread. Finally she tiptoed back into the family room with the soup to find him fast asleep. He needed food, though. She put the bowl and spoon down on the coffee table and gently shook his shoulder.

"Matt. You need to eat."

"Lemme sleep."

"I'll let you go right back to sleep after you eat something," she coaxed.

"Sleep."

"You have to eat," she urged.

"Not hungry."

He was talking in his sleep. He didn't open his eyes.

Amy's evening plans consisted of laundry, dishes, and watching the DVRed episode of some show she didn't care that much about. She could stay with him for a little while, but then she absolutely had to go. She'd call his mom or something. His mom could get to his house in a taxi if he really needed her.

The only noises in Matt's house were his soft snores

and the ticking of the clock on the mantel over the fire-place. She knelt down next to him and touched his fore-head once more. Dry and warm. He didn't have a fever. He stirred a little, but didn't wake up.

Amy grabbed the other blanket on the opposite end of the couch and hit the couch across from him.

MATT'S HOUSE WAS dark when she awoke to a loud crash. Her eyes adjusted to the dimness enough, though, to note that the couch was empty, and so was the soup bowl. He'd gotten up.

"Matt?" She called out.

She pulled herself off the couch and glanced around. He wasn't in the room, but she heard the shower run-ning. Dread skittered up her spine. He might have passed out and hit his head. He wasn't especially steady earlier from lack of food and whatever bug he had, so she hur-ried down the hallway to check on him.

Matt's room was huge, dominated by a king-sized bed in a dark, curved wood frame with four posters. The bed was still neatly made. He probably hadn't slept in it lately. The nightstands had the typical lamps and books. Amy's gaze moved over the iPhone docking station that must have been next to the side he most often slept on. An overstuffed wingchair sat in one corner with clothing draped over it, and there was a bench at the foot of the bed; it all sat on a huge braided rug in shades of blue.

"Matt? Are you okay?" she called out again. No answer.

He'd left the door open. Steam billowed out of the bathroom. She would take a look, just to make sure he was fine. There was nothing wrong with that. It was the right thing to do.

Amy inched through the doorway. Matt's bathroom was a masterpiece of high-end fixtures and surfaces. He, or the builder, had spared no expense on the granite countertops, tile flooring, beveled mirrors, cabinetry, and indirect lighting. The toilet had its own room, complete with padded bench. The shower was bracketed by a luxurious jetted tub, large enough for at least two people. Her feet froze to the floor. She was riveted, staring at the nude man standing in a clear glass double shower.

Matt looked like a statue she might see in a museum: long, lean, and bronzed from the sun. His arms and legs were covered with wet, silky-looking dark hair, and she saw a tan line on the wrist he wore a watch on. He braced his hand against the shower wall while the water cascaded over his head. It ran over flexing shoulder muscles, the ripple of muscles in his forearms and his biceps, down his back, over his butt and onward. Instead of realizing he was fine and leaving, her feet wouldn't move. Maybe he hadn't seen her.

"If you wanted to take a shower with me," he called out, "all you had to do was ask."

Amy's mouth dropped open. "Excuse me? I was making sure you didn't drown yourself."

"Let me know if that's working for you."

"I heard a crash. What did you think I should do?"

"I dropped the damn shampoo bottle," he said.

He turned to face her. For one shocked moment, all she could do was stare. Run, she told herself. Just go.

"Come on in. The water's fine," he said.

Her feet unfroze from the floor. She ran out of the bathroom, down the hall, and scooped her purse up off the hall table. She wrenched the front door open, slamming it behind her. She threw herself into the driver's seat of her delivery van, laying rubber as she drove away.

Amy glanced into the rear-view mirror. Matt stood in the middle of the street, wearing nothing but a white towel around his waist in the gathering darkness.

Chapter Seven

TWO DAYS LATER Amy shut herself inside her tiny office at the shop after locking the front door for the evening. Her brand-new brother-in-law, Brandon, was speaking at a fundraiser for Children's Hospital tonight. The entire family had been invited to sit at his table. She looked forward to seeing her family, but she wished she wasn't alone. Being lonely was bad enough. Being lonely in a room full of happy couples was miserable.

She spent all her time keeping her business afloat. She was great at business, but not so great in the dating and romance department. She realized she didn't miss Brian as much as she missed the *idea* of him: someone to talk with and confide in, someone to laugh with. Then again, there wasn't a lot of laughter toward the end of their relationship.

Maybe she needed a dog. They weren't dazzling conversationalists, but they were loyal. They were cuddly. They didn't break your heart.

She pulled a black jersey evening gown with a ruched waistline, scoop neck and cap sleeves over her head, brushed her hair into a sleek ponytail, applied some fire engine-red lipstick, and stepped into a pair of black patent leather flats. High heels and Amy were never friends. Right now, they weren't even on speaking terms. She fastened a pearl bracelet around her wrist, added the matching earrings, and hurried to the delivery van. She threw a candy apple-red cashmere wrap onto the passenger seat.

Maybe she could talk the server at Brandon's event into an extra dessert or something. After all, chocolate was the only cure for a broken heart. "Get over yourself," she said aloud as she swerved around a BMW on the 520 Bridge crossing Lake Washington.

She arrived five minutes before the cocktail hour was due to start. Emerging from the driver's side of a brightly painted delivery van in the valet parking area of one of the more posh hotels in moneyed Bellevue was sure to cause a few stares. This was no exception.

She handed her keys to the parking attendant who opened the van's door. "Don't scratch the paint," she told him. He laughed.

Her newly re-engaged parents met her at the front door of the Hyatt Regency's ballroom. It didn't escape Amy's notice that her dad stood a bit taller as Amy's mom slipped her hand through his arm. He patted her hand in response. She beamed. *Just a couple of lovebirds*, Amy thought.

Amy exchanged hugs with her parents, and Amy's dad gave her an extra squeeze.

"There's my sweet girl. You look great, honey."

"Thanks, Dad. You look nice, too."

She laid her cheek on his scratchy one. She felt an urge to cuddle up to her dad like she used to do when she was little. She needed a few more hugs right now, and maybe a little reassurance, too. Maybe she just had PMS. She'd had another long, tough day. She loved owning a business; she loved what she did. She didn't love being alone, however. Despite Matt's pursuit, she wasn't sure it was going to change any time soon.

"Where's Brian, honey?" her mom asked. "Didn't you ask him if he wanted to come with you?"

She took a deep breath before answering. "Brian moved back to New York two days before Brandon and Emily's wedding."

Amy handed her wrap to the coat check attendant. She turned back to see both her parents' mouths hanging open.

"He just left?" her mother asked. "Why?"

"His dad wanted him to take over the law firm." She swallowed hard. "It was a great opportunity."

Her dad slid his arm around her shoulders. "And that was it?"

"That was it. Can we go inside? It's frosty out here." She tried to smile. She tried to act like she didn't care. Her parents weren't buying it.

"He didn't ask you to come with him?" Meg Hamilton draped the shawl she carried over her shoulders. It really was cold tonight.

"Mom, I wouldn't have, even if he did ask."

Amy's mom dug in her purse for a tissue and handed it over. Amy frowned at this. She wasn't shedding one more tear over Brian. She regretted every tear she'd shed over him before tonight. She longed for a man who made her laugh more than he made her cry, and it was time to explore that option.

"But you were in love with him, sweetheart. I know you were."

"No, I wasn't . . . ."

Her parents weren't listening.

Her dad looped his arm around her for one more side hug. "There will be someone else. He's—he just didn't appreciate what he had, did he?"

"Thanks, Dad." Amy tried to take a deep breath. After all, what was done was done, and frankly, she was done with Brian the moment he'd told her he was leaving for New York. Hot tears rose in her eyes, and she fought them back. Her mom and dad towed her toward Brandon, Emily, and Brandon's parents. An evening with the married people: This ought to be a blast.

"Amy!" A glowing Emily hurried over to throw her arms around Amy. Brandon hugged both of them.

"My two best girls," he assured them.

"Hey! What about me?" Brandon's mom joked. The next few minutes were full of even more family hugging, kissing, and *good to see yous*. Amy pasted another smile she didn't feel onto her face.

Her sister detached herself from her new husband and made her way to Amy's side. "Where's Brian?" Emily asked.

"New York. When's dinner?"

Meg Hamilton said something into Emily's ear. Emily shook her head and glanced over at Amy. "He's a jerk."

Amy agreed with her, but she remained silent. Her family regarded her as if she'd just told them she was terminal. It would have been nice if Emily's marriage had taken the heat off Amy's finding a nice guy and settling down, but it seemed the few weeks of peace all single women hoped for after a family wedding would not happen.

The Hamiltons and McKennas moved into a ballroom dominated by a hundred-foot-tall atrium. It was ringed by a railed catwalk. Tables for ten were decorated by towering centerpieces and custom linens. The lighting was designed to flatter women of a certain age, and an orchestra played Cole Porter and George Gershwin. Servers circulated through the crowd with appetizers and flutes of champagne. Amy wondered if she should slip the conductor a twenty and ask him to play CeeLo Green's "Forget You."

She saw the swish of a seafoam-green chiffon evening gown out of the corner of her eye, and Suzanne McKenna sidled up next to her.

"I'm having a dinner party next week. Do you think you could fit making a centerpiece for me into your schedule?" Suzanne asked. Brandon's parents were now spending part of the football offseason in Seattle.

"Of course I can. Just let me know what you'd like."

"We'll pick it up if you're busy."

"No, no, no. I'm fine. I'm happy to do this for you."

"It's almost spring. How about something simple in springtime flowers, like tulips?"

"I can do that," Amy assured her. "Do you have a specific color or type you'd like?"

The rest of the family was distracted by seating themselves at the table. Suzanne slipped her hand through Amy's arm and whispered into her ear, "Everything's going to be fine, you know."

Amy knew she wasn't talking about the tulips. She wished everyone would stop saying stuff to her that made her want to cry. "Maybe."

"It will. Somewhere in the hundreds of men both my sons and my husband know, there's the perfect man for you." She slid into the chair next to Amy. "You'll see."

Amy wasn't ready to get into the entire sob story of how her relationship had blown up, especially with someone she didn't know that well. At the same time, Suzanne McKenna was nothing like Amy had thought she'd be when they first met.

Suzanne never had a hair out of place. Her manicure was unchipped, her clothes were perfect, but she laughed at her sons' raunchy jokes. Well, just as long as they had no bad language. Above all, she'd probably think paying off the conductor to play something inappropriate for the old money crowd was funny.

Suzanne's husband got up from his chair and took Emily's hand.

"I've already danced with my wife, and now it's your turn, Mrs. McKenna." He led her onto the dance floor as Brandon held out his hand to Amy.

"Listen, squirt, it's time for us to cut a rug."

"No, thank you. I don't need to— Brandon! What are you doing?" He tugged her out of her chair, and swept her out onto the dance floor.

"You have to dance with me," he said. "You're the only other woman besides the moms that my wife won't shoot me for dancing with."

"You're so full of it." His arms around Amy were comforting, though.

Brandon was the only person in her family she didn't feel like the Jolly Green Giant with. She had to tip her head back to look him in the eye. After all, he was six-four in his bare feet.

His blue-green eyes currently reflected concern. "You look a little glum. What's up?"

Amy kept her voice light. "Where'd you learn to waltz, tough guy?"

"Nice try at changing the subject. My mama made me go to dancing school when I was a kid." He regarded Amy with a teasing smile. "You'll need a derogatory nickname for me, you know." He moved a bit closer to speak into her ear. "So, I'm a guy, but even I can see something is wrong. Spill it."

Amy bowed her head again. One minute she was giving him crap, a minute later she was choking back more emotion. She was not going to burst into tears in the middle of a crowded dance floor. She worked hard to have a successful business, but deep down—and no matter how hard she'd shoved Matt away—she wished for a man to share it with.

"Heyyy," he murmured, "it's not that bad. Tell me what I can do." He tipped her chin up with his fingertips. "Let me help."

She heaved a gusty sigh. "It's really stupid. You're going to laugh at me."

"I promise I won't laugh, squirt. Just tell me." He took his hand off her waist long enough to give her ponytail a gentle tug, which made her smile.

"I can't find someone to go out with. It doesn't work. I meet guys. I don't know what to do," she said into his ear. "I must meet the wrong ones." She tried to take a deep breath past the lump in her throat. "Don't you know a lot of guys from the team?"

Brandon's halo of golden-blond curls shimmered as he shook his head. "There's nobody from the team I'd send you out with," he insisted.

"What do you mean?"

"Let's see. There's several guys who are single, but they are not for you, squirt. Zach? No. He stands women up. Damian? I love him, but you'd be miserable."

"Why?"

"You would. Jon's a player."

"Dylan seems nice."

Amy had met Brandon's younger brother, Dylan, at their wedding. He was as dark and quiet as Brandon was sunny and extroverted. It was bizarre. If Amy hadn't seen both of their parents, she would have never believed they were brothers. Dylan was an orthopedic surgeon who lived in Los Angeles, and traveled all over the world in his spare time for Doctors Without Borders.

"Married to his work, and you're not going out with him. He'll break your heart."

"Who *can* I go out with?" she groaned.

"Well, Matt Stephens is a good start."

"Matt Stephens of *NFL Today*. Your friend, Matt," she said. Her stomach dropped. She hoped Brandon didn't pick up on the trembling in her voice.

"Yeah. Tall, dark haired, TV guy." Brandon spun her out from him, and reclaimed her with a flick of his wrist. She saw the smile spread over his lips. "Now that I think of it, you're perfect for each other. He told me the other day there's someone on his radar screen right now, but I don't believe it. He needs a woman who's smart, funny, caring, and will keep him on his toes. Someone like you, squirt." He steered her away from two people who should have never been allowed access to a crowded dance floor. "Have you met him?"

Now she was babbling. "Yes. He ordered flowers from the shop." She felt weird about telling her brother-in-law she'd spoken to Matt almost every day since Brandon and Emily's wedding. She was still resisting Matt's advances, but maybe that should stay between the two of them. She was definitely not informing him that she'd seen Matt naked in the shower.

"Is that so? He says he doesn't know you."

Amy tried for confused outrage. "Excuse me? That's bizarre. Why would he say that?" She could feel a telltale flush spreading over her cheeks. When you couldn't dazzle them with brilliance, baffle them with BS. If she didn't at least try to remember what she was doing at the moment, she was going to step on Brandon's toes. Maybe that was a good idea.

"We had lunch a few days ago at The Met; I showed him one of the wedding photos, and he acted like he'd never seen you before." Brandon's chuckle was warm in her ear. They danced in silence for a few more minutes. "If you two should run into each other somewhere, give him a chance. He's a good guy. Plus, I know for a fact he's left his player days behind, and I'm not talking about football."

"How do you know? He might just be telling people that."

"I get the impression there's things you're not telling me, so I'll tell you how this is going to go. Here's your choices, squirt. You can either work it out yourselves, or Emily and I will set you up. Which would you prefer?"

Brandon burst into laughter at the look of horror that must have crossed her face. He twirled her.

"Does Emily know you can do this?" she finally burst out.

"Of course she does." He dipped her, smirked when she grabbed for his arms, and straightened up again. "You know, come to think of it, it wouldn't be all bad if I made sure you stayed single. We'll need a babysitter, Auntie Amy."

Amy's mouth dropped open, and her heart skipped a beat. "Is there something you're not telling me?"

"Well, no. Not yet. It's not for lack of trying." Brandon spun Amy again as he spoke. "Practice makes perfect, you know."

"Eww! Too much information," Amy protested and batted at his shirt front. Her brother-in-law had a huge, booming laugh, and other people on the dance floor turned to look at them.

Brandon offered his arm as the song ended.

"Shall we? I have to find my wife. I'm sure she misses me." He patted her hand with his much bigger, warmer one. "Let's go see if we can get you married off before football season starts again."

She let out a groan.

Chapter Eight

AMY WAS DUSTING the front counter at the shop the next day. Last night's pity party faded in the cold light of morning, and shortly after she had taken five new phone orders the bells on the front door rang. A tall, slender, dark-haired teenage girl walked in, and approached the counter.

"Hi. Are you Amy?"

"Yes, I am. How can I help you?"

The young woman stuck out her hand, and Amy shook it.

"I'm Samantha Stephens," she said. "Thank you for the flowers you took to my dad when he was sick. He said that you stayed to take care of him, too." Her eyes were perfect replicas of her dad's. She rolled her gold-flecked, navy blues in exasperation. "I can't believe he didn't call any of us. He could have *died*. We wouldn't have even *known*."

"He would have been okay," Amy rushed to reassure her. "He's just stubborn."

"My mom says that all the time." She brushed long bangs out of her eyes. Even if Samantha hadn't introduced herself, she might as well have been wearing a sign. Besides the long legs, similar facial features, and Matt's dark hair, Samantha, it seemed, was a bit of a rebel. She'd lined her eyes with smudged black pencil, which clashed with the demure school uniform she wore. She'd also applied a thick layer of pink lip gloss. There were cobalt-blue streaks in her long, black-as-ink curls, which matched the uniform. She carried a vintage Louis Vuitton satchel. She wore leather booties on her feet, which Amy was sure were non-regulation as well.

"My dad's pretty . . . Well, he can be stubborn, too."

Samantha put both hands on her hips, fixed Amy with a look, and raised one eyebrow. "So. We're not here to talk about that. You're dating Matt, aren't you?"

Once Amy managed to recover from the shock of being called out by a child in a school uniform, she choked out a response. "You call your dad by his first name?"

"Obviously." When this failed to get a rise, Samantha drummed her fingers on the counter a little. "You didn't answer my question."

"He's asked me out, but we're not dating."

"You told him no? Everyone wants to go out with him," she insisted. "Why?"

Maybe Amy could stall. "Samantha, what grade are you in?"

"Ninth. How come?"

Amy did some quick math: She was fourteen or so. "Just wondering."

"How old are you?"

Amy considered notifying Samantha that asking a woman her age wasn't the best policy, and realized it was a waste of breath. "Thirty-five. I'll be thirty-six soon."

"So, what's wrong with Matt?" Despite Samantha's efforts to affect worldliness and even a tiny bit of boredom, Amy saw hurt in her eyes. She thought her dad was being insulted. It was enough to melt the cold, cold heart of a non-dater. Almost.

Amy's lobby wasn't huge, but there was enough room for a small round metal table and a couple of chairs. Her clients used the table to look through books of flower arrangements. Today, it was just right for a brief visit with Matt's daughter.

She indicated the table with a nod. "Let's sit down for a minute. Would you like some bottled water or a soda?"

"I'd like some diet pop, please," Samantha said.

Amy pulled two Diet Cokes out of the flower cooler and they sat down. She didn't typically spend much time with teenagers, especially the teenage daughter of a guy she'd turned down multiple times now. It was uncomfortable. She also mused on how a fourteen-year-old had managed to score a Louis Vuitton satchel bag.

A few moments passed while Samantha busied herself with opening the can and taking a sip. Amy noted the chipped blue nail polish she wore. Samantha also left a smear of lip gloss on the can.

"Hey, Samantha, got a question for you," Amy said as casually as she could manage. "Does your mom know you're here?"

"I called her earlier and said I was going to drop by. The bus stops right at the corner. I can get one home, so it's no big deal." She took another sip of soda. "It's a good thing Matt's not here right now. He'd be pissed off about the pop. He doesn't like it."

Amy wondered idly if she should say something about inappropriate language. That was definitely her parents' problem.

"Why not?"

"He's obsessed with healthy stuff. It's boring." Samantha rolled her eyes and heaved a sigh. "At least he lets me have pizza once in a while." She leaned over the table. "He likes tofu, and this nasty green juice he gets at the smoothie place."

"I'm sorry," Amy deadpanned.

"It's awful. He tries to get me to eat that stuff, too. My grandma says that Matt thinks if he eats the healthy stuff, he'll live forever, but she thinks it'll just feel like it."

Amy couldn't control her snort. She tried to cover it up by taking another sip out of her pop can. Samantha looked around the shop. "Have you always been a florist?"

"No. I used to be an accountant."

"Why did you change?"

She'd been dying inside, but she knew Samantha would not understand that answer.

"I was bored and wanted something different. This

is a lot more fun." Amy fiddled with a pen on the table. "What would you like to be when you're older?"

"I want to be a fashion designer. My mom says that it's hard work and I'm going to have to go to college first, but I really want to do it." Samantha glanced at the LV satchel resting on the table. "That's my mom's old handbag," she explained. "Matt said that if I didn't wreck it or lose it, we could talk about a designer handbag when I'm sixteen."

"Old" or not, Amy would be more than happy to take it off her hands. She dragged her eyes off the handbag.

"Most sixteen-year-olds would ask for a car."

"I want a car, but I'd have to pay for my own gas and insurance." Samantha wrinkled her nose. "That's not so bad, but if I get a job, I can't do sports, and I really like sports. Plus, if I don't keep my grades up, the insurance is a lot more money, and Mom and Matt won't be happy with me." She squeezed the sides of her pop can. "Did you have a car when you were sixteen?"

"My sister Emily and I shared a car."

The look on Samantha's face was wistful. "I don't have any brothers or sisters, so I won't have to share." She swirled the soda can in her fingers, and blurted out, "Do you want to have kids?"

"Someday."

Samantha's smile was impish. "My dad wants to have more kids." Amy wondered if Samantha was attempting to recruit her to be Matt's baby mama. There were lots of other women who would volunteer for the job in a heartbeat.

"Uh, that's nice." If she felt awkward before, now she wondered if she should hide somewhere till Samantha gave up and went home. Amy shook her head so hard she felt something rattle. "Samantha, your dad and I can't be in a room together for more than a few minutes, or we argue with each other."

"Why do you fight with him?"

"He's the most unreasonable man in the world."

Samantha barely kept from spewing a mouthful of soda all over Amy as she tried to stifle her laughter. She clapped one hand over her mouth, swallowed, and wiped away a stray tear with her fingers.

"Are you okay?"

"Oh, yeah." Samantha grabbed a tissue from the box Amy had on the table and wiped her nose. "He doesn't like it when anyone disagrees with him," she admitted. "He says that he's just watching out for me. So he tries to tell you what to do, too?"

Amy heaved a sigh. "All the time."

"I think he likes you," Samantha observed. "He says that he wouldn't bug me so much if he didn't love me."

Amy's stomach churned. She wasn't even going to let herself think about the reasons behind Matt's behavior toward her.

She let out a long breath. "I think he enjoys it."

"Maybe you could have dinner or something and agree that you wouldn't argue," Samantha said.

Amy realized she was getting fixed up by a fourteen-year-old. Then again, Samantha had paid her a pretty high compliment: She was obviously at the shop to check Amy out, and for some unknown reason, she'd passed Matt's daughter's inspection.

Amy took another swallow of soda and leaned back in her chair. "So, what's your mom like?"

Samantha's face lit up. "She's great. She and Matt got married when she was still pretty young, so she likes the music I do, she lets me wear her clothes, that kind of stuff. We get along really well. She streaked my hair. Matt freaked out when he saw it." Samantha leaned forward and put one elbow on the table as she spoke. "He said if he hears one more word about getting my eyebrow pierced—"

Amy was saved from additional discussions about dating and babies when Samantha's phone rang. "Just a moment," she said, and she consulted the screen of a pink cell phone. "Hi, Mom." Amy couldn't make out what was said, but Samantha nodded. "Okay. I'm at Crazy Daisy. Do you want me to meet you there?" She listened for a few moments, and then she said, "I'll use the crosswalk. I'll be there in ten minutes." She used a finger on the touchscreen to end the call. "My mom wants me to meet her at Urban Outfitters, so I have to go." She picked up her bag, and dropped the phone back into it.

Amy got to her feet. "Samantha, it was so nice to meet you. I'm glad you stopped by."

"So, it's okay with you if I drop by again?"

Maybe Samantha just wanted a free soda. Why else would she be visiting? At the same time, Amy had to admit Samantha appeared to be fourteen going on thirty-five. It was like talking with another adult, as long as Amy forgot about the strategies employed by a teenage girl who wanted her way.

"Of course it is. Anytime."

"Cool!" Samantha exulted. "Thanks!" She threw her arms around Amy, who realized she and Samantha were the same height. Matt's genetic material was obviously superior.

"Why don't I walk outside with you and make sure you're across the street?" Amy asked.

"I'm not a baby," Samantha said.

"I know. I want to make sure—"

"You're just like Matt," but she started to laugh.

Amy stepped outside the shop to watch Samantha's progress to the corner. Urban Outfitters was almost directly across the street and it was broad daylight, but she felt oddly protective of Matt's daughter. The woman who'd taken the flowers at what must have been their home was waiting outside the store. She embraced Samantha, waved at Amy, and they went inside.

An hour and a half later, Amy was sweeping the floor in the workroom when the phone rang.

"Crazy Daisy," she said.

She heard Matt's voice. "So, you met my little princess, did you?"

"Excuse me?" Obviously Matt needed to update his glasses prescription. Amy had to smile, though: Her dad still called her the same thing.

"My daughter informed me that I should really consider dating you."

"I told her it wouldn't work—"

He interrupted her. "Why not, Amy? You won't know until you try."

"We argue all the time."

"We're not arguing now."

"Yes, we are. I told you I—ooh!" She stomped her foot on the workroom floor. "I do *not* get you."

She heard the laughter in his voice. "There's one way to end this once and for all, you know."

THE NEXT MORNING was even crazier, if it was possible. Estelle was out sick. Amy's new delivery driver was stopped behind a wreck on 520, the floating bridge connecting downtown Seattle to the moneyed Eastside, and she had no idea when traffic might start moving again. In the meantime, the list of arrangements that needed to be made was epic. All she could possibly do was work as quickly as possible and hope her driver returned to the shop before closing. She was also crossing her fingers that the finicky flower cooler unit she'd purchased from a retiring florist before she opened her doors was not about to go tits up. It was making noises she'd never heard before.

"Sucks to be me," she muttered to herself as a stray thorn she'd neglected to strip off a long-stemmed white rose left a long scratch on her forearm as she worked. An anonymous cubicle in a large corporate accounting firm was sounding better and better. The worst injury she'd had there was a particularly egregious paper cut.

Crazy Daisy was a minefield of work-related injuries. She'd slipped on spilled water, stabbed herself with wire, fallen over junk in the storeroom, burned herself with hot coffee . . . and that was just last week. The best part was trying to explain the resulting bumps and bruises to assorted friends and family. They all thought being a florist was a profession that did not require additional health insurance coverage and a physical therapist on retainer.

Shortly after lunchtime Amy had just stashed the last arrangement in the still-working cooler, wiped down the worktable, and poured herself a cup of coffee when she heard the bell over the front door jingle again. She bit back a groan. Even though she needed the business, she wanted five minutes to drink a cup of coffee in peace.

MATT STOOD AT the front counter, holding the biggest bouquet of sweet peas she'd ever seen. Amy forgot the coffee.

"Hey, Amy."

She came to a halt behind the front counter. "Hey, yourself."

He was clumsy as he moved around the counter and laid the bouquet in her arms. To Amy's amazement, the arrogant, blustering, take-no-prisoners Matt had been temporarily replaced by a shy, gentle suitor. He moved closer. She forgot to move away. She buried her nose in the bouquet, breathing in the heavenly scent.

"These are for you. Thanks for taking care of me. I appreciate it."

"What? Why?" she blurted out, and then wished she hadn't said a word. He took her cheek in his hand.

"I wondered if anyone brought you flowers lately."

In that moment, she was undone, vulnerable, at his

mercy. Her heart opened. She tried to string together anything even remotely self-possessed to say, but mostly, she wanted to cry. He'd managed to hit on the one gesture that would mean more to her than almost any other. After all, she sent flowers to other people. They didn't send them to her.

"These are my favorite. How did you know?"

"You told me." He stroked her cheek with his thumb.

She didn't know what else to say, and she really didn't know what to do. She couldn't imagine where he'd managed to get them, especially since they were out of season, and cut sweet peas lasted only a day or so. Years of training finally kicked in, though, and she murmured something to the effect of, "Maybe I should put these in some water."

Amy turned away from him, but then she turned back. He hadn't moved. He watched her. She took a few steps toward him before she realized what she was doing. She reached up to brush a kiss across his cheek.

"Thank you. They're beautiful."

His arms slipped around her. He laid his scratchy cheek on Amy's as her arm slid around him in a hug. She could smell the flowers she still held, but even more, she could smell him: the warm, clean scent of his skin, the starch in his shirt and shampoo, the hint of aftershave. It also dawned on her that she had relaxed into his embrace.

"Amy," he said into her ear. "There's a card."

"What does it say?"

She was obviously stunned stupid at this point. After all, she was exhausted. If Scott the driver did not materialize momentarily, she was going to have to call twenty-five customers to say their deliveries would be late. When she wasn't freaking out about that, she kept trying to remember every reason why she'd believed dating Matt was one of the more stupid ideas in the history of the universe.

She couldn't seem to pry herself away from him. He was warm. She listened to his heartbeat beneath the button-down shirt he wore. He held her close, but it wasn't creepy. It was nice. He laid one hand over the stress ache in her lower back. Ahhh.

"You might want to take a look." He watched as she pulled the small white envelope out of the profusion of flowers, ripped it open, and silently read, "Have dinner with me, Fifi. Matt."

"And?" he asked.

She was in a daze. It didn't even occur to her to argue with him. He brought her sweet peas! She couldn't imagine where he'd gotten them. Plus, he remembered she loved them. He *remembered*.

Brian hadn't even remembered her birthday, and she'd dated him for a year.

It had been an awful day before Matt showed up. Even his daughter was pleading his case these days. He persisted long after any other guy would have given up and walked away, and he brought her something that must have been next to impossible to get.

Maybe she needed to give him a chance. Just once.

"It's only lunchtime," she said. She looked up into his face, and watched the smile slowly spread over his mouth.

"It's eight o'clock in London," he suggested helpfully.

"We're not in London, are we?"

"We could be."

"They—they won't let me bring my flowers on the plane."

"I would get you some more." He took her face in both hands. "Tonight. I'll be here to pick you up at six."

"I have to change."

"No. Just be here." His thumb slowly stroked her cheek, his mouth moved toward hers, and she closed her eyes. He kissed the corner of Amy's lips. His stubble tickled. She let out a laugh.

"What if I want a real kiss?" she whispered.

"Later," he said.

THE REST OF the day was so busy that Amy didn't think much about her date with Matt. Actually, that wasn't true. She caught herself staring off into space multiple times for no apparent reason, and she had her nose in the sweet pea bouquet when she wasn't staring off into space. Nice flowers. Even better kiss, despite the fact his aim was bad.

Good thing she'd finished most of the orders for the day before Matt happened in.

At four o'clock, Emily called.

"Hey, Ame. Brandon and I are leaving the doctor's office. Can we meet you for dinner somewhere?"

It was somewhat odd that Brandon was at a doctor's appointment Emily told Amy was "routine," but Amy would get it out of Emily later.

"Right now?"

"Well, yeah, pretty soon. How about Coastal Kitchen? I think we can find something that Brandon might like to eat there." Amy could hear Brandon's laughter over the phone. Brandon would eat almost anything that didn't run away from him, so this was a bit of a joke.

"I wish I could. I can't make it."

"The shop's busy?"

"Yeah, but that's not it." Amy cleared her throat. "I have a date tonight."

"A date?" Emily cried out. "That's wonderful." She must have hit the speaker on her cell phone; Amy heard Brandon's voice.

"Who's the lucky guy, squirt?" he said.

"Oh, some guy." If the date went well, she might mention it. If it didn't, she'd prefer licking her wounds in private.

"She's not going to tell us, is she?" Brandon asked his wife.

"Baby, we shouldn't interfere," Amy's sister cautioned.

"Hey, your dad and I will show up over there to check the guy out. Don't think we won't do it," Brandon warned.

"Hush," Emily told him. "So, you'll tell me about it later, right?" she said to Amy.

"Sure." *Not on your life.*

"No kissing on the first date," Brandon insisted, and the word "date" sounded a little muffled. Emily must have put her hand over his mouth.

"I don't know what we'll do if I have girls," she fretted. "Our poor daughters will have no social life at all."

"Everything will be fine." Brandon's voice was firm. "They're not dating until they're thirty-five."

"I was barely thirty-six when *we* started dating, Buster," Emily told him.

"That's right, and you were much too young to date me, weren't you? Listen, Amy, we'll get together with you later this week." Brandon said into the mouthpiece of the phone.

"Let's do that. Give Em a hug from me."

"I will. You be good."

Amy hung up the phone, and walked into the coolers. It was time to make a list of what she needed at the wholesaler tomorrow morning. She might be able to concentrate that long.

AMY SPENT THE rest of the afternoon cleaning up in the workroom to burn off her nervousness, but it wasn't working. This was the same guy she'd spent almost a month now arguing with. It made no sense that her heart was racing and her hands shook. It was dinner. She had to eat, didn't she?

The bells on the shop door jingled as Matt walked in, five minutes before six o'clock. As she turned to face him she wiped her sweaty palms on the apron she still wore.

Matt wore a sport coat, jeans, and a medium blue button-down shirt. He looked like any other guy that dressed for a dinner out, but she hadn't seen him quite like this before. He'd shaved. He'd had his hair trimmed sometime in the past six hours. His exterior announced "mild-mannered guy with money," but the look in his eyes was predatory.

He walked over to Amy, took the broom out of her hand, and kissed her cheek. "Hi."

"Hi."

"Ready?"

"Are you sure?" she burst out. "This is a very bad idea. I'm not dressed—"

"It's a great idea. Let's go." He leaned the broom in a corner. "Well, let's take the apron off first." He reached for the bow tied at Amy's waist with his other hand and pulled it free.

She tugged the apron off over her head, smoothed her hair, and hoped the makeup and lip gloss she'd hurriedly applied wasn't smeared. He took her hand.

"I'll be back in a minute, okay?" She tried to pull away from him, but he didn't let go.

"You're going to the ladies' room to check your makeup and comb your hair, aren't you?"

"You're all dressed up and I—"

"Amy." His voice dropped to almost a whisper. "You look great." She could have sworn she felt electricity arc between them. "Let's get out of here." He drew her toward the front door of the shop. "You put the cash in the safe, right?"

"Yes."

Amy snagged her purse off the hook beneath the cash register, grabbed her keys off the front counter, and he held the door so she could pass through it. Two minutes later they were in his car, and he was pulling out into traffic. She dropped her keys into her purse and resisted

the impulse to grab a mirror and check the makeup Matt
didn't seem to care about.

"So." Matt glanced over at her. "How was your day?"

"Busy. There were lots of deliveries, but the driver was
able to handle it, so things were fine."

"How's he working out?"

"He's good. I don't have to worry about whether or
not he's doing what I tell him to do. The customers seem
to like him. Plus, it's nice for the surrounding neighborhood to know there's a guy in the store."

Matt stopped at a light and turned to her. "Are you
worried about being robbed?"

"No. I just . . . Oh, it's fine." She waved a hand toward
him. His brows knit, but he stepped on the gas when the
light turned green.

"Well, Fifi, I'm relieved to hear it."

He pulled off onto a street Amy didn't immediately
recognize and stopped in front of what looked like a resi-
dential home. She expected someplace like the Dahlia
Lounge or El Gaucho; somewhere Matt could show off.
She'd guessed wrong.

Matt opened the car door for her and took her hand as
they climbed a small staircase stepping inside.

"Hey, Matt! How are you doing?" The hostess picked
up two menus. "Good to see you again."

"I'm fine, thanks. This is Amy," he told the hostess.
She'd never had a guy introduce her to a restaurant's
hostess before. Maybe he considered it important she was
known here. Amy reached out to shake the hostess' hand;
she looked a little surprised.

Matt and Amy were seated at a table for two in a se-cluded alcove. Amy glanced around. For a smallish res-taurant, she couldn't believe how peaceful it was. Even though it was late afternoon, lit crystal candleholders graced each white cloth-covered tabletop. The walls were painted a buttery yellow and covered in framed antique-looking family photos. The windows were draped in old-fashioned cotton floral prints. Grape vines wrapped around the curtain rods. For the moment, Matt and Amy appeared to be the only customers.

"I think you'll like the food," Matt said, picking up his menu.

"I'm sure it's delicious. Do you come here often?"

"They know me," he said. His voice was dry, and Amy let out a laugh. "You like Italian food, don't you?"

"I thought everyone did."

The server appeared, a bottle of pinot noir was or-dered, and Amy leaned back in her chair.

"So, what do you think?" Matt asked.

"It's nice here." He reached across the table, and laced his fingers through Amy's. "It's like having dinner at home."

His eyes lit up. "I hoped you'd like it."

Amy wasn't accustomed to quiet dinner dates. When she dated Brian, he wasn't interested in conversation. He liked showing off. Their first "date" was running a 5K. She couldn't find him at the finish line, and didn't hear from him until he sent her a text later that night: GREAT RACE. LET'S GET TOGETHER AGAIN.

Amy had stood at the finish line of more half-marathons than she cared to count in the past year. When Brian wasn't running, he was lifting, riding his bike, or swimming. She couldn't keep up with him. She wasn't opposed to physical fitness, but she wished for some time with a man who found what she might have to say as worthwhile as how much he could bench press.

Matt still held her hand, and an easy silence fell between them. He was as calm and relaxed as if he and Amy sat in his living room. He leaned toward her, but she squirmed away. The nerves began to churn in her stomach as a result.

She'd been on many first dates in her life. The biggest difference between this first date and every other she'd had, though, was the fact Matt wanted to spend an evening getting to know her at a place they'd both be comfortable. The restaurant they were sitting in was nice, but it wasn't somewhere to see or be seen. He was out with the woman he'd chosen, but he made it clear he focused on her.

Despite the scores of reasons she kept reminding herself of why dating Matt wasn't a great idea, she was beginning to wonder why she'd resisted him for so long.

The contrast between Matt and Brian could not have been more jarring. Matt was drawing Amy into conversation by spending the evening in a cozy and intimate restaurant. Brian made it clear over and over that he wasn't interested in her as a person. She was just someone to show off to, or someone that looked good on his arm at the professional functions lawyers in a big firm were required to attend.

Normally, Amy would push back on Matt's control. She wasn't good at expectations. She was even worse at feelings, especially the kind that could leave her crying again. She knew how it would end. He was going to make her fall in love with him, and then he'd decide he wanted someone else. It was inevitable.

He broke into her fearful thoughts with a soft, "Hey, Fifi."

"I can't believe you're still calling me that."

His smile started with the dimples on either side of his mouth, and made its way to his eyes. "Of course I am. Isn't Fifi your alter-ego?" he teased. "Plus, if I called you 'honey' or 'darling,' you'd either barf into my entrée or ask me if I was feeling all right. What's a guy to do?" He stroked the back of her hand with his thumb.

"Well, then, I guess I'll have to come up with a ridiculous nickname for you as well," she said.

"I look forward to that." He squeezed her hand. She couldn't stop the grin that spread over her face. They had a private joke, and she was elated.

The server arrived with the bottle of wine Matt ordered, fumbled with the wine opener, and almost knocked a wine glass onto the floor when the bottle slipped on the tablecloth.

Matt gave the server an encouraging nod. "They get away from me sometimes, too. Let me try."

"I'm so sorry," the woman said. "Usually I'm really good at this."

"Of course you are," Matt said without a trace of irony or sarcasm in his voice. Amy looked on in amazement. The server handed him the corkscrew and the bottle. A few deft motions later, he opened the bottle and handed it back to her. "Here you go."

"It's my first night here. I'm pretty nervous." The server poured a few drops into Amy's glass. Amy almost told her that Matt was supposed to taste the wine, but she lifted the glass to her nose instead. It smelled fine. The first taste wasn't bad, either.

"What do you think, Amy?" he asked.

"It's very nice."

The server poured them both a glass. "I'll be back in a few moments to take your order," and hurried away.

"That was interesting, wasn't it?" She saw him smile again, and she had to smile, too. If Matt wanted everyone in the restaurant to know what a star he was, he'd just passed on a pretty big opportunity. She was sure most other people wouldn't have been so calm and patient with the server and her mistakes. She started a mental list: *Great Things about Matt*.

"What are you going to eat, Matt?"

The look in his eyes told Amy food was the last thing on his mind. He seemed more interested in holding her hand. He laid the menu down by his plate.

"I like the *ragu bolognese*. What sounds good to you?"

"I think I'd like the gnocchi."

"We'll get some salad, too." He took another sip from his wineglass. "Are you blushing?"

"Probably," she muttered. The image of Matt in the shower remained burned onto her brain pan. He was gorgeous all over. Of course she couldn't stop thinking about that, either.

"It's just me."

"I know." She took a sip of ice water, resisting the impulse to dunk her napkin in it and apply it to her burning cheeks.

"We could argue about something. Would that make you feel more at ease?" Matt teased.

She couldn't stop the laughter that bubbled out of her. He looked pleased.

"There she is. I was wondering where you were hiding," he said.

Matt gave their order to the server, who had just reappeared, and they looked out the window at the pinks, dark blues, and violets of dusk smudged over the sky. There were other diners in the restaurant now, but the world had shrunk to their little table for two. She leaned forward in her chair, seemingly pulled by an invisible string. She ran her fingers over the calluses on his hands. They must be from the gym, she told herself. He wasn't splitting wood or building something behind the desk at Pro Sports Network. Amy realized Matt had spoken. "Are you enjoying this?"

"Yes. I am."

Considering he was a man she'd done nothing but spar with, it all felt like a dream. They sat together peacefully. She gave Matt's hand another squeeze. Her hand felt so small inside his. He squeezed back.

A few seconds later Amy's reverie was broken by motion she saw out of the corner of her eye. Their server was practicing picking up a large platter in the kitchen area, flipping it around on her wrist, and laughing at a conversation Amy couldn't hear.

Their salads arrived. The server poured them each another glass of wine. Amy rested her chin in her hand. Matt glanced up from his plate. "What's on your mind?"

"Matt Stephens, is this who you really are? Why do I think I don't even know you?"

"I'm full of surprises." He lifted his glass and touched it to Amy's. "To exploration." They both took a sip, and he gestured toward her plate. "The salad's good, Fifi. Try it."

Amy took a bite. The flavors of fresh spinach, sliced strawberries, and a tangy dressing exploded on her tongue. She took another bite, and tasted a hint of crumbled blue cheese and sliced almonds. If the salad was this delicious, she couldn't wait to try the entrée. Although she was fairly absorbed in her food, she still noticed their server approaching.

The woman carried a very large tray of food. She flipped her wrist as she lowered the tray to a standing holder. Well, she tried.

It all happened so slowly. Panic spread over her face as the server realized she'd lost her grip. She grabbed for the rim of the tray with her other hand. The tray slid away from her, full plates slipping off the tray and flipping in mid-air, and Amy had just enough time to grab her head in a panic. What if they hit her? Matt reached over the table for her, knocking over his wineglass, and half-rose from his chair.

"Oh, God. Oh, no!" the server exclaimed. "*Shit.*"

By some miracle, the heavy plates missed Amy, but their contents didn't. She was showered with four plate-fuls of hot Italian food. The glassware smashed on the floor as it fell, spilling contents everywhere, and the tray bounced off the floor.

The server was still talking. "I am so sorry! Let me help—"

Amy had spaghetti in her hair, penne in her lap, lasagna everywhere else. A large chunk of rigatoni lay in the middle of her salad plate. The penne in her lap was marinated by the glass of white wine that drenched her as it flew off the tray. The server pulled a towel out of her belt and offered it to Amy, while frantically motioning to another server.

"Please—please let the kitchen know we need clean towels—and more food!"

The chaos swirled around Amy. She knew people were talking to her. The customers at the next table whose entrees and wine had taken a dive were all up out of their seats. The expressions on their faces registered either shock or hilarity. She could see the commotion, but all she could focus on was Matt. He didn't yell at the luckless server, or freak out in any way. He braved the mess on the floor, crouched down next to her, and cleaned sauce off her face with his napkin.

"What do I do now?" she asked him.

His voice was gentle. "You're supposed to eat it, not wear it." He pulled a chunk of spaghetti out of Amy's hair, and dropped it onto the ruined dinner table. He kissed the tip of her nose. "Let's get dinner to go."

Chapter Nine

AFTER A SPONGE bath in the restaurant's ladies' room, Amy managed to pull herself together enough to make the trip home. The restaurant provided an unopened bottle of wine and a free t-shirt. It would have been even better to get a shower and a change of clothing from the skin out. However, beggars—or people covered in marinara sauce and wine—couldn't be choosers. The labor-intensive cleanup would have to wait till Amy got home.

She tried to look at the bright side: Nobody was hurt. By the time she emerged from the ladies' room, the restaurant was mostly back to peaceful enjoyment of some delicious-looking Italian food. She loved Italian food. She just didn't imagine wearing it.

Matt's contemplative mood seemed to be gone, along with the largest chunks of pasta, cheese, and sauce out of Amy's hair and off her clothing.

"Are you okay? You weren't burned or anything,

right?" He had her arm and held the shopping bag full of entrees they hadn't had a chance to try, and he was pulling her toward the car. "They gave you another bottle of wine, too?"

"I'm fine. I—I need to go home and take a shower. I'm going to have to cut our date short." He opened the car door for her. "Maybe another time."

"You still need to eat." He got into the driver's side. He didn't flinch over Amy's stained clothes touching the leather seats of the Mercedes, which she thought was nice. "There's some tiramisu in that bag."

"I'm not really hungry right now."

Matt turned to her at a stoplight and touched her hand. "The evening didn't quite turn out as I envisioned."

"Well, you never know when you're going to be dive-bombed by a plate of lasagna." She wondered how much it would cost to get the interior of his Mercedes detailed. "What was your original plan?"

"We'd have dinner, we'd go for a walk on the waterfront or something. How does that sound?"

She glanced out the window to see moonlight rippling over Lake Washington. It would have been incredibly romantic if she didn't smell like she'd been bathing in tomato sauce. Amy knew this was her cue to say, "We should try this again sometime," but she couldn't shake the feeling she'd had during the glass of wine and the few bites of salad they shared.

Even if her relationships had a bad habit of blowing up, she still wanted any emotional involvement to be her decision, especially with a guy who seemed to see right through her. She wanted to find the guy she trusted enough to be herself with, on her own terms. She hoped for a man who would woo her with patience and tenderness.

Amy was tired, and it had nothing to do with lack of sleep. She wished that somehow he was everything she'd glimpsed in that few minutes earlier at the restaurant. Her *Great Things about Matt* list was still growing, too. She knew the definition of insanity was doing the same thing over and over while expecting a different result. Maybe she should try something different, just once. Maybe she should give him another chance.

She bit her lip, and inched one toe off the high-dive.

"That would have been nice."

A few moments later he reached out and took her hand. Just holding his hand, Amy broke out in a cold sweat. This was the real thing. She was out with a man, not a boy. He made her long for something she'd never known and had wanted desperately. When it ended, she'd never get over it.

Matt stopped in the driveway at her townhouse and shut the engine off. He stared out of the windshield. "This is about more than having food spilled all over you, isn't it?"

"Yeah."

"Want to tell me about it?"

She fidgeted a bit. "Not right now."

She opened the car door and slid off the seat. He grabbed the bag of food and followed her up the walk. They stopped at her front door. Normally she would have had the keys in her hand before she even got out of the car, but she was so dazed by his nearness it was difficult to remember the most basic things right now. He tipped her chin up with gentle fingers.

"Let's have another glass of wine. I happen to have a bottle right here."

"No, thank you. I need to go get in the shower." She tried to take a breath. "Thank you for—oh, just thank you."

He wasn't letting go. "Amy." His voice was beguiling. "Don't leave."

"I need to go."

"Talk to me." He moved closer.

"I—I have to go." She pushed the key into the door-knob, gave it a shove, and tried to move away from him. He didn't let go. His hold on her was gentle, but he wasn't moving away, and he wasn't letting her pass. He set the shopping bag down beside them on the front porch, and Amy heard the slight "clunk" of a wine bottle on cement.

She studied her shoes. He spoke into her ear. "This didn't go the way I wanted it to. I wanted to talk with you some more. I wanted to find out why I can't seem to stay away." He left a trail of tiny kisses over her cheek. "I want another chance, Fifi."

"I've got to go," she whispered.

"I know." He kissed the sensitive patch of skin behind her earlobe. She shivered. "I want one more thing, though."

Her eyelids fluttered closed. If she could get in the house, she could mop up from there, and it wasn't her clothes that needed the most help. When she needed

Matt to be a blustering, arrogant, uncaring ass, he melted her heart instead with quiet words and gentle kisses. She could still get away. All she had to do was take a few steps, and she would be inside, behind a locked door. His hand slid to the side of her neck: Danger, Will Robinson.

He was a snake charmer, and she was the little cobra that wanted to sleep in the warmth and comfort of her basket in the sun. He was a tomcat, and she was the sparrow drawn to his lair for food. He was a backyard bug zapper, and she was a moth. She could conjure analogies all night long, but they all added up to the same thing: Her attraction to him—and there was a lot of it, she had to admit—couldn't overcome her anxiety, or the scent of tomato sauce.

Matt went after what he wanted, and she was no exception. His mouth covered hers. He nibbled and teased, stroked and sampled. His tongue found its way into Amy's mouth. He tasted like the wine they had drunk. She discovered that alcohol was not necessarily the most intoxicating taste she'd ever known, too. She fisted her hands in his shirt front.

She tried to pull any breath at all into her lungs, and used most of it to tell him, "This is so unfair."

"What do you mean?" His lips hovered half an inch from hers. Maybe she should shut up and kiss him again.

"You're a great kisser, too? It's just so—"

He cut off whatever she was going to say with another kiss. She felt his smile against her mouth. His arms wrapped around her. She hung onto him despite her best intentions. A few minutes later Amy's defenses were melting like a snowball in Palm Desert, and Matt lifted his head.

"I'll pick you up day after tomorrow at the store. Don't dress up."

She found her voice. "What do you mean?"

"Saturday. Six o'clock. Bring a jacket." He stepped back and handed her the shopping bag. She was so shocked she took it as she backed over her threshold. "Goodnight."

He pulled the front door closed as he walked away.

She resisted the impulse to pull the door open, tackle him on the front lawn, and do a few things to him that would bring a substantial fine from the homeowner's association at the very least. She reached for the doorknob as she heard Matt's car drive away.

AMY PUT THE untouched food into the fridge before she hit the shower. She didn't sleep well that night, either. She kept remembering the look in Matt's eyes as they sipped wine at the restaurant, how his nearness had been enough. There was only a little conversation before she found herself showered with Italian food, but that wasn't necessarily a bad thing. Despite her trepidation, she wondered what it was about Matt she couldn't seem to resist. Obviously, he was handsome. He had money. He was charming (most of the time), funny, and intelligent. He was everything any woman would want, but there was something deeper than the exterior attracting her, and maybe she needed to find out what that was.

She didn't want to lean on anyone else. She didn't want

to lose herself in a man, either. She wanted to do things herself, be in control and succeed on her own terms, but the temptation to rest against Matt's broad shoulder and let him take over was almost irresistible. The most frightening thing of all: She liked it.

Chapter Ten

AMY LET HERSELF into her parents' house after work the next day. Even if she didn't live here anymore, she still had a key. Plus, it was March Madness. Her dad wasn't moving from his recliner unless the Dallas Cowboys Cheerleaders were coming over for dinner. The cheerleaders showing up for dinner was doubtful, but he'd still get to see the main event: The University of Washington men's basketball team was playing Duke for a spot in the Elite Eight, and nothing else—besides beer—would make him glance away from the TV.

"Mom and Dad," she called out. "Is anyone home?"

She moved into the kitchen, and began unloading her grocery bags. Beer, tortilla chips, avocados for guacamole, and her dad's favorite, wings. His doctor had recommended Mark Hamilton find another favorite snack food. Amy's dad's response was to cut down to a few times a year. Obviously, the doctor didn't know that

March Madness was as much a religious observance as Christmas Day to Mark and his youngest daughter.

Amy and her dad bonded over sports. They had to find something to do during the football offseason, so the ritual of watching college basketball's biggest show began.

Meg Hamilton hurried into the kitchen. "There you are. Your dad thought you were going to miss the tipoff." She embraced Amy. "Did you close the shop early?"

"Yeah. We're not getting as much walk-in as phone business right now. Plus, everyone's glued to their TV tonight."

Amy's mom's brilliant copper hair had gray in it now. She didn't move as quickly as she did when Amy was younger, but she was no less graceful. Meg was a former ballerina who had given up a promising, red-hot career to marry her one true love, Amy's dad, Mark. One divorce later, they were now engaged. Again.

Meg scooted around her daughter, reached into the refrigerator, and produced a baking dish. "I made seven-layer dip for you two, with low-fat sour cream. Your dad will love it."

"Mom, I brought some avocados. You didn't have to do that. Plus, I have take-out from the Wing Dome." The Wing Dome's selection of sauces ranged from mildly spicy to seven-alarm hot. On an occasion like tonight, supermarket deli wings weren't going to cut it.

"I know you both enjoy this, so I wanted to. A few snacks won't hurt him once or twice a year. Let me get this stuff set up in the family room, and then I'm going outside to pull some weeds." Needless to say, Meg Hamilton did not share Mark and Amy's love of sports. She patted Amy on the back, and her eyes narrowed.

"When's the last time you got eight hours of sleep, Amy Margaret? There are dark circles under your eyes. You look like you haven't slept in a week! You're exhausted, and you're putting in too many hours at the shop."

"Mom, I'm fine. I get plenty of sleep. Everything is going well."

"I don't think—". Margaret stopped, shook her head, and changed the subject. "I think your dad wants some time with you, honey. He misses you."

"I miss him, too." Amy let out a sigh and then pasted a smile on her face. "Things are going great at the shop. I'm really pleased with the increase in business. It's great to see the things I've worked so hard for happen." She'd like to add, *"I'm a huge success and you should be as proud of me as you are of Emily,"* but this would certainly start an inquisition about how successful she was, and why she would think they weren't as proud of her as they were of her sister.

Her mother glanced up from the tray of food and drinks she was assembling. "What's this I hear about a date? Emily called me to find out if I knew anything."

"Mom, I had dinner with a friend of Brandon's. It's not a big deal."

"Are you going to see him again?" Meg asked.

Amy let out a groan.

"I'm just teasing you. I am curious, though. I can't remember the last time you didn't tell Emily or me all about a date. What's the big secret?" Meg's amber-brown eyes, the same color as Amy's, sparkled in the dimly lit kitchen.

"There's no big secret. I'll tell you all about it when there's something to tell." There was definitely something to tell. Right now, though, there was something more pressing on her mind.

"So, Dad moved back in?"

Amy's parents had split up when she was a teenager, in a fusillade of bitterness and arguing. It was the defining event of Amy's teen years. Her parents' divorce still reverberated in Amy's life, years later. She knew the divorce wasn't her fault. Her parents had told their two daughters that, sometimes, two people just couldn't get along. Amy wanted her life to be different. Unlike Emily, though, the information hadn't made it from Amy's head to her heart.

After years of fighting, Amy's dad left as the result of Meg's belief he was cheating on her. He wasn't, but that information didn't come to light until the damage was done. If Amy's dad would leave her mother, some man would leave Amy, too, sooner or later. She realized it wasn't normal to believe this, or to do or say whatever it might take to force the latest guy away from her. She knew she was picking guys who weren't right for her in the first place, but trying to understand why she did it left her bewildered and heartbroken. Again.

Even more confusing, her parents had reconciled. She was torn between happiness for them and the residual anger that came when she realized they had fought for years instead of talking it out.

Amy's mom wiped her hands on her apron. "The lease on his apartment was up—"

"Mom."

"Amy Margaret, our living arrangements are between your father and me." She picked up the tray. "Speaking of your father, I'll bet he's looking for a beer."

Amy picked up the plateful of wings and trailed behind. She loved her mom, but she longed to ask her why Amy's social life was always open for discussion, while her parents' relationship was off-limits. After all, it wasn't like the years and years of acrimony had any effect on the family or anything.

Mark Hamilton got up from his recliner, took the heavy tray out of his ex-wife's hands, and set it down on the coffee table. "Thanks, honey. Are you sure you don't want to sit with us for a few minutes? We'd love your company."

His now-fiancée reached up to kiss his cheek. "That's very sweet, but I'll be right outside. Our little girl's here. Didn't you want to spend some time with her?"

Amy's mom stroked her cheek. "Have fun. I'll check on you two in a little while."

Amy's dad reached out for her. "Hey, where's my hug?"

AMY OBVIOUSLY GOT her height from her dad. At five-nine she towered over both her mother and Emily. Mark Hamilton was over six feet tall, and kept his lean, rangy frame with jogging and racquetball. His chestnut-colored hair was graying, too, but he rose out of his chair swiftly.

Her dad wrapped his arms around her, gave her a breath-stealing squeeze, and kissed the top of her head.

"I've missed you, Twinkletoes. Let's watch some hoops."

Amy and her dad concentrated on food and basketball till halftime. The Huskies were up by eight points. Mark wiped the wing evidence off his face with a well-used napkin, and glanced over at his daughter.

"Dad, do you need another beer? Maybe I should grab some now."

"It can wait. How are you doing? Your mom said she talked to Emily, but all I heard out of that conversation was something about wedding photos. How's it going at the shop?"

"It's fine. It's busy. I'm happy about that. Just the usual stuff," she assured him.

"Have you heard from Brian?"

"No. I don't think he's going to be calling me again." Amy resisted the impulse to slam the rest of her bottle of beer.

"I wondered if he was the guy you had a date with last weekend. Your mom mentioned something about it, and that you wouldn't tell anyone who you were with."

"No, Dad, he wasn't. I had dinner with one of Brandon's friends."

"Did you have a good time?"

"Sure. It was fun." She tried to keep her voice casual. Of course, her dad saw right through that.

Mark pulled the lever to sit up straight in his recliner. "Do you think you'll see him again?"

"We have a date tomorrow night."

"We want to meet him," he said.

"Dad. He's just a guy I had dinner with. I promise I won't marry him without telling you first." She got up from the couch. "The second half's going to start. I'll be right back."

Amy made a beeline toward the powder room on the first floor of her parents' house, followed by a quick stop in the kitchen to grab some beverages. Her dad wasn't going to give up on this. Then again, if the second half was exciting enough, he might forget all about it.

The Huskies ran away with the second half. Even with more beer, Mark Hamilton proved to be more than a bit curious about Amy's dinner date.

"So, tell me about him. What does he do?"

If the words "He works in sports broadcasting" left Amy's lips, her dad would go bananas. He wouldn't ask for game tickets or anything. Her dad was a sports fan who was most likely quite familiar with Matt and his reputation with the ladies, well-deserved or not. He tended to take a dim view of that kind of thing, especially when it involved his daughter.

"He lives in Redmond. He's in communications. He's divorced. Dad, what is the deal? I know you guys loved Brian, but he didn't love me. There's not a lot I can do about that."

"Brian's a coward. If he didn't want you to come along to New York with him, he should have cut things off a long time ago. So, what's the difference between him and the new guy?"

"The new guy wanted to have dinner with me?" She saw her dad's grin. "It was just a date. He's nice. I don't believe he has a police record. If things get more serious, I'll bring him over here so you and Mom can meet him." Amy took a breath. "Dad, when are you and Mom getting remarried?"

Mark slid one arm over the back of the couch. "So, sweetie, I'm not sure how to answer your question."

"Why?"

"Your mom and I discussed it. We're going to live together for a little while first." He gave her shoulder a squeeze. "We're also seeing a counselor, to get a handle on some of the things that went wrong before."

Amy's head snapped up. She knew she must have looked startled. "But Emily said you didn't really cheat. She said that you and Mom just fought all the time, and— Dad, is there something else I don't know?"

"No. Of course not. The rest of the things that went wrong were between your mom and me, and they were mostly due to the fact that I'm still not the best at the talking thing. She needs to talk when she's upset, and I didn't understand that. See? We've been talking for less than five minutes, and you're about to jump out of your skin." He pulled her closer. "Listen, I have something I want to tell you."

Amy swallowed hard. "What's wrong?"

"Nothing's wrong. First, though, I'm going to answer your question." He thought for a minute. "This is between us. Don't tell your mother."

"Okayyy." Her dad wasn't usually a secrets kind of a guy.

"I want to take her on a really nice honeymoon this time, so I've been putting some money away. I should have enough in a couple of months. We're going to New York for a week, and then Paris, if she'd like to go. We want to have a small wedding in the backyard. Your mother wants to show off her garden, but we have to wait until it stops raining long enough." He looked into Amy's eyes. "No matter what, we're getting married again, and we'll stay married for the rest of our lives. How's that?"

Amy hoped her expression was blank, that she'd rapidly concealed her apprehension over what he might say, and forced a smile.

"Dad, that's great. She loves New York, and I know she's always wanted to go to Paris. Maybe you all can go to the ballet. She would love it—"

"There's something else I need to tell you."

She nodded, studying her clenched hands.

"Even an old dog can learn new tricks. The counselor has been a lot of help." She heard the sounds of his whiskers as he rubbed one hand across his mouth. "I've thought for a long time on how to say this. Maybe the best thing is to just say it. Amy, honey, I'm sorry. I'm sorry about what happened between your mom and me, and I'm sorry that I moved out instead of staying and trying to fix it. I thought that if I made the extra effort to spend time with you, you'd understand, but mostly, I wimped out, as you kids would say."

She still couldn't look at him. She didn't glance at the TV.

"I know it was really hard on you and Emily, maybe harder than it was on us. I should have apologized to you a long time ago. I was wrong. I hope you'll forgive me."

She put one hand over her mouth. Her shoulders were shaking. She saw her dad hit Mute on the TV remote and wait.

AMY LET OUT a sob. Her dad had said the words she'd waited twenty-one years to hear. During her teenage years, she prayed her parents would get back together like some girls prayed for a date with the Backstreet Boys. She was reminded of the old cliché: *Be careful what you wish for. You might get it.* Mostly, she was attempting to avoid a crying jag of epic proportions.

She'd prefer to have some kind of breakdown by herself, thanks.

Her dad rubbed her back, just like he had when she was a child and had skinned her knee. "Shhh." He comforted her. "Everything's going to be all right."

If she looked at him right now she was going to cry and cry and never stop. She covered her face with both hands.

"You're not too old to cry on my shoulder."

She gathered every bit of self-control she'd ever had. "Could we talk about this later?" She choked the words out.

She heard the effort in his voice. He wanted to sound casual. "Sure. Why don't we sit here and relax? Good game, huh?"

She felt the movement as her dad leaned back against the couch cushions. He was still rubbing her back. The only sounds in the room were their breathing and the ticking of the anniversary clock that had sat on the mantel since Amy was young.

There was no moisture left in her mouth. All at once she was freezing cold, and she was shaking. She fought the impulse to grab her purse and run out of the house, but even more, she had to say something. She knew her dad loved her. She knew he was trying to make amends. She also knew she would spend the rest of her life regretting it if she didn't speak up.

"Dad," she rasped, "how could you leave us? Didn't you know how much we needed you?" She mangled the napkin that had been in her lap with both hands. "I needed you. Why?" Of course, the tears gushed forth. "I kept hoping that you would change your mind. You never did. Emily was gone, and Mom was so sad . . ."

"Come here." He reached out and pulled her into his chest. "I'm right here."

By the time she managed to drag in a lungful of air, the front of his Oxford-cloth shirt was soaked. The shredded napkin was soaked. She was boneless.

"Daddy, I was alone," she said.

"I know, baby. I know." He held one of the unused paper napkins Amy's mom left on the side table up to her nose. "Blow," he prompted.

She gave it a try. The napkin was soaked with tears and snot when he pulled it away from her face.

"Ewww. Gross," she said.

She managed to sit up straight, even though she felt like she'd been wrung out and left to dry. Her father looked a little wrung out, himself. Men of his generation really didn't cry, but she saw some telltale redness in his eyes.

"Don't worry about it." He took his glasses off, and pinched the bridge of his nose. He laid the glasses on the side table. "The only answer I have for you is that I thought your mom would be happier if I wasn't here. We couldn't talk to each other without fighting, and I did a lot of things wrong."

Amy wiped her nose again with the sleeve of her sweatshirt.

"I know you're mad, and you're hurt. You should be. There's something else I want to say, though." He kissed her forehead. "I loved you before you were born. I'm going to love you till my last breath. I wish I'd been better at showing it and saying so."

Amy wrapped her arms around him and squeezed. "I love you, too."

Chapter Eleven

The shop's doorbell jingled late on Saturday afternoon, and Matt strolled in. He wore jeans, a Seattle Sounders jersey and scarf, and a confident grin.

"Hey, Fifi. Ready to go?"

"What—what are you talking about?"

Obviously he'd made the date with her, but he hadn't called. He hadn't stopped by over the past forty-eight hours to make sure she was fine after their ill-fated dinner date. The flower orders even slowed down over the last couple of days. He and his ghostwriter must have been taking a breather, or maybe he was mad when he found out how much it cost to clean his car's upholstery. Amy alternated between pining for him and feeling disgust with herself. After all, admitting she was looking forward to the date meant she planned on moving forward with him.

She hated women who whined about how they

couldn't make up their minds about some guy, or how they couldn't stop thinking about him. Now, she was one of them.

Matt rounded the counter and reached out to stroke her cheek.

"It's you, me, and a soccer match. I even have a team scarf for you. We can join the crowd walking to the pitch. If you play your cards right, I'll buy you a hot dog and a beer. Think you can handle that?" He leaned over and murmured into her ear, "I promise there's no Italian food there." His arm slid around her waist.

"I can't go. I got a last-minute order, and I need to take some flowers to the site." She fiddled with the pens in her apron pocket.

"We'll stop on the way."

"I can't."

"Yes, you can. Let's go." He laid his fingers over Amy's lips.

"I—maybe another time," she tried to say around his fingers.

"You promised."

Amy pulled away from him. "I did not. I did nothing of the kind. You TOLD me—"

"Shh." Those maddening fingers were over her lips again. "You're going to hurt my feelings. Who will yell at the opposing team with me, huh? Plus, I'd like to see if we could get through an entire evening in public without a disaster." He gave her his most enticing smile. Of course she was powerless to resist it, dammit. "C'mon, Fifi."

So, Matt wanted to "stop by on the way"? She'd show

him. After all, he told her he really hated weddings. Wait till he found out where she was going.

"Fine," she said, smiling back at him.

"Ahh. Now we're making progress. Where's the stuff you need to drop off?"

"The cooler." She grabbed her purse off the hook under the register. She yanked her work apron over her head, dropping it on the front counter.

He pulled the floral box out of the cooler, grabbed the ring of keys off Amy's wrist, and nodded toward the front door. "You know where these have to go?"

"Yes. I don't think you're going to like this idea."

"It's an excellent idea." He took her elbow in his fingertips. "Ready?"

MATT AND AMY pulled up in front of a large, three-story, nondescript beige building about twenty minutes later. The sign out front advertised it as an assisted living facility. Amy resisted the impulse to laugh out loud when she considered what was waiting for Matt inside.

She opened the box to check everything was there one last time. It held one bridal bouquet of red and white roses, one boutonniere, and a flower for the retired judge that was performing the wedding.

"I take it these are wedding flowers," he said.

"Yes, they are," she sang out.

Amy barely stifled her laughter at Matt's horrified expression. His brows knit. He passed one hand over his face and rested one hand on the small of her back. He actually appeared nervous. Wedding ceremonies seemed to be Matt's Kryptonite for whatever reason.

"We're just dropping the stuff off, aren't we?"

"I think you'll want to stick around. There's supposedly cake, and the coffee here isn't bad. Plus, the newlyweds may get a kick out of seeing you. Come on, Sparky. It'll be fun."

FIVE MINUTES LATER, Matt Stephens was officially in Hell.

He hadn't seen the woman for almost thirty years, but he remembered the deceptively soft voice, and the black-and-white attire. Hopefully, someone had relieved her of her favorite weapons: Guilt, and a wooden ruler.

"Matthew Stephens! What are you doing here?" Sister Mary Margaret, his eighth-grade French teacher, gave him a brisk pat on the arm. "How's your mother?" She didn't wait for an answer. "Matthew, I was surprised to get your flowers, and even more surprised at the note. It made me sound like some kind of trollop. Why would you do such a thing?" Even if she was stooped with old age, she reached up and grabbed his chin in her pincer-like fingers. "Have you been attending Mass? When was your last confession, young man?"

"I thought you'd like getting flowers, Sister Mary Margaret."

"Oh, they were lovely. I shared them with some other people here. The note, though, was—Matthew, does your mother know about this?"

"I'm not living at home anymore. I haven't lived there for a long time now."

He was a grown man. He'd been out of school for a while. If it wasn't bad enough that Fifi was dragging him to some kind of wedding, he was in hot water with one of his former teachers. This was *not* how he envisioned his Saturday night unfolding.

A flock of conservatively dressed, short-veiled women descended on him.

"Matthew! What a nice surprise!" one of them called out.

This just kept getting better. He saw the principal of his high school, Sister Theresa. He'd sent her flowers, too, and a card saying something to the effect that he missed their late nights together. It was actually more "late afternoons" because of detentions, but hell, who was counting? Sister Mary Helen was his art teacher. The card that came with her flowers read, "You are a work of art." Sister Barbara was his math teacher; she still wore thick glasses and rubber-soled shoes, and he was sure she'd loved the card that read "It all adds up to you and me."

By now he was surrounded by elderly nuns, who seemingly all remembered him, remembered more than he would like about his exploits in parochial school, and also remembered his mother's phone number. Evidently his mom had already had an earful about the bouquets he sent from Amy's shop, but she hadn't mentioned it to him.

He might have made a few targeted donations here over the years at his mom's request. She never told him why she wanted him to give money to this particular assisted living facility, either. He didn't associate the name out front with the street address his mom gave him when he asked where some of his old teachers might be living now. He might have to make a few more donations—anonymously, of course. There had to be something they needed.

Maybe he should stop in here to visit once in a while, too. His former teachers and the school administrator always made sure his mom had a little extra help with his tuition via a "scholarship." A few flowers were nice, but he wanted to know their last years would be worry-free.

Even Sister Mary Margaret's.

"There's a retired priest here, too, Matthew." Sister Mary Helen had him by one elbow, steering him toward a doorway marked "chapel." "He can hear your confession," she told him.

Matt would hate to imagine the effect of his confession on an elderly priest, considering the fact he hadn't been to confession at all in at least twenty years. It might take all day. Obviously it was best to distract them while he formulated some kind of plan. Of course, Fifi disappeared with the wedding flowers the minute they walked in the front door.

Revenge would be sweet.

He held out one arm for Sister Barbara to hook a thin, gnarled hand through. She moved more slowly than the others, who were all still trying to ask him questions about whether or not he'd been to Mass lately, and if he prayed the rosary. She'd always been so sweet to him when he was in school.

"Sister Barbara, how long have you been here?"

"Our convent had to close a couple of years ago, Matthew, and we all retired. The Church was kind enough to help us find a nice place to live. We were all surprised you still remembered us." Her cheeks flushed a pale pink. "I loved the flowers. Your naughty message made me laugh, too."

Matt settled his hand over her frailer one. "That's good. I'll have to send a naughty message more often, then."

Maybe he could talk Amy into a weekly flower delivery or something.

The nuns stopped badgering Matt long enough to make a beeline toward Amy, who was pinning a boutonniere on an older gentleman in a military dress uniform. Sister Mary Margaret was in the lead.

"Amy," she called out, "Katarina's daughter brought a cake this morning. It's all set up in the cafeteria. The coffee's already made. She even made a nice punch for us."

"Oh, that's wonderful," Amy told her. "The bride must still be getting dressed."

"Oh, yes," Sister Theresa assured her. "She wants to make a grand entrance. The wedding should start in about fifteen minutes. We'd better get a seat."

Sister Mary Margaret sat down next to Matt, in the chair he'd saved for Fifi.

"Sister, my date might want to sit with me."

"I'll shove over when she gets here. Did she tell you that she donated those lovely flowers? Katarina will be just thrilled. She and Bill don't have a lot of money. We all chipped in to pay for the flowers, and Amy wouldn't take a dime. Plus, she's been here a couple of times already to help with the dinner service in our cafeteria."

Matt was betting that Amy was coerced into it by the ex-nun goon squad, but he did his best to maintain a neutral facial expression.

"Your mother says you were married. You're not married now?" Sister Mary Margaret said.

"No, Sister, I'm not."

"Amy's not dating anyone. She's a nice girl. So sweet. She owns her own business, and she's pretty, too."

If his mother ever found out his former teacher was matchmaking him and Amy, he'd never hear the end of it. His mother was chomping at the bit for more grandchildren. Even better, the sheer entertainment value of Amy's dodging his pursuit would leave his mother helpless with laughter.

Matt pulled the non-restrictive collar of his Sounders jersey off his neck for the fourth time in ten minutes. It was hotter than Hell in here. He could really use a beer. Even better, a tequila shot. Or five. If they didn't move it, they were going to miss the game. They'd already missed the crowd that walked to the pitch before each Sounders game, singing and chanting. Soccer in Seattle approached religious fervor for the fans, who held up team scarves and sang through most of the match.

Maybe he was so uncomfortable because they'd turned up the heat for the old people. That's it.

"Thanks. I'll take that under advisement," Matt said.

He heard a commotion in the back of the room. It

seemed the other residents were making their way to their seats. It looked like a ten-walker pileup out there. If he went to help, he and Amy might have a chance of making it to the stadium before the game started.

"Hey, Sister, I'm going to go see if there's anything I can do to help those people find a seat."

"Well, aren't you nice? Your mother would be so proud. She told me just the other day—"

Matt strode away before he found out what else his mom had to say about him. He took the elbow of an older gentleman who wore a military uniform jacket over hospital sweats.

"Hello. May I show you to a seat?"

The guy smiled and stood up a little straighter. "Are you Bill's son? He talks about you all the time."

"I'm Matt. I'm not Bill's son, but I'd like to help. How about that end seat in the second row? It's got your name on it."

For the next twenty minutes or so, Matt acted as an usher. He seated men and women with canes, walkers, motorized scooters, and wheelchairs. They were in varying states of wedding-type finery, too. They expressed how happy they were about the wedding and how much they appreciated his help; the hot, sweaty, awkward feelings he'd had about being here in the first place began to fade.

His former teachers were amusing. He had to admit it; he was happy to see them. He friggin' hated weddings, though. They reminded him of the one thing in life he'd failed at. He didn't like being reminded of failure—especially his own—in any way, shape, or form.

Amy waved him over to the seat he'd gotten up out of. "They're going to start. Would you like to sit with me?"

One of the seniors sat down at the piano on the left-hand side of the altar and coaxed a passable version of Lohengrin's *Wedding March* out of the instrument. An older guy in black robes took his place at the front of the room, and Bill the groom stood on his left. The best man, wearing what Matt would consider a go-to-hell sports jacket in an interesting burnt orange plaid, stood next to the groom.

The bride made her entrance in a cornflower-blue chiffon floor-length dress, clutched the rose bouquet Amy brought for her, and leaned on a cane as she walked. She never took her eyes off Bill. If there were family members there, nobody got to their feet to walk with the bride.

Matt made another split-second decision as she paused in the back of the chapel for her big walk up the aisle. Obviously, nobody here was going to do anything about this but him.

"I'll be right back," he told Amy. He stood, walked to the back, and offered his arm.

"May I escort you, young lady?" he asked in a low voice.

She beamed at him. Her pale blue eyes twinkled. "Aren't you sweet? Yes, you may." She slipped her hand through his arm, leaned against him, and they set off together on the slow trip up the aisle.

"I'm Matt," he explained. "I'm here with Amy. The florist."

"Oh, yes. We love Amy."

The bride took two more slow steps. "Take all the time

you need," he said into her ear. She smiled at him again. "Now, I've heard I'm supposed to ask. Are you sure about this?"

She squeezed Matt's forearm. "Absolutely."

He patted her hand. "You could marry me, you know."

"I don't think so. You're pretty handsome, but I'm in love with Bill. He's the only one for me."

Matt and Katarina took a few more steps, and they were at the altar. Bill shuffled forward, and Matt put Katarina's hand inside of his. He waited for the justice of the peace to open his book.

"Dearly beloved, we are gathered here today to witness the marriage ceremony of Katarina and Bill. Katarina, are you here of your own free will, and do you intend to be faithful to this man as long as you shall live?"

"Yes."

"Bill, are you here of your own free will, and intend on being faithful to this woman as long as you shall live?"

Bill cleared his throat. "Oh, yes."

"Who gives this woman to be married to this man?"

"I do," Matt said. He kissed the bride on the cheek, turned, and went back to his seat.

Amy was dabbing at her eyes. "I can't believe you did that," she whispered to him.

"I asked her to marry me. She said no. I'm off the hook with my mom," he whispered back. She rolled her eyes, but she slipped her hand through his elbow.

His heart skipped a beat. He glanced over at her. He saw her lips curve into a smile. He laid his hand over hers.

The judge asked all the usual questions, and then said,

"It is an honor to officiate at this wedding. Some of our guests may not know Bill and Katarina's love story. They met at a USO dance on a military base in Germany. Bill was a young soldier, fresh from World War II. Katarina was a girl from a prominent German family. Her parents didn't want her to marry an American. His parents didn't want him to stay in Germany. They parted, each married others, but they couldn't forget the love they'd found."

"After many years Bill's wife died, and he wondered what happened to the vivacious, beautiful girl he'd met in Germany. He looked her up. Her spouse was gone, too, and she wondered what happened to the dashing soldier she met so long ago."

"Katarina moved to America. They got engaged. This just goes to show that love is only for the young, the middle-aged, and the old."

All too soon, the ceremony was over. The pianist played something that sounded like a recessional. The guests watched the newlyweds make their way back down the aisle and followed them out of the chapel. Amy was still sniffling a little. He reached out for her hand.

"Now you're going to tell me we should stay for the reception, aren't you?" Matt said.

"Listen, father of the bride: Don't you have to offer the toast?"

MATT TOOK ONE look at the pitiful display of three bottles of cheap champagne on the table in the facility's cafeteria and pulled the smart phone out of his pocket.

"Amy. Don't let them cut the cake till I get back."

"Huh? Where are you going?"

"Grocery store. I'm not letting them drink that sh— Oh, just make them wait."

"Matt, don't get a case," Amy warned. "They're old. They're not getting drunk."

He sprinted out the front doors of the facility, jumped in the driver's seat of his Mercedes, and popped the hands-free earphone in. He arrived at a local upscale grocery store less than ten minutes later, purchased a five-hundred-dollar American Express gift card, half a rack of fairly good champagne, and a "congratulations on your wedding" greeting card, which he signed his and Amy's names to. Samantha would call it "power shopping." He called it convenience.

He arrived back at the assisted living facility to find Amy helping with the dinner service. He invaded the kitchen, found himself a bus tub, and started dumping ice into it.

"What are you doing, goofball?" Amy whizzed by him with another cart full of covered plates. "No, wait. I saw that box of champagne. Veuve Cliquot? Nice."

"It's not getting opened till it's chilled."

He hauled the bus tub back into the dining room, made sure the table would support the weight, and started burying bottles in the ice. The greeting card and the gift card were in his back pocket. If he could manage to pull Fifi away from her dinner duties, they could make a presentation.

He still hated weddings, but he'd decided he liked this one.

Katarina's bouquet sat on the table next to the uncut

cake. The only other evidence a wedding had just taken place were the lit candles on the tables. Songs from the forties played over the sound system. The bride and groom were seated at a table with what appeared to be a few family members. His former teachers appeared to be spread out amongst the other residents. The retired priest still wore his collar. Amy was setting a dinner plate down in front of him as Matt watched.

Fifi was working her ass off, and he needed to help. If it meant coming within a three-foot radius of more quizzing about his last confession, so be it.

"Hey. What would you like me to help with?"

Amy glanced up from putting another plate down in front of a woman who patted her hand and said, "Thank you, dearie."

"We're almost done. Are you hungry?"

"I'm always hungry."

"Great. Steak or chicken? The chef made a couple of extra meals for us. I already gave the director some cash for our dinner." Amy moved the salt and pepper shakers closer to an older guy, who winked at her. She seemed to know what these people needed before they did.

"I can pick up the tab for dinner—"

"You were getting champagne when all this happened. Again: Steak or chicken?"

"Steak. Let's nab that half-empty table in the corner, too."

MATT AND AMY managed to get a table to themselves. He was pleasantly surprised at how good the food was.

Even better, he had a chance to grill the cornered Fifi for a few minutes.

"So, when were you going to tell me that you managed to find most of my teachers in one place?"

"Imagine my surprise to learn that you were sending flowers and suggestive messages to a bunch of nuns." She dug into her mashed potatoes. "Isn't there some kind of law against that?"

"Revenge will be painful, Fifi. I will repay." He narrowed his eyes, flared his nostrils, and all but pawed the floor with his hoof. She just laughed.

"Now you're sounding like a bad action-adventure movie. I hate to tell you this, but the Sounders game is probably almost over." She stabbed at the "vegetable medley" on her plate. "Wait till your buddies find out you spent Saturday night at a retirement community. Maybe they'll think you're making plans."

"That's a long way off. Hey, I got the happy couple a gift. From us."

"You already bought champagne."

"Yeah. I'd better check on that. In the meantime, they can stay a night or two at a hotel, or use it for something they'd like. Here." He pulled the card out of his back pocket and pushed it across the table. "I'm going to go find out if the champagne is cold. I'll be back."

AMY PULLED THE card out of the envelope, opened it, and read, *Please use the enclosed for an overnight stay at a hotel, or whatever else you might want. Our best wishes for a long and happy marriage. Your friends, Amy Hamilton and Matt Stephens.*

She flipped the gift card packaging over, and stared at the gift card amount. He'd lost his mind. He was going to argue with her for paying the retirement home for their dinners, but he'd spent, by conservative estimate, almost a thousand bucks today? Plus, she really needed to repay him for her half of the gift card. It wasn't right. She thought she'd inflict all his old teachers on him, they would drop the flowers off, stay for the little wedding, and leave.

Maybe the joke was on her.

She slid the card and enclosure back into the envelope, and sealed it.

Matt made sure the champagne was cold, and now he was chatting with the few family members at Bill and Katarina's table. The staff was doing the after-dinner cleanup. They'd evidently deputized someone to cut the cake and pass it out, so they probably didn't need her help.

Matt loped back to their table, dropped into the chair, and grinned at her. "Katarina's daughter is giving a toast. I believe we can escape."

"Don't you want to have some champagne?"

"I can get more. I have the technology." He waggled his eyebrows at her.

"Speaking of technology, I now owe you two hundred and fifty dollars. Will you take payments?"

He leaned over the table, and took her hand. His voice was low. He spoke rapidly. "No. I made that decision on my own, and I can afford it. Do not even think about paying me back. This is a gift."

"It's a lot of money! I—"

Amy's protests were cut off by someone rapping silverware against a wine glass. The facility's director, a roundish woman, had possession of a cordless microphone. "It's time for our newlyweds to cut the cake. Come on up here, Bill and Katarina. By the way, the cake was donated by Katarina's daughter, Heidi, and the champagne was donated by Amy's friend, Matt. Let's give them a hand."

Matt shook his head and made the "waving off" sign with one hand, but Amy saw him smile. Despite his protests, he managed to choke down a piece of cake and half a glass of champagne. A few minutes later, he took Amy's elbow and helped her out of her chair.

"Come on, Fifi. It's time for the guests to leave so the newlyweds can enjoy their privacy." He hauled her across the dining room, stopped in front of Bill, and held out the card. "This is for you and your new wife."

"You didn't have to bring a gift." There were a few other cards on the cake table. The seniors were milling around and chatting with each other. It was the most low-key wedding Amy had ever attended. It was also the most heartfelt.

"We wanted to," Matt told him. "We hope you'll enjoy it. Nice to meet you." He stuck out his hand, and Bill shook it.

Matt grabbed Amy's hand, two plastic cups, and one of the unopened bottles of champagne and walked her to his car.

Chapter Twelve

MATT'S ORIGINAL PLAN for the evening was not going to work out, so he pulled up in front of the Admiral Way lookout in West Seattle a few minutes later. The half-a-block long strip of land offered a perfect, unobstructed view of Seattle's skyline, and there was a convenient park bench to sit and take it all in. The lookout was busy day and night with tourists taking pictures. Even lifelong residents of Seattle never got tired of the view.

"Hey, Fifi. Let's do something illegal."

"What did you have in mind?"

"Open container law. Champagne. Us. How about it?"

"I'm not really into spending the evening getting bailed out of jail." He saw her lips twitch into a smile, though. "Let's go somewhere a little less public, shall we?"

Ten minutes later, Matt stopped in a deserted park at the top of Magnolia, an upscale neighborhood that also overlooked the Space Needle. It seemed so close he wondered if they could reach out and touch it.

"How's this?"

"Great. It's gorgeous out here."

After a quick examination of a somewhat dirty picnic table, they decided to stay in the comfort of his Mercedes. Matt settled back into his seat, turned toward Amy, and said, "So, tell me about yourself."

"Oh, you're good," Amy told him.

"Maybe I should ask you what you plan to be doing in five years instead."

"If you were a tree, what kind of tree would you be, Matt?"

"Let's start with the easy stuff," he said. "How about some champagne?"

Just like millions of other adults on a second date anywhere in the world, as Matt and Amy talked and laughed together, the minutes turned into hours. Moonlight dusted the unkempt little park with magic. She realized she was having fun. Even more, she liked him.

They covered a lot of subjects that night: His career. Her career. Their families, friends, and a little about previous relationships. She kept it light. After all, it was their second date, and she'd like to keep her romantic misadventures to herself for the time being. She quizzed him to her heart's content about playing in the NFL and whether or not his job now made him miss his playing days. Her curiosity got the best of her, though. She wasn't sure how he would react to the next question, but she had to ask.

"I'm sure Brandon probably told you that I'm a big football fan."

"He mentioned that. It was kind of a selling point, Fifi," he said, and she laughed. She'd spent a lot of time laughing tonight. "I didn't get this kind of in-depth interviewing from reporters during my entire career."

"What was it like when you retired?"

"Well, it's a long story."

His voice was carefree, but for the first time since they met, she noticed he was obviously rattled by her question. He wouldn't look at her. He shifted repeatedly in his seat, glanced out the car window, and fidgeted. He stared at the plastic cup of champagne in his hand like it held the answers to the universe.

"So. You want to know what it was like when I hung it up."

"I've read before that it's rough."

"Has Brandon said anything to you about his retirement?"

"A little. He mostly talks to Emily."

Matt heaved a sigh. "Every guy's different, but most don't know what to do with themselves. It's all they know. They have to find something else to do with most of their time, and some don't make good choices." He regarded the sky. "I was one of them."

"What happened?"

The only sound for several minutes was their breathing, and the breeze rustling the tree leaves above them. Amy tucked one leg beneath her and turned toward Matt. He closed his eyes.

"I knew it was coming. The team drafted a tight end for me to work with the last two seasons I was with Seattle. I announced my retirement before my last game. I was getting out when I was still fairly healthy. I'd made all the right choices. I thought I knew what I was doing after football, I hadn't blown every cent I ever made, Laura and Samantha would stick with me. My life was going to be perfect." He took a long swallow from his cup. "Yay, me."

Amy was silent, and more than a little shocked. She'd asked him the question. She wasn't prepared for the answer, it seemed. He poured another slug of champagne into his cup, and put the bottle down on the console between them.

"I couldn't talk to Laura about it. Every time I tried, it must have scared her. We got married when she was twenty-two. It wasn't my first trip to the rodeo as far as realizing things don't always pan out as we want them to in life, but it sure as hell was hers, and I didn't get that. She was in her mid-twenties; she'd never lived on her own at all before we got married. Now she had to deal with a husband who didn't know what to do with himself all day."

Amy bit her lip. She was watching football with her dad in those days, but there was not as much emphasis on life for ex-NFL players at that time.

"What happened to your post-career plans?"

"The field I planned to go into couldn't have been more wrong for me," he said. He didn't elaborate.

"I did the same thing. It took me ten years to realize it," she blurted out.

Matt nodded. He took a long swallow, finished his glass of champagne, and offered the bottle to Amy. She made the "inch" gesture with her thumb and forefinger.

He poured a bit into her cup, poured a little into his own cup, and abruptly poured the rest of the bottle out of the car window onto the pavement below them. In other words, he was driving, and the subject under discussion was sufficiently upsetting to him he'd drink the rest of the bottle if it was still available.

Amy appreciated the fact his opening up to her meant he trusted her. She got the impression it didn't happen a lot. Listening to the story of someone else's life cracking apart, though, wasn't light or fun at all. She realized she wouldn't be able to hide her own less-than-perfect life if she kept dating him, either.

"Laura didn't know what to say, so she said a lot of 'it'll be fine' crap. It wasn't going to be fine. I tried to explain this. She'd cry or something, and I'd—I couldn't do it." He passed one hand over his face. "Samantha was a toddler. On top of everything else, we were learning to be parents. She did a much better job than I did. I . . ." He shook his head. "After my ignoring her or being an asshole for months, after she spent so much time alone with a baby, she just couldn't take it anymore. The day after I officially retired, I was in Mexico, drunk off my ass. I didn't come home for almost a month. I was drowning myself in tequila, and she had an affair."

"What? Why?" Amy shifted in her seat. "Did she even know where you were?"

"Yeah. I called home to say where I was, but I realize there's no excuse for my behavior at the time. It took me awhile to figure this one out, but women don't like it when you ignore them. We were divorced soon after." He let out a sardonic snort. "It didn't help that she was involved with someone affiliated with the team, but she got my attention. We couldn't talk without fighting. I'd yell, and she'd cry. We spent a lot of money arranging visitation and basic stuff through our attorneys, too." He took a sip of champagne. "She's the mother of my child, I will always care about her, but we're two different people. Laura is the sweetest woman on the planet, but she could not stand up to me. I can't be with anyone who doesn't." He shifted in his seat again. "So, I came home and cleaned myself up. I went back to school, got a master's, and went to work. I got to know my daughter. I tried not to be such a shit."

She wanted to be reassuring, but she wasn't sure what to say to behavior that any woman would find objectionable. She'd read several instances of ex-NFL players having significant personal and financial problems when they retired, though. Maybe she should cut him a little slack. She had never disappeared to Mexico for a month and left a wife and daughter alone, but she wasn't perfect, either.

Matt leaned back against the driver's seat.

"I learned my lesson, though. I was an embarrassment to my mom, to my daughter, and to myself. It took me a long time, but I apologized to Laura. I'm so damn grateful Samantha was too young to understand what was going on."

Amy reached out and squeezed his hand. To her surprise, Matt squeezed back.

"I told her about it last year. Plus, Laura will talk to her about what happened on her end when Sam's old enough."

"What made you and Laura finally try to get along with each other?"

"Samantha. She asked me why I hated her mommy." He'd shown little emotion while unpacking what had to be some pretty embarrassing skeletons in his closet. To her shock, Amy saw tears in his eyes. He blew out a breath.

They sat silently for a few moments. Matt's brows knit as he watched what looked like a bunny hopping through tall grass.

"She's amazing, Matt. She's funny and smart and mature."

His voice was gruff. "She's her mother."

"No, she's you, too. The stuff that comes out of her mouth—it's you."

"That's what you think."

"She adores you."

"I can't believe she's still calling me 'Matt,'" he muttered. "There are some days I'd give my left nut to hear 'Daddy' or 'Papa.'" A pensive smile turned up the corners of his lips. "She knows it bugs me. Maybe she's more like me than I originally thought."

"So, what do you think you learned from all this?"

Matt let out a snort. "Is this an ABC Afterschool Special?" His expression grew thoughtful again. "I learned that there are other things I love besides a football field and Super Bowl rings. I wanted to be someone my family was proud of, and I worked till I got there. I realized I needed to find a woman who knew me better than I knew myself."

"That's interesting." Amy sipped a little of her champagne. "Do you believe that any of us can know someone else better than we know ourselves?"

"You and your sister know each other that way."

Amy wasn't going to tell him her deep, dark secret. She was tired of living in Emily's shadow. Amy loved her sister. She was her best friend. It was time for Amy to do something for herself and succeed on her own terms.

Her business didn't depend on being Emily Hamilton McKenna's younger sister or Brandon McKenna's sister-in-law. It helped that Brandon sent Amy business, but it wasn't the only reason her doors remained open.

She squirmed a little.

"We do. Mostly." Amy finished off the drops of champagne at the bottom of her cup. "Do you regret not having a brother or a sister?"

"Yeah. I know my mom wanted another child. Plus, I'd have someone else to spend time with." The smile reappeared. "Samantha wants a brother or a sister. She's made it clear that I'm not producing fast enough."

"She talked to me about it, too."

"What did she say?"

"She wants you to get married again and have a baby. She thinks it's time. She says her mom works all the time and will never meet anyone, so it's your problem."

He opened the car door and moved a short distance

away to drop the empty champagne bottle into a nearby garbage can.

"She likes you," he called out to Amy.

She got out of the car to stretch her legs and followed him. The stars looked like white diamonds tossed over a purplish-blue night sky. The moonlight lit silver streaks in Matt's hair.

"I like her."

He looped his arm around Amy's shoulders and pulled her close. "So, how's this week for you?" His voice dropped. "I think I can fit you in."

"Hey. Knock it off, Stephens."

"I know you want a baby," he cajoled.

"Forget it."

"Come on. Think how cute you'll be with a baby bump."

"You're ill," she said, but she was laughing.

Amy gave him a playful push and walked away from him. It wasn't like the thought hadn't crossed her mind, too, but he exhausted her when they weren't officially a couple. Even though she gave him a ration of crap over sperm donors, Amy wasn't having a baby without being married. Call her old-fashioned, but she wanted her children to live with their father. He caught up to her in a couple of long strides.

"Hey, Fifi. Don't you want to keep me off the streets? Have my baby."

She whirled on him. "We're not even officially a couple. You and me . . . Well, we're socializing. That's it."

"Who made that decision?" His face was a mask of

injured innocence. "Not me. I've been asking you out for a month now. You keep telling me no. Why is that, anyway? I shower. I dress reasonably well. I can be taken out in public. Plus, I'm fairly sure we'll get along nicely in the bedroom, if that whole thing at your front door the other night was any indicator."

"I can't even believe you brought that up—"

"Even though you claim you're not, you're looking for a man. Why not me?"

"You don't want me."

"Yes, Amy, I do." He slid his arm around her shoulders. "Give me a try. Let's date each other some more and see what happens."

"I won't buckle under your pressure, Matt," but she smiled as she said it.

"Of course you won't," he murmured into her ear. "Bring it on."

"I want someone who respects me enough to realize that I mean what I say." Amy stopped walking and poked her finger into the middle of his chest.

"Of course I respect you and what you have to say. That doesn't mean that I don't reserve the right to talk you out of it."

"This is exactly what I'm talking about!" she fumed.

He caught her around the waist again. He took her cheek in his palm. His voice was as calm and quiet as the night surrounding them.

"I was just teasing you. Someday, you're going to know when I'm teasing, huh?"

"I don't like it," she informed him.

"Sometimes we all need to laugh at ourselves." He rested his chin on the top of her head, sniffing her hair. He kissed her temple. "Come on, sweetheart."

The old-fashioned endearment melted her heart. She wasn't going to consider how many other women he'd probably called "sweetheart" before. Right now, it was just for her.

"Stop trying to distract me with kisses and . . . Just stop."

"Do you really want me to?" His fingertips rubbed the back of Amy's neck. "I could dream up a few other things you might enjoy."

"You—you make me mad, then you kiss me, then I can't remember why I was mad. Why? There must be another woman you can torment."

"I want the one in my arms right now."

"What if I don't want *you*?"

"Oh, you do, Fifi."

His mouth touched hers, and she forgot to pull away from him. Even more, she didn't want to. She wrapped her arms around his neck. His tongue slid into her mouth. His hands skimmed down her back, landing on the twin globes of her butt. He pulled her into him.

"I know you want me," he whispered.

She rested her forehead on his shoulder and listened to the night surrounding them. A breeze moved through the trees. Frogs greeted each other. They heard the indistinct hum of traffic in the distance. She breathed in cool air and the faint scent of Matt's shaving cream.

Matt's cell phone went off, playing ten seconds or so of Paul Simon's *Father and Daughter*.

"It's my little princess, calling to say goodnight," he said.

"Answer it," she told him.

He pulled it out of his pocket and hit the speaker function. "Are you having fun, Sam?"

A tear-clogged voice responded, "Hi, Mr. Stephens, it's Morgan. We need your help."

Chapter Thirteen

MATT FELT AN immediate and almost overpowering surge of fight-or-flight adrenaline as he listened to his daughter's best friend attempt to control her tears. *If Samantha was hurt or sick, she would have called Laura first. They would have called from the hospital,* he told himself. *Stay calm.*

"Morgan, what's wrong?"

"Natalie's parents went out to dinner while we were watching a movie. Her older brother's here. He brought a bunch of his friends with him, too. They're drinking and they're doing dumb stuff." He heard her sniffle. "We want to go home."

Multiple underage girls alone in a house with high school boys, alcohol, and no adult supervision—He dragged breath into his lungs. If the adrenaline surge wasn't enough, he was scared and disgusted with himself for not laying down the law; He didn't want Samantha spending time with Natalie, let alone staying overnight at her house.

He stepped away from Amy.

"Where's Samantha?"

"She's in here, too."

He heard his daughter's voice in the background. "I— I was afraid you'd be mad at us. We didn't know they were going to be here—"

He interrupted her. "Where are you now?"

"We're in the parents' bathroom."

"Is Brittany with you, too?"

"Yes. She doesn't feel good right now."

Amy was listening with a concerned look on her face, but he could only concentrate on Samantha right now. "Lock the bathroom door. I'll be there in twenty minutes."

He heard his daughter's voice. "I'm sorry. I know you said you were going on a date tonight. Mom isn't answering her phone right now, and we didn't know what to do."

"Don't be sorry. You did the right thing to call me. Stay in the bathroom. Lock the door."

He hung up his phone, let out a "God DAMN it," and turned to face Amy again. To his surprise, she moved closer and took his hand.

"I'm guessing we're going to go get Samantha."

"And two of her friends." He shoved his phone into his pocket, and passed his hand over his face. "I guess this is the end of our date. Do you want me to drop you off at your place first?"

"Hell, no. We need to go get the girls." Amy tugged him toward his Mercedes.

MATT MANAGED TO keep it together while he made phone calls to both Brittany and Morgan's parents through the in-dash voice command cell phone in his car. He also managed to drive the speed limit as they took the exit to Medina, one of the wealthier and most exclusive communities on Seattle's Eastside. Matt knew Medina's police force frowned on underage drinking. Hell, they frowned on anything that would cause a disturbance or danger to homeowners who most likely boasted a high eight- or nine-figure balance in their checking account at all times.

Natalie's parents didn't have the right to endanger his daughter or her friends by their inattention. He'd be taking this up with them in person at another time. Right now he was holding onto his temper with fists of iron. He realized his anger was a byproduct of being frightened as hell. Men weren't supposed to be scared. They were supposed to handle this kind of fear with an overpowering show of strength and fury.

Those guys probably didn't have a fourteen-year-old daughter that they would do anything to protect.

Amy had been quiet through most of the ride. She turned in the seat to face him.

"Would you like me to go to the door with you?" she said.

He was flooded with completely different emotions in seconds: disbelief, surprise, gratitude. The previously skittish Fifi wanted to get involved. He'd be giving this additional thought shortly after he made sure his daughter was safe and sound, but he knew his initial impression of her was right.

She was worth whatever he had to do to keep seeing her.

He turned into Natalie's parents' driveway and hit the brakes. He couldn't believe there weren't cop cars here already; the music was turned up so loud he was sure the neighbors in the next block were singing along with Macklemore. Then again, cars clogged the driveway, double-parked all the way to the street. Maybe the cops couldn't find a place to park.

"You don't really want to do this," he said.

"I was a teenage girl." She unsnapped her seat belt. "Let's go." Her lips curved into a slight smile.

He grabbed the keys out of the ignition and popped the driver's side door open. She walked around the front of the car. He reached out for her hand as they approached the front door.

MATT RANG THE doorbell three times. No response. He'd resorted to banging on the heavily carved wooden door with a closed fist when it opened to reveal a tall, lanky teenage boy who snapped, "What the hell is your problem?"

"What the hell is yours?" Matt didn't wait to be invited in, and any pretense of good manners or courtesy at someone else's home was gone. He pulled Amy across the threshold with him as he shoved the door open further. "Where is my daughter?"

The kid smelled like a brewery, even from a couple of feet away. His eyes were bloodshot. He backed up a few steps unsteadily. The music was so loud they had to shout at each other to be heard. "Who are you?"

"I'm Samantha's dad. Who are *you*?"

Amy knew that the kid must have been powering down whatever alcohol he could get his hands on. He was weaving around like he was about to fall down. She also knew it was no use arguing with him about the fact they'd waited ten minutes at the front door, or maybe he shouldn't be drinking at all. The fastest way out of this was to find the master bathroom.

She resisted the impulse to gawk at the most opulent house she'd ever been in. The entryway was probably bigger than her entire townhouse. A chessboard marble floor gave way to richly patterned, wallpapered walls and a staircase framed by a hardwood banister that probably took more time to carve than the ceiling of the Sistine Chapel took to paint. The beveled prisms of a huge crystal chandelier tossed shards of light around the room. Right now, those prisms were swaying with bass turned up high enough to rattle the house.

The noise was coming from what she imagined was a basement. It was probably called something else in a house with this price tag.

She dragged her eyes off the scenery. Right now, Job One was getting the girls and getting out of here before Matt lost his shit completely. It seemed that the teenagers of the very wealthy did the same dumb crap that every other kid did when their parents' backs were turned, or when those parents made it easy on them by conveniently leaving the house.

"May I use your bathroom? Which way is it?" she asked.

"Down the hall." The kid hooked a thumb toward a hallway. He stared at Matt again. Amy saw his upper lip curl. "Why are you being such an asshole? We didn't hear the doorbell."

Someone downstairs must have decided they'd heard enough of Macklemore; the music halted abruptly.

She saw a flush spreading up Matt's neck and over his cheekbones out of the corner of her eye. Matt's hands balled into fists. She stepped between him and the kid.

"Maybe you need to go back to the party," she suggested to the kid.

"Maybe you should party with us," the kid said. "He's fuckin' boring."

"Thanks, but no thanks." She tugged Matt toward the staircase. "Why don't you go tell your friends that Samantha, Brittany, and Morgan are not feeling well, and we're taking them home."

The kid loped away, throwing "They're not going to care" over one shoulder. He vanished around a corner.

"The only thing saving that kid right now is that he's a kid, Fifi," Matt said.

They hurried up the staircase.

MATT WAS STRIDING down the hallway of Natalie's parents' house, with Amy on his heels. She still had his hand. Every step felt like he was sinking into quicksand. He knew this was just the start of Samantha's teen years, but he wondered if he was going to spend the next five or six years mired in this kind of fear every time she was out of his sight.

He told her he didn't want her to go to Natalie's. She went anyway. He wondered how he could explain to her without shouting that being a parent was like spending the rest of your life with your heart walking around outside of your body. He realized he was probably overreacting. His daughter was smart. He'd done his best to teach her how to take care of herself, but she was just so young still.

A set of double doors at the end of the hallway must have been the parents' room. Amy tugged on his hand. "Matt. Are you okay?"

"I'm fine. Let's get in there."

"Wait," she said. She reached out for his other hand. "You're not fine. Take a deep breath."

"Excuse me?"

She put her hand in the middle of his chest.

"Your heart's pounding. Take a breath."

He knew she was just trying to help, but he felt a bit annoyed. Maybe she was right. He concentrated on his breathing and listened to her talk.

"Samantha's scared to death right now. So are her friends. In two years she'll have a driver's license, and there will be a lot more going on than some teenage boy who wants her to have a sip of whatever alcohol he could get and maybe kiss her." Amy hauled air into her lungs. "There are guys who could drug her drink, or try to get her into a car even though they've been drinking. You can't control every situation she'll end up in. You can be as mad as you want later, but right now, you're the guy she knows she can call, no matter what's wrong, where she is and what time it is."

His eyes narrowed. "Don't tell me I don't know how to parent."

"I'm not attacking your parenting. I'm telling you what it's like to be fourteen and to know you're going to get it from your dad because you made a bad decision." She took another deep breath. "Morgan called you because Samantha already knows she's in trouble. She knows she screwed up by coming here." Her amber-brown eyes pleaded with him. "Scold her all you want tomorrow, but right now she needs to know you're on her side."

Matt felt some of the adrenaline draining off as she held his hand. He shoved himself off the wall. "Okay," he said. "Let's do this." He laced his fingers through hers.

MATT AND AMY found the master bathroom and the three girls in short order. Brittany was clutching her stomach. Morgan was texting. Samantha wouldn't meet his eyes. She shuffled her feet a little. He watched her edge toward him.

"Brittany, are you sick? What's wrong?" he asked.

Brittany blushed a deep red and muttered, "I—I'm fine. Can we leave now?"

Matt had a feeling he knew what the issue was. Sure enough, Amy made a beeline for her. The two talked for a few moments in lowered voices while Amy dug through her purse. She pulled out a paper-wrapped tampon and slipped it into Brittany's hand. She glanced up, caught Matt's eye, and made a shooing motion.

"Hey, Matt, why don't you take Morgan and Samantha to round up everyone's stuff? We'll be out in a minute."

"Got it."

Samantha and Morgan led him to Natalie's room. The girls' things were still in the corner they'd dumped them in. If Fifi and Brittany were done in the ladies' room, they could be gone in a couple of minutes. He'd just grabbed the last backpack as he heard an angry voice in the hallway.

"Why are you leaving? You're ruining my party!" A drunk, crying, and inappropriately dressed Natalie had managed to make her way upstairs.

Matt herded four females down the stairs as Natalie continued to shout at them.

"I'm going to tell everyone at school that you're a bunch of babies!"

Natalie's face was streaked with running mascara. Lip gloss was smeared everywhere but her mouth. Natalie was still crying and shouting at them from the stairs as they hurried away from her.

"You're all losers. You ruined my party! I can't believe how lame you are. Nobody wants to kiss you, Samantha. At least they want me!"

"Thank you for inviting us," Samantha called out.

Matt's vision was tinged red with anger. He told himself he was an adult and any argument with a drunken fourteen-year-old was pointless, but he turned at the base of the stairs to face her.

"Natalie, you need to go upstairs right now. Wash your face and change your clothes. You might feel better if you got some sleep, too."

"You're not my dad," she snarled. She wiped her face with the back of her hand. In that moment he remembered her comment at breakfast with the three other girls about her dad. He knew what it was like to know your dad didn't give a shit about you. He was willing to bet she did, also.

He forced himself to lower his voice. "No, I'm not. I'll tell you what, though," he said. "If I was your dad, I'd make sure you were safe. I wouldn't leave you here to handle this alone. I would make it clear every day that you are more important than anything else to me."

Her mouth dropped open. She stared at him for a minute or so.

"Go upstairs and wash up," he said. He saw the sheen of new tears in her eyes, but she turned and raced up the stairs again.

He strode out the front door.

Matt longed to invade her parents' basement and dump every remaining bottle of alcohol down the sink, but the best thing to do was to leave as quickly and quietly as possible. He didn't want to be there when the cops showed up. He backed the car out of the driveway, drove a block or so, pulled over and dialed 911.

MATT COMPLETED HIS phone call.

"Okay. You all have your overnight stuff, your phones, anything else you brought?" Amy said. She turned toward the back seat of Matt's car, noting three girls who were still unusually quiet.

"Yes," Brittany said.

"Thank you, Amy," Morgan said.

"You're welcome," Amy said.

"What do you say, Samantha?" Matt said.

Samantha mumbled something like "Thank you." At the next stoplight her father turned to give her a look Amy could only classify as disappointed. Four cop cars raced by in the oncoming lane, sirens screaming.

Amy reached out to pat Matt's hand. He didn't respond.

"When they find out my dad called the cops, they're going to be so mad," Samantha said. Amy saw Matt's hands tighten on the steering wheel. "Everyone will hate me."

Amy heard whispering in the back seat, but she couldn't make out what was being said.

"Mr. Stephens," Morgan said.

"Morgan, it's okay to call me Matt."

"Well, okay. *Matt*. What are you going to tell our parents?"

"I already talked to your parents." There were a few panicked *oh nos* from the back seat. "They know I'm bringing you home. Were you girls drinking tonight?"

"No," Morgan said.

"We left when they started drinking," Brittany said.

"I didn't drink," Samantha said.

"Well, then. It looks like all I have to tell them is that you left when the boys started drinking and you didn't drink. Is there anything else you want to tell me?"

"Thank you for coming to get us," Brittany said.

"Yes, thank you," Morgan said.

"Thanks, Dad."

He didn't miss that, but he played it cool. "You're welcome, ladies."

Matt pulled up in front of Morgan's house minutes later. Both her parents were waiting on the doorstep. She grabbed her things out of the back of Matt's car and ran to them. Brittany's house was a few minutes away; her parents came to the car to shake Matt's hand and thank him for bringing their daughter home.

"I'm happy to do it," he said. "Maybe it's best if the girls don't make plans with Natalie."

Brittany's dad nodded, and shook Matt's hand again. "We've already called Natalie's parents. They have a houseful of cops right now. I don't think their kids will be making plans with anyone for a while."

"Probably not. Enjoy the rest of the evening," Matt said.

Matt got back into the car and turned to his daughter. Tears ran down her face. She wiped her runny nose on the sleeve of her sweatshirt.

"I know you're mad at me," she said. Of course, this made her cry harder. Amy started digging through her handbag for some damn thing.

"Yes, Samantha, I'm angry. I told you I didn't think you should go to Natalie's house. You did it anyway. I told you I've never met her parents and had no idea if you and your friends would be safe there. You weren't. What would you have done if both your mom and I were unavailable tonight?"

"I don't know," she said in a small voice.

He made a conscious effort to lower his voice again. Amy was right; yelling at Samantha would do nothing but alienate her. "I was mad, but even more, I was scared. I didn't know if you were okay. I was afraid someone tried to hurt you or put something in your drink. Can you understand why that would scare me?"

He turned to look out of the windshield again and turned the key in the ignition. He didn't mean to be harsh with her. She was surrounded with love every day of her life, and she wouldn't understand the hole that still existed inside him from the worst rejection of all—the rejection of a parent. He could hear Samantha sniffling. So could Amy, who pulled a package of tissues out of her handbag and turned to hand them to his daughter.

"It sounds like the party wasn't much fun tonight. Did you girls eat before you left?" she said.

"No. Natalie's parents said they were ordering pizza, but they didn't." Samantha said. She blew her nose.

"You must be a little hungry, then," Amy said. Samantha didn't answer her.

Matt and Amy exchanged a look. "We'd better stop and pick something up," he said. He took the exit to what he knew was Samantha's favorite burger place. He detested fast food, but he liked theirs.

BURGERMASTER WAS THE kind of drive-up restaurant his mom took him to for a splurge when he was a kid.

The customers ate in their cars. The differences between Burgermaster and another fast-food place were pronounced. The menu boasted grass-fed, hormone-free beef, handmade shakes, and vegetarian options. Burgermaster fed those who founded Microsoft as the company got off the ground, and it was possible to see Seattle-area celebrities enjoying the food year-round. Matt got out of the car to stretch his legs while he waited for the to-go order to be brought out to his car. Samantha got a meal. He and Fifi ordered a couple of shakes.

He understood his daughter was fourteen and tended to blurt out things she hadn't thought through. He also knew she wouldn't understand what it was like to believe your child was in danger of any kind. He didn't support underage drinking by any means, but he didn't call the police on those kids to be a gigantic prick. He called the cops because of the sheer number of cars in that driveway. The unsupervised teens would decide they wanted to leave sooner or later, and there was nobody home to determine if they were too drunk to drive.

He wasn't Samantha's pal. It was his job to protect her from things and people that might hurt her. The thought of one of those boys touching her made him want to flip out. At the same time, she was growing up. It was natural for her to be curious about boys and kissing, but he didn't have to like it.

He heard the car door open, and a still-sniffling Samantha got out. She waited until he turned to look at her.

"I'm sorry," she choked out. "I didn't mean to scare

you." She shuffled toward him, and threw her arms around his waist.

"I know," he said. She burrowed against him like she did when she was little. People were probably staring. He didn't care. "I'm glad you called me, princess."

"You're not mad I interrupted your date?"

"No. Amy's not mad, either. Next time, though, I need you to listen to me. Can we work on that?"

"Yes." She nodded vigorously.

"Okay, then. The food should be here soon, so why don't you get back in the car." He kissed the top of her head. She gave him another squeeze and reached out for the door handle.

A minute or so later, he felt someone touch his upper arm.

"Hey," Amy said. "Samantha went to the ladies' room. How are you doing?"

"I'm fine." He slid his arm around her waist. "How are you doing?" He felt her body move as she laughed.

"I hope I didn't step on your toes by trying to help a little with the girls. My dad had to rescue me once upon a time, too. Let's just say I didn't have texting capability then." She let out a sigh. "I was never so grateful to see him in my life."

"I need to thank you as well."

"No, you don't."

His voice dropped. "Like I knew how to handle Brittany's situation! It's not like I carry the necessary supplies around in my back pocket."

"You would have been fine."

He let out a chuckle. "Oh, hell, yeah. Ask my daughter about that one."

They stood quietly for a moment, watching the commotion of cars pulling up, carhops bringing already-ordered food to other customers, and Samantha getting back into his car.

"Listen, Fifi. We're not going to get a lot of privacy at your front door later."

"There's not a lot of privacy *here*."

"No, there's not." He dropped her hand, tipped her chin up, and brushed his lips over hers. She trembled. "Let's go to Jazz Alley. I will do my best to make sure there's no flying Italian food, wedding guests, or teenage girls there. What do you say?"

She could hear Samantha's "Ewww" from where they stood.

"Everyone's going to start holding up numerical paddles next, Matt," she said.

"Is that so? Better make it good." He swept her into his arms, his mouth covered hers, and he kissed her until she was breathless. They heard applause and whistles from the surrounding cars. Amy felt her face superheat in response.

She reached up and took his face in both of her hands. "Matt Stephens, you've got yourself a date."

Chapter Fourteen

Amy unlocked the front door to the shop the next day, and relocked it as she slipped inside. It was already an expensive morning, and it wasn't even seven o'clock. She'd made a huge dent in the flower wholesaler's bill before ordering the supplies she needed to construct the wedding order she'd be making next week. But even after paying her delivery driver and Estelle, the bottom line—and her business bank account—looked better than she thought it would. She could almost afford to call the HVAC guy to fix whatever was making the weird noise in her cooler.

She turned from the front door and realized she could hear the proverbial pin drop. The constant hum of the refrigerated unit in her miniscule lobby area was silent. She squeezed her eyes shut. *This could not be happening. Shit!* Maybe the cooler had miraculously repaired itself. Maybe the Flower Shop Fairies had dropped off a new one during the night.

"It could happen," she muttered.

Maybe she wasn't going to throw up all over her freshly mopped shop floor.

She opened her eyes, rushed to the cooler, and groaned aloud.

It was dead. It made no noise at all. The glass was warm when Amy laid one palm on it. Even worse, the arrangements ready for delivery this morning were obviously dead, too. They'd have to be remade. *Now*. She could stash the remakes in her other walk-in, but there wasn't a lot of room in there, and she wasn't sure she had enough flowers. *Oh, shit*. What was she going to do? And a brand-new unit cost at least five thousand dollars . . . .

She should have called the HVAC guy last night when the sound had gotten worse, but having an HVAC guy on retainer rivaled the cost of hiring U2 to play at a backyard barbecue. The last time she'd spoken to him, he told her she'd have to "nurse that baby" when she opened her doors, and she'd tried, but it hadn't been enough. She should have bought a new cooler when she opened, and before she had hired two employees.

Amy hugged herself. "Just take a deep breath," she said. "Just breathe." She wanted to scream, cry, and run around in little circles, but hey, the only thing that would get her was stared at by people passing her storefront on Broadway. Maybe it was a stroke of marketing genius: She could change her name to the Crazy Florist, send dead flowers to people who had made her customers mad, and hey, she wouldn't need a cooler at all.

She moved into her workroom, fired up her laptop, and looked up the HVAC guy's number. She tried to tell herself that it wasn't going to be all bad, but somehow the lump in her stomach got bigger with every passing second. She had to get those balls back up in the air.

TWO HOURS LATER, the HVAC guy emerged from the cooler. "Well, Amy, do you want the good news or the bad news?"

Amy was up to her ass in alligators, otherwise known as madly assembling replacement arrangements. The flower wholesaler had been nice enough to drop off another order after a semi-frantic phone call. He was offloading the delivery in the alley outside her store as she tried to do four things at once. Estelle and Scott the driver would not be here for another half-hour. She rubbed her hands over her face. If she could just live through the next thirty minutes without screaming or crying, the day was bound to get better.

She wondered how much chocolate she'd have to eat before none of this bothered her anymore.

"How about the bad news? I like living dangerously," she told him.

"It's dead, honey. You'll need a new one. The compressor's fried. It's cheaper to replace the entire unit than to install another compressor."

She swallowed hard.

"What's the good news?"

"Just think how great the new cooler will look in your shop."

Oh, yeah. One of those half-full guys. "Well, that's something to think about."

He packed up his tools, picked up his toolbox, and touched the brim of his baseball cap. "Good to see you again, Amy. I hope everything else is going well. The office will send your bill next week." He was out of the shop in less than thirty seconds.

Another bill. On top of the existing bill. On top of the bill she was going to have for another delivery of the same flowers she'd picked up yesterday. She flattened both palms on her worktable, leaned over it, and tried to remember why she'd thought this all was a good idea.

The guy she bought the cooler from in the first place was retiring. He wasn't a bad guy. She knew he'd taken excellent care of his equipment. If she didn't want these problems, she should have just bought a new unit, but she knew his family needed the cash they could raise from selling off their fixtures, and she was a sucker, and again, she had nobody to blame for this but herself.

Where was she going to get five thousand dollars?

"Amy, are you okay?" The wholesaler was a somewhat gruff older guy, but he gave her a tentative pat on the back. "Cooler's dead, isn't it?"

"Yeah. It is." She tried for a laugh. "Services are pending."

"Those sons-a-bitches die when you least expect it. I lost eight grand in orchids once. Let's just say I was afraid my wife and I were going to have to give the HVAC guy our firstborn to pay off the bill, too." He nodded at her walk-in. "I put everything in there while he gave you the good news."

"Thank you." Amy stuck out her hand.

He brushed it aside and held out his arms. "How about a hug? You look like you need one." He gave Amy another clumsy pat on the back and stepped away from her. "Listen. You pay your bills on time, and you remind me of my daughter. Just for today, there's a discount. I'll send you a bill, but let's just say a few things will get left off."

Amy just stared at him.

"Now, don't let it get around. People will think I'm a nice guy, and we can't have that." He turned to leave and raised one hand. "See you later."

"Thank you so much—"

Amy's words were cut off by the back door's slam. Tears rose in her eyes. A few seconds later, she heard his voice again. "You need to lock this back door now, you hear?" It slammed again, and there was silence.

ESTELLE BREEZED INTO the shop twenty minutes later. "Hey, Amy, I'm here," she called out. "What's wrong with the cooler?"

"It's dead," Amy shouted back. "I'm remaking the arrangements right now."

Estelle dropped her coat and purse on the loveseat that sat in the corner of Amy's workroom. It doubled as a break area. "Let me help." She glanced at two finished arrangements. "Which would you like me to tackle first?"

"How about the one that's going to the little girl at Children's Hospital? I was going to send that out first thing, but I had to wait for another wholesaler order."

Amy was going to have to make a tough phone call later, but right now, making sure everyone got their flowers was much more important. One of her most popular arrangements was a "cupcake" made out of carnations and delivered in an oversized coffee cup with a one-pot package of ground coffee. The worst part of the construction was making sure the stems were the perfect height. She'd had the idea two weeks ago. The people who got them kept calling and re-ordering for co-workers and friends, which was great for her. She stuck two more carnations in the dampened oasis. She glanced up to see Estelle's brows knit as she regarded Amy.

"Is everything okay?"

Amy waved one hand at her. "Sure. It's all fine. How are you doing?"

"That had to be kind of a shock." Estelle nodded toward the cooler.

"It is, but right now I can't think about it. If you could make the little girl's arrangement, we can send Scott out with it right away when he gets here. He's filling the van up before today's deliveries. The woman that ordered it wants it to be there when the little girl gets back to the room after her surgery." Amy glanced over the six other order slips lined up on the worktable. "The arrangements for the law firm dinner are going to be the most labor-intensive. I can't decide if we should start them first, or get the smaller stuff out of the way so they have our undivided—"

The shop phone rang. Amy snatched it up off the base.

"Crazy Daisy."

"Hello. Is this Amy Hamilton? This is Officer Phillips of the Seattle Police Department."

There was nothing like a caller identifying themselves as being from the police department to get one's heart rate up. Amy's skipped a beat as well. An icy shiver skittered down her spine.

"Y—Yes, this is Amy. May I help you?"

"Ms. Hamilton, your delivery driver's been in an accident."

"Oh, my God." Amy sat down hard on the stool next to her workbench. "Oh, God, no. Is he okay?"

"He's not badly injured, but he's being taken to Harborview as a precaution. He was very concerned that we call and let you know."

"Is he there? Can I talk with him?"

"He's already enroute to the hospital." The police officer paused for a moment. "He was making a legal left, and another driver blew through the stoplight. The airbags saved him from a lot more serious injuries."

"It's a good thing there were airbags." If she was having a bad day, Scott's was worse.

"I'm pretty sure he'll call you himself when they let him out of the emergency room. He had some cuts and scrapes, he'll be sore, but he'll be fine. On the other hand, your delivery van won't be." He let out a low chuckle. "You might want to call your insurance company, if you have any preference on where the van should be towed."

Maybe she was just having a nightmare. She'd wake up from this any minute, everything would be fine, and she would go back to complaining about the little things, like a dead compressor on her refrigeration unit. After all, the compressor could be replaced; Scott the delivery driver couldn't.

"Yes. Yes, I'll do that right now." She tried to sound calm and pulled together. "Thank you so much for calling. I really appreciate it."

"Thank you, Ms. Hamilton. I hope it all works out."

"If Scott is fine, it will."

Amy hung up the phone in a daze. "What's wrong?" Estelle asked.

"Scott's just been taken to the hospital. He—" Amy slapped both hands over her mouth. *Breathe*, she told herself. It wasn't going to help anyone if she passed out. She concentrated on taking in gulps of air, one after the other, until she was reasonably sure she was going to get through the next ten seconds without some kind of medical emergency. "The van's wrecked. Scott has some cuts and scrapes. We can talk to him when he gets to the hospital."

The next hour was a blur of phone calls to Scott's cell and the van's insurance company; doing anything about the cooler was going to have to wait. The body shop that received the wrecked van was doing an estimate. The guy that Amy talked to, however, wasn't hopeful. Estelle worked on the arrangements. Amy would take the little girl's flowers to Children's herself when she finished with them. The phone rang, and Estelle grabbed it before Amy could.

"Crazy Daisy. Yes. Yes, she is. One moment, please."

Estelle handed Amy the phone, and she heard Matt's voice.

"Hey, Fifi, how are you doing this morning?"

She wondered what he'd do if she burst into tears. Just hearing his voice soothed her. She took a deep breath and dropped onto one of the stools in her workroom.

"Awful. Matt, things are falling apart here, and I really can't talk right now. Do you need to make an order?"

"No. Not now." He paused for a moment. "What's up?"

Amy closed her eyes. "It's a long list. Can I call you back later?"

"Absolutely. I hope whatever's wrong gets better. Be good."

He hung up the phone, and she stared at the buzzing receiver. Okay, fine, so she'd been a little short, but what the hell was that? She shoved the phone back in its cradle and concentrated on the teeny bouquet she was making out of pink tea roses. It would go in an equally teeny clear plastic vase, then into a basket along with a plush brown teddy bear named Truffle, a few children's picture books, and a Mylar balloon depicting a teddy bear holding a pink rose.

Hiring Estelle was the best fifteen bucks an hour she could hardly afford. Estelle was saving her butt right now. She assembled the basket, made sure the balloon was secured to the handle, and grabbed her purse.

"Hey, Estelle, I'm going to run this over there. I should be back in half an hour. If the insurance company or Scott needs to talk with me, I have my phone." She dug into her jeans pocket to make sure this was still the case. Her hand closed around her Droid, and she let out a sigh of relief. At least one thing had gone right for her today.

"Okay. I'll get the law firm stuff started. The rest are ready to go when you get back." Estelle glanced up from her work. "Be careful."

"I will."

Amy was currently driving a new-to-her 2004 Volkswagen Bug that she purchased shortly after hiring a delivery driver for her business. It wasn't much, but it was paid for. It was wheels, although it was another huge dent out of her savings account. She picked up the arrangement and started for the door. She heard the bells on the front door ring, and Matt strolled in. She felt a surge of happiness, despite her awful day.

"Hey, Fifi. Going somewhere?"

He paused just inside the doorway of the shop. Instead of his usual beat-up jeans or very expensive suits, he had on a pair of Under Armour sweat pants, running shoes, and an NFL "Play 60" t-shirt. His hair was still a tousled mess. Someone would have to address this, but right now, she didn't have time.

"I have a delivery."

He stepped aside as she opened the front door, and followed her out onto the sidewalk. The sky was cerulean blue. The sun was warm on her skin, but she didn't have time to enjoy it. She had to handle this. She had to get back.

"Where's Scott?"

"He's at Harborview."

"What the hell happened?"

"Car wreck."

She dug her car keys out of the mess she called a purse and unlocked the passenger side door. The basket would fit in the back seat; she'd have to be careful while she was driving. Matt was still talking to her. She couldn't listen to it right now. Well, she didn't listen till he took her car keys out of her hand.

"I'll drive," he told her.

It finally penetrated the fog in her head that no, this was not what she wanted. She straightened up and tried to take the keys out of his hand, which he held high over his head. She was torn between kicking him in the shin and bursting into tears of frustration.

"You can't drive. My business insurance won't cover you. I shouldn't even be driving right now, but I have no other choice. If I get in a wreck, it's on me, but if you are hurt—"

"Okay, then. Let's take my car," he said.

"Matt, I don't have time to mess around with this today. I have to do this—"

"Let me help," he told her. He grabbed the basket out of the back seat of the Bug, evaded her easily, and yanked open the back door of his Mercedes M-Class. "We'll go together. Get in the car, Fifi."

She didn't have the strength to keep arguing with him, so she got in the passenger seat, slammed the door, and buckled her seatbelt.

"Where to?" he asked.

"Children's Hospital."

Matt pulled out into Broadway's traffic without further comment. In some distant recess of her mind, she knew it was a good thing he was driving. She was too distracted to get behind the wheel of any car. Mostly she was bracing herself. Everything that could go wrong today had, and it wasn't even eleven o'clock.

When she had time to think about it later, she'd consider the fact that Matt dropped whatever he was doing to stop by and help her. He was making sure she got where she needed to go safely. He overlooked the fact she'd barely talked to him earlier.

Her phone was ringing. Again. She pulled it out of her pocket and hit the "answer" button.

"Amy Hamilton."

"Hi Amy, this is Trudy from Superior Insurance. How are you doing today?"

"Oh, I'm fine. How are you?" Small talk with the insurance adjuster was always something she looked forward to.

"I'm fine. Listen, I wish I had better news. Your van's totaled. The body is shoved two inches off the frame; it would cost more to fix than the van's worth."

Amy squeezed her eyes shut. She clutched the cell so hard she was surprised it didn't shatter in her hand. "It's *totaled*? Oh, God."

"We'll write you a check for the Blue Book value today. Unfortunately, that leaves a balance on your loan amount. You'll have to work with the bank on that one."

"I bought gap insurance—"

Amy heard paperwork rustle at the other end of the phone. "I see no evidence of a gap insurance addendum on your policy, Amy. I'm really sorry." There must have been something in the insurance adjuster's manual about trying to sound sympathetic. "I know this is a tough blow for a small business owner. Luckily the hospital assures me that your delivery driver sustained only minor injuries in the accident, so that's positive."

"Yes. Yes, it is." Amy fell silent. She wasn't sure what to say next. Mostly, she needed to get off the phone. She felt Matt's car stop, and heard him pull the keys out of the ignition. "Thanks for your call. I have to hang up," she said.

"We still need to discuss—"

"I will call you back later. Thanks for calling. Goodbye." She hung up, pried her eyes open, and glanced over at Matt.

"So, Fifi, I take it you are short one delivery van."

Amy attempted to follow Matt's long strides into Children's Hospital. Children's was one of the more highly regarded pediatric hospitals in the country, and a magnet for current and former professional athletes in the city of Seattle. In other words, he'd been here before, most likely visiting kids he didn't know. He glanced down at the order form he'd managed to pry out of her hand as they crossed the parking lot.

"Okay. The little girl is on Green Whale floor. We have to stop at the desk; they won't let us take the basket to her room." He reached back to grab Amy's hand. "We'll do this, and then I'll take you by the car dealer."

"Why?"

"You need a new delivery van. Try to keep up, Fifi."

"I can't go van shopping today. I have to talk to the ba—"

"Hey. We can look. Plus, I have a buddy that might be

persuaded to give you a deal." He came to a halt at a reception desk. The floor they were on was called "Giraffe." Amy glanced around at art pieces, lots of light streaming in from the windows, and an older woman whose nametag read "Connie."

Matt set the basket on her desk. "Hi, Connie, I'm Matt Stephens. We have a delivery for a little girl on Green Whale named Madeline. What do you suggest we do?"

Connie's eyes lit up. "It's nice to meet you, Mr. Stephens. My husband is your biggest fan."

"Is that so? I like him already."

Amy was so freaked out about the refrigerated unit, Scott, and the wrecked van, all she had the strength to do was cross her arms. She felt Matt's fingertips brush the small of her back.

"Need a map?"

"No. I've been here before. Tell your husband I said hello."

Matt pointed Amy toward the elevator bank. A few minutes later, they were advancing on another reception desk. The scent of disinfectant hung in the air, but the corridor was dominated by bright colors and lots of light. Seattle tended toward shades of gray nine months a year. The kids likely didn't notice the architecture, but their parents probably did. The décor was as cheery as a hospital could get.

It was a good thing Matt was handling the delivery chores right now. The thoughts were whirling through her brain at a hundred miles an hour: *Dead cooler. Scott in the hospital. Wrecked van. How was she going to make deliveries and help with arrangements for an indefinite period of time?* She needed to focus.

Matt held the delivery basket up so the nurse sitting at the desk could see it. "I have something special for a little girl named Madeline."

"Wonderful. She'll be back from the recovery room soon, so I'll take it in there and put it right where she'll see it." The nurse got to her feet and rounded the desk. "She will love this. It's adorable."

At that moment, the metallic sound of wheels rolling over a polished vinyl floor, penetrated Amy's panicked thoughts. She heard a little girl's voice. "Is that for me?"

Amy and Matt turned.

She wasn't tall. Her face had the rounded, puffy look of serious illness. Her honey-colored hair was wispy. She wore flower-print pink pajamas, which hung on her, and slipper socks. The wheels belonged to the IV stand she pulled along with her as she walked. Her dark brown eyes lit with excitement as she glanced over the basket.

"Sarah, honey? I'm so sorry, but this is for Maddy," the nurse told her. "Did you take a good nap?"

Sarah's face fell. In that moment, no matter what else happened today, Amy realized that her worst day couldn't compare to a very sick little girl's disappointment that the special treat wasn't for her. She also wasn't spending her days sitting at a hospital bedside and praying that somehow, God would give her child another chance. Scott would get better. She could get another damn van, and another cooler.

She was doing something for this little girl, if she had to clean out her walk-in and crawl back here on her hands and knees to do it. Today.

She crouched down next to Sarah. "I'm Amy. I have a flower shop. I made something for you, too, but I forgot it. Isn't that silly?"

Sarah's mouth curved into a smile. "It is silly! My mom forgets stuff, too." She let out a giggle.

"I'm going to have to go and get it. It might be a few minutes. Will you still be here when I get back?" Amy asked.

"Oh, yes. I have a treatment, and they'll make me stay in bed," Sarah assured her. "I'll see you then." She padded into her room once more.

AMY PRACTICALLY RAN to Matt's car. He threw himself into the driver's seat, glanced over at her, and a smile twitched over his mouth. "I'm guessing you want to go back to the shop, and van shopping will happen another day."

"Yes, I do. And yes, it will." Her business would survive. Right now, she had a very important appointment with a little girl named Sarah.

Amy glanced over at Matt while he waited at the stoplight. "I'm sorry I haven't been the best of company. I haven't even asked you what you've been doing today," she said.

"I've seen worse." He reached out to take her hand. "I spent some time this morning at a promo event for

Play 60. You sounded like you needed a knight in shining armor, so I stopped by."

"Thank you for the help." She blinked away the tears that threatened to spill over.

"We'll get through this, Fifi," he said.

Chapter Fifteen

THINGS WERE SLOWLY getting back to normal at Crazy Daisy by the next morning. Scott the delivery driver was taking a couple of days off to recover. Besides bumps, bruises, and a little remaining soreness, he was going to be just fine. Amy put an ad on Craigslist to sell her Volkswagen. She'd owned it less than a month. The proceeds would help her pay off the remaining balance on the wrecked delivery van and fund a down payment for a new van. She'd be dealing with finding the money for a new cooler right after she qualified for the loan to get another van. She wasn't sure where that additional five thousand dollars was coming from, but she'd better think of something, and it had better be damn quick. Selling her car wasn't the perfect decision, but she didn't have a lot of other choices at the moment.

She was currently tooling around town in a rental van, which wasn't cheap. She was also going to have to figure out how she could be at least two places at one time; she was going to have to make deliveries today. Estelle was a huge help, but she couldn't make arrangements, answer the phone, and deal with the walk-in business alone.

When Amy wasn't busy juggling her shop's financial and personnel woes, she stopped by Children's Hospital with flowers, a teddy bear, and a copy of *The Velveteen Rabbit* for Sarah. She ended up playing Candy Land with the little girl, too. It was good to spend an hour or so focused on something other than her own problems.

She'd have to do it more often.

Amy was rearranging the flowers and awaiting delivery to make more room in her walk-in when she heard the shop's phone ringing. She wasn't due to open for another hour and a half, so she let it go to voice mail. A few minutes later, the phone rang again.

Maybe it was Scott, or Estelle couldn't come in today, which would be an even bigger disaster. She skidded across a damp—it would be good to mop a little more often—workroom floor to grab the phone off its base.

"Good morning, Fifi," Matt said.

"Good morning, Matt." She had to smile. "How are you?"

"Spectacular. Listen: I found you a delivery driver for a few days. He'll be there in an hour."

"What? Matt, I can't afford—"

"It's Glenn Testerman's oldest son." In other words, his dad worked as an assistant coach for the Sharks. "He's climbing the walls before the NFL Combine, and you'd be doing his dad a favor. He can't take any cash because of NCAA rules. He has a clean driving record and he's over twenty-one."

"What could I do for him in return? It's not fair."

"Send him home with some flowers for his mom. Seriously. He's a nice kid. He'll do a good job."

She was going to have to call the insurance agent and do the paperwork to have him put on her business policy, but it wasn't a terrible idea. "Are you sure?"

"Positive. Plus, I have an ulterior motive." She heard his low laughter. "How the hell are you going to be able to go to Jazz Alley with me later if you're too exhausted to keep your eyes open? I'm only thinking of you here."

"Oh, I see."

"I'm sure you do. I'll pick you up at six tonight."

"I'm not dressed appropriately. I don't have anything here to change into—"

"We'll work it out later. See you then, Fifi." He hung up the phone.

MATT LED HER out the front door of Crazy Daisy at ten to six that evening.

"We have a reservation for the 9:30 PM show. We'll get you home, you can do whatever it is women do before they go out, and we'll be back in Seattle in plenty of time."

Even with someone else doing her deliveries that day, she was exhausted. She sat up a bit in the seat and pinched her underarm to force herself awake. "It sounds like fun."

She was, of course, lying through her teeth. Her idea of fun right now was eight hours of sleep. Actually, a back rub would be even better, followed by eight hours of sleep. She'd started fantasizing about sleep like some women wished for a date with Ryan Gosling.

She also fantasized about Matt, though, and he was less than a foot away. She could always sleep when she was dead.

"It will be," he said. He reached out to pat her hand. "What did you do today?"

She saw his grin. "I met with my accountant. It was fascinating."

She couldn't stifle the laughter that rolled out of her.

"Funny, huh? I bet you dealt with guys like me all day long in your former profession," he said.

"I mostly met with CFO's. They're a real blast. When I wasn't talking with them, I was compiling reports and analysis and taking phone calls and—"

"Things are different now, aren't they?"

"Just a bit. Plus, I don't have to deal with the IRS all day long anymore."

Matt must have had some kind of magic traffic scattering ability. He'd made it across the bridge to Redmond in record time. He braked at the stoplight in front of Amy's townhouse development.

"I treated your temporary delivery driver to lunch, too. We talked about the NFL Combine and what he could expect from the draft. It's a lot different now than when I was drafted." He made the right turn onto Amy's street. "He's expected to go in the first round, so he'll be invited to New York City for the festivities. I told him to do whatever he had to do to stay out of trouble between now and the end of April."

Amy was listening to Matt, but she'd just had a horrible realization. He was fully intending to wait inside her house while she changed her clothes. It was currently a gigantic mess. She had a list for the grocery store, but she hadn't been there yet. She had no beer, no coffee, and the kitchen was a disaster.

"Matt?"

She saw the dimples on either side of his mouth flash. "You sound a little panicky. What's wrong?"

"Would you be terribly offended if I asked you to go get a cup of coffee and meet me back here in half an hour?"

"Why would I do that?"

"My house is a mess right now. It wouldn't be comfortable for you. There's a Starbucks half a mile down the street."

He got out of the driver's seat, hurried around the front, and opened her car door for her.

"I don't want you to have to *see* this," she finished.

They walked to her front door hand-in-hand. "I'm sure it's fine. I've heard this before." He mimicked a woman's voice. "'Ooh, Matt. It's such a mess in here. Really. It's usually a lot cleaner.' There might be a coffee cup in the sink and a few envelopes on the kitchen table, but every woman I've ever met thinks her house is right out of *Hoarders*."

"I know you think you're hilarious." She dug through her purse for her keys.

"That's because I am. Come on. You saw my house when it looked like hell. I want to see your place."

"Fine." She fit the key in the front door lock, and heard him laugh again as she swung the front door open.

MATT STOOD IN the entryway to Fifi's townhouse, a little shocked he'd actually managed to persuade her to let him inside. She worked so hard to keep him at arm's length. He was wearing her down like Marshawn Lynch running the ball for four quarters against Green Bay's defense.

He glanced around. Her house was mainly neutral tones, if the taupe carpeting and pale walls were any indicator. She had a few framed pieces of art along the hallway leading into the living room. The dining room table to his right had mail stacked on it and a goldfish bowl with a somewhat large goldfish swimming around. A faint wisp of lemon tickled his nose.

"I'll give you the tour," she said as she dropped her purse on the table. She gestured toward the fish. "This is Payton. You can feed him if you'd like. His food's next to the bowl, and he gets a pinch."

"Payton? Don't tell me you're a Peyton Manning fan."

"Walter Payton, actually." She gave him a smirk. "Old-school football. Try to keep up, Sparky."

She knew who Walter Payton, one of the greatest running backs to ever play pro football, was. She named a pet after him. She was, officially, a keeper.

She moved into the galley kitchen. "As you can see, dishes in the sink. I need to wipe down the counters, too. Good luck finding anything edible in the refrigerator."

Her kitchen featured white appliances, white tile countertops, and neutral vinyl on the floor. He saw some colorful dishes in the sink, so it seemed she was not completely in love with white. He wondered what she thought about the décor of his house. One thing was for sure: Payton would fit right in on the island in his kitchen.

He followed her into a greatroom-style living room. Love seats flanked the wood-burning fireplace. A flat screen TV hung on the opposite wall. He glanced around at framed photos, plants, a few books, and knick-knacks. He wondered where the mess was. It certainly wasn't downstairs.

"Here are the remotes. I know you know how to work a flat screen. Would you like me to get you some water or something to drink while you wait?"

"What happened to the rest of the tour?"

He saw a flush creeping over her cheekbones. She didn't meet his eyes.

"Oh, there's nothing else to see right now."

"Sure there is. You've seen my room. I want to see yours."

She blushed even harder, if it were possible. He had to admit it was kind of cute to see a woman worried about showing a guy her room.

"My bed isn't made and my clothes are all over the place. I need to do a bunch of laundry, too. I'll be ready in twenty minutes, and we can go."

Matt tangled his fingers with hers. "You're scared."

"No, I'm not," she said, but she still wouldn't meet his eyes. "I don't know where you got that, but it's not true." She melted his heart when she got skittish. He didn't think she was scared of him, or didn't want to get physically involved. Maybe he should find out for himself.

He'd been waiting to hold her all day, and he didn't want to wait a second more. He drew her a little closer when he felt her wrap her arms around his waist. She laid her soft cheek against his scratchy one, and he felt the warmth of her breath on the side of his neck.

She had a goldfish named Payton. Where had she been all his life?

He tipped her chin up. He saw mischief in her amber-brown eyes as he cupped her cheek in one of his hands. He also noticed the circles forming beneath those eyes, which he knew better than to mention to her. She was exhausted after what must have been one hell of a day.

He'd make her forget.

He sealed his mouth over hers. He felt her stiffen a little at first with what must have been surprise, and then he felt her hands sliding up his chest, and her arms wrap around his neck. He slid his tongue into her mouth. She let out a moan.

God, she felt so good.

MATT'S MOUTH MOVED over hers. Her heart pounded, her knees turned to water, and there was a very real possibility that she'd spontaneously combust. She reached up to slide her fingers through his hair, which curled around them. Kissing him while fully clothed was beyond wonderful. She could only imagine what would happen if they were both naked.

They were alone in her place, they'd spent the past week together, and reservations at Jazz Alley or not, she knew what was going to happen next. She *was* scared, but it wasn't the getting naked with him part. They would go to bed. They'd go out for a while, he'd decide he couldn't live with her schedule or the fact she wanted to do things on her own, and she would get her heart broken.

The problem was—and right now, it really didn't seem like much of a problem—she didn't want to say no. Amy dreamed about Matt. Actually, she dreamed about his left eyebrow. His eyes would sparkle, he'd say something moderately raunchy, that eyebrow would lift in a toe-curling *come here* invitation, and every part of her would superheat in response.

He slid his mouth to her neck, and she was wondering if she should lie down before she fell down. He was really good at this.

"You're shaking like a leaf." His hands stroked up and down her back, and she laid her head against his shoulder.

"It's our third date," came out of her mouth in much the same tone as if she had said, "The IRS called, and there's a little problem with last year's tax return." Every adult knew what this meant.

"And?"

Why was she letting him dictate the encounter? This was not her first time. It wasn't his, either.

"Amy, if you don't want this, tell me no," he said. "I

can take it." Despite the fact he spent most of his time trying to talk her into something these days, she knew he wouldn't touch her again if she told him no.

Oh, she wanted him all right. It was positively infuriating that he managed to hang onto all his faculties while leaving her a wreck. She felt him nibble the hollow where her neck and collarbone joined. She couldn't resist him anymore. Even more, she didn't want to.

She could feel herself blushing again, but she whispered, "I don't want to say no."

"Maybe it's time to continue the tour, then."

MATT FOLLOWED HER up the staircase to the second floor. Her room was visible from the landing. Her bed was unmade, but at least the sheets were clean. She thought she had a new box of condoms in her bedside table. The bathroom was a mess, though. Maybe she should kiss him again, before she lost her nerve.

She was still worried physical involvement with him would signal the end, but if Matt made love like he kissed, at least she'd have a memory that would last a lifetime. In the meantime, she was going to enjoy every second. He was hotter than the invention of fire, and every cell of her body was screaming for relief right about now.

Matt grinned at her. "Let's go, Fifi." He caught her up in his arms, and strode into her room.

She let out a startled shriek. "What are you doing?"

It ranked right up there with the more stupid questions known to mankind, but maybe she should put up some kind of token protest: *You are the sexiest man I have ever met, but of course I don't want to sleep with you. Ohh, noooo.* Then again, she was limp as an overcooked spaghetti noodle due to nerves and lust, so any kind of rally was going to take superhuman effort.

Amy opened her mouth to remind him they had to be back in Seattle in an hour or so, and she saw his dimples flash. "You're not going to argue with me right now, are you?"

"What about the reservation?"

She heard his low chuckle. "I don't care about it if you don't."

She couldn't stop the smile that spread over her face. "I don't."

"So, you don't care if I wine and dine you first?"

Amy had to laugh, too. "That would be a no. Dazzle me, Matt Stephens."

"Oh, I intend to."

He kicked the door shut behind them, and deposited her in the middle of her bed. Twilight bled through the blinds at her window. The room was dim in the gathering darkness, but she could see him just fine.

Matt flopped down on his side inches away from her, kicked off his shoes, took her face in his hand and said softly, "It's just us."

He captured her lips with his. His mouth was firm but gentle on hers; she opened her mouth to give him better access as his tongue slid over the seam of her lips. Amy's arms slipped around him as he pulled her closer. She felt his hands, warm and sure, on her bare skin as he pushed the sweater she wore over her bra.

He trailed his tongue down the side of her neck as he unhooked her bra. Other guys fumbled around with the whole bra-removal project. Not Matt. "I know you're dying to argue with me about some damn thing, too. You'd better kiss me again."

Amy had a crushing retort all lined up—well, until he teased one of her nipples with gentle fingertips. She caught his face in her hands, feeling the scratch of stubble against her palms. She slid her fingers into his hair. He yanked her sweater up and over her head, pulling her bra with it. He dropped them onto the floor.

"There. That's much better." He laid one big hand on her belly. "Now. Where was I?"

His eyes traveled from Amy's shoes, over her calves, up her thighs, and stopped when he reached bare skin. He took a deep breath, and did nothing more than look his fill. He stared at her while she kicked off her shoes, and propped herself up on her elbows.

His voice was low and rough. "You're still wearing too many clothes."

"And you're still fully dressed, Sparky."

"What are we going to do about that?" he asked.

Matt watched her tongue as she licked her lips. She saw his eyes glitter. He slicked one hand through his hair. God, this was fun.

"Strip for me," she said softly.

"So, that's what you're into . . ." he teased, but his voice was ragged.

"I want to watch you."

"Really." He infused a world of lust and desire into one word. "What's it worth to you?"

He got to his feet, reached behind his back, and pulled his polo shirt over his head with agonizing slowness. She watched the muscles in his forearms bunch and flex. The shirt moved over his abdomen, up his chest, and finally, over his face. It fell from his fingertips to the floor. His chest looked like it was carved from stone. It was lightly covered with dark curls, and a long, thin trail of hair moved vertically from his belly button to disappear beneath the waistband of his jeans.

Her mouth was instantly dry, unlike other parts of her body. She was breathless, and she licked her lips again with the little bit of moisture she had left. Amy couldn't take her eyes off of him. His shoulders were broad, his waist narrow; he still had a six-pack, and everything was covered with smooth, tanned skin she had to touch.

"More," she managed to croak out.

"I don't know if I should be showing my package off to a woman who's not naked yet," he said, but he unbuttoned the waistband of his jeans, lowering the zipper one tooth at a time. She saw darker, curling hair, and he pushed the jeans off his hips to reveal black boxer briefs, already straining to cover his erection. His big, long, hard, bulging . . . He gestured to the boxer briefs with one hand. "I guess you want me to take these off, too, don't you?"

Duhhh. *Just get them off*, she wanted to yell. Maybe she could tear them off with her teeth. He hadn't touched her for at least two minutes, and she couldn't have stood up right now if she tried. There was nothing on the planet she wanted more than she wanted him, right now. She unbuttoned and unzipped her own jeans, and writhed around as she attempted to shove them off.

"You're the floor show," she reminded him.

He reached down, grabbed the cuffs of her jeans, and removed them with a flourish.

"So, you're going to strip me naked and have your way with me."

She gazed into his eyes. "You could always say no, Matt."

All she heard was his low laugh. He skimmed off his boxer shorts, stepped out of them, and knelt beside her on the bed.

He caught the elastic waist of her thong panties in his teeth, and tugged them slowly down her legs. He kissed and licked his way back up via her calves and inner thighs. By now, she'd abandoned propping herself up on her elbows to see what he was doing. She was too busy writhing around on the pillows to care. Frankly as long as it involved his lips, his tongue, and his hands, she wasn't picky.

"Want more?"

"God, yes!" she burst out.

"I love a woman who's enthusiastic," he said. He pulled himself up and over her once more. Amy stretched her arms over her head, and he quickly restrained both wrists in one hand.

"I want to touch you," she pleaded.

"Maybe."

Oh, God, his eyebrow. She tried to sit up. She had to

kiss him, right now, or she was going to die from an over-load of adrenaline, hormones, and whatever else was currently swimming in her bloodstream. She was breathing hard already. He was, too.

She wondered if it was possible to die of great sex. She had a feeling she was about to find out, and she was willing to take the risk.

"I'll think it over," he said, and Amy wriggled beneath him. She wrapped both legs around his waist, and ground herself against him. "Jesus."

"You're not leaving me a lot of choices," she managed to gasp out.

She arched her back a bit more, cradled his pelvis against hers, and gripped his thighs with her legs. He groaned, "Okay. You win."

He let go of her wrists. She found a few things to do with her hands, which he seemed to enjoy. His mouth claimed hers, and she was lost in a lengthy, incendiary kiss. She was already sweating, and all they were doing was kissing.

In all honesty, there was some rubbing and friction involved as well. If he didn't do something, like find a condom damn quick, she was going to come.

"More," she breathed into his ear.

He rolled onto his back and pulled her atop him. She straddled him, bending over him to kiss him again, and tangle her fingers in the heavy, dark satin of his hair. She felt him against her, hot and hard, and she sat up once more. He found the small, slick button between her legs with his thumbs.

All she could manage to get out was, "Oh, God, don't stop." He tipped her onto her back and replaced his thumbs with his tongue.

"Oh, Matt. That—oh, don't stop. Please don't stop."

He said something she couldn't hear, and she felt the rumble of what had to be his laughter against the most sensitive parts of her body. He was enjoying himself, too, and she loved it. For the most part, though, he licked, he sucked, his tongue tickled her, he slid one finger and then two inside of her, and she was reduced to thrashing on the bed, calling out his name, and praying to the orgasm gods that the neighbors were not going to call the cops when she screamed. She was definitely going to scream.

He laid one big hand on her abdomen as he returned to his labors. She'd locked her legs around his hips.

"Easy," he told her.

Amy felt it in her fingertips and her toes. It moved up her body, strong, unstoppable, and it would drag her under. She'd go happily. She felt the clench of her womb, the ripples throughout, the fireworks bursting behind her eyelids. She was hotter than the surface of the sun, despite the fact her room was cool. She heard herself scream, and she saw Matt's triumphant grin when she opened her eyes. He pulled himself up to lie down next to her, slipped his arms around her, and waited for her to come back to herself.

She laid her head on his shoulder. There was the perfect space, right there, just for her. She felt herself relax against him. She trailed her fingers over his six-pack, which he—and his penis—seemed to enjoy. She'd like to embark on a leisurely exploration of his body. The chances were fairly good he'd agree to that.

His voice was low and amused. "That was quite an orgasm, Fifi."

"Yes, it was. I loved it." Her hand slid lower on his belly. She heard his quick intake of breath. "I think I have a condom."

"If you don't, I might." He kissed her eyebrow. "I loved it, too."

She dug through her bedside table with one hand. Her fingers closed around a small cardboard box, which she extracted out of the slightly messy drawer. At least she'd remembered to buy some the last time she went to the grocery store, even if she had to endure the disapproving glare of a female checker who probably hadn't had sex since the last century.

"Let's just do a little kissing and see what happens," he said.

He rolled over on top of her, and things started happening really fast. Amy tried to tell herself it was because she hadn't had sex with anyone for over a month now. Maybe all the bickering she did with Matt was some kind of aphrodisiac. A little while later, he grabbed the cardboard box away from her, ripped it in half, and extracted a foil-covered packet.

"Voila," he told her as he waved it in front of her nose. She pulled it out of his hand, tore off the foil, and rolled the disc of latex over him. Slowly.

"Are you trying to kill me, Fifi?" he groaned. Of course, that required a little additional attention to the long, thick penis in her hands. "If you keep this up, you'll be waiting even longer."

"You were just telling me to take it easy," she said in the most innocent tone she could muster. "Waiting is not necessarily a bad—"

He flipped her onto her back again and positioned himself between her legs before she could finish her sentence.

"More like it," he ground out. He was inside her with one long, hot, slick slide. She wrapped her legs around his hips. He moved slowly at first as they got used to each other. She reached out to pull him into her.

She couldn't get close enough to him. Even more, she wanted to give him as much pleasure as he was giving her. She realized with a shock there was more going on here than mutual attraction, body parts that just happened to mesh, or something that felt good. She felt her soul open to him, as much as she'd just welcomed him into her body.

She let out a moan.

He picked up the pace. Just a little bit. Enough for her to know that if he kept it up, she was going to come again. She gripped him in her arms with her body. She squeezed him.

"Do it again," he groaned.

She did. He moved just a little faster. His mouth sought hers. His tongue did a complicated dance with Amy's. She raked her nails down his back, the skin damp with sweat. She felt the beginnings of another orgasm, and arched up into him. His chest hair rubbed over nipples hard enough to cut glass. Her head tossed on the pillows.

"Oh, God, Matt!"

"You're going to come," he told her.

And she did.

MATT WRAPPED HIS arms a little more tightly around Amy as she recovered from another huge orgasm. She'd left him a little stunned, too. He'd never had a woman ask him to strip for her before. The delight in her eyes as she looked at him made him feel like he could leap tall buildings at a single bound. He'd never been with anyone who made love with such joy and abandon, either. He laughed with her. Most of all, he knew he'd never be able to get enough of her.

She tangled her long legs with his again. He let out a contented sigh as she sank into him.

"Happy?" she whispered. Her fingertips slid over his arm, outlining the muscles there.

"Yes."

"Me, too." She rubbed the tip of her nose on the side of his neck.

He had the urge to tell her this was already one of the better evenings of his life so far. He could tell her that he'd never forget what she tasted like, the sounds she made, or how she looked when she came. Most of all, he wanted to tell her something that scared the hell out of him, too: She was the one he wanted to come home to.

TWO HOURS LATER, Matt and Amy had ordered a pizza, taken a shower together, and were back in her bed. They both needed a little rest between bouts.

She'd listened to her girlfriends bragging before about how great some guy they were with was in bed. She'd had enough experience to know she enjoyed sex. She'd been with guys who were somewhat proficient at it, but he was something else. Matt was like a drug. Maybe her attraction was all about the forbidden. Maybe it was because he'd had lots of practice, because he persisted and chased her, or because she'd gone without for a while. She was resisting the impulse to leap on him again.

She was still fairly worried that having sex with him was the beginning of the end. It wouldn't be the first time she slept with a guy and things didn't work out so well afterward. But, dammit, at least she was going to have some great memories if it was. She wondered if it was possible to get enough of him in the meantime. Maybe she should find out.

Before she could do something to him that would bring a rapid and significant response, Matt reached over to wrap his arms around her waist.

"Sleep," he said.

The only light in her room was the reflection of the full moon off the blinds over her window. She snuggled against him in the darkness. She didn't ask if he was spending the night. Obviously, it would take some doing to pull herself out of his arms, and right now she didn't want to.

He kissed the back of her neck once more.

They'd get some rest, and then she was *definitely* going to talk him into it again.

AMY AWOKE TO her cell phone ringing on the nightstand. The call went to voice mail while she tried to disentangle herself from the sheets and Matt's massive arm. The clock on her phone read 1:33 AM.

"What's up?" Matt asked sleepily. She was thrilled he was still there, but that happiness was quickly replaced by a jolt of fear as the phone rang again. Brandon's face popped up on the screen. He wouldn't be making a social call at 1:34 AM.

"I don't know. Something's wrong." She felt alarm skitter up her spine. Was something wrong with her parents? She hit "answer."

"Brandon?" she said. "What's going on?"

He sounded stressed and almost panicky. "Where are you right now?" Whatever was going on, it wasn't good.

"I'm at home. Why? What happened?"

"We're at Evergreen Hospital."

"What's the matter?"

"It's Emily." Brandon's voice broke. "Someone hit our car. She's going to be okay, but she's asking for you. We're at the emergency room."

"I'll be there as fast as I can. Just—just tell her I'll be there," Amy said. She hung up and started scrabbling around for her underwear. The room was dark and she bounced off a few things, which freaking hurt, but bruises were nothing in comparison to the panic that gripped her.

Amy threw her phone back into the blankets while rushing around her room. She grabbed up her clothes.

"What's going on?" Matt asked.

"Brandon and Emily were in a wreck," she told him as she shoved her legs into the jeans Matt dropped on the floor earlier. "They're at Evergreen. Emily's hurt. Brandon says it's not a big deal, but I—I have to go there."

Matt scrambled out of the bed, and his arms surrounded her. "She's going to be okay," he soothed. He let go of her, flipped on the bedroom light, and gathered up his clothes.

"I'll drive you," he said.

"No. No. I can drive the Bug. It's still out in the garage."

"No, you can't. You're upset, and you shouldn't be behind the wheel. Let me get some clothes on, and I'll get you there."

"I can drive—"

"Don't make me take your car keys." He slid into his jeans. He jammed his feet into socks and dress shoes, pulled his shirt back on and said, "Let's go."

Amy finished dressing and followed Matt as he negotiated her house like he'd lived there his entire life. She tried to tell herself he'd probably scrambled out of many other women's homes in the dark before, but this seemed different. She liked having him in her space. He'd spent the day helping her out when things went so wrong at the shop, they'd spent a great evening together, and he insisted on accompanying her to the hospital to see Emily in the middle of the night.

This called for some serious thought, but she didn't have much time right now.

They hurried through a silent house and down the walk, and then he helped her into his car.

"We'll be there before you know it," Matt said as he pulled on his seatbelt. "Did he say anything else?"

"No. He just told me to come over." Hot tears raced down her cheeks. "He sounds really upset."

Matt's lips formed a solid, bloodless line. "I know she's going to be okay, Amy." He squeezed her hand.

The rest of the ride was silent. Amy fidgeted. She glanced out the window, but she saw nothing but pictures in her imagination of Emily lying on an emergency room gurney, bloody and seriously injured.

"I'll park the car and find you," he said.

Matt pulled up in front of the Evergreen Hospital emergency entrance shortly afterward.

"Okay. Thank you."

He stroked her cheek. "Everything's going to be fine."

"I hope so." Amy threw the passenger door open and sprinted through the entrance.

EMILY LAID ON a bed in one of the emergency room cubicles. Brandon had his arm around her shoulder, and was murmuring into her ear when Amy skidded through the doorway. Her right foot was wrapped in a significant number of bandages and sported an ice pack. A sparkly pair of sky-high Louboutins sat on a rolling table next to the bed.

"Brandon said he called you. You didn't have to get up and come over here, you weirdo. I'm fine."

Amy felt like a rock rolled off her back. If her sister was well enough for insults and had put her shoes where she could see them, she was going to live. "What happened?"

"Oh, some doofus drove through a stop sign and hit us. The airbags all went off. Brandon doesn't have a scratch on him."

"What happened to your foot, then?"

"My handbag fell on it."

"You're kidding me."

"Absolutely not. It's a bad sprain. Plus, the doctor lectured me about wearing stilettos at this stage of my life. *Excuse me*? I am not old." She let out a sniff and pointed at the bandages. "I am *not* wearing these for a month."

"You're going to have to wear them till the doctor says you can take 'em off, sugar."

"Brandon McKenna, I love you very much, but no. Maybe I can get something more stylish at—"

"Do you want me to call Mom and Daddy?" Amy interrupted. "Are you in pain?"

"Let's call them tomorrow. Mom will freak out, and Dad will ask us why we were out driving around at midnight." Emily let out a sigh. "I wanted a burger. And no, I'm not in pain. They gave me a shot."

"I'll say," Brandon muttered. Amy almost laughed out loud at the expression on his face—tired, stressed, but amused.

"Are they making you stay here tonight?" Amy asked.

"They're releasing her as soon as the nurse comes in with the paperwork. That Town Car I called should be here too, sugar."

Amy heard a slight commotion behind her. Matt strolled into the room. She felt his arm slide around her waist. Emily's eyes got huge as she watched.

"So, Mrs. McKenna, I heard there was a little accident. How are you feeling?" Matt said.

"Matt Stephens, what are you doing here?" Emily said. "It's a little late for a social call." She beamed at him. "I *love* the espresso maker you sent us. Thank you so much."

"You're welcome. I'm glad you're enjoying it."

Emily glanced back and forth between Matt and Amy several times. Even under the influence of hospital-grade pharmaceuticals, her eyes narrowed. Matt and Amy were saved from what was sure to be an interrogation by the arrival of a nurse.

"Okay, then, Mrs. McKenna. Let me get you back into your clothes, and you'll be free to go. I have some discharge information for you as well. The doctor says that you will want to consult with your primary care physician if you need additional medications for pain control tomorrow. Right now, though, you'll want to keep that foot elevated and stay off it. Ice will help the swelling." Amy saw her smile at Emily and nod toward the pair of Louboutins. "Those might be off-limits for a while." She handed her a small white plastic sack, too. "Here's a souvenir. Congratulations."

Emily grinned at her. "Thank you." She stuffed the little plastic bag into her handbag before Amy could figure out what was in it. In the meantime, Brandon was off his chair at the speed of light.

"Sugar, it's late. Let me see Amy and Matt out," he said. "I'll be right back," he told her.

"What's going on?" Amy called out as she was propelled from the room by both Matt and Brandon.

Brandon finally slowed almost fifty feet away.

"What's in the little white plastic bag?" Amy asked him.

Brandon ignored her question. "Okay, squirt. I kept my mouth shut long enough. I know someone who told me you and Matt had been on a couple of dates recently. Your secret is out."

"Speaking of secrets—"

"You can tell my wife you're seeing Matt or not, but I'd advise 'fessing up. You're busted." He turned toward Matt. "'Someone else on my radar screen?' Nice. I don't know whether to punch you or hug you."

"I know which one I'd prefer." Matt slid his arm around Amy's waist. "Let us know if you or your wife needs anything."

"Oh, I will." Brandon hugged Amy, and shook hands with Matt. "Let me get her home, and we'll catch up with you tomorrow." He made a shooing motion with his hands. "See ya."

MATT AND AMY climbed back into his car a few minutes later. He relaxed against the seat.

"I'm glad Emily's going to be just fine. She's going to hit that doctor with her crutch if he tells her she can't wear those shoes again." He reached out to turn the key in the ignition. "Let's go home and go back to bed."

"That works for me," she said. She reached out for his hand. "Should we bet on what's in the little white bag the nurse handed her?"

Matt shook his head. "We both know what's in there. Let's wait till they decide to tell everyone."

Amy couldn't wipe the grin off her face. It sounded like she was going to be an auntie a lot sooner than she had anticipated. This was definitely worth getting out of bed in the middle of the night and rushing over to the hospital for. Plus, her little secret was out, too. She and Matt were officially An Item. Speaking of bets, she was willing to bet Emily was texting their mother right now.

In the meantime, Matt brought the back of her hand up to his lips and kissed it.

"I kind of liked being your dirty little secret, Fifi."

She turned to look at him. "Are you serious?"

"Sneaking around still sounds pretty sexy, don't you think? We could get trench coats and dark glasses. We could meet up in hotel rooms. We could have a password." He grinned over at her. "You know what this means, don't you?"

"No."

"There's going to be a fourth date, and I want to meet your parents."

Chapter Sixteen

AT SEVEN O'CLOCK the next morning, Amy's cell phone rang. She reached over to the bedside table, grabbed it, and pulled the blankets around herself as she hit the button to send the call to voice mail. "Unknown caller" could wait. She felt an unfamiliar weight next to her in the bed and heard a sleepy male voice seconds later.

"Good morning, Fifi."

He rolled over to pin her in his embrace. He planted a kiss on her forehead.

"Good morning." She trailed her fingertips over the stubble on his cheek. He'd been awake for two minutes, and he looked dazzling, despite being rumpled and sleepy. She wasn't going to think about how she looked. He reached up to smooth the hair out of her eyes. "You're still here," she blurted.

"Where did you think I'd be?"

"Oh, I—you might have wanted to—oh, hell," she

said. She pulled the blankets over her face. It didn't work. He was bigger, stronger, and took them away from her in a hurry.

"I had to work hard to get here," he said. "I wasn't going anywhere." She watched his lips twitch into a smile. "Staying in bed sounds like a great plan, but I have appointments today, and you have a business to run. How are we going to work this out?"

"Carefully."

"Good answer," he said. Morning breath wasn't sexy, but right now she was willing to overlook it. She felt him against her, hard and ready. She rocked against him. Just a little. She was rewarded with a look that made it clear he got her message.

She could get used to waking up to Aroused Matt every morning.

"I have to be at the airport at ten. I'll be back from LA tonight, though. What does your day look like?" he said.

"I need to be at the store at 9:00. I'll be here a little after seven," she said.

"I'll meet you here at eight-thirty. We'll go find some food and maybe a bottle of wine." He smirked. Just a little. "I'll bring a toothbrush."

"Perfect," she said. Her insides quivered. It was only a toothbrush, though. It wasn't serious until he asked her to clean out a drawer in the bathroom vanity for his use.

She even braved morning breath for another one of his kisses at the front door. She resisted the impulse to pull him down on the entryway floor and tear his clothes off. Her concern about what was going to happen as a result of their taking things to the next level was fading by the minute. She couldn't believe her entryway didn't burst into flame from the sparks flying off the two of them.

"I'll be back tonight, Fifi."

"I guess this means I'd better buy more condoms."

"That's my girl."

AMY DRAGGED HERSELF out of the shower a short time later to the sound of her phone ringing. Maybe he forgot something on his way out the door. She grabbed the phone to see Emily's smiling face displayed on the screen. She hit the "speaker" function as she answered.

"Hey, Em. How are you feeling this morning?"

"When did you start seeing Matt Stephens? My husband tells me that you both pretended like you didn't know each other, and now you're dating?"

They were also sleeping together, but Amy could only handle one confession at a time before she had some coffee. Normally, she would have been on the phone with Emily since the day Matt walked into her shop and started asking her out, but this time, she wanted to keep things to herself and see where it went before notifying everyone she'd ever met that she—and her heart—was definitely involved.

"It's kind of a funny story. What's going on with your ankle? And, oh, by the way, I think I know what was in that little plastic bag the nurse handed you last night. Congratulations, Em. You both must be so excited."

"You're trying to distract me, and it won't work," her

sister informed her. "What's happening between you and Matt?"

"We're spending some time together. He asked me out, and I accepted." She could also mention that Matt spent three weeks asking her out, she finally said yes, and now she was wondering why she'd waited so long.

Her sister let out a sigh. "According to Brandon, this has been going on since our wedding. Why didn't you tell me? We tell each other everything!"

"You've been busy, and I—I wanted to keep this to myself for a little while."

"What do you mean?" Emily sounded a little breathless. She must have been attempting to move around despite the sprain. "I can't believe you didn't tell me. I'm a little hurt about it, too," she added.

"I'm sorry that you feel hurt," Amy said. "I never meant for that to happen. I wasn't sure what to say to anyone, and I needed some time to work that out for myself."

"That's *ridic*," Emily said. Amy almost laughed. There must have been a teen in the cast of Emily's latest production. "Why?"

Things were silent for a minute or so.

"I wanted to make sure things were going well before I told anyone else. Kind of like what you're doing right now."

Emily ignored that. She must have been taking lessons from Brandon.

"So, here's a question. Did you know Matt has a daughter from his previous marriage?" Emily asked.

"Yes. I've met Samantha. I really like her."

"How do you feel about being an instant step-parent? If you let this get any further, it's going to happen. I'm also a little curious about the fact Matt's older than the guys you've dated before. What do you think about that?"

Amy threw herself down on the side of her bed, which still wasn't made. She'd have to toss the sheets in the wash before she went to work today.

"Em, we're just dating. It's pretty early to be speculating on being a step-parent." She took a deep breath. "Matt isn't that much older. It doesn't matter."

"Ten years is a lot if you're looking for someone to have a family with."

Amy shoved her temper down with both hands. "If I didn't know better, I'd think you weren't happy about this."

"I *am* happy for you. I'm kind of wondering what you think you're doing here, though," Emily said.

"I'm having fun. I'm seeing someone I enjoy. What's the problem?"

"Why won't you talk about it, then?"

The next few minutes were more of the same—Amy trying to ask Emily how she was feeling, if her ankle was better, if she got any sleep at all after being at the hospital so late the night before, and oh, by the way, was she experiencing morning sickness yet?

Finally Emily heaved another sigh and said, "Here's the official position on the item in the white plastic bag. We agreed we're keeping it a secret from everyone for another month and a half."

Amy let out a squeal.

"You can't tell Mom. You can't tell Dad. Don't even talk about it in your sleep," her sister joked. "And just for the record, morning sickness sucks. Back to you, though. When do you think you're going to trust me with your information?"

"Em, I—I'm trying to figure out how I feel about all of this. I didn't mean to shut you out. It's not that at all. I'm more worried about you right now."

For the first time since Amy and Emily had had a huge fight over Emily's breaking her engagement to Brandon, Amy heard her sister say, "Let me call you back later. I've gotta go." Her phone clicked as Emily ended the call.

She couldn't figure out why Emily was so hurt when Emily and Brandon had a secret of their own. Wasn't she entitled to a secret, too? She longed to confide in Emily, too, but she was now a little nervous about Emily's comments on step-parenting and the fact Matt was a bit older than Amy was. It didn't matter that much, did it?

Defending him to a member of her family was a bit different, too, especially since two weeks ago she would have agreed with Emily. She finally admitted to herself what she'd been running from ever since the moment she saw Matt in the hotel ballroom after Emily's wedding.

"I want him," she murmured. "I must be insane."

Even if he acted like a caveman and tried to run her life, even if he bossed her around and meddled shamelessly, even if she occasionally longed to get her hands around his neck and squeeze, she couldn't get past Matt. It wasn't just the sex; she had to admit it was spectacular. It wasn't how he looked, even though that helped. It was *him*—the maddeningly self-assured, frustratingly overprotective, irritatingly arrogant Matt, who was also deeply thoughtful, uproariously funny, overwhelmingly generous, and a loving, concerned father. He probably thought there wasn't a woman alive who'd managed to figure out that he wanted nothing more than to be needed.

Even though Amy hated to admit it, she needed him.

Chapter Seventeen

ONE WEEK LATER, Matt and Amy pulled up in front of her parents' house. It was a rare sunny spring day in Seattle. Birds were chirping, flowers were blooming, and Amy resisted the feeling of impending doom.

Matt reached out for her hand as they climbed the steps to her parents' front door. He had a bottle of wine in the other hand. Matt's insistence on meeting her parents was very sweet. It was also a very, very bad idea. Amy loved her mom and dad, but she'd seen how things could rapidly fall apart at the Sunday afternoon dinner table before.

She was fairly sure her parents were watching them approach the house. As a result, the explaining why she had turned and ran would be more difficult than just getting this over with.

"Nervous?" Matt gave her hand a squeeze.

"A little."

"For God's sake, Fifi, it's just dinner. What could possibly go wrong?" He rang the doorbell.

"I can't believe you asked me that."

Matt let out a chuckle. "Flying Italian food . . ."

Amy's mom pulled the front door open. "Sweetheart!" She threw her arms around Amy. "Come in!"

Amy found herself dragged over the threshold by her hundred-and-ten pound mom, who seemed to be a bit overexcited. Despite the fact they were divorced, Amy's dad still appeared each Sunday for dinner with his ex-wife and their daughters. Amy typically brought whomever she'd been dating for more than a month to Sunday dinner, but her mom was acting like she hadn't brought a guy home since the high school prom. Matt walked into the front hallway behind them and waited for Amy's mom to quit hugging and kissing her.

Brandon and Emily were out of town today, too.

"It's so good to see you. We've missed you," her mother said.

Amy had seen both parents last week. Evidently, something was going on she didn't understand. What else was new? Her mom finally backed off a little and extended her hand to Matt.

"You must be Amy's guest." She gave him a faint smile.

"Yes, I'm Matt Stephens." He unleashed the full force of his dazzling smile, dimples, and charm, which were set to "stun," on her. "You must be Amy's mom. She is as beautiful as you are." He took her hand in both of his. "It's great to meet you."

Meg Hamilton gave Matt an icily polite smile that Amy knew could mean only one thing: He'd managed to rub her mother the wrong way already, for some reason.

"Amy, why don't you let your guest visit with your dad for a few minutes, and we'll bring the food to the table."

Meg clamped one hand around Amy's forearm and pulled her down the hallway. Amy's dad emerged from the family room.

"Hey, Matt, let's sit down," Amy heard him say as she was tugged past.

"Mom," Amy said into her mother's ear. "What's going on?"

Meg rounded the corner to the kitchen, turned to face her daughter and said, "I do *not* like that man."

Amy hadn't seen her mom this upset over an introduction to a friend since she brought home a guy who informed everyone at the Sunday dinner table he thought the arts were a waste of taxpayer dollars. He and Amy's relationship was over before her mom brought out dessert. The guy was lucky he made it out her parents' front door before being stabbed with a fork.

"Why not? Mom, you just met him five minutes ago. I know he can be a little arrogant."

"A *little*?" Her mother poked her finger in Amy's belly for emphasis. "Amy Margaret, your sister has told me before that Mr. Stephens brings a whole new definition to the word arrogant."

"Emily was the one who thought I should go out with Matt in the first place!" Amy exclaimed, but her mother cut her off.

"That can't be true. Why are you seeing him? Can't you go out with someone a bit more . . . We'd been hoping you'd meet someone else, but you're dating *him*? Why don't you want to go out with that nice Damian?"

Damian was another of Brandon's former teammates. Brandon brought him to dinner a couple of months back; it was all Amy's mother could talk about for weeks. She fell in love with him on the spot. Even better, she wanted to mother him, which Damian thought was wonderful. His own mother was across the country. Amy also knew Damian would go home with anyone who would feed him, but maybe it was best to keep that fact private.

"Damian's pretty serious with the woman he's dating right now. I don't think he's interested in me."

Her mother shook her head and walked away from Amy. She opened the oven door and grabbed a couple of hot mats to retrieve the casserole inside, setting it on top of the oven to cool.

"What's *that*?" Amy blurted out.

"It's tuna tetrazzini," her mother said. "You'll like it."

No, she wouldn't, and she was willing to bet Matt and her dad weren't going to be overly enamored of it, either. Prior to today, she'd never seen a can of tuna in anything her mother made.

"I know you think you don't like Matt, but you made lasagna for Brandon the first time he came over."

"That's different," her mother sniffed. "How could I feed something awful to my potential son-in-law?"

"Excuse me? When Brandon was here the first time,

he and Emily weren't really engaged, and you didn't like him at first."

"It was momentary."

"*Mom.*" She made the conscious effort to lower her voice a bit. "You don't even know Matt, so you're going to feed him something that has a week's worth of cholesterol and sodium, and he'll miraculously disappear?" Amy shook her head in disbelief. "Dad's doctor would have a fit, too. I can't believe you're doing this."

Meg pushed a napkin-lined, wicker breadbasket into Amy's abdomen.

"Go put this on the table. I'll bring the rest in a few minutes."

Amy knew her mom wasn't going to answer her. She was also wondering if she needed to hire a food taster. She could hear Matt and her dad laughing about something in the other room. At least her dad seemed to like him. Her mom was bustling around the kitchen and ignoring her, so Amy hurried into to the dining room and surveyed the rest of the table.

At least there was a salad. Matt wouldn't starve to death. Today's calorie-fest meant Amy was going to spend the rest of the afternoon resisting the impulse to fall asleep, though.

Amy heard Matt's heavy footfalls behind her, and his arm slid around her waist. She leaned against him. She could only imagine what he was going to think about the way her mom was acting, and an entrée she hadn't had to force down since middle school hot lunch. Then again, maybe it was a good thing: If he was going to spook, this would just about do it.

"Hey, Fifi. Why don't you c'mon in and sit with your dad and me for a few minutes? The baseball game's on."

"My mom probably needs some help." *He had no idea.*

Meg appeared with her casserole, and called out, "Honey! Dinner's ready!" She put the baking dish down on the hot mat with a slight *bang* and seated herself at the table. She also managed to glare at Matt again. He gave her a gentle smile in response.

"Thanks for inviting me to dinner, Mrs. Hamilton."

Meg made some kind of snorting noise.

Mark walked in and sat down in his chair. He took one look at the casserole and said cautiously, "Meg? Honey? You must be trying out a new recipe."

"Hand me your plate, honey, and I'll dish some up. It's hot."

Amy noted her dad looked a little confused, but he handed over his plate. "It looks delicious," Matt said, and glanced across the table to Amy.

Meg barely resisted spewing the sip of water she'd taken across the table. She spooned casserole onto Mark's plate and handed it back to him. Her evil plan was not only failing; her ex-husband, and now-fiancé, was looking at her as if she'd lost her grip.

Mark took a bite. The look on his face was indescribable. He managed to swallow, but picked up his water glass. "Of course, honey."

Matt dug into the gigantic portion of casserole Amy's mom put on his plate like he hadn't eaten since last month. "It's delicious," he insisted between mouthfuls.

Amy knew his stance on processed food. His nose was going to start growing any minute.

Matt's face was the embodiment of innocence until Meg looked back down at her plate, and then he winked at Amy. Mark was pushing his dinner around with his fork. Amy took a bite. It tasted good, but she hadn't eaten tuna in years. She could fill up on salad, and if she couldn't, they could find something to eat on the way home.

Matt was polishing off his dinner, and doing everything in his power to charm Meg. Meg was having none of it.

Maybe it was time for a conference.

Amy shoved her chair back from the table. "Mom, I think we forgot something in the kitchen. Maybe we should go and get it."

"No, no, sweetie. You go get it," Meg said.

Amy reached out for her mom's hand. "We'll be back in a minute. Matt, Dad, do you need anything else while we're gone?"

"I'd like some of that raspberry vinaigrette salad dressing your mom got at the store the other day," her dad said.

The two men exchanged glances. Mark handed the salad bowl to Matt once more.

AMY CORNERED HER mom in the kitchen seconds later.

"Mom, what are you doing?" she stage-whispered. "Brandon must have mentioned to you that Matt's one of his best friends."

"Brandon has obviously been hit in the head one too many times, hasn't he?" her mother hissed.

Amy couldn't help it. Despite her embarrassment and frustration at her mom's behavior, she laughed.

"Does Emily know this is what you think about her one true love?"

"Don't sass me, Amy Margaret. There are other men. Better men. You should find one of them."

There was an expression in Amy's mother's eyes she'd never seen before. Meg was trying so hard to find fault with Matt, and Matt had been at his most charming since he set foot in her parents' house. She had to know she was fighting a losing battle, especially since Amy's dad and Matt bonded like old college buddies almost instantaneously.

"Mom, what if I like *him*? I want to keep seeing him." Mother and daughter stared at each other. "Please. Just give him a chance. If you still don't like him, I'll deal, but Mom, he didn't have to come over here and meet you and Daddy. He wanted to."

Her mother stared at the floor for a minute or so. She folded her lips together. Finally, she glanced up at Amy. "Okay." She let out a sigh. "If he says anything about teaching the arts in public schools being a waste of taxpayer dollars, though, all bets are off."

Amy gave her mom a gentle hug. "Got it."

Meg reached inside the refrigerator, grabbed the bottle of salad dressing, and marched back into the dining room.

MATT PICKED UP the bottle of pinot gris when they sat back down at the table and said, "Mrs. Hamilton, would you like a glass of wine?"

"Yes, I would, and Matt, please call me 'Meg,'" her mother said.

"I'd love to," he said. Her mom actually smiled at him. Amy stifled a sigh of relief.

"How did you and Amy meet?" Mark asked Matt.

Mark loaded his plate up with the remainder of the salad, and used a good amount of the raspberry vinaigrette over it. Amy noticed his serving of casserole was almost untouched.

"That's a funny story, Mark." Matt's smile was warm. "Amy and I met after Emily's wedding. She was having a couple of drinks."

"I was not," Amy protested. "I was having *a* drink."

Meg's head snapped up from her plate.

"Of course you were—"

Meg cut Matt off.

"We tried to call your room, and you didn't answer. Amy Margaret, what were you doing?"

Matt glanced up from his plate and caught Amy's eye. She could read his mind: *Amy Margaret*, huh?

"Mom. Everything was fine. I had a couple of drinks at the bar, Matt made sure I got back to my room safely, and then he left. It was nice of him to watch over me."

That wasn't the whole story, but if Amy's mother ever found out what really happened that night on the hotel balcony, they'd have to call 911. Meg was studying Matt with now-wary eyes. After all, he was evidently some kind of corrupting influence, and she wasn't happy about it.

"So, I made sure Amy was safely in her room for the

rest of the night. After that, I spent three weeks persuading her to go out with me."

"Three weeks?" her father said.

The previously distrustful look on Meg's face was replaced with warmth. "You must think she's pretty special," her mother said. For the first time since Matt walked into her parents' house, Meg gave him a heartfelt smile.

"Yes, Meg, she is. I'm very happy she finally said yes."

Her dad's brows knit in concentration. "Now I know who you are," he said to Matt.

"Daddy, what's wrong?"

"Brandon told me that you showed up at the hospital with Amy. What were you doing together at two o'clock in the morning?"

"I drove Amy there," Matt said.

"We had a date," Amy burst out. "We spent the night together."

Amy's father could live with Amy's mother, but just the idea that his daughter actually spent the night with a member of the opposite sex was enough to make him lose it. Both her parents were wide-eyed now.

"Amy Margaret Hamilton, how could you?" her mother gasped.

"Matt and I have a few things to discuss, young lady. Maybe you should be excused from the table."

"Dad, I'm an adult. I own a home and a business. I'm registered to vote, and I pay taxes. If I want to spend the night with a man, it's my business, isn't it?" Amy said.

"Honey," her mother pleaded. Amy's father pushed

his chair back from the table and got to his feet. Matt was still taller than he was.

"Mr. Stephens, I'd like to speak with you in the family room," her father said. He hooked his thumb toward the hallway, and Matt followed him out of the room.

AFTER AMY'S FATHER corralled Matt in the family room and demanded to know "his intentions," Matt drove Amy home. His relationship with both of her parents was a bit dented at the moment, but her dad backed off quite a bit when Matt told him—privately, of course—that he wouldn't be meeting her parents unless he planned to take his relationship with their daughter as far as it could go.

In other words, he knew he wasn't going anywhere, and now Mark Hamilton knew it, too. Matt would also be talking with Amy's mom about "his intentions" at his earliest opportunity.

He pulled into a parking place in front of a local pub he enjoyed. Hopefully, Amy would enjoy it, too. She needed more to eat than the cup or so of salad he'd seen vanish off her dinner plate. They stepped inside, seated themselves at a table, and ordered some food and drinks.

"See?" Amy's voice was miserable. "I told you. My mom is probably trying to get me signed up for some counseling session with the minister of their church right now. My dad actually asked me how long we dated before we slept together. What kind of question is *that*?"

To Amy's surprise, Matt let out a laugh.

"What is so freaking funny, Stephens? You're the one that was getting bitched out in there. Aren't you the least bit mad?"

Matt regarded her over his vegetarian burger.

"You know what? I'd do the same damn thing."

"You would not. You'd be calm, and you'd talk to the boy in question like an adult—"

"I'd have to resist the impulse to knock him into next week. My little girl? Nobody's touching her. I'm not even sure I'm going to let her get married, let alone have sex." Matt took another huge bite of his burger. "Absolutely not."

"You can't be serious."

He wiped his mouth with a napkin and helped himself to a swig of Amy's microbrew. "Oh, I am. I appreciated what your dad had to say. I didn't like it, but I like him, and I know why he did it. He wanted me to understand that he won't tolerate your being treated with disrespect."

Amy rolled her eyes. "I am a grown woman. Isn't it my idea what I do and whom I see?"

"Not to your dad, it isn't. You should be grateful, Fifi. I gotta hand it to him. He got in my face."

"So, what happens now?"

He wadded up the half-wrapper from his burger, dropped it in the middle of his empty plate, and took her hand.

"I think I'll stick around. I can't wait to see what you're going to do next."

Chapter Eighteen

A FEW DAYS after dinner with Amy's parents, Matt was pulling plates and silverware out of drawers in his kitchen to serve up the organic Mexican feast he'd stopped to get on the way home when he realized he hadn't heard her in the family room for at least ten minutes. Maybe she had to use the bathroom or something. Maybe she was watching the news. He darted out of the kitchen to see what she was up to.

Maybe nothing. She was fast asleep on his couch.

He moved closer. The glass of wine he'd poured sat untouched on the coffee table in front of her. She'd curled up with the throw some interior designer insisted he couldn't live without. The few minutes between twilight and nightfall cast her features in shadow, but he heard her deep, even breathing.

He sat down next to her. She didn't stir. He knew she was burning the candle at both ends these days, but this was insane. She fell asleep on the way home, too. Thank God he was driving. Between working at the shop and spending her evenings with him, Fifi was wearing herself out. She accepted his help with the delivery driver, but she was still resisting any other offers of assistance, which frustrated him.

He wondered how he could make her understand that seeing her like this brought back everything he remembered about his own childhood. He'd done his homework in the corner of a diner while his mom worked double shifts; she couldn't afford a babysitter. She had a second job as a cashier at a gas station until he was out of high school. He'd gotten a paper route as soon as he was old enough, but he couldn't make enough money to make a dent. She worked so many hours, but she got paid so little that keeping up with the bills and the groceries was a constant struggle. His mom never knew he'd seen her hiding her tears because she wasn't sure how she was going to pay the utility bill, or because the car needed fixing again.

He wasn't going to stand by and watch while another woman he cared for had a rough time financially, not if there was anything he could do to help.

He made sure his mom's bills were paid to this day. Samantha had half a million dollars in her college fund, and an additional trust fund which would kick in when she was 30. He wished Amy would let him shoulder some of her burdens, too.

He reached out to gather her close. She was warm. She smelled like the shampoo she used, fabric softener, and a whiff of some citrusy perfume he loved. She rubbed her mouth against the side of his neck as she snuggled against him.

"Sweetheart," he murmured. "You hungry?"

She jumped a little. "Oh. Oh!" She reached up to rub one eye, must have realized she was still wearing eye makeup, and tried to repair the damage with her fingertips. "I didn't mean to doze off."

"We didn't get a lot of sleep last night."

He saw her smile in the faint light from the kitchen. "No, we didn't, and somehow I'm fine with that." He had to grin. She tried unsuccessfully to stifle a yawn. "I guess this means we're not going to make the 9:30 show at Jazz Alley tonight."

"Probably not," he said.

She let out an amused snort. It was now a private joke. They'd been out for dinner or other public dates several times now, but they didn't cross the bridge into Seattle in the evenings. They hurried home at the first available opportunity, ending up in her bed, in his shower, or on the living room carpet instead. He wasn't complaining.

He couldn't get enough of her. It seemed she couldn't get enough of him, either. When they weren't making love, they were talking, or they watched rebroadcast football games on NFL Network. Her running commentary was hilarious.

He put his feet up on the coffee table. Maybe he should relax for a few minutes, too. "I realize it's a poor substitute for dinner in a white tablecloth restaurant, but I have a burrito bowl for you in the other room."

"I love burrito bowls." She leaned against him. "Is it bad to want to stay home and veg out on the couch when we've only been seeing each other for two weeks?"

"I thought the purpose of dating was meeting someone you'd like to stay home with."

"Well, then, we're overachievers, Sparky."

He rested his cheek against her hair. She laid one hand over his heart.

"Speaking of dating, Fifi, I have to go to Indianapolis for the NFL Combine next week. I was wondering if you'd like to come along."

He could hardly wait to see what she'd think of the most high-stakes job interview in professional sports. Any football fan would spend the weekend gorging on all things NFL. Maybe he could get her into some of the behind-the-scenes stuff. She'd love it. Sure enough, she almost jumped into his lap with excitement.

"The Combine? You'd take me there?"

"Of course. We'll have to leave on Wednesday, and we'll be back on Monday night. I'm interviewing some of the draft picks and coaches for PSN. We'll fly in the corporate jet, have some expense account dinners. It'll be fun." He leaned back against the couch cushions. "I'll make sure they have plenty of tequila for you."

He felt her stiffen against him. He hoped she wasn't mad about a gentle joke. Maybe she was cold. He pulled the blanket around her. She sat up and looked into his eyes.

"I can't go."

"Why not?"

"I can't be away from the shop for that long."

"It's just Wednesday through Saturday. You're closed Sunday and Monday. Estelle and Scott can handle it for a few days." He reached up to stroke her cheek. "Couldn't we find a shop babysitter or something? I want you with me."

"I want to be there too. I can't leave things alone for so long, though. It's not just the walk-in business. It's wedding planning season. I have to be there to take those orders. If Estelle and Scott get overwhelmed, there's nobody to help. I've been open less than a year, and being closed six days in a row right now would be disastrous for my business. Customers find out you're closed, and they go somewhere else."

"Got it." He stifled his disappointment. "Maybe next year, huh?"

"By next year, I'll have more employees. Next year, it would be great. Thank you for asking me, though. It sounds like so much fun. I've watched it on TV so many times, and I never thought I'd actually get to go."

She'd forgotten her exhaustion for a few minutes and was talking excitedly about the things and people she wished she could see at the combine. Other guys' girlfriends lost it over a piece of fine jewelry, a shopping trip to New York City, or a weekend in Paris. The woman in his life would be ecstatic watching football practice.

He couldn't wipe the grin off his face.

ONE WEEK LATER, he boarded the PSN jet with his iPad and a tote bag Amy left for him before she went to her shop that morning. She made him promise he wouldn't look inside till he was on the plane.

"There's nothing illegal in here, is there?"

"Of course not." She threw her arms around his neck. "I'll miss you when you're gone."

"I'll miss you, too. I'll be home Monday night. I promise."

He still felt her softness against him and the sweet scents he breathed in whenever she was near. He couldn't imagine facing the next six days alone. Maybe he should call her when he got to the hotel, just to say hi. She'd probably think he was whipped. Truth be told, he didn't give a shit if he was.

The pilot announced over the PA that they were cleared for takeoff. Harry McCord, Hall of Fame defensive end and one of Matt's co-workers, glanced over at the tote bag in Matt's lap.

"Someone must have packed you a lunch, Stephens. Maybe she pinned a dollar in your shorts for milk money."

"That would mean I'm actually wearing shorts," Matt said.

McCord looked annoyed, yet one more thing Matt didn't give a shit about. McCord had a bad habit of sticking his nose where it didn't belong. He didn't bother with basic manners, and Matt returned the favor. He imagined anyone else would call it a "personality conflict," but mostly, McCord went out of his way to piss people off— especially Matt.

Matt waited till the jet climbed to cruising altitude, set the bag down on the seat next to him, and reached inside.

His fingers brushed an envelope. He pulled it out and slid a fingertip under the flap to open it.

Matt, I thought you might need a snack or two for your trip. Just in case you're wondering, I made the cookies with organic peanut butter.

I'll be thinking of you. I miss you already. Fifi

He slid the note back inside the envelope and glanced inside the bag. A disposable plastic container filled with cookies. A produce bag with an apple, a pear, a peach, and a half a pound or so of cherries. A lacy, silky red thong.

He slid the envelope back into the bag, zipped the top, and pulled out his iPad. He was going to give Miss Fifi something to think about while he was gone, too.

MATT HAD BEEN in Indianapolis only forty-eight hours, and Amy missed him like she'd miss an appendage. She'd hardly slept last night. Her pillowcase still smelled like him, but it wasn't enough. She couldn't cuddle with a goldfish. She finally resorted to hugging the pillow until she drifted off for a few hours.

Things were crazy at her shop, too. She could hear the "chirp" of texts received on her smart phone as she worked, but she didn't have time to look at them. She heard the bells jingle on the shop's front door as the FedEx guy walked in. He held up a medium-sized box. She put her shears down for a few seconds to sign for it.

"Thanks," she said, and she took the package out of his hands. He left, and she continued to stare at the box.

It was light, too light to be ribbon or enclosure cards. There were only initials in the upper left-hand corner, and she wasn't familiar with the mailing address. She was tempted to leave it on the workbench while she started the next arrangement, but curiosity got the best of her. She opened the Fed Ex box to reveal a much more luxurious box inside. It was a vivid pink, wrapped with black satin ribbon tied into a gorgeous bow. The top of the box read "Agent Provocateur."

She glanced around. Estelle was on a coffee break. She untied the bow, pulled the lid off of the box, and let out a gasp. A delicate pink and black lace slip was nestled in a bed of barely tinted pink tissue paper. She lifted it out of the box. The straps were thin black ribbons that ended in bows. The cups of the bra were the palest pink lace. The bodice was sheer, and the skirt was flounces of Chantilly lace and tulle. Hopefully she wouldn't snag something so beautiful and delicate on her work-roughened fingertips. The tiniest pair of panties she'd ever seen lay undisturbed in the tissue paper along with an envelope that read "Amy."

She pulled a notecard out of the envelope.

They named these after you, Fifi.

You are more beautiful.

Matt

Four days later Amy stood at Matt's front door in the trench coat she hadn't worn since she left her corporate job and a pair of Emily's stilettos. She knew Matt was home; he'd texted her from the Town Car that dropped him off half an hour ago. Samantha was spending the evening with her grandma.

Amy had spent the last two evenings practicing walking in the loaned pair of stilettos. She hardly had any bruises as a result, and last night she was really getting the hang of it. She made it from the van to his front door without wiping out. All she had to do was make it over the threshold of his house.

She tapped at the door. Matt pulled it open seconds later.

"I've missed you so much," he said. The joy on his face made her heart leap. He reached out for her and attempted to pull her inside.

One of Emily's heels snagged in the doormat.

"Ow!"

"You're wearing heels? Since when do you wear heels?" he asked, trying to disentangle her from the rubber doormat's surprisingly tenacious grip on the shoe.

"I wanted to surprise you—*ow*!" She yanked her foot out of the shoe and pulled away from him. "Now the surprise is spoiled. Why can everyone else manage heels, and I'm just a big mess in them? I don't get it. I—"

Matt's mouth covered hers. He was already working on the trench coat's belt with impatient hands. He stopped kissing her long enough to say, "If this is what I think it is, I'm enjoying it already."

"The panties," she whispered into his ear. "They— They're so teeny. I can't get them off by myself."

She managed to shut his front door with one elbow, yanked the trench coat off, and dropped it at her feet. She wore nothing but one shoe, toenail polish, a spritz of Jo

Malone's Orange Blossom, and the panties he'd sent her. He looked, and then he stared.

She bit her lower lip and glanced up at him. He seemed a bit awestruck.

"This is the best day of my life," he said. "Don't move."

He grabbed the heel out of the mat, shut and locked the door, and knelt at her feet to slip Emily's shoe on her foot again. Seconds later, he scooped her up in his arms, and carried her to his room.

Chapter Nineteen

ANOTHER SUNDAY AFTERNOON, another trip to meet the parents, or in his case, *parent*. Six days after Matt arrived home from the NFL combine, he pulled up in front of a modest-looking, white ranch-style house with blue-gray shutters and a green enameled front door. Roses climbed a trellis on one corner. The small garden in the perfectly mowed front yard was weeded, edged and staked to an inch of its life.

"Ready?" Matt got out, came around to Amy's side of the car, and opened the door. "She doesn't bite," he assured her, and laid his hand in the middle of her back as they walked up the path.

"I'll bet you say that to all the women."

MATT RANG THE doorbell, and Amy resisted the impulse to fidget.

"Keep your pants on!" a voice shouted from inside the house. "I'll *be* there!"

"That's my mama," Matt murmured. Amy took another deep breath.

The door swung open and framed a tall, slightly rounded woman with long, teased, carefully sprayed black hair, a makeup application that didn't skimp, and the most gold jewelry Amy had ever seen outside of a jeweler's shop. Matt had led her to believe that his mother was a fragile, modest, and conservative older woman. Evidently, he'd lied. She wore stretch jeans, spike heels, and a hot pink tunic made out of a shiny fabric that accentuated her cleavage.

"Are you coming in?" she asked her son.

"I don't know. Am I?" Matt moved forward and wrapped his arms around her. "So, hot stuff, how's the terror of the gardening club doing these days?"

"Honey, those women need to either get laid or buy a Harley. Talk about wound tightly. Who's your friend?"

Matt reached out to pull Amy over the threshold. "Mama, this is Amy. Amy, this is my mom, Pauline."

Amy stuck out her hand, but Pauline brushed it aside. "What's that crap? I need a hug."

Amy was enveloped in a wave of old-fashioned scent she should have known but couldn't immediately place. Pauline stroked her hair.

"Matty, you are so predictable. A blonde. When are you going to date a redhead? I'm telling you, for what you're in the market for, you want a redhead."

Amy laughed before she could stop herself. She'd met Matt's mom less than five minutes before, but it was evident that the filter that most people seemed to have between their brain and their mouths wasn't standard equipment with Pauline. Behind the makeup and the thick fan of fake eyelashes, Pauline's eyes were the same navy blue as her son's. He had her smile, too. Pauline was tall, but Matt was still a head taller than she was. He wrapped his arm around Pauline's shoulders.

"So, what's for lunch? Ritz Crackers and Cheez Whiz?" Matt was glaring at a stack of envelopes on the hallway table, for some unknown reason. "And what are these?"

"You must have me confused with one of those fancy restaurants you like to go to. You know damn well I don't cook. Maybe you should take your poor mama out for a bite to eat once in a while."

"You like to go to 'family restaurants,'" Matt said, making air quotes with both hands. "Maybe we should go somewhere there isn't a kiddie menu for a change."

"Matty, those aren't my people. I don't like *nouvelle cuisine*, or stuff I can't pronounce. Plus, those guys you work with would just die if they found out you spent ten minutes at the IHOP." She turned to Amy. "He probably takes you all those fancy places, too, doesn't he? Amy, you look like a woman who'd like a medium-rare steak and a beer. How do you feel about the Sizzler?"

"It's pretty good."

Amy knew it might be best to keep the information she'd never been to Sizzler to herself. She studied a black velvet painting of Elvis Presley wearing a white fringed jumpsuit in the hallway of Pauline's immaculate house. Pauline's house was cozy. She'd bought the kind of overstuffed, plaid-upholstered furniture that was popular in the last century with people who were raising a lot of kids. The back of her couch was draped in a multi-colored afghan Pauline had knit herself, judging by the selection of yarn and needles in a tote nearby. Amy wondered what the neighbors thought of her décor ideas.

"I like her already," Pauline told her son. She held out her hand to Amy. "C'mon, honey. Let's go open a couple of cold ones, and Mr. High and Mighty here can make up his mind where he's feeding us today."

Besides being an Elvis fan, Pauline really liked Harley-Davidson. Her kitchen was bedecked with chrome and Harley insignia-laden items. A framed photo of Pauline on the back of what must have been her Fat Boy hung over the kitchen table. She reached into the refrigerator and pulled out three Bud Lights. "Church key." She grabbed the bottle opener off the front of the fridge, opened all three, and handed one to Amy.

"Mom," Matt made a face. "I bought you some Pyramid Hefeweizen. What'd you do with it?"

"I served it to those snotty country club bitches you sent over here." Her lips curved into a smug grin. "I'm sure they thought I couldn't even pronounce "microbrewery," let alone buy some beer from one. Why did you ever think I'd want to belong to a country club?"

"*Mom.*" Matt was suddenly transformed into what Amy imagined he must have been like as a teenager. "There's some people there who ride. You might like them. Plus, it's a good place for you to meet people and get out of the backyard once in a while. Just give it a chance," he pleaded.

Pauline ticked off her objections on long, airbrushed fingernails. "They don't like me. They don't like my clothes. I *know* they think I wear too much makeup. I get out. I ride on the weekends. I've known those Harley folks for a long time. Plus, they don't bug me for game tickets or your autograph."

"*What*? Who did this?" It was interesting to watch as Matt's expression changed. He evidently believed someone was mistreating his mother, and he wasn't going to stand for that.

"Matty, you don't seem to understand. My name is Stephens. Your name is Stephens. There are people who remember seeing me at your games, and they still see you every Sunday on that pre-game show. They think they can get to know you through your ma." She took a long swallow of beer and leaned toward Amy. "You'd hate 'em, too."

Amy liked the business she got from Seattle's Eastside, but dealing with some of its young, wealthy housewives could be trying at times for a woman whose schedule consisted of a few other tasks besides a workout, lunch, and squeezing in a Botox injection before instructing the nanny to pick the kids up from school.

"Maybe we should let Matty go find something else to do, and I'll take you to Target. Do you like that place?" Pauline said.

Obviously, Matt's mom liked to shop.

"Yeah, I do. I'm not rich, so the price is usually right," Amy said.

"We can get some chicken tenders or something when we're done. What do you think?"

Amy opened her mouth to tell Pauline, "Yeah," and Matt spoke before she could.

"Mom. I wanted to take you to lunch so you could get to know Amy."

"We can go shopping. There's no law that says we have to take you. Plus, we'll spend two hours fighting off every football fan in the store."

"People hardly recognize me anymore—"

"Matthew Thomas Stephens, that is a lie and you know it. Amy and I are going to Target for a couple of hours. Why don't you go hit a bucket of balls and have one of those microbrews you like so much, and we'll meet you at Claim Jumper in Redmond?"

"I hate that place—"

"You hate everywhere there's chicken fried steak and a portion that'll actually feed someone." She patted his cheek, and dropped her empty beer bottle in a small recycling tub beneath a writing desk in the corner of the kitchen. "We'll call you when we're done." She propelled Amy out to the garage. "Love you!"

The last thing Amy saw before the door slammed was Matt's mouth dropping open.

PAULINE SLID BEHIND the wheel of a fire engine–red Cadillac STS.

"Matt bought this damn car for me. I wanted a Mustang. He said I'd race." She raised one heavily penciled and perfectly arched eyebrow. "I can race in a Cadillac." She hit the button on the garage door opener, and backed out of the driveway. Amy saw Matt crossing the yard to his Mercedes. "Look at that. I told him if he bought me a Mercedes, I'd just drive it into Lake Washington. I didn't want a BMW, either." She let out a sniff. "What do you drive, Amy?"

Amy watched Matt staring after them in the side mirror as Pauline drove away. She wondered if his mom had done this before. "I have a minivan. I also use it for my business."

"Do you have any kids?"

"No." A bit of explanation might be nice. After all, a minivan wasn't the typical ride of choice for a single woman. "I'm a florist. I use the back for deliveries. Plus, it's nice to ride around in."

"It's probably American-made, too. I like that." She hit the "on" button for her radio. She evidently liked oldies. "You own a business?"

"Yes. I own Crazy Daisy. It's on Capitol Hill."

"I love flowers," she sighed. "Matt sent me flowers from your shop."

"He sent every woman he's ever met flowers from my shop."

She shot Amy a quick grin. "Sounds like a story I need to hear."

Pauline and Amy spent the next two hours wandering through Target. She filled a cart. Amy bought some socks. They settled at a table in the food court, chatting over burgers and fries.

Pauline squirted a little more ketchup over her fries, glanced over at Amy, and said, "So, you like my son, huh?"

"I enjoy his company."

"You've met Samantha."

"Yes, and she's wonderful. You must be crazy about her."

A soft light came into Pauline's eyes. "Yeah. I am. She's a good girl. We have fun together. She stays with me for the weekend every month or so. We get the girly works: manicures, pedicures, the whole thing. She tried to give me a makeover last weekend." Her smile was wistful. "If I would have known a granddaughter was this much fun, I would have had her first."

"It sounds like you have a great time together." They both glanced down at their food for a minute. Pauline set a tankard-sized cup of Diet Coke on the table.

"We do." She met Amy's eyes. "Listen. I like you a lot. You're a lot different than the women Matty usually dates, and that's good. They pretend to like me, they don't laugh at my Elvis pictures and my motorcycle stuff, and maybe that's the best I could hope for. At the same time, I've always hoped he'd meet someone that might be willing to have a few more of those grandkids for me."

"I want kids," Amy assured her.

"I know you do, or you wouldn't be caught dead driving a minivan, flower shop or no flower shop." Pauline played with a french fry. "I have to tell you, though; I'm going to give you the same speech I've given every last one of them."

Amy took a sip of her soda. This didn't sound good. Pauline looked like she was gearing up for a lecture. Even more, the expression in her eyes was a bit sad.

"It's been just Matty and me for a long time now, Amy. His daddy left us when Matty was two. I loved that man, but I knew right then I never wanted to marry again. I wanted to know I had the cash to be independent, so I worked until two years ago. Matty's always felt guilty about it." She let out a sigh. "He wants to fix everything for someone he loves. I love him with all my heart, but I'm the first one to admit he can be a real handful at times."

Amy covered her mouth with one hand to hide her smile.

"If I could pick out the perfect woman for Matty, she'd be someone who isn't bowled over by who he is or the fact he's on TV. She'd be his partner, instead of being someone who gets her entire identity from being with him. She'd be someone who's smart and ambitious enough to have something to call her own. Something that absorbs her." Pauline took another sip of her soda. "I really love Laura, but she didn't learn to stand on her own two feet until after their marriage was over."

Amy sat up straighter in her chair. "I—I have my own goals. I'm working toward them every day."

"Talk's cheap, Amy. If you let him rescue you every time things fall apart, then I'll know you're no different than the rest of them. If you make it on your own, I'll know you are. He needs someone that's as strong as he is."

Amy wasn't sure if Pauline was insulting her, or giving her advice. She really wasn't sure what to say. She took a deep breath and clasped her hands on the tabletop.

"I think you'll find I'll succeed on my own, Pauline. I wouldn't even let my family help me."

"Every last one of his girlfriends and his ex-wife ran to him when things weren't going well, sweetie. He likes to take care of the people he cares about. He doesn't think it's a big deal. It is, though. He doesn't let them make their own mistakes, and he won't let them stand or fail on their own, either."

Pauline gave Amy a nod and started stacking the trash from the table on the tray the food had arrived on. Amy took one last swallow of soda, wrapped her leftovers in a napkin, and rose to dump it in the garbage can. She dumped the tray's contents as well. Pauline studied her for a few seconds, and rose from the seat. The stacked bracelets she wore jingled in the momentary silence.

"Let's go find Matty. He's probably asking the bartender at the restaurant if they have wheatgrass juice or some damn thing."

The car ride to Claim Jumper was mostly silent, but Amy knew she had to speak up before they rejoined Matt.

"Pauline, there's some things you need to know about me."

She pulled into a parking place in front of the restaurant, shut off the car, and turned to Amy. "Okay. Shoot."

"I'm Emily Hamilton McKenna's sister, and Brandon McKenna's sister-in-law. My sister is a diva. She's internationally famous. I've been living with her success for years now."

"I know Brandon. I haven't met your sister yet."

"I'm sure you'll understand when I say I have lots of experience with family members who have huge personalities and sign autographs as part of their jobs. I'm happy for Emily and Brandon, but it wasn't what I wanted. I was a CPA before I started doing this. I saved until I could start a business with my own financing. More than anything else, I want something that's mine." She stared into Pauline's eyes. "I care for your son. I'd like a partner in life, too, and I want someone who's as self-motivated as I am. He's pursuing me, not the other way around." Amy paused to take another breath before she continued, "I don't need to sign autographs or show up on TV to feel good about myself and my achievements. I'd like to think that you and I could be friends, especially if I'm going to continue seeing Matt."

"It's not just Matty," Pauline said. "It's Samantha, too. They're a package deal. Can you handle that?"

"I wouldn't have it any other way," Amy said. She reached out for the door handle, and got out of the car. "Let's go get some onion rings. My treat."

Chapter Twenty

CRAZY DAISY WAS insanely busy with upcoming wedding orders and the usual business, but Amy had a very special invitation: Samantha had asked her to come to her basketball game this afternoon. Matt had sweetened the deal by inviting her out to dinner afterward, too. They'd been officially dating for one month today. After making sure Estelle could handle it on her own for a couple of hours, Amy savored the idea of a little free time and Samantha's elation when she said, "I'll be there."

She and Matt were currently walking through the parking lot of the same school he'd also attended, once upon a time.

"The gym's over this way," he said.

Matt's fingertips closed around Amy's elbow. He didn't seem to notice some of the other parents turning to stare at him, or the flirtatious smiles from women who seemed to have nothing better to do than to give him the eye. He was with her. Obviously, they'd seen him before today.

"If Emily was here, she'd be laughing at them," Amy muttered, realizing one second too late she'd spoken aloud.

"What's that, Fifi? Talking to yourself again?" he joked. She curled her lip in response.

"They had their chance," she said.

Matt laughed out loud. More people turned to stare at them. She wasn't going to put the smackdown on the women who obviously found Matt fascinating, but she pulled her elbow from his fingers and took his hand instead.

He squeezed her fingers in his. "Holding my hand?"

She tilted her chin up. "Maybe."

He grazed the top of her head with his lips and slid his arm around her shoulders. "That'll fix them."

"What are you talking about?"

"You're giving those women over there with their mouths hanging open something to stare at, aren't you?" He pulled her a little closer. "I like it. Let's make out." They came to a halt a short distance from the gym doors, and Amy leaned into his chest.

"That must be what the kids are calling it these days," she said.

She took a deep breath. He smelled like clean skin, freshly washed cotton, and a hint of outrageously expensive cologne. She rested her cheek against his, feeling the scrape of his omnipresent five o'clock shadow. This was a little public for the kind of spit-swapping Matt had in mind.

"Then again, if I get into some kind of clinch with you on school grounds, the nuns will kick my ass," he said.

"You were in the NFL for eleven years, but nuns scare you?" Amy watched Matt glancing around as if he expected a ruler to hit his knuckles any minute.

"Oh, hell, yeah. My mom had a rough time paying for a private all-boys school, but she was determined I was going to stay away from girls long enough to actually learn something."

"So, did you?"

"Did I what?"

"Learn something," Amy said.

His voice dropped. "I'll show you later." She shivered a little.

He reached out to pull the gym door open for Amy, and they glanced around the bleachers. Laura Stephens stood and waved at them.

"Come on. She's saved us a seat."

Amy wasn't sure about sitting with Matt's ex-wife, but it appeared she was going to be doing exactly that. Matt and Laura seemed to be friendly. If she wanted to spend time with Matt, she'd be dealing with not only Samantha, but her mom, too.

Amy had never dated anyone before who had a child from a previous relationship. It was an adjustment which sometimes left her bewildered. She spent most of her time with Matt when Samantha was visiting her mom. It seemed he'd like to slowly bring his daughter into the mix, and Amy hoped Samantha would see her as an ally and friend instead of competition for her dad's affections.

"Are you sure this is okay?" Amy said into Matt's ear.

Matt tugged her up the bleacher stairs. He stopped next to Laura, kissed her on the cheek, and pulled Amy forward. "Laura, this is Amy."

"We've met before. It's good to see you again, Amy." Amy wasn't sure what to expect, but Laura reached out to give her a hug. "Samantha really likes you."

Amy hugged her back. "I like her, too."

Matt was glancing around for Samantha. "Where's my little girl?"

"Chill out, Dad. She'll be here in a minute," Laura said.

Amy crawled over Matt's knees to sit down on his other side. The gym smelled like any other gym she'd ever been in—musty, with an overlay of cleaning products and sweat. She was favorably impressed at the sheer numbers of parents who'd turned out to see a junior varsity game.

Laura pulled a video camera out of her purse, switched it on, and trained it on the basketball court where both teams were warming up. Samantha seemed to be pointedly ignoring her parents as she trotted around the court. The whistle blew, and she glanced into the bleachers as she sat down on the bench, surrounded by her teammates.

"She saw us," Matt told Amy. "She's pretending like she's not happy we're here."

"Does this happen often?" Amy asked. She was a little mystified. Samantha invited her to come to the game, and now she was ignoring the adults? Maybe it was a teenage thing.

Matt and Laura looked at each other, and Laura reached out and patted his knee.

"It depends on the day. Her friends are embarrassed that their parents are here, so she's embarrassed, too." Laura rolled her eyes. "When we go home later, she's going to snuggle up with me on the couch and watch TV."

The teams assembled on the court. Samantha snatched the ball, dribbled down the court, banking the ball off the backboard and into the hoop like she was trying out for the WNBA. Matt beamed.

"One scholarship to UConn, coming right up," he said.

"You'd have heart failure if she chose that school," Laura told him. "She's not going anywhere outside the state of Washington."

"Don't you want to see our little princess in March Madness?"

"Again, you're on drugs, Matt Stephens." Laura leaned forward to lock eyes with Amy. "There will be significant financial bribery to keep her here, at least through undergrad."

"That's not true," Matt assured Amy. "I want her to pick the school she wants."

Laura let out a snort but concentrated on her video camera. Amy watched Samantha and her teammates run up and down the court. It was already looking like a rout. The girls from Samantha's school were scoring at will, were bigger, and were defending their end of the court with ease.

"Isn't there some kind of mercy rule?" Amy asked nobody in particular.

"The coach will slow this down," Matt assured her. The coach in question had just gotten to his feet and gestured to the referee for a time-out. "They don't allow the 67-10 beatings we took in middle school basketball anymore."

"Yeah, I got my butt kicked in basketball, too." Amy leaned forward. "Hey, Laura, did you play?"

"I was a cheerleader. My boyfriend was on the team, though." Laura fiddled with the video camera. "I thought I charged the batteries in this thing . . ."

Matt took it out of her hand. "Let me see." He flipped it upside down, pulled the battery out, put it back in, switched the device on and handed it back to Laura. "Fixed it."

"Thanks." She resumed filming.

Matt turned to Amy.

"How do you feel about seafood?"

"Okay, I guess."

"Great. We're going to the Brazilian steak place." He turned back to watch the game.

SAMANTHA'S GAME ENDED with a final score of 45-20. The last several minutes consisted of her team dribbling up and down the court, and the starters sitting on the bench. Even though it was a bad loss, the other team exchanged fist-bumps and hugs with Samantha and her teammates.

Laura, Matt, and Amy left the bleachers and waited

on the court for Samantha to sidle over to them. She wrapped her arms around her dad's waist.

"Can we go to Pagliacci Pizza? Please? It's sick." She rubbed her face against Matt's shirt. "You like the chop-chop salad, too."

"Not tonight, princess. You're going home with your mom, and we'll spend some time together tomorrow."

The previously excited Samantha's face fell like the Dow. "I thought I was coming to your house tonight." She fixed Amy with a stare. "We were going to go to Frankie's Pizza and Pasta when we talked about it."

Laura reached out to rub Samantha's back. "We can stop at the Dilettante Café on the way home and pick up some dessert for after dinner. How's that?"

Samantha didn't respond to her mother. She was too busy looking up at Matt as if he'd just run over her designer handbag. "But I thought I was going home with you," she protested.

Laura reached out for her daughter as Matt detached himself from her.

"You'll see me tomorrow night." He ruffled her hair. "We'll have fun. I'm looking forward to it."

"I'm staying over at Cindy's tomorrow night!" She was getting progressively more agitated. Her mom was saying something into her ear; Samantha pulled away from her and folded both arms over her chest.

Matt's voice was hard.

"I understand that you are disappointed, Samantha, but you will not be rude to your mother. You need to apologize."

Amy watched the typically smiling and confident Samantha regress into someone much younger in seconds. "But I miss you. I haven't seen you for a week." She glared at him. "You're going out on a date. What about *me*? Aren't I important, too?"

Matt pulled his car keys out of his pocket and put them into Amy's hand. "I'll be with you in a few minutes. I'm sorry for the wait."

Laura glanced over at Amy and shook her head. Laura's eyes said it all: *Teenage tantrum. It'll pass.*

"Laura, it was nice to see you again."

"Nice to see you, too." Laura watched her daughter with a bemused expression. Amy remembered being a teenager. She also remembered the punishments she got when she acted out. It seemed Samantha was about to receive one, too.

Samantha was in the midst of what looked like a fairly serious whispered conversation between herself and her dad; she stomped her foot, and Matt took her elbow in his hand. She was about to be escorted out, it seemed.

"Goodbye, Samantha. Great game," Amy called out to her.

"Bye, Amy," she responded.

Her expression spoke louder than anything she could have said. Amy knew Samantha wanted her dad to find someone special to fall in love with and maybe give her a few siblings while he was at it. At the same time, she'd had her dad's undivided attention for the past fourteen years. It was a big adjustment, and it might take some time.

It looked like the next few minutes weren't going to be fun for Samantha. Her face registered such hurt and anger. Anything Amy said or did wasn't going to help. Then again, she could try.

Amy had been heading toward the double doors that led to the school's parking lot. She spun on one heel and walked back to Samantha. Samantha, Laura, and Matt stopped talking and glanced over at her.

"Hey, Samantha, I have an idea, if it's okay with your mom." She jingled Matt's car keys. "Maybe we should go out for pizza and invite your dad along. What do you think?"

Laura and Matt exchanged glances. He didn't look especially happy, but he let go of Samantha's elbow. The smile spread across Samantha's face like sunshine after a torrential downpour. "Best idea *ever*! Let's go." She reached out for Amy's hand. "I'm starving. Are you hungry? They have this really sick pizza that's all white."

SAMANTHA WAS STILL jabbering away. It sounded like she was giving Amy the rundown on Pagliacci Pizza's entire menu. Matt listened to her excitedly telling Amy about some pizza with pears and God knows what else on it. He was glad she seemed to be a bit happier now, but he knew there was going to be a discussion about her behavior later.

Samantha learned a long time ago it was best to not play him and Laura off against each other to get what she wanted. She'd end up with a punishment instead. She was about to learn the same lessons with Amy, but he wasn't sure how to convey them without pissing Amy off. He knew she was only trying to help. He knew she was nervous about showing Samantha she wasn't a threat or competition for his affection. At the same time, he wasn't especially happy with Amy's contradicting him right now, either.

His ex-wife moved a short distance away from their daughter and his date and beckoned him over. She lowered his voice. "Hey, I don't mean to start something here, but Amy didn't do that to piss you off."

"I wish she'd discussed it with me first. Samantha probably thinks it's going to work for her if she tries it again."

"Let's be happy she seems to enjoy our daughter's company," Laura said. "Did you, or did you not tell Samantha that you'd have pizza with her later? I seem to remember you telling her this three days ago, Matt. You double-booked yourself, and Sam wanted her to come along, too."

Matt blew out a breath. Good thing he talked to Laura before he went apeshit over what he saw as Amy's trying to interfere in his parenting again.

Laura stowed the video cam in her shoulder bag. "So, let your daughter and your girlfriend take you out for pizza. Talk to Amy later. If you two are going to stay together, you're going to have to discuss all this stuff."

"If I didn't know any better, I'd say you want this to happen."

Laura stared at the floor for a minute or so, and looked

into his eyes again. "No matter what happened between us, Matt, you're not a bad guy."

He still remembered how much he loved her when they married. He remembered the laughter, their happy family of three, and the certainty they would be together for the rest of their lives. He also remembered the knife in his gut when he discovered she wanted someone else more. It took years, but he knew their marriage wasn't meant to be, and he couldn't hate her. Their friendship was built slowly as a result.

He hoped Amy could accept the fact he'd always have a bond with Laura. They shared a daughter. He'd like to believe he'd learned enough from the crash and burn of his first marriage to make sure he wouldn't make the same mistakes a second time. He was encouraged by the fact Laura thought enough of Amy she'd stick up for her.

"Thanks for the ringing endorsement, Laura. You're not so bad yourself."

He saw the smile creep over her lips. She patted him on the back. "I'll see you both tomorrow."

Laura walked over to hug and kiss their daughter goodbye. She hugged Amy, too. Matt was ambushed by an overly excited Samantha while he watched Laura walk away from them, alone.

Chapter Twenty-One

SEVERAL DAYS AFTER her pizza date with Matt and Samantha, Amy stared at the stack of bills on her worktable and glanced at the balance left in her business account. She was getting orders—a lot of them—but service on her debt load was killing any progress she made. She'd been sitting here for a while now. After all, she was closed for the day. Estelle and Scott had gone home, and she could brood in private.

Amy wasn't sure what to do, but there was one thing—actually, one *person*—she needed: Matt. She wanted the comfort of his arms around her, the broad shoulder to lay her head on. She told him that afternoon that she had bookwork at the shop and she probably wouldn't see him tonight as a result.

She couldn't believe she was doing it, but she let herself out of the shop, locked up, and threw herself into the driver's seat of the van.

The trip across the 520 bridge wasn't bad after seven o'clock at night. Unfortunately, though, it offered time to think. It wasn't the best idea to go running to Matt like a little girl who'd fallen down and skinned a knee. He'd already expressed reservations about the amount of hours she worked and the fact she was tired most of the time as a result. He had no idea about the continuing money issues; Well, she hoped he didn't anyway.

It was her business, damn it, and she could handle it herself. She couldn't fall apart any time something went wrong. Adversity would always be part of owning a small business. The worries about where the money was coming from every month, even with the added business, were wearing a hole in her spirit.

She didn't sleep well. She didn't eat much. She worried all the time. Maybe Matt was right about the toll stress was taking on her, and it was better to go back to the way things were. Get another accounting job and have a boss. The risk would be on whomever it was she worked for. Amy was so unhappy working in the corporate world, but she had something outside of the office to look forward to. Right now she wanted a break, even if just for a little while.

She pulled into the driveway at Matt's, shut off the van, and sat behind the wheel. She hadn't even called him first, which was rude. Maybe she could rest for a few minutes, and then she'd turn around and go back home. She closed her eyes.

A few minutes later, Amy heard tapping on the driver's side window, and Matt's voice.

"Hey, Fifi, are you coming in? Want a beer?"

"Thanks, but I'll just go home," she assured him. "I should have called you first. You're probably busy." She scrubbed her face with her hands.

He pulled open the driver's side door. She threw herself into his arms.

"Hey. Hey. What's this?" he said.

"I—oh, forget it," she muttered.

Amy tried to pull away from him. He didn't let go. He stroked her hair, he kissed the top of her head, and she blinked back the tears.

"Let's go inside." He tucked her inside his arm. "Bad day at the office?"

She tried to answer him, but she could only manage an unintelligible sound. She pressed her face into his chest. He walked her through the front door of his house, down the hallway, and steered her out onto the deck that overlooked the lake. She glanced up long enough to note that the neighbor's swans were out cruising around in the water. Matt sat her down on a porch swing.

"When did you get this?" Amy indicated the swing.

"Does it matter? What's going on?"

Matt wrapped his arms around her again, and she realized she couldn't speak or she was going to cry. Her chin quivered. Her lips trembled. If she could get it all under control, she wouldn't make a fool of herself by crying like a two-year-old. Matt didn't seem to realize this, however.

"Come here." He pressed her head down onto his shoulder. His warm breath brushed her face. "It's just me. I promise I won't tell anyone that the iron woman cried."

Amy swallowed hard. He rocked them back and forth, rested his scratchy cheek against her forehead, and the hot tears finally overflowed. "So, are you going to tell me what's wrong?"

She sniffled, and let out a sob. "Shhh. Everything's going to be fine," he crooned.

"You're being so nice," she managed to choke out.

"I'm a nice guy. I'm just misunderstood," he assured her. She couldn't stop the laugh that burbled out of her. "See? There's that grin. Things aren't so bad."

He took her face in his hands and touched his lips to each tear. "We'll get through this." Little by little she relaxed against him.

"Matt?"

"Yes, Fifi?"

"I'm afraid I screwed everything up."

"Everything? It can't be everything." His voice was gentle. "Maybe I can help."

She stiffened against him. She didn't want him to rescue her. She just wanted him to listen. Why couldn't he seem to understand this?

"No. I can handle it. I have to do this myself."

He held her silently until she relaxed again. "Why don't you tell me what's happening, and we can discuss it?"

"You don't have to fix it."

"I'll just listen. I promise. I might have to kiss you, too. That's okay, right?"

She nodded, wiped tears off her face with both hands, and rooted around in her jacket pocket for a tissue. If she sat up she could discuss things like a somewhat competent adult. Right now, though, she wanted to lose herself in the comfort of his big, warm body, the arms wrapped around her, the lips that were inches from hers. She longed to hold him, and be held in return.

She let out another sigh. "The shop is doing well, but it's not doing well enough. I'm afraid I'm going to have to look for an investor."

"Why do you think you need additional funds?"

"I hired a driver. I hired a designer. I couldn't keep up with the work. I think I need another designer, but I don't have money for that right now." She closed her eyes as she wadded up the Kleenex in her hands. "I didn't have it in my plan to hire anyone for at least another few months while I built up capital, and I have two people now. I had to replace the van. Just the paint job cost a butt load. I replaced the cooler, too, and that wasn't cheap. I could take it out of my savings—"

"No. You never take business expenses out of your own money, Amy."

She moved away from him; he pulled her close again.

"Okay. I forgot. I'm not supposed to comment." He kissed the tip of her nose. "Keep talking."

"I don't want to go into further debt. It scares me. What if I can't do this? Plus, my parents will be horrified. They think I took such a risk. I had to take a risk. I have to succeed." She was succeeding for a first-year business owner, but she wanted more.

He was quiet for a while, and she wrapped her arms around his waist. "Matt?"

"Hmm?" The rumble in his chest when he spoke tickled her cheek.

"Can I stay with you tonight?"

His chest shook with laughter. "What do you think?"

"Well, then, thank you for your generous offer."

"I'm sure we could work something out. Let me think about it," Matt teased. "Do you want any advice or not?"

She tipped her face up to murmur in his ear. "Do you know what I really want?"

"Why don't you tell me, and I'll try to make that happen."

She couldn't control her yawn. "I'm so tired, and all I want is to be with you."

He stood up from the glider and held out his hand. "Come on. It's time for bed."

All her fight was gone, at least temporarily. He led her down the hall to his room, and gave her one of his old t-shirts to wear. He was starting to accumulate items at her place. She had a toothbrush here. He'd cleaned out one of the drawers in his bathroom for her to use, but she hadn't yet.

Amy stripped her clothes off in the bathroom as quickly as possible, pulled the t-shirt on, and crawled into his bed. She laid her head on his shoulder. It was like sleeping on a skin-covered rock, but she listened to his steady heartbeat and the rhythm of his breathing.

"So, Amy, do you want advice yet?"

"Tomorrow." She rubbed her face in the clean, fresh-smelling t-shirt he wore. "Definitely tomorrow."

She heard the smile in his voice. "I'm going to hold you to that."

Her eyelids slid closed. She took a deep breath. Matt's bedding smelled like him, too, and it was comforting. "I know I'm acting like a big baby—"

He cut her off. "No, you're not. You're just worrying."

"Don't you worry?"

"I have people for that."

"Oh. Maybe I should get some people." Another yawn. "Are they expensive?"

"If you want the good ones, they are."

He kissed her. His lips were sweet and tender on hers; she traced his bottom lip with her tongue and slid her tongue inside his mouth. As always, he tasted wonderful and felt even better. She wanted him so much, but she needed to sleep more. She pulled the blankets up over her shoulders.

"Don't let go of me," she whispered.

"I won't. I promise."

AMY OPENED HER eyes to dawn's peeking through the sheer fabric blinds in Matt's room, and the beeping of his alarm clock. He stirred next to her.

"Hey, Fifi. Up and at 'em."

She'd awoken with him many times now, but she'd never get used to the fact he was breathtaking with rumpled hair and morning stubble. Couldn't he at least have the dried saliva dribbles on one side of his mouth, for instance? It was freaking unfair.

As usual, she didn't even want to dwell on what she

must look like right now. He didn't seem alarmed by her less-than-perfect current look.

After a shower, Amy put on a clean pair of Matt's sweat pants and another t-shirt advertising some NFL event. He seemed to have an inexhaustible supply. She offered to cook breakfast for them. She had to be back at the shop in a couple of hours, but she had a little time still. Matt just laughed at her offer.

"Is that a threat?"

"I can cook," she informed him. "How hard is it to screw up some scrambled eggs and toast?"

"I suppose we're both going to find out." He made a beeline for the coffee pot. "Want some?" He waved the carafe in her direction. Matt had one of the automatic grind-and-brew coffee pots, so his coffee prowess was more due to the fact he had $150 and a pound of coffee beans than some kind of culinary talent.

"Of course I want some." She put both hands on her hips. "Excuse me, Mr. Health and Nutrition, but you are not the only one that can find his way around a kitchen."

He reached into the refrigerator and pulled out a glass pitcher with some nasty-looking green juice inside. "Okay, then. You cook, and I'll drink some of this to counteract it."

Amy managed to assemble scrambled eggs with shredded cheese, sliced fresh fruit, and toast without burning down the kitchen. Matt ate like he hadn't seen food for several days. He also attempted to get Amy to try some of the nasty-looking green juice he had in the pitcher. He desisted when she told him she'd be happy to try it just as long as he didn't mind a manscaping waxing appointment in return.

She wouldn't have actually gone through with the waxing appointment. She loved running her fingers through his chest hair. He was the only guy she'd been with since college who hadn't waxed it all off.

Matt and Amy lingered at the kitchen table over one last cup of coffee.

"Listen, Fifi, about the investor: Do you know how much money you're looking for?"

She gulped. She couldn't help it. "Twenty-five thousand dollars." She pulled in a lungful of breath. "It'll give me a chance to pay down the most immediate debt I have. I'm pretty capped out with the Small Business Administration, so hopefully I can find some good terms with an investor. It'll mean less money for me to live on till the loan's repaid, but that's the way it is."

She realized it was a huge mistake to confide in a man who couldn't wait to whip out his checkbook for anyone he loved that needed cash. She needed to talk about her struggles with someone who cared for her, but she knew she'd made a serious tactical error by even bringing it up. There was a gleam in Matt's eyes she wasn't sure she liked. She also wasn't overly fond of the slight smile playing about the edge of his lips at that moment. He reached across the table and grabbed her hand.

"You know, I just happen to have a few bucks in the bank, and I'm happy to write you a check right now. I offer easy repayment terms, too." He waggled his eyebrows at her.

THE THOUGHTS CRASHED into each other in Amy's mind: *Oh, no.* Her conversation with Pauline flashed through her head in milliseconds. Her determination to make Crazy Daisy a success without depending on family and friends to do so wasn't for sale, either. Amy knew paying off such a debt would cost much more than twenty-five thousand dollars, and it had nothing to do with possible interest charges. It was all about her independence. It meant a lot to her that she was slowly emerging from Emily's shadow, too. Even if she loved her sister, she wanted something that was hers alone. She took another sip of coffee, and put the cup down on the table.

Her hand was shaking. Matt was going to be pissed, but there was no other way around it.

She'd already seen that he wanted nothing more than to be needed. He thought that meant his checkbook. She chose her words carefully and spoke slowly.

"Matt, thank you. I really appreciate your offer, but I'm going to have to say no."

He leaned forward in his chair. His voice enticed her. "Why? If you're going to get crazy about it, we can sign a contract. It's a good investment for me. I always wanted a florist on speed-dial for those flower-sending emergencies." He played with her fingers. "Come on, Fifi," he coaxed. "I don't want to think of your freaking out every day and pacing the floor at night when I can fix it."

She leaned forward and reached out for his other hand. "I really appreciate your offer. It means a lot to me that you want to get involved, and it means even more that you'd try to help." He opened his mouth to speak, and she held up one hand. "But you're not fixing it. Even with a contract, it's not going to work."

"Why do you say that? Amy, that's ridiculous." She saw a flush climbing up his neck. He gripped her hand. "You needed a new van. You needed a new flower cooler. You put the cooler on a charge account. You're paying a ton of interest every month, which is crazy. I care about you, and I don't want to watch your business fail because you are too stubborn to accept help. Do you get that?"

The delicious breakfast she'd just cooked and eaten was churning in her stomach.

"I'm not doing this just to wreck your day. I need to be independent. When I take money from a guy I'm dating, even with a contract, I'm no longer independent. There are nasty names for women like that," she said.

He dropped her hands.

"Twenty-five thousand dollars is one week's interest on my investment portfolio. It's one of several income streams I have. I offered because I want to help, not because I'm attempting to wreck *your* day."

"Matt. I appreciate it, and you, a lot." She reached out to grip his hand. At least he didn't pull away from her touch. "Thank you, but I can't accept. It's not going to work."

He let out another long breath. "Fine. I think you're making a mistake." He shoved his plate away. She saw hurt in his expression, and her heart sank. "May I make another suggestion, or will you reject that, too?"

"Matt, come on. I'm not doing this just to hurt you."

He must have rethought his approach in the past five seconds. He laced his fingers through Amy's again.

"Do you want me to ask around a little? I know guys who would write a check for twenty-five thousand bucks before they have their first cup of coffee in the morning."

"I know you do. Can I look around a little first?"

"Of course you can." He took another sip of his coffee. "Another thing: You need to start eating and sleeping, so maybe you should stay here for a few days."

"I'm fine at home. I—"

"No, you're not. You get out of bed and pace." She opened her mouth to argue with him, but knew there wasn't a lot she could say. He was right. She thought he didn't know. "You actually sleep and eat while you're here."

THE SHOP PHONE rang late that afternoon.

"Hi, Amy. My name is Clint Andrews. I'm a friend of Matt Stephens's, and he told me at lunch this afternoon that you might be looking for an investor for your business." Clint cleared his throat a bit. "He sent my wife flowers from your shop a few months back. You do nice work."

"Thanks, Clint. I'm glad you liked the arrangement. Would you like to get together for a cup of coffee, and talk about the opportunity? What does your schedule look like later this week?"

"Well, I was hoping you might have some availability

tomorrow. My wife and I are leaving for Hawaii at the end of the week. We'll be there till July, so time's of the essence."

In other words he could afford Amy's piddling twenty-five thousand dollar investment opportunity. They set a time, agreed to meet at the neighborhood Starbucks, and hung up. Matt hadn't wasted any time. Then again, Amy knew he wouldn't. She wouldn't borrow money from him, so he was going to fix it, as usual.

The shop bells jingled again a few minutes later, and Brandon walked in. He held out his arms.

"Hey, squirt. Get yourself over here, and give me a hug." He squeezed the breath out of her, patted her on the back, and said, "I needed that."

She grinned up at him. "So, you thought you'd stop by? Where's my sister?"

"Emily is having something called a 'spa day' with my mama. I'll see her later."

"How's she feeling?"

"You know I can't comment on that," but he was laughing while he said it. "Listen. I understand you need some cash. I just happen to have some." He pulled a checkbook out of his pants pocket. "How much do you need?"

"Did Matt call you?"

"Is it good or bad if I say yes?" Brandon tried to look innocent. "I want to make sure I don't stick my foot in my mouth."

Amy sank down into one of the chairs at the little table in the lobby. Brandon parked himself across from her and leaned over the table. "He's just trying to help."

He grabbed a pen out of the container of them she always kept on the table. "How much?"

"I can't take money from you. I can't take money from Matt. I need to be independent, and you can't talk me into it."

"Amy, we'll never miss the money. Why do you do this stuff? Em and I can afford it. You don't have to do this alone. Let us help you."

"You didn't ask for help with your career, did you?"

The teasing grin faded from his lips. His voice was firm.

"Yes, I did, squirt. I had mentors. I still have them."

"Did you borrow money from them?"

His eyes narrowed. "I didn't need their money, and this is not a loan!" It seemed that Amy had finally succeeded in pissing off the typically easygoing Brandon. "I'll be back in a few." He hauled himself off the little chair and stormed out of the shop.

Ten minutes later, he was back. He must have gone for a walk around the block to calm down. He followed Amy into the workroom. Estelle's eyes were bugging out of her head, but she made herself scarce. Hopefully Estelle would get used to seeing Sharks players showing up at her shop someday.

"Listen," Brandon coaxed, in his most beguiling tone of voice. "Em wants this, and so do I. We never would have met if you hadn't sent her over with that delivery, and you bet we know that. We owe you, not the other way around." He reached out to pat her hand. "We're investing in your shop, but truthfully, we're investing in you. You've done real well with your business, and we don't want to see problems later because you won't let us help you."

"Thank you, but no, thank you. I told Matt no, and I'm telling you no, too."

Brandon shook his head. "Aw, honey. He doesn't give up. He chased you till you agreed to go out with him. Why do you think this will be any different?"

"What do you mean?"

"He will find a way around you," he warned. "He fights dirty, too." Brandon crossed the room and looped his arms around her. She found herself squished against his shirt front again. "I gotta go, but this is not over." He tried to look menacing, but the effect was completely spoiled by the mischievous twinkle in his eyes. "Why don't you think about it for a few hours? My offer still stands."

"The answer is still no."

"Have I told you lately you're more stubborn than your sister?"

"It's part of my charm."

He let out a laugh. "See you later," he said and loped out of the shop.

One hour later a courier arrived at Crazy Daisy with a cashier's check made out to her for fifty thousand dollars and a note from her brother-in-law: "Don't hurt my feelings, squirt."

She was going to kill him. Or Matt.

CLINT ANDREWS'S LAWYER wrote a one-page investment contract for Amy to sign. She paid another lawyer three hundred dollars to review it. She offered monthly payments, a small percentage of Crazy Daisy, which would sunset when the loan was repaid, and a free two dozen red roses every year for Clint's wife on their anniversary in perpetuity. He took it. Twenty-five thousand dollars was deposited in her business account two hours after everything was signed.

She paid off her business credit card ten minutes later, heaved a huge sigh of relief, and asked Estelle to watch the store for a few minutes while she took herself out for a caramel macchiato to celebrate.

Matt was still mad at her for not taking his money. Her brother-in-law did not find it amusing that she returned his cashier's check the next day inside a box of homemade chocolate chip cookies. They were both going to have to get over it. She had a business to run.

Chapter Twenty-Two

A FEW DAYS later, Amy unlocked the front door of her shop a little after ten AM. She heard the bells jingle seconds afterward. Matt strolled into her lobby with a carry-out tray and an enigmatic grin.

"So, Fifi, I was wondering if I could interest you in a Top Pot doughnut and a latte." He put the tray with coffee and a bag of doughnuts down on the little table in Amy's lobby. "Brunch for two."

She resisted the impulse to run across the lobby and throw herself into his arms.

"When's the last time you ate a doughnut, Matt Stephens?"

"I heard their maple bar frosting is so addictive people have broken into the shop after hours to get one. Let's find out if it's true." He nodded toward the empty chair across from him. "Join me."

"Are you asking me out on a date? I have work to do,

you know," but she sat down at the table. "Plying me with sugar and caffeine? Who are you, anyway?"

His eyes sparkled. He lifted his left eyebrow, which made every hormone in her body sit up and scream for relief. "I'm the guy who misses you." He opened the bag and held it out to her. "What would you like?"

She extracted a maple bar. "Are you still mad at me?"

He shook his head no. "It's your life."

"Yes, Matt, it is, and I love this right now." She took a bite of the maple bar and almost moaned aloud as the frosting dissolved on her tongue.

"Why don't you drop by my place after work tonight, and we'll go to the concert at Marymoor Park? I just happen to have a ticket with your name on it. Then again, I know you're popular. Can you fit me in at the last minute?"

"Will you *quit*? I'll ask Estelle if she minds closing, and I'll get over there in plenty of time." She thought for a moment. "I have one question for you, Matt."

"What's that?"

"Will we actually make it to the concert this time?"

He took the maple bar out of her hand, and bit off a chunk.

"I promise I won't tear your clothes off till it's over."

AMY ARRIVED AT Matt's a little after six, only to realize she'd forgotten to place one last wholesaler order for tomorrow morning, and her phone was dead. The charger was back at the shop. Dammit.

"Hey, Matt, may I use your laptop for a minute? I need to do something over e-mail."

"Knock yourself out," he shouted from the kitchen. "It's in my office."

Amy rounded Matt's desk. He'd framed a photo of them they asked a guy to take with Matt's cell phone a week or so ago. She smiled to think Matt had a picture of her where he could see it every day. Something else caught her eye beside Matt's laptop. She stared at the check lying on Matt's desk blotter, and sank down into the leather chair behind the desk.

Her legs didn't seem to be working right now. Hot and cold raced over her skin, twisted her stomach in an invisible fist, and she told herself to breathe. One hand rose to her mouth.

Maybe she was seeing things. Then again, she wasn't seeing much of anything right now, besides a check printed on pale green safety paper, payable to Clint Andrews, for twenty-five thousand smackers. The guy who'd just—coincidentally, of course—"invested" in Crazy Daisy.

Why the hell did Matt have a twenty-five thousand dollar check for Clint, anyway? Obviously, twenty-five big ones was a lot of money to lose for eighteen holes of golf. Matt didn't spend much time and money gambling. They'd had that discussion, among others. Something was wrong.

Maybe there was some other reason Matt wrote Clint a huge check. Maybe Clint sold him something, or maybe Matt was lying to her and had been all along. Oh, God. The icy, invisible fist clutching her stomach twisted once more.

Sometimes the shortest distance between two places is a straight line. She tried to find another breath.

Brandon warned her that Matt would "find a way around her." She blew him off. She should have listened.

It was crystal clear: Matt lied to her. There was no way in hell Matt was going to let this happen without his interference; he'd funded Clint's "investment," and she'd better figure out some way to calmly confront Matt on this fact.

She could hear him rattling around in the kitchen. "Fifi," he called out. "You almost done in there? The concert starts in an hour and a half." His voice was getting closer. "You'll like these guys. Plus, there's dancing. I can't wait to see you on a dance floor. This will be epic. I should bring the video camera."

"Hey, Matt," she called out, in the most casual tone of voice she could muster. "Would you come in here for a minute?"

"The laptop should be on. I just used it fifteen minutes ago. We'd better get on the road." Matt blew through the doorway into his office. "Do you need something else?"

Amy got to her feet. *Stay calm*, she told herself. *Breathe.* "Maybe you could explain what this is." She tapped the check with her index finger.

"It's nothing." He glanced at the desktop and back to her. "You ready? Let's go."

She glanced up at him. "So, that's your entire explanation? 'It's nothing'?"

Matt snatched the check up from the blotter. "Let's see here. It looks like a check. It's printed on lined green paper. It's made out to a friend. What else do you need to know?"

Matt was going to BS his way through this. She saw the guilt in his eyes, the way they didn't quite meet hers. She just shook her head.

"You just happen to have a check for twenty-five thousand dollars written to a guy who invested in my business at your suggestion. This is after you tried to talk me into taking twenty-five thousand dollars from you, and I told you no. Wouldn't you agree that's somewhat odd?"

He stared at her for a moment. He folded his arms over his chest.

"Hey, money's money. The stuff in my office really isn't your business, Amy."

She closed her eyes. Matt wasn't going to admit to it, and he'd busted out the "Amy" when he'd normally call her "Fifi." Any hope that she had of an innocent explanation, some kind of mistake or misunderstanding, was over. He'd lied to her. Plus, now she was in a position she couldn't get out of as a result. The cold, clammy, sick feeling that rushed over her might drown her.

He watched her as she struggled for words.

"Did you fund Clint's loan to me, and lie about it?"

"I wanted you to have the money, and I couldn't think of another way to get you to take it."

She felt like someone had slugged her in the stomach.

"I told you how important this was to me. I *told* you that I wanted to do this myself. It's my business. You went behind my back, after I told you no. How could you do this?"

She didn't think it was possible, but he appeared even more frustrated and guilty. His voice dropped again.

"Amy, I want your business to be successful, too. It's just money, and the problem was solved. I didn't want to think about your driving the van into a tree from exhaustion or worry, and you could concentrate on other things, like the additional business. I didn't expect you to sign a thing. When anyone I care about has problems, I want to help. It's who I am. Why are you acting like this is a crime?"

"But you lied to me about it." Amy was gasping for breath. She pounded one finger into his desktop. "What else have you lied to me about besides this?"

"I didn't lie. I asked someone else to write a check, so you'd take the money. Why can't you understand that I can't stand to see you struggle? I watched what my mom went through."

"I know you did. I really like your mom, Matt. But I'm not her, and you can't fix everything for someone else. I feel like you didn't think I could handle it on my own, so you thought you should take care of it instead." The belief that he thought her inept and incapable hurt more than anything else, even more than the fact he lied to her. She hauled breath into her lungs. "I needed to do it myself, and now you've taken that away from me." Amy pushed off from his desk and moved around it toward the door. "I'll get your money back to you as soon as I can."

"No," he said. "That's not why I did this."

She moved out from behind the desk. It felt like she was walking through wet concrete. Hurt and anger were melting her bones. "I have to leave."

He caught her arm as she walked past. "Where do you think you're going?"

"I don't know." She had to get out of here before she started screaming. "Let go of me."

Matt dropped her arm like it was on fire. She ran down the hallway, snatched her purse and keys off the hall table, and wrenched the front door open. Matt grabbed the door.

"Fifi. Let's talk about this." He reached out to stroke her cheek with one hand. "Can't we even talk about this?"

Her head bobbed back and forth like one of those dog figurines people used to put in the back window of their cars. "No, I can't. You don't believe you did anything wrong. I can't be here, and I can't be with you." She forced herself to jerk away from him, ran down the front steps to her van, and threw herself into the driver's seat.

He was right on her heels. "That's it? You're just going to leave. You're not even going to listen to what I have to say?"

"I've heard what you've had to say. You don't listen to what I have to say. After all, it's all about what you want, or how you think it's going to go. Not this time."

She grabbed the steering wheel till her knuckles showed white.

He gripped the window frame. "Fifi. Please. Don't go."

She jammed the key in the ignition, started the van, and slammed the door.

"Bye, Matt."

He grabbed for the door handle, but she'd locked it. She stepped on the gas and drove away from him. She didn't look back.

Chapter Twenty-Three

THREE DAYS LATER, Amy dragged herself to the shop after a night of tossing and turning. She wished she had someone to talk to about it. She could call her sister, but she knew Emily would side with Brandon, who sided with Matt. Her mother would tell her to sell the business and go back to being an accountant. Her girlfriends would think she was insane to refuse Matt's money. Even more, she couldn't explain to anyone else why the thought that Matt had lied to her about anything shook her even worse than his arranging her "loan."

Today went somewhat smoothly. She was happy to get an order from yet another Sharks player with an angry girlfriend. Five dozen roses and a rapidly obtained teddy bear later, the guy tipped her a hundred bucks and walked out with a handful of her business cards for his buddies. She could close in an hour. She could go home then and try to sleep.

The bell on the front door of the shop jingled, and Estelle called out, "Hey, Samantha. How are you doing?"

Samantha's response was unintelligible. Amy moved further into the walk-in. She knew Samantha wasn't visiting just for the fun of it, and Amy knew she wasn't up to this today.

"Hey, boss." Estelle tugged on her shirttail. "You have a visitor. Want me to take over on the arrangement?"

Amy heaved a sigh. "Tell her I'm busy."

Two seconds later, she heard footsteps behind her, and Samantha's voice.

"I'm staying till you talk to me."

"This really isn't a great day for a chit-chat." Amy didn't even turn around.

Samantha cut Amy off, just like her dad. It must have been genetic.

"I'm waiting. Hey, Estelle, want a coffee?"

"No," Estelle told her, "but I'll bet you want a Diet Coke, don't you?"

Amy pulled another bucket of Gerbera daisies out of the walk-in as Estelle handed Samantha a soda.

"Estelle, if you could trim those roses and make sure they're ready to go, I'll finish it later. Thanks."

Estelle gave Amy an abbreviated wink, and moved further into the workroom.

Amy gestured toward the little table and chairs in the front of her store. Samantha took the seat across from her.

Amy fiddled with flower arrangement photo books, straightened order forms, corralled pens in a holder, and did whatever she could to make sure she wasted a few minutes. Samantha popped the top on her soda, took a sip, and tapped one toe.

Amy wasn't big on Samantha's behavior right about then. She had a feeling Matt would have sent his daughter to her room for being rude, and rightly so.

"So, what's up?" Amy finally asked her.

"What's going on with you and Matt?"

Amy rested her elbows on the table and rubbed her hands over her face. She should just stop wearing makeup. She wiped it off every day anyway.

"You know, Samantha, I don't think it's appropriate to discuss this with you. It's an adult thing."

"That's what my mom said, but I want to know." Samantha took another sip of soda, and regarded Amy over the rim of the can.

"Your mom is right—"

The pop can hit the table with a bang.

"Come on, Amy. You've always been really honest with me. Why won't you talk about this?"

"It's hard to explain adult relationship issues to a teenager. Plus, he's your dad."

Samantha's eyes narrowed. "Try me."

Amy knew what Samantha was up to. Even with the teenage behavior, she was hard to ignore. It was an inappropriate discussion, but Amy was going to have to tell her something.

Amy thought for a few moments. The shop phone rang, and she heard the murmur of Estelle's voice in the workroom as she spoke to whoever was on the other end. Samantha's behavior was masking her anxiety, or so she believed. She twisted her fingers together in her lap, when she wasn't folding her arms across her chest.

"Samantha, your dad and I have a disagreement over his involvement in my business. That's what happened."

"That's *it*?"

"That's what I'm willing to tell you."

Samantha slumped in her chair and gave Amy a mutinous look. "He's been really cranky."

"I'm sorry to hear that," Amy murmured diplomatically.

"He misses you," she insisted.

"Not really," Amy burst out, and immediately regretted it. Samantha seized on this.

"Yes, he does. Your picture is still on his desk. I think he loves you. I know it."

Amy shoved back from the table and pulled herself to her feet. This conversation needed to be over ten minutes ago.

"Samantha, I love it when you come to visit me and I enjoy talking to you, but this is something we're not discussing. It's not appropriate."

To Amy's shock, tears rose in Samantha's eyes.

"You don't get it. I want—I want a little brother or a sister," she blurted out. "My mom isn't dating anyone, and you are the only person my dad's ever gone out with that I even like! He's not going to meet anyone else like you. Can't you work it out?"

Amy laid a comforting hand on Samantha's shoulder.

"I know this is really disappointing."

"No, you don't." Samantha jumped up from her chair. "Can't you even *try*? I always thought that once you fell in love, you were always in love. Isn't that true? My mom says she still loves my dad, just in a different way."

Amy grabbed her head in both hands. She didn't have the first idea of how to comfort Samantha when she couldn't even explain any of this herself. She had no idea what to say to Matt's daughter. After all, love confused her, too. Her anger at his lie was confused with the fact she missed him so much already. It was obvious she wasn't great at romance, either. And right now, meeting someone else was out of the question. She certainly wasn't telling Samantha she loved Matt.

God, what a day.

Samantha was digging through her handbag for something, and Amy saw tears fall onto the leather.

"Hey, sweetie. Don't cry." Amy grabbed a few tissues out of the box sitting on the table and reached out to embrace a now-sobbing Samantha.

Between the sniffles and sobs, she heard a plaintive, "Don't you love my dad?"

Social security number, number of guys she played Spin the Bottle with in high school, amount of money she made each month: Amy would have answered any other question than that one. Her stomach made a perfect square knot. She hoped the ground would open and swallow her whole, but so far, no luck. She hadn't told Matt those three little words yet, but she knew she loved him.

Samantha was rubbing her eyes, smearing an amazing amount of Kohl pencil from eyelid to cheekbones.

"Your eye makeup might need a little attention right now."

Amy tried to steer her toward the bathroom. Samantha didn't move. The only sounds out of her were sniffles, and that hiccupping thing all females did after they cried. Reddened, tear-filled eyes met Amy's.

Amy would have to answer her.

"Okay, Samantha, you're right." Amy folded her arms across her chest. "I'm in love with your dad, but it's not going to work."

Samantha started shaking her head before Amy was even done speaking. "How can love not work? If you love someone enough, don't you want to work it out?"

There was no possible good way to explain this. Amy knew what happened between Samantha's parents. Samantha had the sanitized version. She would never understand that by this age, maybe it wasn't the other person involved. Maybe it was you. Maybe it was something you could never, ever fix, no matter how badly you wanted to, because justifying the reason why Amy was shoving away the best thing that ever happened to her with both hands was more important than opening herself up to even more emotional pain.

Amy dragged air into her lungs.

"Sometimes even if you love the other person, and they care for you, too, you can't overcome your differences. I wish I had a better answer, but it's true. It doesn't make you bad, or wrong. It just means you can't fix it."

Samantha thought about this awhile. The shop phone rang again; Estelle was handling things. Amy knew she needed to get back to work, but right now there was a fourteen-year-old in her shop who was making her skin crawl. She could hide in the walk-in, but Samantha would follow her, and there would be more questions.

She was an adult and struggled with the same things that made Samantha cry, and dammit, she wondered why.

"Does anyone ever fall in love and stay that way?" Samantha said.

"I hope so. My sister has."

She nodded. "She's Brandon's wife."

Amy inclined her head in response.

"He used to babysit me. Did I ever tell you that?"

Amy wondered where this all came from, but Samantha stopped crying, so maybe it was best to let her talk.

"My dad says he really loves kids, and my parents would leave me with him and his ex-girlfriend when they went out for dinner sometimes." She gave Amy an impish grin. "He took us to the park and out for ice cream. My dad says that I asked Brandon to be my boyfriend. I wanted to marry him when I grew up."

"Emily might have something to say about that."

"Maybe I can be their babysitter when they have a baby."

Amy practiced her poker face. "You'll have to talk to them. I'll bet they'd appreciate the offer." Amy stuck her hands in her jeans pockets. "Samantha, I know it's hard to understand this stuff, but you'll see it when you're a little older." Samantha glared at Amy a bit, and Amy added, "I know, I know. It used to piss me off, too, when adults would say that to me."

Samantha picked up her handbag, walked past Amy, and made a beeline for the workroom's bathroom. The door shut behind her. Amy followed her into the workroom.

"I made an appointment for two o'clock tomorrow for you. The woman's wedding is in six weeks, and she wants a bouquet and a few boutonnières," Estelle told Amy.

"Okay. Thanks for setting it up for me." Amy leaned over the worktable. "How did I do there?" she stage-whispered.

"You did as well as you could under the circumstances." Estelle patted her hand. "The teenage years are tough, especially when your parents are dating other people."

Amy closed her eyes. "She's not going to quit asking me questions."

"No, she won't." She heard the smile in Estelle's voice. "It's up to you, though, how much you want to put up with."

After the usual bathroom noises, Samantha emerged.

"I have to go home," she informed Amy and Estelle. "My mom's not going to be happy if I'm late for dinner."

"Do you need me to drive you there?" Amy said.

"No. There's a bus in about five minutes."

Samantha had cleaned the smeared black pencil off her cheeks and eyelids. Her eyes were still red from crying, though. Amy reached into the walk-in cooler, fished out a cold can of Diet Coke, and handed it to Samantha.

"Here's one for the road. I'll walk you to the bus stop. Come on."

Amy gestured toward the front door. Samantha waved goodbye to Estelle, and stuck the unopened can of soda into her handbag.

THE SIDEWALK BUSTLED with young urban professionals who must have wrapped things up in the office a bit early on the gorgeous late-spring day. Some had already staked out sidewalk seating at a few of the cafes close to Amy's shop, and settled in with friends for a chat. Samantha glanced into the shop windows of Broadway as she and Amy walked along.

"I'm glad you came to see me," Amy told Samantha.

"So, we'll talk again?"

"We will." Amy breathed a sigh. "Listen, Samantha, I just want you to know that I don't think I can fix this, but it's not that I don't care about what you had to say. I wish things could be different." She reached out and ruffled Samantha's hair. "I like spending time with you."

"I like you, too." Samantha tried to look bored. "You'll still be my friend?"

"Of course. That's never going to change." Amy dug around in her pocket. "Do you have bus money?"

"I have a pass." Samantha pulled it out of her purse.

Amy could see the bus ahead; it stopped at the curb, the doors opened, and Samantha turned to her once more. "I think you should give Matt another chance." She stepped onto the bus, showed the driver her pass, and was heading toward the back before Amy could even respond.

An hour or so later, Amy finished the arrangement she started before Samantha's visit. She took a few more orders that would need to be made for tomorrow's deliveries, and she had a cup of coffee. She was still thinking about Samantha's comments. After all, it was a bit surprising that Samantha would actually come to Crazy Daisy to plead Matt's case. Amy was sure Matt would be less than happy to learn about Samantha's visit. Estelle was out of the shop, so Amy grabbed the phone when it rang.

"Crazy Daisy."

"Amy? It's Laura Stephens. How are you?"

"I'm fine, Laura. How are you? Did Samantha make it home? She stopped by a little while ago."

"That's why I'm calling." Laura took a deep breath. "Do you have a few minutes? We probably need to talk."

"My employee is out on a delivery, but things are quiet. What's on your mind?"

Amy liked Laura, even if she was Matt's ex. Obviously Amy enjoyed Samantha's company, but she and Laura had something else in common: They both owned a small business, and probably had most of the same problems as a result.

"Sam told me what she did. I apologize."

"Laura, I'm not mad. I know she's upset about this. I knew it was something that shouldn't be discussed with a teenager, but I—I'm—I wasn't sure what to tell her."

"We had to have a long talk about how adult relationships are nobody's business but theirs." Even if Laura couldn't see her do it, Amy shook her head a bit. "She has been told that whatever happens between you and Matt, it's private."

"I appreciate that. You know, I really like Samantha. You're doing a great job."

"Thank you. That means a lot to me. Matt is so strict that I worry she's going to rebel, but so far, we've managed to keep it under control." Laura took another deep breath. "Listen. Now that I've scolded my daughter for prying, I'm going to do it. I have to tell you she's not the only one that's sad that it didn't work out. Out of everyone that Matt's dated, I was so happy when I met you. You love our daughter, you're easy to get along with, and you have a life of your own." She cleared her throat. "Are you sure it's over?"

"You must know better than anyone what it's like to deal with Matt." Now it was Laura's turn to laugh. "He knows I told him I wanted to run my business myself, and he meddled. Even worse, he lied to me about it. I know it sounds ridiculous and unforgiving, but I'm still so mad at him I could spit."

"He tried to run my life, too."

"Annoying, isn't it?"

"Amy, it's up to you, but listen. He's not a bad guy. He does it because he takes care of everyone he loves. I had a bad month at the salon about a year ago. Two of my stylists quit with no notice, my rent went up, I had to replace some equipment, and he was there with his checkbook. He wouldn't talk to me for a week after I told him no. He took care of his mom for so many years . . . It's the way he shows love."

"I know that. I just—I'm just so mad still, and he would not discuss why what he did was wrong."

"He still does this to me, too. He finally backed off, but it took him years to do it. Obviously I still love him, because we're friends. At the same time, I wanted to kill him. I know it is hard to deal with someone who won't listen to your concerns as well. It took us a long time to get there. He's going to have to learn the same lesson with you." There was silence on the phone for several seconds, and she finally said, "I know you love him, too."

"Sometimes it's not enough."

"Think it over, Amy. I know you're probably hearing from your sister and your friends. You heard it from Samantha today. He's like a bear with a sticker in its paw. I know he loves you." Amy could see Laura's smile through the phone. "It's hard on his ego to have the woman he wants walk away from him."

Laura and Amy chatted a little more about how their respective businesses were doing. A customer came in, so Amy had to hang up. After she sold the guy a hand-tied arrangement of irises and calla lilies, Amy was still thinking about what Laura had to say. She'd been dealing with Matt for almost fifteen years. Amy was surprised, though, that she'd go to bat for him with another woman.

Chapter Twenty-Four

AMY SPENT THE next week ignoring Matt's phone calls and immersing herself in work. She slept three or four hours a night before she was up and pacing again, so she'd started taking the bus to her shop. She knew she wasn't safe to be behind the wheel. She didn't feel like eating. Everything in her room smelled like Matt, no matter how many times she washed it. She was too numb to cry.

Mercifully, it was Sunday. Amy finally closed her eyes as the first light of dawn warmed the skies outside her bedroom window. She awoke to the sound of Emily's voice.

"Hey, get out of bed. We're going to Cannon Beach for a couple of days." Emily was pulling Amy's overnight bag out of her walk-in closet.

Amy sat up in bed and rubbed her hands over her face. "Who let you in?"

Emily jingled her key chain. "I still have a key." She crossed the room to Amy's dresser. She tossed items into the open suitcase. "Let's see here. Underwear. Socks. A bra. Where are your toiletries?" She stared at Amy in shock. "What's with the huge dark circles under your eyes? You look like you took up boxing."

"It's nothing." Amy shook her head. "I'm fine."

"The hell you are. When was the last time you ate something?"

"I can't go to the beach right now—"

"You need a break. I have some days off. Brandon's doing something called 'organized team activities,' so we're outta here." Emily opened the closet door again. "How do you even find your clothes? You don't hang anything up. How do you tell what's dirty from what's not?"

Emily and Amy had been having this same argument since elementary school. Amy was fairly sure they'd still be having it when they both lived in a retirement home.

"Dirty is in the laundry basket. Everything in the closet's clean," Amy pointed out with exaggerated patience. She rubbed her eyes again. It was just past seven AM, she'd finally managed to fall asleep for a couple of hours, and she'd kind of like to go back there for a while.

"Listen, Mrs. Clean, don't you have something else to do?"

"Probably. Right now, though, you're getting out of bed, and we're going on a trip," Emily said. She pulled stuff off the clean laundry pile and folded it into the suitcase. "If we leave now, we'll get there by noon."

Emily couldn't cook, but she was a neatnik. There was no clutter in the McKenna residence. Amy strongly suspected there was no dust there, either. Brandon greeted

Emily's cleaning mania with amusement. She could not understand how he could mess up a room thirty seconds after she left it. Amy was sure they didn't fight over it. After all, Brandon could employ methods of distraction the rest of their friends and family had no access to.

"Em, I know you're pretty bent on this, but I really can't leave."

"Yes, you can." She glanced up at Amy, and ticked reasons off on her fingers. "It's Sunday. You're closed till Tuesday morning. Your employees are opening the shop now; I talked to Estelle yesterday, and she says they can handle it for a day. We'll be back on Wednesday. You need a break. I need to spend some time with you, so get your ass out of bed."

Amy resisted the impulse to laugh. Her beautiful, poised, perfect older sister, the toast of opera companies all over the world, was trotting out the obscenities this morning. In other words, she was serious.

"You talked to *Estelle*? This is *my* business . . ."

The rest of Amy's comments trailed off as Emily walked into the bathroom, flipped on the shower, and shouted over the spray, "Don't make me drag you in here."

An hour later, Amy was showered, dressed, and packed, and the sisters were speeding down 405 toward Oregon. The only way Emily had managed to get Amy into the car at all was by promising she could sleep until they got to the hotel. Even more, Amy knew this was Emily's way of provoking the Showdown at Matt Corral. Emily wanted to know what happened. Amy wasn't sure she wanted to share that information quite yet.

Sleeping was a convenient way to avoid it.

Amy awoke as Emily's phone rang, but kept her eyes shut while Emily chatted with Brandon. If she was any more of a chicken, she'd have enough eggs for an omelet.

The next time Amy woke, her sister stood inside of the open passenger door, shaking Amy's shoulder and telling her, "Hey, wake up. We're here."

AMY AND EMILY walked Cannon Beach together, watching kids and a few dogs running and playing. Amy took deep breaths of the salt-tinged air. The ocean breeze blew their hair around. She scrunched her toes in the sun-warmed sand. The sky was a brilliant forget-me-not blue, and the puffins celebrated the good weather on Haystack Rock.

Emily glanced over at Amy. "You need to call Matt."

"I'm not calling him," Amy said. "We broke up. It's over."

"And this is the same woman who rode me until I called Brandon."

"That was different. Brandon's wonderful. Matt is a lower life form."

Emily stopped, and grabbed her sister's arm. "You're in love with him." Her voice was flat. "There's never going to be anyone else for either of you but each other. Why are you being so stubborn?"

"He lied to me. He meddled in my business. He—"

"He wanted to help you. You threw it back in his face. Honest to God, Amy, where do you *get* this? He wants you to succeed, just like Brandon and I do. And by the way, Brandon said to tell you you're more stubborn than I am."

"Matt needs to understand that he is not the boss of me!" Amy finally burst out. Emily started to laugh, which made her even madder. "I'm not talking to you."

Amy tried to stomp away. Sand didn't really lend itself to stomping. Emily caught up with her.

"You have to talk to me. We're staying in the same room," she pointed out.

"I'll get another room. Just leave me alone."

Again, Emily grabbed her arm and swung Amy around to face her.

"I'll never leave you alone," Emily said.

They stared at each other for a few minutes. Amy must have gotten sand in her eyes. They were tearing up.

"Why can't everyone just drop this? You and Mom, and Samantha's even on my butt," Amy pleaded. Emily reached out and pulled her sister into her arms. "I'll just meet someone else. I don't need him. I don't need anyone—"

"Anyone but all of us," Emily interrupted. "We all love you, you weirdo. We all want you to be happy."

Amy tried to move away from her, and Emily held her fast. Those workouts with Brandon must have been paying off. She stuck her fist in her mouth, and tried to think of anything that would stop the hot tears from streaking down her cheeks.

"Fight all you want," Emily said into her ear. "I'm not letting go of you."

"The kids are starting to stare."

"Who cares?" She patted Amy's back. "I've cried on your shoulder more than once."

"It's been six months," Amy said. "And you've been disgustingly happy ever since then."

She heard Emily laugh a little. "The next time I have a crying jag, I'll give you a call."

As usual Emily had seen past whatever it was Amy was trying to cover up. Emily gave her one last squeeze, dropped her arms, and started walking again. Amy trotted after her, while attempting to control her emotions. They weren't cooperating.

Matt's absence was a physical ache. Even more, Amy kept remembering the look on his face when she hit the gas and drove away from him. Losing him was the worst pain she'd ever experienced, but she didn't know how to fix it. She was like a wild animal caught in a trap. She would do anything to keep other people from finding out about the pain and loneliness inside of her, and she'd do anything to get away from them while she did it.

The only time she felt comforted was when Matt was near. He knew pain and grief well. He talked with Amy about the things in his life that still hurt: his dad's abandonment of their family; the fact his mom struggled for so many years alone, and he could do little to help her until he got older; his regret that he couldn't make it work no matter how hard he tried with his ex-wife; and the fact he worried his failure would impact Samantha. He also knew joy, and he shared his with her.

She wondered why other people fell in love so effortlessly. Maybe they had some kind of special coating on their emotions—heartbreak didn't hurt as much, or they were able to quickly forget it. Not her. She'd take any financial risk, but a risk with her feelings? Absolutely not.

Emily turned to her. "Let's get some food."

"I don't need to eat."

"You haven't eaten a thing since we got here."

"Are you keeping track?"

"I don't want to have to carry you." She turned toward the restaurant beyond the beach. "I heard they have flourless chocolate cake and a full bar."

Chocolate was still Amy's Kryptonite. "Let's go."

AMY AND EMILY sat at a hardwood bar. The back wall was floor-to-ceiling windows looking over the ocean view. There were a few people scattered throughout the restaurant enjoying the snacks and libations, but everyone else must have been romping on the beach. Obviously, it was five o'clock somewhere, even if it was still early afternoon in Oregon.

Emily gathered the long skirt of her cotton turquoise sundress around her, cradled her brand-new baby bump, and took another sip of her virgin Cosmopolitan, otherwise known as cranberry juice with some lime. Her pea-sized diamond stud earrings flashed in the recessed lights.

"Brandon makes fun of me when I order one of these."

"Did you tell him to get over himself?" Amy said.

"That's what you're for."

"Come on. I know you tell him once in a while he's not God."

Emily swirled the juice in her martini glass, and let out a sigh.

"I miss him. Even if he can make me completely insane, the house is so quiet without him. Plus, I don't sleep well when he's not there."

"What do you do when you're out of town for a performance?"

"That's different. I don't expect him to be there." Emily made a moisture ring on her bar napkin. "We talk before we go to sleep. Every night." She concentrated on lining up the bowls of bar snacks on some invisible marker. Amy loved her sister, but wow, Emily had a thing about organization. "If there was one thing in life I would wish for you, it's that."

"Talking to Brandon every night before I go to sleep?" Amy said. Emily stared at her. "Okay. It was a bad joke. I was just trying to lighten the moment."

Amy had picked at her food for over a week now, but she'd decided in the past thirty seconds she was ravenously hungry. She'd seen all the sweeps-week news reports about bacteria thriving in bar snacks. Maybe she should risk it anyway. She wondered what Emily would do if she messed up her sister's carefully aligned bowls of peanuts and pretzels on the bar.

The restaurant's kitchen door was visible from where they sat. She wondered if anyone would mind if she ran in and helped herself to whatever was ready to eat. The bartender and servers must have been on some kind of extended break.

"I never thought it would be like this. I *never* thought I'd be one of those sappy women crying into my drink about how much I miss my husband." Emily let out another sigh. "See? I've been away from him for a grand total of less than eight hours, and I'm already having some kind of meltdown."

"You can't wait till I'm experiencing the same sort of misery?" Amy decided to take a risk, and grabbed the bowl of peanuts. Emily took it away from her before she could eat any.

"That stuff's nasty. Let's find the server." Emily swiveled in her bar chair to face Amy, and laid one hand over hers. "This is all about someone who knows everything about me, even the stuff I wish I could hide. My faults. Things I wish I were better at. He loves me anyway, or maybe I should say, despite it all. I know all of his faults, too. It doesn't matter. I could never imagine this kind of love before it happened to me." She tapped on the bar with one finger. "That is what I mean, Ame. That's what I'm talking about. That's what I think you could have with Matt."

"Matt doesn't understand me. He doesn't even want to try."

"I think you're wrong." Emily took a sip from her glass. "Do you understand where he's coming from?"

"Oh, let's see: Arrogant, bullheaded, testosterone poisoned, knuckle-dragging freak? Oh, yeah. I know exactly where he's coming from—"

Emily interrupted her. "You are just hurt. Whenever I

said something critical of him, you were all over me. You stuck up for him with Mom and Dad, too."

"Mom and Dad don't like anyone I go out with." Amy needed something to eat. *Now.* Where the hell was that bartender? She glanced around.

"That's not true. They really liked Brian."

"They sure as hell don't like him now. He's not even an option."

"Amy, does it occur to you that the reason you fell in love with Matt was because you finally met a guy you can't shut out of your life?"

Amy's mouth dropped open. "I can't even believe you said that. It's BS."

"And it's not true?" The bartender reappeared, and Emily signaled for another round of drinks.

"You are so paying for this," Amy said while pointing at her drink. She called out to the bartender, "May I have a menu, please?" She needed some nourishment, and a lot of sleep, before she continued this conversation.

"You haven't answered my question," Emily said. "Before Matt you never dated anyone you trusted with your heart, let alone your plans for the future. You never confided in Brian, for instance. You never shared your hopes and dreams with him, either."

"That is completely untrue," Amy hissed. She took a healthy swig of her cocktail. "I dated Brian for a year."

"You *dated* him. You didn't *love* him. And you were over him a week after he left for New York, weren't you?" Emily tossed back the last few ounces of her virgin Cosmo. "Brian wasn't the one. Matt's the one. Just admit it."

"Okay, ladies, one more virgin Cosmo, right?" The bartender indicated Amy's half-empty glass. If Brandon would laugh at Emily's choice, she knew ordering a second "Sex on the Beach would leave him in hysterics."

She gave him a nod on the drink refill, and he dropped a menu on the bar in front of Amy. She wondered if Emily would be alarmed if she ordered one of everything.

Emily polished off her drink and slid the glass away. "We'd better eat."

"Maybe I should get drunk enough to forget that Matt exists," Amy muttered.

Emily's voice was tart. "I don't think there's enough alcohol in the world for that."

"Let's find out."

Their friend the bartender was back with two freshly made drinks and a basket of what smelled like bread and butter. Amy grabbed a hunk of steaming-hot, fragrant bread out of the basket, and dragged it through the butter. She took a gigantic bite.

It was currently the best thing she'd ever tasted. It was all she could do not to moan when the hot bread and melted butter hit her taste buds. Her eyes might have rolled back in her head a little.

"More bread, please," she called out to the bartender.

"You're cut off," Emily said.

AMY AND EMILY ate a huge amount of food. Well, Amy ate most of it. The ocean air seemed to revive her appetite.

She was full and a little sleepy when two guys approached their table.

They were nodding and smiling at Emily and Amy before, but she tried to ignore them. They parked themselves in the two empty chairs at the sisters' table. The tall blond sported artfully rumpled hair, board shorts, and a Cannon Beach Surf Shop t-shirt. His dark-haired buddy had a crew cut, camo board shorts, and a black t-shirt that read, "Any way we can speed this up?" They both appeared to be in their late thirties, which was much too old for their current attire. Plus, anyone who wasn't legally blind could see the gigantic rock on the third finger of Emily's left hand. The blond must have been giving Stevie Wonder a run for his money.

"So, ladies, how about another drink?"

The blond spoke to both of them, but he couldn't take his eyes off Emily. Actually, he couldn't take his eyes off her cleavage. He thrust out a hand. "I'm Justin. This is Matthew."

Emily gave him a polite smile. "Shouldn't you both be out on the beach? The waves look great today," she said.

"We surfed this morning." Matthew stretched an arm around the back of Amy's chair. She moved away. "You surf, blondie?"

If there was one thing in life Amy wanted to avoid more than any guy named "Matthew" right then, being called "blondie" was it.

"Nope. I don't surf."

"I'll teach you."

Amy was fairly sure there were plenty of things he

wanted to teach her, seeing as how he continued leaning toward her, and she continued to move away.

"Thanks, but no thanks. We're here for a little relaxation," Amy said. She took another sip of her drink.

Matthew wasn't taking the hint. "Relaxation, huh? I've always been a fan. How 'bout you, Justin?"

Justin still couldn't seem to remove his eyes from Emily's chest. "It's good to kick back," he said.

Emily picked up her drink with her left hand. Amy could have told her that subtle wasn't going to get rid of these two. Justin flashed Matthew a smile. In other words, he couldn't tell that Emily was simply being polite; he thought she was interested.

Amy was also allergic to guys spouting seventies cool-dude speak. Matt teased her with it sometimes, but on him it came off as ironic. On these clowns, it was just scary.

"So, mama, why don't you finish up that drink, and we'll go find something more fun to do," Justin said.

The idiot had just asked Emily out. This called for desperate measures. Amy and Emily locked glances, and Amy gave her sister a slight nod.

Amy leaned over the table and gave Justin a conspiratorial smile. "Hey, Justin, when's the last time you had your eyes checked?"

"Huh?" He tried to look confused. "We're just trying to spend time with some pretty ladies."

Amy's voice dropped to a sensual purr.

"You seem to have gotten off at the wrong bus stop. Let me redirect you," she said. "My sister is married. To an NFL

All-Pro defensive lineman. When he walks through that door and sees you sitting at our table, he's going to rip your arm off and beat you with the wet end." She gave him an innocent smile. "You might want to leave before he gets here."

Shortly after Emily stopped laughing at the sight of two grown men running out the door of the restaurant like something was on fire, Amy and Emily retreated to their hotel room. Amy lowered herself onto a chaise lounge on the balcony overlooking the ocean, dropping a bag of assorted mini chocolate bars and two romance novels onto the small, round table between them.

Amy opened one of the books to the dedication page. Of course, the author wanted to thank her wonderful husband, who brought flowers and candy on Groundhog Day because it meant something to her. How sweet. She heaved a sigh. Another woman with something Amy couldn't even pretend to have: a successful relationship. Emily had cracked open a book as well. They listened to the sounds of seagulls, crashing surf, and other people's screaming little kids as they pretended to read.

Emily glanced up from her book. "Do you think they're still running?"

"Maybe they sustained a groin pull." Amy reached into the bag for some chocolate. "I can only imagine what would have happened if Brandon really walked in on that whole thing."

Emily let out a snort, and dropped her book back onto the table. "Speaking of Brandon, I have a message for you from him. He says to quit screwing around and call Matt."

"Not going to happen."

"You're miserable without Matt. He's miserable without you. How long do you think you can keep this up?" Emily said.

"As long as I have to."

"That's not an option. I have two days to fix this."

"Excuse me? Are we going to talk about your schedule again?" Amy pushed off the chaise lounge, sat up, and glared at her. Her patience was at an all-time low. "Why don't you remind me again how insignificant I am, how important *you* are, and how I'm just lucky to be sitting here, breathing the same air you do?"

Emily laid her book down. "That's not what I meant, and you know it. What are you talking about?"

"You know what I'm talking about. You are beautiful. You are famous. You are wealthy. You have a gorgeous husband, a baby on the way, and the future's limitless. I own a small flower shop. I'm alone. I share my time with a goldfish, and I will never measure up."

"You've lost your mind." The color was draining out of Emily's face. "You can't believe this."

"I do. I always have." Amy ripped open the bag of chocolates, shredded the wrapper off, and crammed candy into her mouth. "You have it all. I don't."

"How did we go from 'Call Matt' to this?" Emily asked. "You—you don't know the first thing about my life."

It was muffled, but she could still speak. "I've been your sister for the past thirty-five years. I think I could write a book about your life." Amy needed more candy. She'd never been an emotional eater, but if there was ever a good time to start, this was it.

"No, Amy, you couldn't." Emily pulled her knees up to her chest and wrapped her arms around them.

Amy held up one hand, and ticked her reasons off, finger by finger. "Let's see here. Emily is born. The music teacher sends a note home when she's in second grade that Emily shows unusual aptitude, has perfect pitch, and is learning to read music. Emily starts voice lessons. She gets into a training—"

Emily cut Amy off. "Stop it. Just stop it."

"No. Do you want the rest?"

"No!" her sister shouted. To Amy's shock, tears were streaking down Emily's face. "Let me tell you the real version. I was a freak! The other kids wouldn't even play with me. After all, I was a teacher's pet. Mom and Dad took me to appointment after appointment with voice teachers. I just wanted to be normal. Nobody would let me!" She took a long, shuddering breath. "I had to have a tutor. Then I had to leave home. I wanted all the stuff the other kids got to do—they got to go to dances, play sports, and just hang around. I knew that if I didn't succeed, it—I— oh, fuck it. I sound like every bad cliché on daytime television." She reached over. "Give me that."

Emily grabbed the bag of chocolate out of Amy's hand, reached in for a handful, and got the wrappers off in a record amount of time. She crammed them into her mouth.

"Do you know where I got my first kiss?" Emily demanded through a mouthful of candy.

"No." Amy poked through the candy bag again for a Midnight Milky Way. Dammit. Where were they?

"I was onstage. I had to kiss another guy in the production. I didn't know how. He told me what a bad kisser I was. He tasted *awful*. I don't think you get it. I just—I wanted the things you probably had and you don't care about. I wanted to kiss a boy my own age, not some older guy with bad breath and an attitude. Isn't that how you're supposed to learn how to kiss—that stumbling, bumbling kind of stuff, where you don't know how to move your head or whether or not to use your tongue, but you're learning together? I never got any of that stuff." She let out a gusty sigh. "I never slow danced until I met Brandon."

"That can't be true," Amy argued.

Her sister was crying, shoveling chocolate into her mouth, and blushing. "I asked him if he would dance with me. We had to go to this fundraiser, and I was afraid I wouldn't know how if we had to slow dance together. I thought he was going to laugh at me. He was"—she rubbed her runny nose with the back of one hand—"He was wonderful." Amy loved her sister, but that was one more reminder of her saintly brother-in-law, who always seemed to know exactly what Emily needed before she did. "Did you dance?"

"Uh-huh."

"And Josh gave you your first kiss?"

Josh and his family had moved next door to the Hamiltons when Amy was five. Amy had no fear of dirt, so playing outside with the neighbors' son wasn't unusual to either set of parents. They failed to notice, though, their kids were growing up. Josh and Amy were outside in her parents' backyard one warm, clear summer night when they were both thirteen. Their parents were in the Hamiltons' kitchen, playing canasta.

Before Amy knew what was happening, Josh tipped her chin up and kissed her.

She still remembered the softness of his lips, his fingers in her hair, the taste of the strawberries they'd been eating from her mom's garden, and the sweetly clumsy way his arms finally slid around her.

Amy had been kissed more than a few times since, but the only man who ever made her feel that way again—pounding heart, weak in the knees, safe and cherished—was Matt.

"Everyone is proud of you. Everyone! Mom and Dad—" Amy burst out.

"You don't think they're proud of you?"

"No. They want me to go back to being a CPA. According to them, what I'm doing is just too risky."

Emily crammed some more chocolate into her mouth.

"Mom told me that they never knew how much determination you had. They brag about you all the time. Me? I get good reviews. They hand out your business cards."

"They're just being nice."

"No. They said all their effort went into me, and they still feel badly about it," Emily said.

"So, they feel sorry for me."

Emily reached out, grabbed Amy's shoulders, and shook her once. "They are proud of you. *We* are proud of you. When will you get it through your thick head?" She stared at Amy. "How long have you felt this way?"

"All my life."

"Why didn't you ever talk to me about it?"

"What was I going to say? 'Gosh, Emily, I'm pissed off that I live in your shadow. You'd better not achieve. After all, I'll feel bad'?" Amy said. Emily pressed one hand to her mouth. "How can I ever do anything that equals what you already have?"

Emily was speechless. Even more, she sat motionless.

"How in God's name could each of us get what the other one wanted?" she finally said.

"It's a cosmic joke."

"I wonder which one of us is the actress." Emily sprang up from the chaise lounge, and walked to the railing that surrounded the balcony. "So, you were just going to go through the rest of your life and never talk to me about this?"

"There's nothing you can do about it." Amy got to her feet as well and crossed to the railing. Emily whirled to face her.

"This is what you'll do about it." Her sister's invisible tiara was back. Emily drew herself up to her full five foot four, and gave Amy the look she'd perfected while crossing hundreds of stages in her career.

"I don't have the courage to operate my own business. I have five different people telling me where to go, what to do when I get there, dressing me and making me up, making my travel arrangements. You have a thriving business that you built yourself." She moved closer to her sister. "You've succeeded in an area I never could. I am so proud of you."

"Brandon fell in love with you." Amy stared out at the

deep blue water of the Pacific Ocean, and the puffy clouds overhead. "What if I never have that? I love my business, but I want someone to go home to." She bit her lower lip.

"You already have it. Reach out and take it."

"You don't understand." Amy's voice was desperate. "I'd be stepping into Matt's shadow instead. He'll get bored, and he'll leave me."

"Now I know you've lost your mind. You're certifiable. He's in love with you. He's not leaving."

"Every man I've loved has left me!" Amy burst out.

Stillness came over Emily's face, and she covered her mouth with one hand. She stared at Amy. "This isn't about Matt. It's Mom and Dad. I had to work through my feelings about what happened with them when I met Brandon, and now it's your turn," she said.

"I don't think so, Em. You weren't in love with a man who gives a whole new meaning to 'testosterone poisoned.'"

"Oh, yeah? You think Brandon's so perfect?" She flung the words back at Amy. "I fell in love with him because he's not. Matt isn't perfect, either. Why don't you focus on the fact that maybe you don't see him as everyone else does?"

Amy turned to grab her unread book. "I can't listen to any more of this. I'm going to bed."

"Not yet." Emily caught her hand. "Does it occur to you that the reason why Matt came after you was that he was tired of the façade? He wanted you, not someone he'd seen in a magazine or on a TV show. He wants someone he can be who he is with."

"He takes over."

"He takes care of the women he loves."

"It's suffocating."

"You're just making excuses now." Emily let out a long sigh. "Do you want to spend the rest of your life running? He'll spend the rest of his life chasing you."

"Until I get that restraining order," Amy muttered.

Her sister laughed in her face. "Oh, there's a threat. You finally met the guy you can't live without—"

"Oh, yes, I can."

"I'm going to tell you exactly what's going to happen. You're going to let him catch you. You're going to overcome your fears, you're going to fall in love for the rest of your life, and you're going to be disgustingly happy, too. Then you'll have to come up with something else to worry yourself to death about."

Chapter Twenty-Five

MATT SHOULD HAVE known that everyone else's comments about his love life were tame compared to the reception he received on the *NFL Today* set. He and his colleagues were taping a pre-season look at this year's pro football schedule. They were playing that Adele song on the overhead PA when he walked in—the one with the lyrics that felt like a punch in the gut every time he heard it. He wasn't going to be able to find anyone else like Fifi.

The best defense was always a good offense with these clowns.

"I'll bet that's your favorite song, Falcon," he called out as he walked toward his seat.

"Not really. I thought you might like it. Hey, McCord, I heard Stephens is single again. Maybe we should fix him up."

Hank's upper lip twisted into a sneer. "Oh, hell, yeah. Heard she dumped him, too. I should have no problem introducing her to my big anaconda." He pointed at his groin. "She looks like a great piece of ass. I can't wait to find out for myself." He smirked at Matt. "She needs a real man, Stephens."

The words barely left Hank's mouth as Matt threw himself over the desk and onto his co-worker. He'd left the league ten years ago, but he still knew how to tackle. He also remembered how to punch. He and McCord hit the floor with a "thud."

Six people pulled him off McCord, but not before he managed to mete out some punishment. McCord got a couple of shots in, too. Matt wiped his hand over his mouth, and came away with blood.

He was breathing hard, wrenched away from the men that held him, and told the man still lying on the floor, "There's more where that came from, you son of a bitch. Don't let me hear you say anything about Amy again."

"Settle down, Stephens. That's enough."

"I haven't even gotten started," he snarled. "Anybody else want some?"

The producer arrived on the run. "That's it. Stephens, get out of here. You have the day off. Without pay."

Matt laughed in his face. "You're unaware of the terms of my contract. I get paid no matter what."

"Don't make me call the cops."

"Call them. I don't give a shit."

The only sound he heard was his own footfalls on the highly polished studio floor as he walked away.

Matt threw himself into the back of a cab outside, barking out the name of the hotel he wished the Pro

Sports Network group stayed at when he spent eighteen Sundays a year in LA. He booked a room in the time it took the cabbie to drive the mile and a half, and sent his agent and publicist a text. His phone was vibrating thirty seconds later. He shoved it into his pants pocket.

The cabbie pulled up to the curb in front of the hotel and popped the trunk for Matt to retrieve his carry-on and garment bag. Matt pulled out a pair of twenties to pay the guy.

"Thanks for the ride."

"You might want to get that cut looked at," the cabbie told him.

"I'll do that."

Matt's luggage was snagged by a bellman, who followed him to the reception desk. The woman behind it was visibly shaken.

"Oh, my God, what happened to you? You're bleeding." She grabbed a box of tissues on the credenza behind her, and extended them to him. "Is there anything else I can do to help?"

Matt could think of a couple of things, but one typically got arrested for that. "I'm Matt Stephens," he told her. "There's a very large tip in it for you if I can check in here as Daffy Duck."

"Of course, Mr. Duck. I'll also make sure some first-aid supplies are sent up to your suite." She typed for a few minutes on the laptop in front of her.

"I'd also like a bottle of Herradura Silver, a bucket of ice, lime wedges, and salt. I'll take Patron in a pinch."

"Those items will be in your room as quickly as I can secure them." She nodded at the bellhop as she passed the folio with Matt's room keys inside across the counter. "Welcome, Mr. Duck. I hope you'll enjoy your stay."

"I think I will."

An hour later, Matt poured his second drink. The tequila wasn't helping. He didn't really regret punching McCord, even if he was in pain as a result of being punched in return. McCord richly deserved what Matt had dished out to him. He'd do it again, too, and he'd make sure McCord apologized to Amy as well. He lifted the glass to his lips. He could slam the entire bottle, but he couldn't drink away the real problem.

Matt had to admit his anger with McCord's comments was nothing compared to his torment over his own stupidity with Fifi. It was eating him alive. He couldn't believe he ever thought she would buy his line of crap about the "loan." She wanted the pride of knowing she'd built a successful business by solving her own problems, and he'd taken that away from her. He was too stubborn to admit that he lied to her about where the money came from, too.

His girl was smart. He should have known she'd react like she had when she'd stumbled across the proof in his office. Instead of manning up, telling her he was a dumbass and doing whatever he had to do to convince her he was sorry for meddling and lying to her about it, he made things even worse. He thought he could BS his way past her justified anger and hurt. He had nobody to blame but himself.

His face was still bleeding. He pressed a towel against it, but the cut wasn't closing up. His phone could double as a sex toy, judging by the non-stop vibration since he pulled it out of his pocket and left it on the bedside table. Drinking himself blind would not solve his most immediate problems, but it was a hell of a lot better solution than facing what he would be greeted with if and when he left the friendly confines of a luxurious hotel suite.

Samantha wasn't talking to him. Laura asked him why he thought punching someone else was going to make Amy reconsider. Amy wasn't returning his calls. He was fresh out of the women in his life. Actually, there was one left still speaking to him, and he dialed her number.

She didn't even say hello.

"You'd better have a goddamn good explanation, Matthew Thomas Stephens. My phone's ringing off the hook," his mother said.

"Hey, Mom, nice to talk to you, too." He watched sunlight reflect off the crystal rocks glass on the table in front of him.

She let out a long sigh. Matt would bet the deed to his house she would kill for a cigarette right now. She hadn't smoked for twenty years, but even his mom had her limit.

"You started a brawl at work. Maybe you'd better tell me what the hell happened. Sounds like someone's going to plead "exhaustion" pretty soon here, and check his ass into rehab."

"I don't need rehab. Plus, I need to find out why my daughter is no longer speaking to me."

"Your stock may be improving. Samantha just called. She wants to know why you got in a fight with Harry McCord."

"McCord's a dick." Matt took a long swallow from his glass. "How did Samantha hear about that, anyway?"

"She still likes him from when you brought her with you during last year's Super Bowl broadcast. Maybe you should tell me what happened."

"Harry made some comments about Amy that I took exception to."

"And there was no other way to handle it?"

"Mom, you would have punched him for what he said about her, too."

"Samantha is the least of your problems right now. I suggest you get on the horn with that highly paid publicist of yours. Son, you're in some trouble, according to the Twitter. The LA police evidently want to have a conversation with you, and so does the brass at PSN."

He couldn't figure out what was worse: the fact his mother had discovered Twitter, or dealing with the big bosses over what happened this morning. It wasn't the first time a fistfight had broken out at the *NFL Today* set, and he was betting it wouldn't be the last, either. The police were a bit worrisome. He'd have to call his lawyer.

Someone started banging on the door to his room. "Ma. I'll call you back." He hit the "end" button on his phone and got out of the chair to investigate. Good thing the room had a peephole.

His publicist stormed into the room as he pulled the door open.

"Goddamnit, Stephens, you must think I'm a miracle worker. Harry McCord has facial contusions. He's seen a plastic surgeon and is talking about suing you. PSN wants to terminate your contract, too. As of right now, you're on suspension until further notice." She glanced at the open bottle of tequila, grabbed a clean glass off the tray below the flat-screen TV, and splashed a healthy amount into it. "What the fuck happened to your face?"

"Want some ice?"

"Hell, no. You might want to get that cut stitched up." She slung what he knew was a costly handbag onto his bed. "You're still bleeding. That's going to scar."

Matt dropped into a chair. "Suspension. That makes it all easy."

"I have no idea what you're talking about." Candice the publicist sat down on the foot of his bed. "I can't believe this. You torched your brand in one afternoon. Hell, not even an afternoon." She gulped more alcohol. "Maybe you could explain to me what you were thinking."

"McCord told me—*shit*." He reached for his own glass, and swallowed another gulp. It burned all the way down. Candice's phone rang. Matt slung his feet up on the table again. His face was really starting to hurt. He'd patched it up with a few Band-Aids the front desk sent up, but his handiwork wasn't as effective as he'd hoped.

She got up off the bed and thrust the phone out to him. "Someone you'll want to talk to."

He tried to shove the phone back into her hand. "I have nothing to say to PSN or the police right now."

"Just answer it."

"Stephens."

"Dad?"

TWO HOURS AFTER he hung up with Samantha, the cut on Matt's face was being stitched up by a plastic surgeon. At least they managed to stop the bleeding; facial wounds bled like crazy. His pain level went from *Sweet Jesus, that hurts* to a string of every obscenity he knew.

"Matt, you know I can't give you anything due to the tequila." The doctor adjusted his microsurgery goggles. "You had worse than this in the NFL. Just two more."

"Fucking hurts," Matt said through clenched teeth.

"Uh-huh." The doctor finished closing Matt's wound, and two nurses cleaned up around him. "The bandages need to stay on your face for the next seventy-two hours. We'll send you home with some replacements. It might also be good if you don't get in another fight. The best thing would be to go back to the hotel, order room service, and take it easy tonight. Lay off the booze, too."

"Whatever."

"You'll need to be back for stitch removal in a week."

"Thanks. I'd like to leave now."

Matt shoved himself off the table. One of the nurses handed him a plastic bag full of gauze, cloth tape, alcohol wipes, and he was betting, her phone number. He didn't think the medical establishment encouraged cleavage at the office, or flirting with the patients. Maybe this was something unique to California.

"Here's some supplies. If you need more, give us a call," she said. She winked at him.

He nodded his thanks, shoved the door open, and walked into the waiting room.

"Dad!"

Samantha sprang to her feet, crossed the room on a run, and threw herself into his arms. The side of her head smacked him in the cheek. It hurt so much tears rose in his eyes.

His mother's face swam into his vision. "Hey, Sam, take it easy. He's not as young as he used to be."

He reminded himself he was not twelve, and tried to formulate a response that would not get his mouth washed out with soap.

"I can't *believe* you had to have an operation. I was so *worried*." Samantha's words tumbled out. "We came to bring you home with us." She clung to him. "Grandma Pauline says that maybe you should leave before you have to go to jail. You won't have to go to jail, will you? I can't believe you *hit* someone. You—"

"Princess. Listen. Everything will be fine. Why don't you let me pay my bill, and we'll be on our way."

"I'm scared. Mom said you might lose your job. What will we do?" He felt tell-tale tears against his cheek. Her voice quavered. "Morgan said it took her dad almost a year to find another job." She stopped long enough to take a breath. "You can have my college fund if you need it."

Matt pulled Samantha toward one of the waiting room chairs, yanked the wallet out of his back pocket with one hand, and held it out to his mother. She took it without comment and made her way to the reception desk. Samantha was still clinging to him and parked herself in the chair next to him. He tucked her head under his chin while she sobbed against his chest.

She was at the age where physical displays weren't appropriate. Right now, though, she wasn't going to let go of him long enough to have a discussion about it.

"Thank you for the offer, but I don't need to raid your college fund. Even if I lost my job, I can still take care of you. It's all going to be fine," he soothed.

"Are you sure?"

"Positive." He kissed the top of her head and leaned back in the chair. "Plus, I owe you an apology."

She stopped crying. She brushed the tears off her face with one hand and tried to sit up. He didn't let her. He held her against his chest.

"It was wrong to do what I did. There were other ways to handle what happened besides punching Harry, and I will apologize to him. Mostly, I want to say I'm sorry to you, too."

"Maybe you were just mad."

"I was wrong. I scared you and Grandma. I know better than to do stuff like that."

He glanced down and saw the edges of her mouth curl up.

"When I get in trouble, I get a punishment."

"That's right."

"Maybe Grandma will take away your laptop for a week. Or, maybe she'll ground you."

This was going nowhere good. Fast. He saw a mischievous sparkle in Samantha's eyes. She shoved herself off him. "I'll be right back."

A few minutes later, Pauline and Samantha reappeared in the waiting room. "Let's go, slugger," his mother said. "We'll see if you can stay out of trouble long enough to get back to the hotel."

The cab ride was ominously quiet. The elevator up to his room was silent. He tossed his room key on the table next to the still-open bottle of tequila, picked up the bottle to pour himself another drink, and heard his mother's voice.

"I don't think so. Give me that." She took it out of his hand, re-stoppered it, and gave him a glare he hadn't seen since he tried backing her car out of their driveway at age twelve. "Samantha and I discussed this, and you need a punishment for your behavior. No alcohol for a week."

"I'm over 21—"

"You are damn lucky you're not in jail right now. By the way, your lawyer called. Harry McCord isn't pressing charges, but there's now an agreement between Harry and the ambulance chaser. You'll be donating the equivalent of this week's paycheck to the charity of Harry's choice. PSN says the only way you're getting your job back is to complete an anger management course with an approved instructor, too."

"That's unfair. You know exactly why I hit that asshole—"

"Language," his mother snapped. Samantha's head moved back and forth as if she were watching a tennis match. "No alcohol for a week, Matty, or I send those bearskin rug photos of you to ESPN."

"You wouldn't."

"Try me," she said.

He noticed Samantha edging toward the second bedroom in the suite. Candice the publicist had "errands to run." He was fairly sure she was outside having more than one cigarette. His mother put the tequila bottle back down on the computer table and settled herself into the easy chair next to the couch he was currently lounging on.

"Um, Dad?"

"Let me guess. You want to play video games." He'd like to play video games, too, but right now he needed to relax for a few minutes on the couch. He was wondering if he needed to brace for incoming. His mom had the determined look on her face he knew meant he was about to get a lecture for some damn thing.

"There's an Xbox in here with two controllers."

"Maybe you can teach your grandma how to play a driving game or something later." He pulled on the drawer knob in the end table next to him and grabbed out the room service menu. "Are you hungry?"

"Yes."

"I'll order you some food."

Samantha looked panicked. "Please tell me you're not getting tofu, kale, or that awful green juice . . ."

"It's good for you." Maybe it wasn't nice to tease her this way, but he had to admit it was a little funny to watch the horrified expressions flit across her face. He held out the menu to her. "Well, okay. You did come all the way here to see me. Go ahead."

"Really? Thank you!" She crossed the room on a run, grabbed the menu out of his hand, and vanished inside the second bedroom. The door shut with a *click*.

"No R-rated movies," he called out. "No *Grand Theft Auto*."

It was very sweet that she managed to stifle her groans.

"I'm hungry, too," Pauline said.

Matt picked up the remote for the flat screen across from them. "I have the technology. The room service menu's on the hotel channel, or we can ask to have some food picked up."

His mom took care of the food order. He stretched out on the couch again, and wondered if it would be a good time to take a nap. His eyelids drifted closed. He heard his mother's voice.

"Not so fast, Matty. You and I have a few things to talk about."

"Mom, let me get a nap, and we'll talk when the food gets here."

"I don't think so. You'll be asleep ten minutes after you polish off that thirty-dollar piece of steak the size of a postage stamp." She reached out to shake his shoulder. "Wake up."

He forced himself into a seated position. She kicked off her high heels and tucked her feet beneath her in the chair; she was settling in for a mother-son chat, and he could just guess what was first on her agenda.

"Samantha tells me you and Amy broke up. What happened, son?"

The sick, shaky feeling was back, as well as the knot in his stomach. He did his best to pretend like it didn't matter. "It wasn't working, so we ended it."

"You're going to have to try that with someone who actually believes you, Matty. Why don't you tell me the truth?"

He'd just gotten busted for lying, and now he was trying it with a woman who had a built-in and flawless BS detector. He let out a long breath. "She needed money for her business. I offered her some, and she turned me down. Instead of letting her find an investor on her own, I talked one of my golfing buddies into giving her a "loan" that I actually funded." Matt made air quotes with hands he realized were shaking. He hoped his mom didn't notice. "Needless to say, she found out about it."

He didn't like the look on his mom's face, or the lifted eyebrow. "And how did *that* go?"

"Not well."

"I wonder why."

Anger swelled inside him again. "I just wanted to make sure she was okay. It wasn't that much money in the first place! I offered her a contract and everything. She was too stubborn to take it. Plus, she threw it in my face. Why would she think I—"

"So you lied about arranging the loan, too?"

"It wasn't exactly a *lie*. I just didn't tell her the entire truth."

She was shaking her head before he finished speaking. "Oh, my GOD, Matty. Is this one of these things like 'It depends on what the meaning of "is" is?' Are you listening to yourself? What do you think any woman thinks when you lie to her, honey? I'll tell you what they think: What else has he lied to me about?" She let out a bark of laughter. "You're busted. You finally found a woman who will stand up to you, and you didn't like it."

"This is NOT funny," he fumed.

His mother's voice grew gentle. "Of course it's not, honey. You have to admit it, though. You don't make it easy. I'll bet she told you no, and said 'stay out of it,' and you just couldn't stand letting her handle it herself."

"I didn't think she'd dump me over this, if that's what you're asking."

Maybe his stitches were pulled too tightly. His vision blurred. He glanced away from her. "I'll be fine." He blinked till the tears went back where they came from, and pretended great interest in a hangnail.

He'd had some tequila and he was tired, he told himself. He'd feel better after some food and a nap. Plus, his mom was a champ at getting under his skin.

She got out of the chair, scooted behind the coffee table, and hip-checked him into moving further down the couch so she could sit next to him. She slipped one arm around his shoulders. "Listen. You won't be fine. You're in love with Amy, and she's in love with you. You are going to have to apologize, and you'd better make it good. For starters I'd advise you to tell her you were wrong, you shouldn't have done this, you are sorry, and you will never lie to her again. Right after that, you need to find something else to occupy your time and your money while she runs her business. It'll be good for both of you."

"I can't believe you're siding with her," he said.

"I'm siding with my future daughter-in-law." His mother's smile was heartfelt. "If you let her go, Matty, you'll regret it for the rest of your life. You'd better figure out how you're going to fix this, and how you're getting her back."

Someone knocked at his hotel room door. "That'll be the food." Pauline got to her feet and hurried away from him.

Samantha vanished back into the second bedroom with a tray full of food he couldn't believe he was letting her eat. He couldn't imagine when she'd developed a taste for chicken nuggets, but he was somewhat happy to note she actually ordered a salad for herself. He and his mother talked about everything but Amy while they ate their own room service dinner. Shortly afterward Pauline grabbed her phone out of her bag, stepped back into her shoes, and called out, "Samantha, come on out here."

He heard the racket from whatever video game she was playing shut off abruptly. "What's going on, Grandma?"

"Your dad's publicist just texted me. We're going to get mani-pedis downstairs with her while he takes a nap." She gave Matt a nod. "Get some sleep, son. When I get back, we're going to talk about Amy. You need a plan."

She dumped the entire bottle of tequila down the bathroom sink before she left, too.

THREE DAYS LATER Matt's stitches itched like a mofo, photos of his trip to the local grocery store for supplies ended up on TMZ.com, and he had to apologize in front of witnesses to that dickless wonder Harry McCord, whose "facial contusions" had miraculously healed.

Someone on the show's production staff must have liked the holiday gift Matt gave them last year. A "source" told multiple sports reporters what really happened before Matt punched Harry. PSN withdrew Matt's suspension the following day. Matt asked for a leave of absence instead. He had some things to work on before he went back to the show.

The only thing that kept it all somewhat bearable was the fact Samantha was still with him. It seemed she was infuriated with her mother these days, for reasons that were a mystery to Matt. He muttered something about "hormones," and his mother went medieval on his ass.

Fifi was silent. He had tried calling her. She didn't call him back. Maybe it was time he stopped chasing her. There were other women who would be more than happy to take his calls. Maybe he should find one of them. LA was full of gorgeous, single women.

The only problem was he didn't want any of them.

Chapter Twenty-Six

AMY CURLED UP on her couch after a challenging day at the flower shop. Most of the time the worst thing that happened in her job was someone didn't like their order. But today she had done the flowers for a funeral.

The deceased was a twenty-year-old college kid who fell into a crevasse on Mount Rainier. The young man's mother appeared at the shop herself to order flowers for the pedestal the urn with his ashes would rest on during the memorial service. She glanced through Amy's arrangement books. Amy offered her a cup of coffee.

The woman dug a well-used handkerchief out of her purse and pointed toward a small arrangement of greenery with a few white tulips and roses. "This is the closest I'll get to what I think he'd want," she said. She picked up her coffee with a trembling hand, took a sip, and put the paper cup back down on the table.

Amy reached out and patted her hand. The woman

gripped hers. Amy squeezed in return. "Why don't you tell me what you think he would like?"

"He loved the outdoors. He was outside all the time, even as a little boy. I had to drag him into the house to eat and sleep. He . . . The arrangements in this book are beautiful, but they're not him. He'd want something that reminded everyone of the trees, the sky, water, and mountains, and—"

Amy leaned forward in her chair. "Let me see what I can come up with." She thought for a moment. "Do you have a measurement of the pedestal you'll be using during the service?"

AMY LOADED THE arrangement into the delivery van herself the next morning. She used pine branches and greenery as a base. She raided her mother's garden for old-fashioned wildflowers, like bluebells, digitalis, and forget-me-nots. The arrangement wasn't large, but the urn would be surrounded on all sides by the beauty and fragrance of the outdoors.

Amy clicked the TV on, and she settled in for an hour or so of mindless entertainment. She reached for the remote again to change the channel when an entertainment news show came on. A photo of Matt's face on the screen made her stop.

"Matt Stephens of Pro Sports Network must be wishing for a do-over. The set of *NFL Today* was thrown into turmoil after punches were thrown between Stephens and his co-anchor, Hall-of-Fame defensive end Harry

McCord. We haven't been able to determine what started the fracas, but an unnamed source told us this afternoon, 'It wasn't the first fight on the set, and it won't be the last.' Matt Stephens was suspended from the show, only to be reinstated this morning. He asked for a leave of absence instead. Stephens is licking his wounds in Los Angeles this week. He was spotted inside a local grocery store earlier this afternoon but would not answer our reporter's questions."

The video clip they showed was of Matt and Samantha, pushing a half-loaded grocery cart. Matt responded to the reporter's shouted questions with "No comment," while shielding Samantha under one arm. Amy saw Samantha fling a couple of packages of Pepperidge Farm cookies into the cart while Matt was busy keeping the press away from them. She had to smile.

The bandage on Matt's face looked awful.

She didn't listen to the rest of the report. She got up, grabbed the cordless from the kitchen, and plunked herself back down on the couch.

The entertainment show anchors kept talking. Amy gripped the phone in her hand. All she had to do was scroll down the caller ID, locate Matt's number, and hit "dial." The hundreds of reasons why she thought it was such a good idea to walk out on him fell away while she considered what a mess he was in right now.

He tried to help her. Maybe he'd appreciate whatever help she might have to offer, too. Or maybe he'd hang up on her.

Maybe she should stop being so afraid. Of everything.

She clicked the TV off, and scrolled the caller ID. She hit "dial." She closed her eyes, and took a huge breath.

"MATT'S PHONE," PAULINE barked.

"I'd like to talk to Matt, please," Amy said.

"Who's this?"

"Amy Hamilton. Is he there?"

"Amy, he's a little busy right now. I'll tell him you called, though." Amy heard the phone click off. She redialed the phone number. It went to voice mail.

"Well, that takes care of that," she muttered to herself. Amy got up off the couch, grabbed a beer out of the refrigerator, dispensed with the top, and chugged it.

An hour later, Amy was in bed and falling asleep. The phone rang. She didn't answer it. The call must have gone to voice mail. It rang again. She snatched the cordless off the base in her darkened bedroom, punched "talk," and held it up to her ear.

"Hello?"

"Fifi, it's me. Don't hang up."

"Your mom said you weren't available."

"I'm here now." She heard the mouthpiece rub up against the stubble on Matt's chin.

She sat up in bed. "I'm worried about you. What happened?"

Silence ensued.

"I saw something on an entertainment show—"

He cut her off. "You shouldn't believe everything you hear."

She flopped back into her pillows. "Then maybe you should tell me what wasn't true. Did you punch Harry McCord? What's going on with your job?"

"Harry made a comment about you he won't be making again."

"What in God's name could he have said that was so bad you punched him?"

Matt ignored that. "I'm on a leave of absence from my job while I decide what I want to do. My mother and daughter are treating me like an invalid. I sent them to Disneyland overnight so I could get some peace and quiet." He let out a breath. "You're filled in, Fifi."

She rubbed a trembling hand over her mouth. Any thought of facing this in a dispassionate way was gone.

"Did you find the cookies Samantha threw into the cart at the store before you got to the check stand?"

She heard strain in his voice. "I let her have the damn things."

"I don't even know how to say this."

"You're not backing up the truck on me, too," he said. His words were wary and cautious; the way he'd talk with someone he wasn't letting anywhere close enough to affect him.

"That wasn't what I was going to say."

"Well, spit it out," he said. "I don't have all day." He was going to bluster and give her attitude, but she knew him well enough to know the truth: She'd hurt him, too, and he was trying to pretend like he didn't care.

Amy swallowed hard, and closed her eyes. Just hearing his voice made her long to walk to wherever he was and throw herself into his arms. "I can go over and pick up your mail if you'd like."

"Excuse me?"

"I—you didn't say how long you'll be there, and some-one has to get the mail. I can do it. If there's anything else you need me to pick up or make sure you have on hand—"

The previously chilly tone of his voice warmed. "I have an assistant for that."

"All right. I wanted to make the offer."

"That's all you have to say to me right now—you'll get the mail?" Incredulity replaced Matt's false bravado.

She rubbed one hand over her face. "No. It's not. I don't have any idea what to say, but I'll start with this. You listened to me when I had trouble. Maybe it's my turn to listen for a while."

He still owed her an apology. She deserved that apol-ogy, too. At the same time, just listening to his voice—she was lost. She missed him so much. She'd get her apology, but right now, he needed her help.

She heard his low, sardonic laughter at the other end of the phone. "We're not at the therapist's."

"Do you want to go back to the show?"

He let out a long breath. "No. No, I don't." She heard two thumps as his shoes must have hit the hotel room floor. "Let me stretch out here." Blankets rustled. "I'll bet you're coming up with some psychobabble bullshit that's going to make it all better."

"No. I'd like to think we're still friends."

"Friends, huh? That's funny, Fifi." The tone of his

voice indicated he didn't think it was funny at all. "If that's what you want, though, we'll go that route. Friends. I suppose this means I get to belch in front of you and complain about other women."

"That's up to you." She felt like someone had slapped her in the face. Just imagining him with someone else made her want to scream with pain. She pulled the down blanket over her shoulders with her free hand. "Maybe you should tell me why you're not sure you want to go back to your job."

He was silent for so long Amy wondered if they'd been disconnected. "Matt?"

"I'm still here. I'm thinking." She could hear him breathing. "To be truthful, I'm over it. I loved playing football. I'd still be playing if I could get out there and mix it up with the young bucks, but that's not going to happen. I'm tired of talking about it. I don't want to spend the rest of my life telling the same stories, interviewing guys I wouldn't want to have a beer with in real life, and worrying about my Q rating when my contract's up for negotiation. Football may have defined me in the past, but it doesn't now." He pulled breath into his lungs. "I'd like to do something that made a lasting impact, and I'm not talking about more endorsements."

"Is there something you've been considering?"

"Yeah." She heard him moving around on the bed. He must have sat up. He hit the speaker button on his phone. "Just a second." She heard the hiss as he twisted the top off a bottle of carbonated drink. "By the way, I'm on alcohol restriction for another three days."

"I don't get what you're talking about."

"My daughter decreed I needed a punishment for my behavior. They made me promise them I wouldn't drink alcohol for a week. I'm having some juice drink they got at the store right now."

"You don't have a drinking problem."

"They're concerned. The next time you go to the store, you might try the stuff. It's a little sweet for me, but the blackberry flavor's not too bad. Back to the subject. How long did it take you to decide you'd had enough of accounting?"

"Ten years. I paid off my student loans as fast as I could, started saving, and got the hell out."

"I have an MBA I've never used. I got it shortly after I retired from the league. I'm wondering if it might come in handy."

If one income stream from his investment portfolio was twenty-five thousand a week, he wasn't being truthful about "never using" his MBA, but Amy wasn't going to argue with him about it right then.

"That depends. What do you think you'd like to do?"

"I have a good driving record. Maybe I should drive an ice cream truck."

Amy let out a snort. "That's pretty seasonal."

"Not if I live in another state."

It was all Amy could do to stifle the gasp. He couldn't leave. He just couldn't, and she couldn't seem to ask him to stay.

"You're not serious about this."

"That depends. Should I be, Amy?" Her tongue felt

like it was frozen to the roof of her mouth. Tears flooded her eyes. A minute that seemed to last an eternity passed. Finally he said, "Since the cat's got your tongue, let me tell you what I've been working on."

FORTY-FIVE MINUTES LATER, Matt took another swig of blackberry sparkling juice, and he heard Amy's voice. "It's a great idea. What's stopping you?"

"I've spent the past ten years talking about pass completion statistics and trick plays. There is the slight possibility that those I approach to partner with me in this business might want someone with more of a financial services background." He knew the dripping sarcasm in his voice wasn't going to fool her, but he gave it his best effort. He wasn't a schoolboy, crying to his mother about some girl who didn't want to date him. Fear wasn't an option.

"Do you want to spend the next ten years too scared to make a move?"

He felt that. How ironic that a verbal roundhouse kick should come from Miss Fifi, who was still totally spooked about how she felt about him. She didn't want to live without him any more than he wanted to live without her.

"I don't fail. Ever."

"Then don't," she argued. Her voice got softer. "I know you can do this. If there's one thing I also know about you, Matt, is that you want to be needed. This is perfect for you." He let out a snort, and she continued. "Do it. If you hate it, you can sell the business to your investors and find something else that you'd like better. Don't spend the next ten years doing something you're tired of because you won't take a risk."

He heard rustling sheets. She must have rolled over in bed. His brain flooded with images of waking up with a warm, soft, naked Fifi wrapped in his arms. He was hard as nails in seconds.

"So, you want to talk about taking a risk," he rasped. He'd spent the past hour on the phone with the only person in his life he could imagine talking his idea over with. He wondered if she had any clue.

"I—I—"

"We'll talk soon." His voice was soothing. "Go to sleep." He ended the call, dropped the phone on the bed next to him, and rested a forearm over his eyes. He'd thrown down the gauntlet. What she did with it was up to Fifi.

...

Chapter Twenty-Seven

ONE AFTERNOON SEVERAL weeks later Amy's cell phone rang at the shop. She fished it out of her apron pocket. "Hello?"

"Hi, Amy. It's Samantha."

"Samantha?" Amy sat down on the bench that now graced the shop's lobby. "How are you doing?"

"I'm—I need your help." Samantha paused for a moment. "I was wondering if you could come and pick me up from basketball practice."

"Of course, but where are your parents? Won't they be worried?"

"Mom is at her shop, and Matt is—well, he's unavailable." Her voice dropped almost to a whisper. "I have cramps."

"I'll be there in twenty minutes. Will the school let you leave with me?"

"Yeah, I think so. My dad put you on the list at the

office, and I don't think he ever changed it. I'll meet you outside." Samantha let out a sigh. "Thanks, Amy."

"You're welcome. See you in a few minutes."

Amy hung up the phone, tore off her apron, and grabbed her purse out of the office. Estelle could lock up. Scott the delivery driver was already done for the day.

"Estelle!" Amy called out.

"What's up?" She poked her head around the door-jamb of the tiny office.

"I need to run an errand. I might not be back till after closing time. Would you lock up for me, please? The cash goes in the safe; the lights are left on—"

"I'll take care of it, Amy."

"I also have my cell if there's something you need."

"Everything will be fine." She made a shooing motion. "I'll see you tomorrow morning."

"Thank you so much." To Amy's surprise, Estelle leaned forward and gave her a hug.

"Don't worry about a thing. Just go."

Amy threw herself in the driver's seat of the delivery van and pulled into late-afternoon traffic. Luckily the lights were with her. She made it to the school entrance in twelve minutes. Samantha stood on the sidewalk, waiting. She wasn't wearing either school or basketball uniform. Her hair was dry and styled. She wore jeans, a sparkly top, and what looked like high heels.

Amy pulled to a stop in front of her and called out the window, "Samantha Pauline Stephens, you'd better have a damn good reason for this."

Samantha settled herself in the passenger seat. "I

don't know what you're talking about." She wouldn't look at Amy.

"So, how are your cramps?"

"Fine."

"I'm taking you home, right?"

"I have to stop at Matt's office and pick something up first."

"Really? What might *that* be?"

Samantha stared straight ahead. Amy turned in the seat to look into her face. "Samantha, the car doesn't move till you tell me what it is you're up to."

She was twirling a long strand of hair around her finger. "Can't we just go, and I'll explain on the way?"

"I'm not sure. What if I don't like your little surprise?"

"Please?" Samantha finally turned to acknowledge Amy. "I promise you'll really like it."

"Fine. I want your word, though."

"What?"

"You have to promise me that this has nothing to do with your dad." Eyes as blue as Lake Washington at midnight locked onto Amy's. She didn't say anything. "I mean it."

"Of course it doesn't." She glanced at her lap, glanced up again, and smiled at Amy. She was totally lying. At the same time, Amy had to deliver her to at least one of her parents. This did not mean she had to see him or talk to him.

"You're sure?"

"Yes. Can we go?"

"Maybe you should tell me where I'm going."

"Please drive to Redmond. I'll give you directions when we get closer."

Half an hour later Amy pulled up in front of a beautifully maintained Cape Cod house in Redmond's business district that had been transformed into an office space. There was a new sign on the lawn: *Lifechangers, Inc.* An arch of medium-pink helium balloons was installed over the entrance. The front door stood open, and she could see a lot of women milling about the porch and the inside of the house.

Samantha unfolded herself from the front seat, and got out of the car. "Come on," she coaxed.

"I thought you needed to pick something up from your dad before you went home."

"We'll do that next." She held out her hand. Amy reluctantly took it. Her young friend was obviously up to something.

Amy crossed the threshold and glanced around. A very familiar-looking arrangement of pink roses, freesia, and ivy graced a refreshment table. It had been one of this morning's deliveries from her shop. A server was pouring champagne punch. She saw scores of women talking and laughing together in what must have been a large living room at one time, most holding a copy of the literature laid out on the corner of the refreshment table. Amy saw a conference room on her left in the former dining room.

Laura had just materialized, and she embraced Samantha.

"I thought I told you that your dad and I would take

you out to dinner later to celebrate." She was laughing. "So, you bamboozled Amy into bringing you here?"

"She told me she had cramps," Amy said.

Laura shook her head. "She did, huh?" She held out her hand.

Samantha dug into her handbag and put her iPhone into her mother's hand. "You'll get this back in a week," Laura said to Samantha.

"But she wouldn't have known if she wasn't here," Samantha insisted.

"You heard me, young lady. Go give your father a kiss." So, he *was* there. Amy's heart skipped a beat. She hauled breath into her lungs. Unless she was wrong, Matt had moved forward with the business he told her about the last time they talked. He'd also announced his resignation from *NFL Today* when the season was over. The network hired Brandon to replace him on the show next season, but nobody could seem to get Matt to talk about his future plans, at least publicly.

Samantha gave Amy a pleading look. "Just stay long enough to hear what he has to say."

Laura patted Amy on the back. "I told her not to pull something like this." She reached out, snagged a brightly colored brochure off the refreshment table, and handed it to Amy. "Welcome to Lifechangers, Inc., a microcredit firm loaning start-up funds to female-owned businesses that don't qualify for traditional business financing."

"How did you hear about this?"

"Let's just say I was in on the ground floor. I think you were, too," Laura said to Amy.

Even over the chatter and laughter, Amy heard what had to be Matt's heavy footsteps on the hardwood floor. This would be his scene for sure: a houseful of women. She stepped into the conference room across the hallway. She could hear, but he couldn't see her.

Someone tapped a piece of silverware against a champagne flute. The group fell silent. Amy heard Laura's voice over the small PA system.

"I'd like to welcome you all here today. This is not only a great day for female entrepreneurs in the Pacific Northwest, it's a great day for any woman who has a business plan, a dream, and the start-up funding to make that dream a reality. Lifechangers, Inc. was started as a response by one man who watched three of the women in his life scrimp and struggle to get their businesses off the ground and wondered how he could help others. I'd like to introduce the founder of Lifechangers, Inc., my ex-husband and best friend, Matt Stephens."

Amy let out a gasp. Luckily, nobody seemed to notice. He'd taken her advice after all.

The women present applauded lustily and then grew silent as Matt began to speak.

"I'd like to thank everyone for being here today. Your support, and your efforts to spread the word that we're here, will help women you've never met to achieve success and to improve their circumstances. I found my success on a football field. The reason why I was so driven wasn't the public recognition or the money. It was my mother, Pauline. Mom, where are you?"

"Here, honey." Pauline waved.

"My dad left us when I was two. My mom was a waitress. She worked double shifts to keep a roof over my head and food in my belly. She didn't have the money to get training or go to school, to even try to find a better-paying job. The proudest day of my life was the day I got drafted into the NFL. I came home and told her she'd never have to work again." He was silent for a few seconds. "She thought that was pretty dumb." A wave of laughter moved through the crowd.

"After a lot of arguing, she finally agreed to let me pay for cosmetology school. She became a barber. She opened her own barbershop, and she worked there until two years ago. She finally retired. After listening to my mom's experiences, my ex-wife also went to cosmetology school. She owns Salon Cirrus in Kirkland. Even though we weren't married any longer when she opened her business, I have experienced the ups and downs of a small business owner, because she told me about it. I know that a small loan when she opened helped her get the equipment she needed, allowed her to secure a space, and made it possible to hire one employee." Amy heard him set his drinking glass down on the lectern.

"When I started my career, the only cost to me was physical wear and tear. For the women in my life, it was money. Even a small amount of money made the difference between *just a job* and *success*. They wanted more. They went out and got it."

Amy peeked around the corner. Matt's smile didn't waver, but he looked somewhat lost.

"The other woman in my life managed to open her

business without my help. Amy's a florist. She owns Crazy Daisy on Capitol Hill. When things got bumpy for her, I wanted to fix it all. She wouldn't let me. I didn't understand it, but now I do. She wanted to succeed or fail on her own terms." Laura nodded. "Mostly, Amy taught me a lesson. She made me see that it was time to shake up my life, too. Football was all I knew. Maybe it was time to try something else, something that would be a tribute to the courage and daring of the three women in my life, and be an example for my daughter, Samantha." Amy peeked around the corner again, and saw Matt lift his glass high. "So, let's toast. I'd like to drink to the women I love, and I'd like to drink to the women who will succeed because Lifechangers, Inc., gave them a hand up, not a hand out."

The clinking of glasses greeted his comments. He had his arm around Samantha, who had a flute of what looked like sparkling cider. Pauline stepped over to a ribbon stretched across the far end of the room and snipped it with a gigantic pair of scissors. There was applause, more clinking of glasses, and Amy put her glass down on a nearby windowsill.

Matt was surrounded by women who wanted to hug him, talk with him, and pose for photographs. She slipped out the front door, and hurried to her car.

She needed a plan of her own.

Chapter Twenty-Eight

ON A MISERABLY warm July evening, Amy glanced around another packed hotel ballroom of people dressed in formalwear. The place boasted meat locker quality air conditioning, which she appreciated. Brandon and Emily had bought a table at the Seattle Humane Society's "Tuxes and Tails" fundraiser, and she was told, under no uncertain terms, to be there.

"Listen, squirt, you're going to have to save me. My wife wants a dog, which will not get along with Deacon the cat," Brandon explained. "She wants one of those big dogs, too. No Chihuahua for her. It's yellow lab or nothin'. And you know she winds me around her little finger. There are evidently going to be dogs there. I don't have a good feeling about this."

"I suppose," Amy sighed.

"So, you'll force yourself, huh?" Brandon's laugh boomed over her phone. "She'll probably try to sneak a puppy out of there in her evening bag. If there are two of us keeping an eye on her, she might not get away with it."

"Maybe we could have her frisked on the way out."

"Good idea, squirt. I'll see you then."

She actually enjoyed most of the soirees her sister and brother-in-law invited her to, as a result of having to see and be seen themselves. It was a great excuse to dress up, too. If that wasn't enough, this was the first stage of her carefully crafted plan. Matt always got invited to these things. She was going to do whatever it took to get him back, up to and including public humiliation.

He was worth it.

Amy wore a strapless chiffon ball gown in shades of blue and purple, with a high ponytail, a pearl bracelet, and her typical flats. She'd get to dance, if she didn't knock somebody over on the way to the dance floor. Other people managed to get through an evening out without some incident caused by sheer clumsiness. She wished she knew their secret.

Emily and Brandon were the center of attention, as usual. She watched people tripping over themselves to talk to her opera diva sister and her NFL-player-turned-game-analyst brother-in-law. There was an open bar, the food was good, and the live music wasn't too bad, either. She was looking forward to the parade of pets later in the evening.

Amy saw a familiar head of blue-black, rumpled hair in the crowd, and a shiver ran down her spine. It was time to gather every bit of courage she had and approach him. She needed a drink first, though. She snagged a glass of champagne off a passing tray and drained it with one swallow. She resisted the impulse to barf it up when she saw Matt wasn't alone.

The woman at Matt's side was tall, blonde, graceful, beautiful, and really, really rich. Amy recognized her, too. Paula's family owned the biggest Cadillac dealership in Washington State, and Paula did their TV commercials.

Paula held Matt's arm. They were talking and laughing with a knot of people who were basking in their light. He seemed like he didn't have a care in the world. After all, he'd managed to find the perfect woman. They would have gorgeous, socially adept, athletic children. *She* probably never freaked out about a paltry twenty-five thousand dollars, or managed to stab herself with flower wire.

Amy heard Brandon's voice in her ear. "Get over there and talk to him."

She couldn't stop the icy fear that consumed her, or her clammy palms, or the urge to cry. Maybe she needed another glass of champagne. Then again, she typically wasn't at her best when she overindulged.

"I can't compete with that."

"You don't have to," Brandon said. "I'll bet you ten thousand dollars he'll dance with you if you ask him. I'll bet you another ten thousand he showed up here tonight because he knew you'd be here, too."

She narrowed her eyes as she looked up at him. "I'm sure he didn't have any help finding out."

Brandon's eyes sparkled. "Of course he didn't."

This was going to be the easiest twenty thousand bucks she ever made, despite the fact she wasn't actually taking his money.

She took a deep breath, stuck out her hand to shake his, and said, "I'll take that bet. There's no way he's here to talk to me with *her* on his arm. He's over it."

She heard Brandon's chuckle as she moved through the crowd in Matt's direction.

Matt was leading his companion to the dance floor. For some reason, he glanced in Amy's direction. He froze in his tracks and stared at her. If her heart weren't singing with happiness, she would have been appalled at how clichéd locking eyes across a crowded room was.

Paula must not have been watching where she was going, either. She crashed into him, which almost made Amy laugh out loud. For a minute, she didn't look quite so graceful. Amy actually liked Paula when they'd met at other fundraisers her family asked her to. Paula was with Matt, though, which meant she was not getting anything remotely approaching sympathy from Amy right now.

Matt walked Paula onto the dance floor, drew her into his embrace, and they danced. He kept staring at Amy, though.

Brandon grabbed Amy's hand. "Hey, dance with me."

"I was going to go ask Matt to dance," she hissed. "I have to wait till he's done, I guess."

"The hell you do," her brother in law said. "Watch this." He moved them both around the dance floor until they were a foot or so away from Matt and Paula. "Ready?" Brandon asked. He reached out to tap Matt on the shoulder. Matt didn't respond at first. Brandon tapped again. "I'm cutting in, buddy."

Paula looked a bit surprised, but put her hand in Brandon's outstretched one. Brandon danced away with her, leaving Matt and Amy standing in the middle of the dance floor.

He looked so handsome in his black tuxedo and bow tie. She couldn't look away from him if she wanted to. She opened her mouth to speak, but nothing came out. She swallowed hard. Matt took her hand.

"Dance with me, Fifi."

She shuffled closer to him. He slid his arm around her. There were so many things she knew she should be saying to him at that moment, but she didn't know where to start. Maybe the best thing was to use the two little words she should have used a long time ago. To her surprise, he beat her to it.

"Fifi," he said. "I'm sorry. I acted like an ass. I should have stayed out of it."

"I'm sorry, too," she whispered. She couldn't say any more, or she'd start crying like a big baby in front of a thousand people.

He pulled her a little closer. His hand was big and reassuring wrapped around hers. She wondered how she'd gotten through the days since the last time he held her. His scent washed over her. She resisted the impulse to slide her fingertips under his collar and stroke the skin on the back of his neck. She wanted to savor and remember every moment with him like it was the last.

He laid his cheek against hers. All the other things

she'd planned to say, to explain why she'd acted as she did and how wrong she was, seemed to stick in her throat. He wasn't talking, either. They swayed together to the music. The song ended, and the couples on the dance floor applauded. There was an announcement that the auction would start in a few minutes. The dance floor cleared as a result.

Matt and Amy stood alone. Matt didn't move.

"I can't let you go," he whispered into her ear.

He rested his forehead against hers. She looked up into his eyes. The longing and the loneliness there took her breath away. She slid her fingertips into Matt's shirt collar after all, and slowly stroked the back of his neck. She tangled one hand into his curls. People were probably pointing and staring. Let them. She'd stand out here all night, feeling the comfort of his arms around her. She hoped he felt comforted, too.

Amy heard a woman's voice over the PA. "Ladies and gentlemen, this one goes out to the couple still on the dance floor." The singer sat down at the piano, accompanying herself as she sang *How Deep is the Ocean*.

Amy had heard the song before. Her parents probably danced to it when they were falling in love, too. She glimpsed Brandon and Emily standing at the edge of the dance floor. He handed Emily the pocket square from his tuxedo jacket; she dabbed at her face with it. Amy could hear people walking back onto the dance floor and feel movement around them, but her world was the circle of Matt's arms. She closed her eyes. She felt the scratchiness of his cheek against hers, the way he always laid his hand on the small of her back over the stress ache. She pulled breath into her lungs.

"I miss you so much," she said.

His voice was soft. "I miss you, too, Fifi. Every moment of every day."

Amy felt a tap on her shoulder. "My turn," a woman said.

Chapter Twenty-Nine

AMY SAT DOWN in the same seat she'd been sitting in for the past five football seasons at Sharks Stadium. She couldn't afford the expensive covered seats. Then again, the real football fans sat in the elements. She prided herself on being a *real* football fan. No pink jerseys and Bedazzling for her, dammit.

"Hey, Amy." George called out to her as he arrived at his seats. "Good to see you." George was the informal leader of the row's season ticket holders. He'd had his two seats since the 1990s. He and his wife had kids older than Amy. He told anyone that asked that he'd be sitting in those seats as long as he lived.

"I'm happy to be here, George."

He glanced at Amy. His eyes narrowed. "You okay?"

"I'm fine. I can't wait for the game to start."

Amy forced a smile she didn't feel onto her lips and fixed her attention on the field. The players had just run out to start their warm-ups. It was just like every other football game she ever attended, with one major exception. Typically, she was excited to see her friends, drink a beer or two, and scream for the Sharks. Today, it was hollow.

Matt hadn't called or stopped by after they danced at the fundraiser a week ago. She finally broke down and called him twenty-four hours ago. He didn't call her back. She couldn't seem to tell him all the things she'd wanted to say that night, and now it looked like she'd lost him forever. Just remembering how it felt to hold him again made her want to bawl. Even more, she had nobody to blame for this but herself. And didn't that just suck? Nobody could compete with him. If she took a risk, she wouldn't be facing her life alone. The thing she was most afraid of had happened, and it was her own damn fault.

A knot of people materialized from nowhere at the bottom of the seating section, blocking the entire concourse. She couldn't imagine what was going on. She craned her neck to see what was happening, but the mob seemed to be dispersing as quickly as it had started, with some help from stadium security.

A familiar figure with wavy, rumpled blue-black hair emerged from the crowd of people and climbed the stairs in her section. Amy's heart started pounding like the drum line over their heads. Somehow, she couldn't imagine Matt wanted to sit outside in the rain in attire that probably cost more than a club-section season ticket. He had on the pressed Sharks polo shirt, dress slacks, and summer weight cashmere blazer the network's stylist dressed him in when he did a game broadcast. He didn't usually work pre-season games, so he must have been filling in for someone else today. He scanned the crowd till he found Amy. If he was working, though, he certainly wouldn't be in the stands.

She tried to pull some breath into her lungs. He didn't take his eyes off of her. She couldn't decide whether to jump the seats and throw herself into his arms, or run away as fast as her legs could carry her.

Matt paused at the row Amy sat in, and extended his hand to George. George got to his feet and clapped Matt on the shoulder.

"I was hoping there'd be a seat left in this row," Matt said.

"I think we might be able to arrange that." George turned to indicate Amy with a nod. "There's an empty seat next to Amy. You two know each other, don't you?"

Amy was going to get on her knees and thank George's daughter Lisa for not showing up to a preseason game, right after her stomach unknotted and her knees stopped knocking. Matt shook George's hand again and moved slowly toward her.

She could pretend like she hadn't seen him, hadn't watched every step he took up the stairs toward her. It would require her to take her eyes off of him. That wasn't going to happen anytime soon. She opened her mouth to tell him she was mad at him because he hadn't called, and she spent the past week wondering if she was going to have to live without him for the rest of her life, but nothing came out.

Matt settled into the seat next to Amy. "Fifi." He slid his arm around the back of her seat. "This place is packed, isn't it?"

"Why are you here?"

She told herself he wasn't going to notice her trembling, or the fact that her voice cracked. Of course he did. He took Amy's hand and kissed the back of it. She thought about yanking it away. She just couldn't.

"Watching the game. These seats aren't bad. There's no free food, but it's a pretty good view." Amy noticed that everyone around them seemed to be ignoring what was happening. *Sure, they were.*

Her voice finally decided to work. "Don't you have a seat somewhere else?"

"I wanted to sit with you."

She heard a roar from the crowd. The team was running back into the locker room. They'd be introduced momentarily, complete with fireworks and cheerleaders. Right now, though, the game was paling in comparison to what was happening in the row Matt and Amy sat in. She loved football, but the real reason her heart kept beating took her hands in both of his and gently rubbed them.

"It's warm out here, but your hands are freezing."

She looked out at the field, into the stands, anywhere else but at the man sitting next to her. He continued to rub her hands and his voice was quiet in her ear.

"So, we have things to talk about," he said.

Her voice dropped, and she leaned toward him. "You never called me. I called you yesterday, and you didn't call me back. I—I thought you didn't want to see me again." She blinked back the tears that threatened. "I felt awful."

"I was out of town on business, and I had to take care of a few things. I wanted to make sure everything was ready before I saw you again."

Usually, there was nothing that could knock Amy down. She was going to make it, no matter what. At the same time, the tough part of her had shriveled and died as far as Matt was concerned. All she knew was a grief more profound than any she'd ever felt. Was he just here to torture her?

It took a few minutes for his words to sink in. "What 'things'? What are you talking about?"

The cheerleaders formed two lines on each side of the tunnel the players would run out of in seconds; the crowd got to its feet. It was time to welcome the team. Matt still had her hands in both of his, and pulled her to her feet along with him. She couldn't even clap. She didn't yell. She watched as Brandon ran out of the tunnel to ground-shaking cheering. It was his last season as a Shark. Emily was probably in the team's suite. She'd taken a red-eye to get here from London.

The crowd noise was almost at the level of pain now. She was shaking. She couldn't control it anymore. Matt slid his arms around her, and he pulled her close.

"You're freezing, sweetheart. Let's see if we can warm you up a bit."

"I'm not cold," she choked out. "I did everything wrong. I—I miss you so much. I don't want to live without you."

Even with a crowd of 67,000 screaming their guts out over the kickoff, he could hear her.

"And now I've lost you, and I'm never going to get over it. You're dating Paula, and I should have told you how I felt about you a long time ago."

He laid his fingertips over her lips. She felt him let out a sigh. A smile twitched over his mouth.

"That's funny. She's Clint's daughter, and I took her to that event as a favor to her dad. She spent most of the night dancing with someone else." He cupped her face in his hands and looked into her eyes. "And you're wrong about something else. I love you, Amy Hamilton. I'm always going to love you. I never stopped." He took a shaky breath. "You are the love of my life."

Amy's mouth fell open. Matt pulled her closer. The kick returner was streaking down the side of the field toward the end zone. There was bedlam all around them, but they might as well have been alone. She couldn't focus on anyone or anything beyond Matt's eyes. Nothing registered but what he was saying to her.

"You didn't call me," she insisted. "I thought you didn't want to talk to me—"

He cut her off. "I wanted to wait till I could see you to say all of this." He stared into her eyes. "I was an idiot. Will it help if I tell you every morning for the rest of my life how stupid and hardheaded I was over the loan and a few other things? I hurt you. I was wrong. I'm sorry." He took a deep breath. "I will not meddle in your business, unless you ask me to. I will never lie to you again."

She stopped shaking and stood there in shock. The

great Matt Stephens, king of the alpha males, was apologizing. Again. Was Hell freezing over? Amy felt sudden and inappropriate laughter bubbling up in her throat. Suddenly she could breathe again. Her world burst into magnificent color.

"I didn't quite hear that. Could you say it again?"

"What do you mean?" He frowned a little, and then she saw the side of his mouth curve up. "I think you heard me."

"Oh, I don't think I did. What was that you said?"

"Amy, you heard me."

"I was wrong? I'm sorry?" She gave him her most innocent smile. "I'll have to hear it a lot more than once a day."

"I see how you are. You get the poor sucker to confess his undying love, and then you bust his chops."

"Not at all. I'm just looking for a little additional groveling."

Matt laughed. Of course, nobody was seated yet; there would be another kickoff. That's what happens when the home team scores on the first possession. He hadn't let go of her, either. It wasn't too bad to watch a football game wrapped up in Matt's arms.

"I love you, too," she said into his ear. "So, so much."

Matt pointed overhead.

"Hey, Fifi, look at that."

The team was still lining up for their kickoff, but the crowd was cheering again. She glanced up. A small plane flew high over the stadium, towing a banner that read: *Fifi. Marry me. Matt.*

Amy swallowed hard. Her heart leapt. The blood

bubbled through her veins. She stared at the small plane, which executed a wide arc over Niehaus Field and flew over Sharks Stadium once more.

"Are you serious?"

"Serious as a heart attack, Hamilton. Are you in?" He kissed the corner of her mouth. "Marry me. Have my babies. Be my love, and I'll be yours."

"Everyone else proposes on the scoreboard."

"That's for losers. I had to get a stadium flyover exemption from the FAA for this."

He pulled a ring box out of the breast pocket of his jacket. People around them were pointing toward the plane, asking each other, "Who's Fifi?" and clapping. The heart Amy was afraid was broken beyond all repair pounded in her chest.

She could tell him she wasn't going to consider his proposal till he got down on one knee. When she opened her mouth to say so, though, something funny happened.

All she said was, "Yes."

Epilogue

Two years later

IT WAS FOUR am and Amy couldn't sleep. She had tossed and turned for hours. Matt had slept like a baby, as usual. He looked like a dark, dangerous, and sexy pirate against the snow-white bedding with his wavy hair, the stubble on his square jaw, his strong brow, and the thick, long eyelashes that lay like fans against his tan skin. She could wake him up. There could be a little plundering going on in their bed, as long as they locked the door and were very, very quiet.

Actually, there'd been some plundering before, and there would be again. Just not right now. Unless Amy missed her guess, she was in labor. The contractions were still ten minutes apart. They had some time. She was alternately thrilled and scared out of her mind. She hoped this was normal.

She tiptoed through the bedroom and down the hall to Samantha's room.

Samantha had kicked off all her blankets sometime during the night. She sprawled on her belly, arms flung over her head. The pink sapphire and diamond band she wore on the middle finger of her left hand sparkled in the faint light peeking through the blinds. Amy and Matt gave her the ring on their wedding day.

"Hey, Sam." Amy sat down next to her and shook her shoulder. "Wake up."

"It's not time for school yet, is it? Too early!"

"It's time to go to the hospital. I need your help."

Samantha shoved a mass of hair out of her eyes and flipped over onto her back. "It's time? It's *time*? Oh, God. Where's my dad?"

"He's still asleep."

"Are you okay? Does it hurt? How—Oh, we have to go!" Samantha jumped out of bed, grabbed Amy's hand and tried to tug her to her feet. "Come on!"

Amy didn't move, and she pulled once more.

"Just a second," Amy gasped.

Her stepdaughter handled it like a champ. "Breathe, Amy. Breathe."

"God, it hurts."

"Let's go get Ma—my dad."

There were so many things Amy wanted to say to her right then, but they would have to wait.

Thirty minutes later, a nervous Matt pulled up in front of the hospital entrance.

"Don't move, sweetheart. Let me help." He jumped

out of the driver's seat, hurried around the front of the Mercedes, and opened the passenger door. "Easy," he cautioned as he reached into the car to help her out of the seat.

"I'm fine, Sparky. I can do this."

"No. You need me," he said, and wrapped his arms around her. "Just take it slow. We'll get there."

A few minutes later Amy was in a wheelchair, being taken to the maternity floor. Matt was hurrying along beside her, holding her hand with one of his and making phone calls with the other. He called Emily and held the phone up to Amy's ear.

"How far apart are they?" Emily asked.

"Five minutes or so."

"I'll be there as fast as I can. Brandon will stay with the babies."

"Hurry," was all Amy could say. She'd been in the room when Emily gave birth to twin boys last year; now it was her turn.

Matt called her mom. He called his mom. Samantha had decided she wanted to see the baby born. After a long talk with the doctor, she'd stay till the transition, and then she'd be in the waiting room with Laura and Pauline. Pauline was probably live Tweeting the proceedings already.

"What's the matter?"

"Oh, God, it hurts."

"Contraction," the nurse said. "Amy, let's get you up on this bed and get the monitors on you."

Matt shoved the phone into his pants pocket. "I've got

you." He swept Amy up in his arms and set her down on the hospital bed. "Take it easy, Fifi. We'll get through this," he reassured.

"Oh, God," she gasped again. She gripped Matt's hand as hard as she could.

"Man, that's fast," the nurse said. "This baby wants out." She stripped off Amy's pants, put her in a hospital gown, put warm stockings on her legs, and put her feet in the stirrups.

"Can I have drugs?"

"I think this baby will be here before they even take effect," the nurse said. "You know Lamaze breathing, right?"

Amy nodded frantically.

"Okay. Let's breathe. Just relax. You're at nine and a half centimeters; the contractions are on top of each other, and the doctor's on his way."

"Can I push?"

"I'd rather you didn't. Let me find out where the doctor is." The nurse hit the call button with her elbow and told someone on the other end to page Amy's doctor.

Matt grabbed Amy's other hand. "How are you doing?"

"I'm—Oh, my GOD, it hurts. It hurts!"

He looked up at the monitor, and kissed the hand that clutched his. "The contraction is over. It's over. Take a breath."

"They didn't tell me it was going to hurt this much!"

Matt seemed to remember the Lamaze breathing. Well, good for him. Amy had forgotten it somehow. She panted. She tried. It still freaking hurt, and here was another contraction.

"Just squeeze my hand," Matt said. "That's it." Amy let out a scream. Something seemed to be taking over, and she wasn't in control. "Almost over. There." The nurse came back into the room. She looked worried, at least to Amy.

"What's wrong?" Amy cried out.

"Everything's fine," the nurse reassured her. She positioned herself at the foot of the bed. "The doctor's doing another delivery, but he'll be here."

"I have to push!"

"I know, darlin'. I know. Let's try to relax," the nurse said.

Another nurse ushered a white-faced Samantha out of the room. Amy heard her wail, "But I want to stay!" all the way down the hallway.

"She'll be fine," Matt assured Amy. "Breathe."

Amy took another lungful of air, only to have a contraction hit in the middle of it. She was going to break Matt's hand if this kept up. He was brushing the hair off her face, telling her how much he loved her, how proud he was of her, how he couldn't wait to meet the newest member of their family. Mostly, Amy wished he had access to an epidural needle, or someone that did. The nurse wasn't going to help.

"You can't wait? YOU can't wait? Which one of us is in pain right now? I want this baby *out*!"

"Of course you do," he soothed. Amy knew he was just trying to help, but right now she'd appreciate a little righteous anger on her behalf. She needed painkillers, dammit.

Another contraction came, even worse than the last one. The nurse had been on the phone, she'd pushed the call button to page the doctor, she'd done everything she could humanly do, and there was nothing left for Amy than to grit her teeth and push.

"Matt Stephens," she screeched in the middle of a particularly bad contraction, "You are never, *ever* touching me again! *Never!* I don't care how cute you are, or how good you smell, or that thing you do with your tongue!"

"They all say this," the nurse reassured him.

"Even the tongue part?" Matt moved away from Amy, and she grabbed him. He looked a little startled.

"Don't leave! Don't leave! I love you! Don't leave!"

"You probably say that to all your husbands."

He sat down in the chair next to her again, though. Amy actually growled at him, which he found even funnier.

The nurse glanced between them. "Where is that doctor?"

"Okay," Amy gasped. "Enough. I am not waiting. You," and she pointed to the nurse. "You and Matt are delivering the baby."

"The doctor's on his way. I promise."

"You'll be delivering the baby, because I'm going to push!"

Before the nurse had time to tell her again the doctor was on his way, Amy pushed as hard as she could. She shrieked like never before—or since.

"The baby's crowning!" The nurse grabbed her other hand. "Take a breath, and push! Push hard, Amy!"

Amy gasped for breath. Matt was still talking into her ear. "I love you," he said. "Let's see our baby."

She pushed so hard she saw stars. She grunted, she groaned, she screamed. She took the deepest breath she could and pushed one more time.

Amy felt the baby sliding out of her.

"That's it!" Matt's voice was exultant. "Baby's head is out. Just one more push, Fifi!"

Amy pushed again, and the sweetest sound she'd ever heard split the air: a baby's cry.

Matt got to his feet, craned his neck a bit, and wrapped his arms around Amy. "It's a boy! It's a boy. He's perfect." Tears rolled down his cheeks. "You did it, Fifi. We have a son."

The nurse laid their newborn on Amy's stomach after she wiped him off a little, and handed the scissors to Matt. "Would you like to cut the cord?"

Matt was momentarily speechless. He reached out to take his son's tiny, goo-covered hand, but recovered enough to nod at the nurse. He made the snip.

"He has your hair," Amy said.

"He's got your nose." Matt traced it with a gentle fingertip. Their son opened his eyes. They were as blue as his father's. He had a dimple in his chin. Oh, he'd be a heartbreaker. He was long and lean, and Matt murmured, "I was like this when I was born, too."

"So, he's going to be a tight end?"

"He can be whatever he'd like to be," Matt assured her. "I

love you. I love you so much." He wrapped his arms around Amy, and they drank in the sight of their healthy baby boy.

"I love you, too." Amy pressed her lips into the side of his neck. "I'm sorry about all the yelling and the—"

"You're going to let me touch you again at some point," Matt murmured into her ear.

"Don't push your luck, Stephens."

"*No?* Is that so? Even that thing I do with my tongue?"

The doctor raced into the room, just in time to deliver the afterbirth. The baby was cleaned up, weighed, given his second Apgar, and returned to them.

AMY KNEW THAT her family would descend on the hospital any minute, but first Samantha edged through the doorway to her room.

"Come on in, Sam," Amy called out to her.

"Are you sure?" Samantha tiptoed in.

"Of course I'm sure. Do you want to hold him?" Amy held her swaddled son up so Samantha could get a glimpse of him.

Matt got to his feet, crossed the room, and pulled his daughter into his arms.

"Mom and Grandma are in the waiting room," Samantha explained. "Grandma told everyone on Twitter that she has a new grandson."

"I'm glad you're here, princess," her dad told her. She edged closer to the side of the bed.

"It's all over," Amy explained. "Come here and sit next to me."

The nurse looked on as Samantha perched on the mattress next to Amy. Amy held Jonathan out to her. "This is your new brother." She got him settled into the crook of Samantha's arm. He didn't even open his eyes.

"He's so little," Samantha breathed.

"He's bigger than you were when you were born," Matt observed.

Samantha peered into her brother's sleeping face. She kissed his cheek and wiped off the smear of pink lip gloss she'd left behind. He opened his eyes and silently regarded her. She opened her mouth, and closed it. She must have finally decided what to say.

"His name is Jonathan, right?"

"Yes. Yes, it is," Amy said.

Samantha cuddled him close. "I've been waiting for you, Jonathan."

Matt reached for Amy's hand.

"I'm your sister, Samantha, but you can call me Sam," she told him. "I can tell you all about Mom and Dad." Jon's lips moved into something approximating a smile, and Samantha turned to them with tears in her eyes. "He smiled at me!"

"Yes, honey, he did."

She stuck one thumb inside his fist. "Look how teeny his fingernails are."

Matt was around the bed like a shot. "Listen, princess, careful." He helped her support Jon's head. "You're doing fine."

"I was fine before," she retorted, but the feigned impatience didn't fool either Amy or Matt. Samantha had just fallen in love with her little brother.

"I'll teach you how to play video games," she said to him. "By the time you're old enough, I can drive you to the store to get candy. We're going to have so much fun together."

The nurse approached one more time. "You know, Samantha, we have a little button we give out. You're probably too old for this," but she extended a powder-blue button reading "I'm the Big Sister" to Samantha. Samantha's chin trembled, and she nodded quickly. "Would you like me to pin it on your t-shirt?"

"Yeah." Samantha tried to roll her eyes and act bored, but she let out a long sigh. "Maybe I'll get less homework or something." She carefully transferred Jon back to Amy's arms and told him, "I got you a present." She dug through her backpack and produced a baby t-shirt that read, *I can't even walk, and I already hate the Yankees.*

"You're not putting that on your brother," her father told her.

"C'mon, Dad, it's funny." Of course, Matt melted into a warm puddle of protoplasm when he heard the word "Dad" from Samantha.

Jon made a gurgling sound, and Samantha looked elated.

"He likes me."

"Of course he does," Amy reassured her. "Go ask your mom and grandma if they want to come in here and see the baby."

"Ask them if they could give us a few minutes, and we'll be all set," Matt said.

Samantha leaned over the bed, kissed Amy's cheek, whispered, "Good job, new Mom," and gave her dad a kiss, too. She darted out of the room.

In the meantime, Amy had a hungry boy on her hands.

"Would you like to try feeding him?" the nurse asked.

"Sure."

Amy pulled her arm out of the hospital gown, propped Jonathan up in the crook of her elbow, and teased her nipple over his tiny mouth. The baby's lips parted. It took a few tries, but he suckled Amy, and Matt wrapped his arms around both of them.

"He wanted some dinner," Matt said. "He takes after his papa."

Jonathan swallowed hungrily, and closed his eyes. One small fist rested on her breast. Matt kissed her one more time while they watched their son eat.

Amy had everything she would ever need. Well, she thought she had everything.

Samantha and Jon's younger sister arrived a year later.

Can't get enough of Julie Brannagh's
Love and Football series?

Don't miss CATCHING CAMERON

Coming May 2014
Read on for a sneak peek!

An Excerpt from

CATCHING CAMERON

ZACH ANDERSON WAS in New York City again, and he wasn't happy about it. He wasn't big on crowds as a rule, except for the ones that spent Sunday afternoons six months a year cheering for him as he flattened yet another offensive lineman on his way to the guy's quarterback. He also wasn't big on having four people fussing over his hair, spraying him down with whatever it was that simulated sweat, and trying to convince him that nobody would ever know he was wearing bronzer in the resulting photos.

He was making eight figures for a national Under Armour campaign for two days' work. He knew he shouldn't bitch. The worst injury he might sustain here would be some kind of muscle pull from running away from the multiple women hanging out at the photo shoot who'd made it clear they'd be interested in spending more time with him.

He was all dolled up in UA's latest. Of course, he typically didn't wear workout clothes that were tailored and/or ironed before he pulled them on. The photo shoot was now in its second hour, and he was wondering how many damn pictures of him they actually needed.

"Gorgeous," the photographer shouted to him. "Okay, Zach. I need pensive. Thoughtful. Sensitive."

Zach shook his head briefly. "You're shitting me."

Zach's agent Jason shoved himself off the back wall of the room and moved into Zach's line of vision. Jason had been with him since Zach signed his first NFL contract. He was also a few years older than Zach, which came in handy. He took the long view in his professional and personal life, and encouraged Zach to do so as well.

"Come on, man. Think about the poor polar bears starving to death because they can't find enough food at the North Pole. How about the NFL going to eighteen games in the regular season? If that's not enough, Sports Illustrated's discontinuing the swimsuit issue. That should make a grown man cry." Even the photographer snorted at that last one. "You can do it."

Eighteen games a season would piss Zach off more than anything else, but he gazed in the direction the photographer's assistant indicated, thought about how long it would take him to get across town to the hotel when this was over, and listened to the camera's rapid clicking once more.

"Are you sure you want to keep playing football?" the photographer called out. "The camera loves you."

"Thanks," Zach muttered. Shit. How embarrassing. If

any of his four younger sisters were here right now, they'd be in hysterics.

CAMERON ONDINE SMILED into the camera for the last time today. "Thanks for watching. I'll see you next week on *NFL Confidential*." She waited till the floor director gave her the signal the camera was off and stood up to stretch. Today's guest had been a twenty-five year old quarterback who'd just signed a five-year contract with Baltimore for seventy-five million dollars, fifty million guaranteed. His agent hovered off-camera but not close enough to prevent the guy in question from asking Cameron to accompany him to his hotel suite to "hook up."

Cameron wished she were surprised about such invitations, but they happened with depressing frequency. The network wanted her to play up what she had to offer—fresh-faced, wholesome beauty, a body she worked ninety minutes a day to maintain, and a personality that proved she wasn't just another dumb blonde. She loved her job, but she didn't love the fact some of these guys thought sleeping with her was part of the deal her employers offered when she interviewed them.

The sound techs unclipped her lavalier microphone and the power pack in the waistband of her skirt. She waited till they walked away and gave Jake Eisen a brisk pat on his upper arm.

"I'm really flattered, but I have several appointments later today. I'm not going to be able to make it." She didn't add that she was a few years older than he was, she'd been married before, and above all, she wasn't interested. "Thank you, though. I hope you're enjoying the visit to New York."

"I'd like it a lot more if we could get together, Cameron. How about tomorrow? I don't go back to Baltimore till Saturday morning." He gave her what she was sure he thought was a seductive grin. "I've had it for you since you signed with PSN. Make my dreams come true."

She resisted the impulse to barf all over what had to be prototype Reebok shoes he was wearing. "That's quite an offer, but no," she said.

She reached out, briefly clasped his hand, shook once, and walked away. She heard the name he called her under his breath. It wouldn't be the first time a guy called her that, and it sure wouldn't be the last.

Cameron rushed down the hallway to her dressing room, peeled off the loaner clothes she wore for a taping, and washed the TV makeup off in record time. She applied makeup with a much lighter hand, added swingy silver chandelier earrings, and bent from the waist to run her fingers through the long, blonde, highlighted hair that cost a fortune to maintain. She flipped it back into the just-out-of-bed tousle the show's hair person had spent forty-five minutes working on this morning. She stepped into black, strappy stilettos, a knee-length fuchsia floral sheath with a bow at the waist, and threw the items she needed into an evening bag: Cash, credit card, house keys, lip gloss, breath mints, and smart phone. She pulled a lightweight silk wrap around her shoulders.

A knock at the door announced her assistant, Kacee.

"Cameron, you need to be here at eight am tomorrow morning for hair and makeup. It's the Zach Anderson interview."

"Got it." God give her strength. She could think of a thousand things she'd rather be doing than spending an hour with Zach Anderson tomorrow, or any other day. She gave Kacee a quick nod. "Thanks for your help today."

"So, have you seen him yet? He's in the building this afternoon at a photo shoot."

"Seen whom?"

"Zach Anderson." Kacee gave her a look as if she'd grown another head.

"No." Cameron frowned at the noise and vibration coming from her bag. Her phone was going nuts. If she stopped to figure out what it was, she'd be late, and she couldn't be late.

"Every woman in the building must have been in the studio during his photo shoot." Kacee let out a sigh. "He's beautiful. Have you met him before?"

"Yes." Oh, they'd met before. She'd spent the past ten years avoiding him, too. If that wasn't enough, she had no interest in dating a professional athlete, especially in her line of work. Female sportscasters had a difficult time in pro sports as it was; she wasn't going to add to the existing problem.

Cameron glanced up from her still-buzzing handbag to catch Kacee's eye as she hurried toward the door.

"If you're interested in talking with him, I'll make sure you get introduced tomorrow," she said.

"Oh, God. I'd love that. Thanks, Cameron!"

"You're welcome. Listen. I've got my phone if something happens, but it's Donna's rehearsal dinner—"

"And Donna will have a fit if you leave in the middle of it," Kacee finished. "Hopefully, nobody in the NFL gets arrested or traded over the next four hours or so."

About the Author

JULIE BRANNAGH has been writing since she was old enough to hold a pencil. She lives in a small town near Seattle, where she once served as a city council member and owned a yarn shop. She shares her home with a wonderful husband, two uncivilized Maine Coons, and a rambunctious chocolate Lab.

When Julie's not writing, she's reading, or armchair-quarterbacking her beloved Seattle Seahawks from the comfort of the family room couch. Julie is a Golden Heart finalist and the author of four contemporary sports romances.

Visit www.AuthorTracker.com for exclusive information on your favorite HarperCollins authors.

Give in to your impulses . . .
Read on for a sneak peek at four brand-new
e-book original tales of romance
from Avon Books.
Available now wherever e-books are sold.

THE LAST WICKED SCOUNDREL
A Scoundrels of St. James Novella
By Lorraine Heath

BLITZING EMILY
A Love and Football Novel
By Julie Brannagh

SAVOR
A Billionaire Bachelors Club Novel
By Monica Murphy

IF YOU ONLY KNEW
A Trust No One Novel
By Dixie Lee Brown

An Excerpt from

THE LAST WICKED SCOUNDREL
A Scoundrels of St. James Novella
by Lorraine Heath

New York Times and *USA Today* bestselling author
Lorraine Heath brings us the eagerly awaited
final story in the Scoundrels of St. James series.

Winnie, the Duchess of Avendale, never knew
peace until her brutal husband died. With
William Graves, a royal physician, she's discovered
burning desire—and the healing power of love.
But now, confronted by the past she thought she'd
left behind, Winnie must face her fears . . . or risk
losing the one man who can fulfill all her dreams.

After last night, she'd dared to hope that she meant something special to him, but they were so very different in rank and purpose. She considered suggesting that they go for a walk now, but she didn't want to move away from where she was. So near to him. He smelled of sandalwood. His jaw and cheeks were smooth. He'd shaved before he came to see her. His hair curled wildly about his head, and she wondered if he ever tried to tame it, then decided he wouldn't look like himself without the wildness.

With his thumb, he stroked her lower lip. His blue eyes darkened. She watched the muscles of his throat work as he swallowed. Leaning in, he lowered his mouth to hers. She rose up on her toes to meet him, inviting him to possess, plunder, have his way. She became lost in the sensations of his mouth playing over hers, vaguely aware of his twisting her around so they were facing each other. As she skimmed her hands up over his shoulders, his arms came around her, drawing her nearer. He was a man of nimble fingers, skilled hands that eased hurts and injuries and warded off death. He had mended her with those hands, and now with his lips he was mending her further.

Suddenly changing the angle of his mouth, he deepened

the kiss, his tongue hungrily exploring, enticing her to take her own journey of discovery. He tasted of peppermint. She could well imagine him keeping the hard candies in his pocket to hand to children in order to ease their fears. Snitching one for himself every now and then.

He folded his hands around the sides of her waist and, without breaking his mouth from hers, lifted her onto the desk. Parchment crackled beneath her. She knew she should be worried that they were ruining the plans for the hospital, but she seemed unable to care about anything beyond the wondrous sensations that he was bringing to life.

Avendale had never kissed her with such enthusiasm, such resolve. She felt as though William were determined to devour her, and that it would be one of the most wondrous experiences of her life.

Hiking her skirts up over her knees, he wedged himself between her thighs. Very slowly, he lowered her back to the desk until she was sprawled over it like some wanton. On the desk! She had never known this sort of activity could occur anywhere other than the bed. It was wicked, exciting, intriguing. Surely he didn't mean to do more than kiss her, not that she was opposed to him going further.

She'd gone so long without a caress, without being desired, without having passions stirred. She felt at once terrified and joyful while pleasure curled through her.

As he dragged his mouth along her throat, he began undoing buttons, giving himself access to more skin. He nipped at her collarbone, circled his tongue in the hollow at her throat. She plowed her fingers through his golden locks, relishing the soft curls as they wound around her fingers.

More buttons were unfastened. She sighed as he trailed his mouth and tongue along the upper swells of her breasts. Heat pooled deep within her. She wrapped her legs around his hips, taking surcease from the pressure of him against her. He moaned low, more a growl than anything as he pressed a kiss in the dip between her breasts.

God help her, but she wanted to feel his touch over all of her.

Peeling back her bodice, he began loosening the ribbons on her chemise. In the distance, someplace far far away, she thought she heard a door open.

"The count—" Her butler began and stopped.

"Winnie?" Catherine's voice brought her crashing back to reality.

An Excerpt from

BLITZING EMILY
A Love and Football Novel
by Julie Brannagh

All's fair in Love and Football . . .

Emily Hamilton doesn't trust men. She's much more comfortable playing the romantic lead in front of a packed house onstage than in her own life. So when NFL star and alluring ladies' man Brandon McKenna acts as her personal white knight, she has no illusions that he'll stick around. However, a misunderstanding with the press throws them together in a fake engagement that yields unexpected (and breathtaking) benefits in the first installment of Julie Brannagh's irresistible new series.

Emily had barely enough time to hang up the cordless and flip on the TV before Brandon wandered down the stairs.

"Hey," he said, and he threw himself down on the couch next to her.

His blond curls were tangled, his eyes sleepy, and she saw a pillowcase crease on his cheek. He looked completely innocent, until she saw the wicked twinkle in his eyes. Even in dirty workout clothes, he was breathtaking. She wondered if it was possible to ovulate on demand.

"I'm guessing you took a nap," she said.

"I was supposed to be watching you." He tried to look penitent. It wasn't working.

"Glad to know you're making yourself comfortable," she teased.

He stretched his arm around the back of the couch.

"Everything in your room smells like flowers, and your bed's great." He pulled up the edge of his t-shirt and sniffed it. Emily almost drooled at a glimpse of his rock-hard abdomen. Evidently, it was possible to have more than a six pack. "The guys will love my new perfume. Maybe they'll want some makeup tips," he muttered, and grabbed for the remote Emily left on the coffee table.

He clicked through the channels at a rapid pace.

"Excuse me. I had that." She lunged for it. No such luck. Emily ended up sprawled across his lap.

"The operative word here, sugar, is 'had.' " He held it up in the air out of her reach while he continued to click. He'd wear a hole in his thumb if he kept this up. "No NFL Network." She tried to sit up again, which wasn't working well. Of course, he was chuckling at her struggles. "Oh, I get it. You're heading for second base."

"Hardly." Emily reached over and tried to push off on the other arm of the couch. One beefy arm wrapped around her. "I'm not trying to do anything. Oh, whatever."

"You know, if you want a kiss, all you have to do is ask."

She couldn't imagine how he managed to look so innocent while smirking.

"I haven't had a woman throw herself in my lap for a while now. This could be interesting," he said.

Emily's eyebrows shot to her hairline. "I did not throw myself in your lap."

"Could've fooled me. Which one of us is—"

"Let go of me." She was still trying to grab the remote, without success.

"You'll fall," he warned.

"What's your point?"

"Here." He stuck the remote down the side of the couch cushion so Emily couldn't grab it. He grasped her upper arms, righted her with no effort at all, and looked into her eyes. "All better. Shouldn't you be resting, anyway?"

Emily tried to take a breath. Their bodies were frozen. He held her, and she gazed into his face. His dimple appeared, vanished, appeared again. She licked her lips with the microscopic amount of moisture left in her mouth. He was fighting a smile, but even more, he dipped his head toward her. He was going to kiss her.

"Yes," she said.

Her voice sounded weak, but it was all she could do to push it out of lungs that had no air at all. He continued to watch her, and he gradually moved closer. Their mouths were inches apart. Emily couldn't stop looking at his lips. After a few moments that seemed like an eternity, he released her and dug the remote from the couch cushion. She felt a stab of disappointment. He had changed his mind.

"Turns out you have the NFL Network, so I think I can handle another twenty-four hours here," he announced as he stopped on a channel she'd never seen before.

"You might not be here another twenty-four minutes. Don't you have a TV at home?" She wrapped her arms around her midsection. She wished she could come up with something more witty and cutting to say. She was so sure he would kiss her, and then he hadn't.

An Excerpt from

SAVOR
A Billionaire Bachelors Club Novel
by Monica Murphy

New York Times bestselling author
Monica Murphy concludes her sexy
Billionaire Bachelors Club series with a fiery
romance that refuses to be left at the office.

Bryn James can't take much more of being invisible
to her smart, sexy boss, Matthew DeLuca.
Matt's never been immune to his gorgeous
assistant's charms, and though he's tried to
stay professional, Bryn—with a jaw-dropping
new look—is suddenly making it very difficult.
And when the lines between business and
pleasure become blurred, he'll be faced with
the biggest risk of his career—and his heart.

Bryn

"I shouldn't do this." He's coming right at me, one determined step after another, and I slowly start to back up, fear and excitement bubbling up inside me, making it hard to think clearly.

"Shouldn't do what?"

I lift my chin, my gaze meeting his, and I see all the turbulent, confusing emotions in his eyes, the grim set of his jaw and usually lush mouth. The man means business—what sort of business I'm not exactly sure, but I can take a guess. Increasing my pace, I take hurried backward steps to get away from all that handsome intensity coming at me until my butt meets the wall.

I'm trapped. And in the best possible place too.

"You've been driving me fucking crazy all night," he practically growls, stopping just in front of me.

I have? I want to ask, but I keep my lips clamped tight. He never seems to notice me, not that I ever really want him to. Or at least, that's what I tell myself. That sort of thing usually brings too much unwanted attention. I've dealt with that sort of trouble before, and it nearly destroyed me.

The more time I spend with my boss though, the more I want him to see me. Really see me as a woman. Not the dependable, efficiently organized Miss James who makes his life so much easier.

I want Matt to see me as a woman. A woman he wants.

Playing with fire. . .

The thought floating through my brain is apt, considering the potent heat in Matt's gaze.

"I don't understand how I could be, considering I've done nothing but work my tail off the entire evening," I retort, wincing the moment the words leave me. I blame my mounting frustration over our situation. I'm tired, I've done nothing but live and breathe this winery opening for the last few weeks, and I'm ready to go home and crawl into bed. Pull the covers over my head and sleep for a month.

But if a certain someone wanted to join me in my bed, there wouldn't be any sleeping involved. Just plenty of nakedness and kissing and hot, delicious sex . . .

My entire body flushes at the thought.

"And I appreciate you working that pretty tail of yours off for me. Though I'd hate to see it go," he drawls, his gaze dropping low. Like he's actually trying to check out my backside. His flirtatious tone shocks me, rendering me still.

Our relationship isn't like this. Strictly professional is how Matt and I keep it between us. But that last remark was most definitely what I would consider flirting. And the way he's looking at me . . .

Oh. My.

My cheeks warm when he stops directly in front of me. I

can feel his body heat, smell his intoxicating scent, and I press my lips together to keep from saying something really stupid.

God, I want you. So bad my entire body aches for your touch.

Yeah. I sound like those romance novels I used to devour when I had more time to freaking read. I always thought those emotions were so exaggerated. No way could what happens in a romance novel actually occur in real life.

But I'm feeling it. Right now. With Matthew DeLuca. And the way he's looking at me almost makes me think he might be feeling it too.

"So um, h-how have I been driving you crazy?" I swallow hard. I sound like a stuttering idiot, and I'm trying to calm my racing heart but it's no use. We're staring at each other in silence, the only sound our accelerated breathing, and then he reaches out. Rests his fingers against my cheek. Lets them drift along my face.

Slowly I close my eyes and part my lips, sharp pleasure piercing through me at his intimate touch. I curl my fingers against the wall as if I can grab onto it, afraid I might slide to the ground if I don't get a grip and soon. I can smell him. Feel him. We've been close to each other before, but not like this. Never like this.

An Excerpt from

IF YOU ONLY KNEW
A Trust No One Novel
by Dixie Lee Brown

Beautiful and deadly, Rayna Dugan is a force to be reckoned with. But when she must suddenly defend her life against a criminal empire, Rayna knows she needs backup. Ex-cop Ty Whitlock never meant for his former flame to get mixed up in this mess—a mess he feels responsible for. Now he's got only one choice: find Rayna and keep her safe. But that's the easy part. Once he finds her, can he convince her to stay?

He leaned close. "Goddammit, Rayna. You could have been killed." He breathed the words, and the anger in his expression morphed into fear as he grabbed her forearms and gave her a shake.

The deep emotion playing across his face tugged at her heart. His tortured gaze held her transfixed. She searched for the words to fix everything, starting with the way she'd botched their relationship, but some things couldn't be fixed.

She hooked her fingers through his belt loops and drew semicircles on his firmly toned abdomen with her thumbs until she found her voice again. "But I wasn't . . . thanks to you and Ribs."

Ty straightened and glanced upward, away from her face. "I thought I was going to lose you. I *won't* lose you, Rayna." His piercing gaze fastened on her again, and he raised one hand to caress her cheek. "Don't you get it? We're a team. I *need* you, and whether you'll admit it or not, you need me too."

Hope flared within her at his words, followed almost immediately by a spark of anger. "If you truly believed that, you wouldn't be trying to keep me out of the hunt for Andre. If we're such a good team, why not act like one?"

Ty swept a hand across the back of his neck. "I'm not

trying to keep you . . ." He stopped and looked away from her. "Shit. You're right. I wanted you out of it so you'd be safe, and so I could do my job without worrying about you. I still want you to be safe . . . but I'm fairly certain Joe was going to side with you anyway." He swung his gaze back to her, and amusement quirked his lips. "Besides, if he takes you home, you'll just spend all your time worrying about me."

"Oh, you think so?" Rayna raised a quizzical eyebrow. Did he mean it this time? Would he let her help take Andre down, or was he simply putting her off again?

Ty grew serious. "Stay with me, Rayna, and we'll get this guy. He won't know what hit him."

His soft words and the sincerity in his eyes melted her heart and filled her with sadness at the same time. It sounded like he was asking her to stay with him forever, but he'd already made it clear that he wasn't returning to Montana. So where did that leave them? The smart thing to do would be to ask, but her courage failed in the face of what his answer could be. For right now, she wanted to believe he meant forever, but the truth was she wanted him for however long he would have her, and she'd convince him later that he couldn't live without her. Did that make her desperate? So what if it did? She grabbed a fistful of his shirt and pulled him closer as she shook her head slowly. "Try getting rid of me."

A genuine smile lit his eyes, and his head lowered slowly. His lips touched hers in a lingering kiss, warm and promising more. His arms slid around her waist, pulled her in tightly, and he rested his chin on top of her head. She inhaled a deep breath, and her wild heartbeat began to slow. The safety and comfort of his embrace was exactly what she needed, and it was surprisingly easy to surrender herself to his care. Of course, there were still things to do. They had to get Ribs back and his wounds treated, but for now—for just a moment . . .

A shrill siren screeched in the distance, disturbing the peace of Nate's uncle's property. Ty tensed and raised his head, listening, then pulled his gun from its shoulder holster.